MAYWOOD PUBLIC LIBRARY

3 1312 00194 80

W9-BUH-394

Maywood Public Library
121 S. 5th Ave.
Maywood, IL 60153

ONE NATION, UNDER GOD

Further Titles by Keir Graf from Severn House

MY FELLOW AMERICANS

ONE NATION, UNDER GOD

Keir Graff

This first world edition published 2008
in Great Britain and the USA by
SEVERN HOUSE PUBLISHERS LTD of
9–15 High Street, Sutton, Surrey SM1 1DF.

Copyright © 2008 by Keir Graf.

All rights reserved.
The moral right of the author has been asserted.

British Library Cataloguing in Publication Data

Graff, Keir, 1969-
   One nation, under God
   1. Presidents - United States - Election - Fiction
   2. Fundamentalists - United States - Fiction 3. Suspense
   fiction
   I. Title
     813.6 [F]

   ISBN-13: 978-0-7278-6623-3   (cased)
   ISBN-13: 978-1-84751-063-1   (trade paper)

Except where actual historical events and characters are being
described for the storyline of this novel, all situations in this
publication are fictitious and any resemblance to living persons
is purely coincidental.

All Severn House titles are printed on acid-free paper.

Typeset by Palimpsest Book Production Ltd.,
Grangemouth, Stirlingshire, Scotland.
Printed and bound in Great Britain by
MPG Books Ltd., Bodmin, Cornwall.

One

Maybe, he thought later, if the Mormon kid hadn't come to Tulsa, the rest of it wouldn't have happened either. Or if it had happened, he wouldn't have been involved. He wouldn't have witnessed anything and wouldn't have been asked to keep a secret. And if he hadn't kept that first secret, maybe he wouldn't have kept all the others. And maybe he wouldn't have hurt anyone.

But the Mormon kid had come to Tulsa. And he had seen what happened. And he had helped with the rest of it.

It was a Friday night in late July. Summer's heat had settled in. Seth Stevens was rehearsing with his band, Salvation, in the music room at the Free Church of God's Slaves. It wasn't really his band—he was the newest member—but after a year and a half, he had finally stopped feeling like he had to apologize every time he flubbed a riff or played the wrong chord.

Seth Stevens played guitar. Kirk Swindoll was the singer. Jimmy Gilstrap played keyboards and sang backup. Ben Badgeley played bass. Owen Rusk played drums. Youth pastor Terry Kinsman wasn't a musician, but he insisted on helping, so he sat at the mixing board. Every minute or two he furrowed his brow and made some inaudible adjustment to the sound levels.

They had been practicing for an hour. Usually they stopped and started each song several times, disagreeing politely about who should have done what, then noodling mindlessly while instruments were tuned and amplifiers adjusted. But tonight the energy was different. Finishing each song without stopping and starting the next song as soon as it was suggested, they played with the same intensity they had when performing during Sunday and Wednesday services. It was at times like these that Seth felt the Lord's Spirit in them. It didn't feel like a band rehearsal. It felt like worship.

Kirk Swindoll was thin and muscular with spiky blond hair. Seth Stevens sometimes thought that Kirk Swindoll's hair was thinning and wondered if the teenaged girls would still swoon over him if he turned bald at thirty. It was a sinful thought, born of envy. Kirk Swindoll was born for the stage, and if he hadn't been a Christian he probably would have been truly famous in a regular rock band.

As the band played the propulsive bridge of their most popular song, 'Take It On Faith', Kirk Swindoll closed his eyes and sang:

> And you've told me what's right
> I take it on faith and I fight
> To do just what You say
> And I live each dying day
> Come Hell, come what may
> Only to stand in Your sight

They lashed the music upward, Owen Rusk making his drum kit shake with staccato bursts that sounded like gunfire, then played the chorus again. Jimmy Gilstrap sang harmony so pure it was indistinguishable from the lead vocal. Seth Stevens tapped his volume pedal, strumming the chords and letting them ring almost until they started feeding back. Ben Badgeley looked up and met his eyes. They smiled and nodded at each other.

And then the song was over. They stood looking at each other, sweaty, euphoric, filled with the Spirit.

Terry Kinsman's slow clapping broke the reverie.

'Amen,' he shouted. 'Amen!'

Then they laughed, high-fiving, feeling like they'd really done something.

They played for another half-hour, but the rest of rehearsal felt almost obligatory. They worked on the arrangement of a new song that Ben Badgeley had been bringing to practice for months but which was nowhere near ready. Even a Christian band had some of the same politics as the bands Seth Stevens had played in before he was saved. Christians didn't get drunk and fight about their differences, but they had egos, too. Though it wasn't clear given his shyness onstage, Jimmy Gilstrap had founded the band and had written all of the songs so far. He'd voiced interest in Ben Badgeley's song but had found all sorts of ways to postpone its debut in church.

Ben Badgeley took it in stride. He was persistent but not pushy. The song was bound to get finished one of these days, he said.

Sometimes Terry Kinsman did more than push buttons. Sometimes he played the role of manager. When he said it seemed like time to call it a night, no one objected. They powered down their amps, wound up their cords, and put away their instruments.

Even after the hundreds of hours he'd spent in the music room, Seth Stevens couldn't get over how clean it was. His old band had shared a practice space in a converted slaughter-house with a thrash-metal band and a black-metal band. The walls had been covered with spray-paint, set lists, and pornography. The sticky concrete floor was too disgusting to sit on. And he would never forget the time he'd reached for his beer and accidentally taken a deep drink of cigarette butts and expectorated chewing tobacco.

The church's music room was big enough to accommodate bands, classes, and even choirs. There were risers along one wall and blonde varnished instrument lockers along another. He would have felt comfortable sleeping on the gray speckled carpet and eating off the gleaming risers. Christians—those at the Free Church of God's Slaves, anyway—actually used the trash cans.

After rehearsal the band usually went to Perkins for coffee and dessert. The ritual was theoretically accompanied by Bible study, but often they were too tired to read scripture. Even so, the simple act of drinking coffee on a night when their peers were guzzling alcohol served as affirmation of their beliefs.

Tonight there were only four of them: Seth Stevens, Terry Kinsman, Ben Badgeley, and Owen Rusk. Kirk Swindoll had gone to his girlfriend's house to watch movies. Jimmy Gilstrap was married and had twin two-year-old girls. His wife allowed him to stay in the band only as long as he didn't come home late.

They ordered ice cream, blintzes, brownies, and bottomless cups of coffee.

'You know, some guy at work the other day told me Christians don't have a sense of humor,' said Owen Rusk.

'What was the joke?' asked Terry Kinsman.

'It wasn't a joke-joke. It was more like he was saying something about me—then he said "just joking"—and when I didn't laugh he said Christians don't have a sense of humor. He could have just said *I* don't have a sense of humor, but no; it has to be *Christians*.'

'So he made fun of you and then gave you crud because you wouldn't laugh when he made fun of you?'

'It wasn't, well, not exact—'

Owen Rusk always had a hard time explaining himself.

'What did he say?' said Terry Kinsman.

Owen Rusk stared at a ruptured blintz bleeding cherry filling on to his plate.

'It was my shirt. He said I looked like a dork with my T-shirt tucked in all the time. And he said I wore grandpa pants.'

Seth Stevens and Ben Badgeley chuckled.

'It's not exactly getting fed to the lions, is it?' said Ben Badgeley.

Terry Kinsman scowled.

'Do you know why we tuck our shirts in?'

'Well, yeah,' said Owen Rusk.

'So we don't look like the metalheads, the speed freaks, and the gangbangers. Because cleanliness is next to godliness. Because one day your shirt-tail is hanging out, next day your underwear is showing, next day you're listening to gangster rap. Because even though we shine with God's light from within, we respect our bodies, which are our temples to Him.'

'Amen,' said Ben Badgeley.

'Terry, you don't have to preach, it's not Sunday,' said Owen Rusk.

A young man walked in and sat down at the booth across from the band. He wore a white, short-sleeved, button-down shirt with a black nametag pinned to the pocket. If it hadn't been for the bicycle helmet he put down on the table he could have been mistaken for a waiter.

Terry Kinsman stopped preaching. From the ceiling speakers, strolling strings played Paul Simon's 'Graceland'.

Utensils clicked on plates. A waitress asked someone whether they wanted gravy on top or on the side.

'It's Elder Dumb,' said Terry Kinsman. 'Or is it Elder Dumber?'

Owen Rusk laughed nervously.

'Terry,' said Ben Badgeley, cautioning him.

The Mormon studied his menu.

'You know what I call Salt Lake City?' asked Terry Kinsman. 'Mo-Town. See? Christians do have a sense of humor.'

'Terry, they're Christians, too,' said Seth Stevens.

He didn't know if that was true or not. He himself had been a Christian only a little longer than he'd been in the band.

Terry Kinsman's eyes narrowed. Though he was the youth pastor, he had never fit Seth Stevens's idea of what a youth pastor should look like: bearded, bespectacled, soft. Terry Kinsman was over six feet tall, with a broad, powerful body topped by a slightly undersized head. His close-cropped hair made him look like a soldier in boot camp.

'Christians? Just saying you believe on Jesus Christ don't make you a Christian, Seth. Walking in the path of the Lord is what makes you a Christian. Mormons is a cult.'

Seth Stevens wished he hadn't said anything. He didn't know anything about Mormons. The young man who sat across from them, his hair crimped and sweaty from the bicycle helmet, didn't look like a cult member. When Seth Stevens heard the word 'cult', he thought of Charlie Manson's family, who he had learned about from an old paperback of his mother's.

'A cult?' he said weakly.

'Do Christians claim the scriptures were written on golden plates? Do Christians wear holy underwear that protects them from evil? Do Christians practice multiple wives? Do Christians baptize the dead? Do Christians claim that when they die they get to be the god of their own planet?'

Seth Stevens looked across the aisle. The Mormon was staring intently at the list of hamburgers and hobo skillets. The back of his buzz-cut neck was red.

'It's one thing when these guys go to Africa to try to convert the animal-worshippers,' continued Terry Kinsman. 'But Tulsa? They think we don't got church here? They think we practice multiple wives here?'

The Mormon looked up, his eyes flashing, about to say something. Then he bit his lip and looked away.

'That's right,' said Terry Kinsman. 'Look away. We don't want your cult here. Go back to Mo-Town.'

After the band had eaten their desserts and drained a pot of coffee each, they stood in the parking lot between the two cars they had come in, talking about nothing. The humid air felt almost chilly in the nighttime breeze. The cars on the Interstate passed in a pulsing hum. In a nearby field, half-filled with water, frogs burped and night birds sang. Seth Stevens wished he hadn't drunk so much coffee. He felt nauseous, high-strung, and tired.

The Mormon came out of the restaurant, pulling his helmet on but letting the chin straps dangle. He bent to put on a pants clip and then clipped lights to the front and back of his bicycle.

Terry Kinsman broke off in mid-sentence and strolled toward the bicycle rack. Seth Stevens, Ben Badgeley, and Owen Rusk exchanged apprehensive looks.

Terry Kinsman hailed the Mormon.

'How's it going?'

The Mormon looked up, unsure of his ground. He stood under a bright security light. The rest of the band, standing in twilight, crossed the parking lot halfway, trailing their friend.

Terry Kinsman read the Mormon's nametag.

'Elder Harbo.'

'What do you want?' asked Elder Harbo.

'Finding many converts here in Tulsa?'

'Mind your own business, mister.'

Terry Kinsman looked back at his friends.

'Hey, I'm a mister!'

Elder Harbo pulled his bicycle out of the rack. He tried to swing it around so he could climb on but Terry Kinsman was in his way. About thirty pounds lighter than Terry Kinsman, Elder Harbo looked frightened, as if the seat and handlebars were the only things holding him up.

Seth Stevens felt nervous even though he wasn't in any danger. He knew a fight was coming. Terry Kinsman wasn't acting godly and Seth Stevens didn't know any scripture he could quote to stop him. Turn the other cheek? Terry Kinsman was the one doing the slapping.

'You're in my way,' said Elder Harbo.

'We don't like ungodly fornicators here in Tulsa,' said Terry Kinsman. 'You're not welcome here.'

Elder Harbo's grip on his bicycle tightened.

'You strike the first blow, because I won't,' he said. 'But I won't turn my back when you're speaking untruth about my God.'

'Your God? Don't make me laugh. You're praying to my God, and he's not listening.'

'You need to pray, period,' said Elder Harbo.

Terry Kinsman threw a punch. Elder Harbo saw it coming and flinched. Terry Kinsman's fist glanced off his cheekbone. Elder Harbo staggered, got hung up on his bicycle, and fell on top of it. He got to his feet like a man climbing out of barbed wire. Then he swung his leg over his bicycle and stood on the top pedal and urged his bike forward. He'd left it in a high gear and he started to roll only slowly.

Terry Kinsman watched, shaking his head. Then suddenly he started running after the bicycle, reaching out for its rider. He drew even after only a few steps. Then Elder Harbo swerved and Terry Kinsman's hands clutched empty space.

The bike's derailleur clicked as it found a lower gear and Elder Harbo picked up speed and pulled away. When he reached the end of the parking lot, he sailed right around the glowing arrow that urged motorists to stop at Perkins and on to the four-lane street running by. He turned to look back, inadvertently drifting into the path of a jacked-up, tricked-out 4x4 pickup. It clipped his back tire and, like a film suddenly broken, he flew into the ditch and disappeared.

Terry Kinsman was already running back toward the band. 'Go!' he shouted. 'Go!'

Without thinking, they climbed into their cars, Terry Kinsman with Owen Rusk; Seth Stevens with Ben Badgeley. They drove out of the lot, turned left, and sped away.

Seth Stevens didn't own a car. If he couldn't get somewhere by walking or riding the bus, Ben Badgeley would usually give him a ride. Ben Badgeley's father taught science at Heartland Academy, the Christian high school, and his mother was a part-owner of The Mustard Seed, a Christian bookstore. Ben Badgeley studied computer programming at

Tulsa Community College and worked part-time at the book-store.

Ben Badgeley checked his rear-view mirror. Seth Stevens checked the passenger-side mirror.

'I don't think he got hurt that bad, probably,' said Ben Badgeley. 'The truck hit his tire, not him. So if he got hurt it was probably from the fall. And he fell in the weeds, not on the road.'

Seth Stevens didn't say anything. He was thinking about the way that Terry Kinsman had advanced on Elder Harbo with his fists ready. He was thinking that he didn't know whether Mormons were real Christians or a cult.

'And anyway, what was he doing on a bike? Why is it the Mormons always ride bikes? Is it in their contract or something?'

Seth Stevens watched the mirror, hoping for the glow of ambulance flashers.

'Don't you think we should go back and check to see if he's all right?' he said.

Ben Badgeley snapped the rear-view back into its regular position.

'Terry said—'

'We don't have to tell Terry.'

'Say someone shows up. An ambulance—or the police, even. You know the TV reporters listen to police scanners?'

'Well, if they show up, good. We can leave.'

'The police will want to know our names. Just think about how that looks. Three members of Salvation involved in some guy getting hit by a truck. Never mind we didn't punch the guy, never mind that we didn't chase him into traffic.'

'We can just tell the truth.'

'And then think of it this way: how's it look for Pastor Grady?'

Seth Stevens didn't want to find out what the answer to that one was. Because if there was someone he owed something to, it was Pastor Grady.

They didn't talk much during the rest of the short drive to Seth Stevens's apartment. Seth Stevens knew that everything they'd done was wrong, even if none of it was his fault. And even excusing himself from blame was wrong. Pastor Grady, he thought, would have said that not stopping a sin from being committed was as bad as committing the sin yourself. Not that he'd decided to do nothing. He just hadn't thought fast enough.

He should have run after Terry Kinsman. They were all weak. They all needed each other's help to keep from sinning.

Ben Badgeley stopped the car in front of Seth Stevens's building and said he would give him a ride to church on Sunday. They exchanged their ritual handshake, an intricately choreographed routine of hand slaps, finger taps, and fist bumps, then said goodnight.

He walked past the manager's office and through the parking lot to his stairwell. The sun-bleached aquamarine building was a former motel and looked like it. It was two stories tall and L-shaped around a drained pool with leaves, twigs, and fast-food wrappers at the bottom. The asphalt of the parking lot was slowly crumbling into gravel.

He climbed the stairs, which were covered in unraveling green indoor/outdoor carpeting. He passed the rusting ice machine and turned right. At 203, he stopped, unlocked the door, and went in. There was a red LED blinking on the answering machine on his kitchen counter. He pressed play before he'd even turned on the overhead light. The computer voice told him that he had One. New. Message.

Seth, it's me, your mom. Listen, honey, I need to talk to you. I know—

He hit the delete button before she had a chance to finish.

Two

H e woke to the sound of a door slamming. His next-door
neighbors were home, their drunken voices clearly audible
through the cinder-block wall.

Can you fucking believe?

Oh, I can fucking believe.

He says that when he knows, when he knows—

Well, you didn't have to go and make it worse.

How worse could it've much got?

Laughter. Their voices grew quieter. He heard pans banging.
He lay on his thin mattress on the floor, watching dust motes
spin in the breeze from the window. A tiny fiber fell off the
fuzzy venetian blinds and dropped, then shot upward again
and disappeared between the slats of the blinds.

Twenty minutes later he heard the woman start to moan,
her voice warm and smiling. Then the man started grunting
and Seth Stevens crawled out of bed. He ran a lukewarm
shower and then turned it cold, trying to soften his insistent
erection.

The couple next door usually stayed out all night. When
they didn't, they watched horror movies one after another, the
volume high enough that he heard every scream and whimper.
Often they fell asleep in front of the TV. He knew this because
the DVD menu cycled in endless loops—a line of dialogue,
a scream, a thunderous clash of music—without stopping until
some time after he went to work.

He didn't know what either of them did for a living. The
man wore a leather vest and a Harley Davidson T-shirt but
usually rode as a passenger in the woman's Ford Festiva. The
woman wore tight jeans and tight tank tops that accentuated
her firm, round breasts. They were both so skinny that he
might have pegged them both as tweakers except for the
pleasant softness of the woman's face. Maybe they were just

drinkers, although he imagined they used something else to keep themselves going all night.

He lathered his washcloth and scrubbed himself all over, then rinsed and did it again. Whatever his neighbors' chemical habits were, he knew more about their lifestyle than they could have imagined. When they passed him on the breezeway, they would nod at the cross of nails that hung from a leather thong around his neck.

'Going out, Reverend?' they'd say, smiling.

He didn't try to explain anything to them. And he certainly never told them he was in a Christian rock band. From the woman's T-shirts—Slipknot, Mudvayne, Insane Clown Posse—he pretty much knew they'd die laughing when they heard about Salvation. One day he'd be confident enough to witness to them, but he wasn't yet.

He was out of shampoo, so he soaped his hair using the bar. He thought that it was interesting how he didn't get to decide what he remembered. If he thought hard enough he could remember the bad parts. But hearing the slam of a door, drunken voices, and sex sounds, his mind played back only pleasurable scenes. Making a mess of someone's kitchen making a midnight snack. Laughing hysterically. A girl's long, slim back, his hands gripping her hips. Thinking he really, truly, would never have to sleep again. Then lying in bed thinking he'd never be able to get up again.

He stood under the icy stream until he started shivering. When he finally turned the water off it was quiet next door.

He toweled himself dry and dressed in navy slacks and a white, short-sleeve, button-down shirt. He fastened a vinyl belt around his waist and slipped his feet into a pair of nearly shapeless black Oxfords.

In the so-called kitchenette—a piece of countertop outside the bathroom—he poured a bowl of cereal and opened a flat, half-empty bottle of Mountain Dew. He sat down at the round table next to his bed. Though he was almost too afraid to do it, he turned on the TV to watch the morning news. He half-expected to see his own picture staring back at him with an all-points bulletin for his arrest crawling across the bottom of the screen.

Instead, the news anchor was talking about early plans for the Tulsa State Fair. There would be a concert by Lee

Greenwood, who would sing his hit song, 'God Bless the U.S.A.'.

The broadcast moved on to weather and sports. He changed to the cable news channels. He knew he was being stupid. There wouldn't be anything on the national news about something that happened outside the parking lot of a Perkins in Tulsa, Oklahoma.

There was news from Oklahoma, but it wasn't about a Mormon missionary who got hit by a truck. It was about politics.

Fox News had a graphic that arrived on the screen with a tympani roll and heralding trumpets: *2008: The Fight to Control the Country.*

'And now we turn to a state we don't often cover: Oklahoma,' said the anchor, Harris Trent. 'Not, of course, because it's not important, but because this Midwestern state's conservative credentials are rarely questioned. Though registered Democrats outnumber registered Republicans by a substantial margin, that fact is seen as little more than a statistical anomaly. In presidential races, voters in the Sooner State have cast their ballots for the Republican candidate since 1968. Their two U.S. senators are both Republicans. And four out of five U.S. representatives are, too.'

The screen was filled with a photograph of a dark-haired man with intelligent eyes and a cocky grin.

'But Ira Isaacs is looking to stir things up. He wants to become the first Democrat to win the office of U.S. senator since 1979. That would be newsworthy in any year. But in a year when many Republican strategists have privately conceded the White House and are focusing their efforts on fighting the Democrats for control of the Senate, it means that a lot of people are going to be watching the Sooner State with eagle eyes. For more, we turn to Byron Dennis in Oklahoma City.'

Normally, Seth would have changed channels by now. But there was no way he was going to pass up seeing his adopted state on national TV.

The camera cut to a handsome, gray-haired man wearing a denim work shirt under a suit jacket. He was holding a microphone and standing in front of a barbecue joint.

'Oklahoma City, Oklahoma—hardly what you'd think of

as a political hotbed. Folks around here, who like to meet over a plate of brisket at Earl's Rib Palace, are more likely to discuss their beloved Sooners than Washington politics. That's because their voice in the Senate has been even more predictable than the outcome of football games—or indeed the ever-surprising Oklahoma weather—until now.'

Finally they got to the story. Seth Stevens had seen Ira Isaacs's name on yard signs but hadn't even known that he was a Democrat. According to Byron Dennis, Ira Isaacs was not only an outspoken liberal and an outsider—he had an actual chance of winning.

Pictures and video accompanied a brief biography. Ira Isaacs had grown up in Muskogee. He had excelled in high school, where a host of plaques still stood testament to his academic excellence. He was captain of the varsity track team—he broke a state record in the long jump—and a very respectable swimmer, too. A summer job as a congressional page had given him a taste for politics, and he headed east as soon as he graduated. He delivered the Latin valedictory at Harvard and then stayed on to attend Harvard law school. Still in his mid-twenties, he'd been hired in a minor role on a Democratic presidential campaign. The candidate lost, but Ira Isaacs was making a name for himself as a tough and clever political operative. He practiced law for a while before becoming the deputy campaign manager for a Democratic presidential candidate who won, a job that led to his appointment as a deputy chief of staff for the president. He served until the end of the president's second term, then returned to his home state to begin laying the groundwork for his own campaign. Establishing residence in his hometown, he ran for the U.S. House of Representatives for the Second Congressional District and won.

Now Byron Dennis was standing in front of a storefront office with *Ira Isaacs: Future U.S. Senator* painted on the plate-glass window.

'Critics claim Isaacs won his seat because of name recognition and the fact that he parachuted into the only part of Oklahoma that still sends Democrats to Washington. They point to the fact that he didn't maintain a residence in Oklahoma from the time he left for Harvard until one year before he filed his papers for his run at the House of

Representatives. Even then, they say, he was more often seen on the streets of New York and Washington than the streets of Muskogee, Miami, and Okmulgee.'

Now file photos showed Ira Isaacs shaking hands, giving speeches, and hard at work at his desk.

'But if some see him as a carpetbagger, he's also seen as someone who can get things done. His years in Washington, his youthful energy, and his impressive pedigree have all given weight to his promises that he'll bring back the pork that Oklahomans love so well. If Isaacs was running against two-term Senator Jim Bynum, those who love to handicap political horse races would give him long odds at best. But with the seventy-three-year-old Bynum retiring for stated health reasons, and with his hand-picked heir apparent, Dean Platt, suffering from a late-breaking case of foot-in-mouth disease, the mood at Isaacs's campaign office in Oklahoma City can only be described as optimistic.

'We talked to some ordinary Tulsans, who shared their thoughts on Isaacs's end run.'

The camera showed an Okie in a sauce-stained T-shirt, squinting into the sunlight outside the barbecue restaurant.

'Isaacs?' said the man. 'Well, they say that old boy growed up around here, but, personally, I don't see it. Personally, I don't think he knows what us Okies think or want or care about.'

The camera showed a blue-rinsed woman with a face like a pecan nut, hanging out her washing on a backyard line.

'I tell you what, the only issue I care about at all is the healthcare. And that fellow running against Isaacs used to be a Washington lobbyist for the pharmaceuticals.'

The camera showed a chubby, thirty-ish woman sitting behind the wheel of a minivan. Middle-schoolers played soccer on the field behind her.

'Well, I've been a Bynum voter since I started voting, but you have to put the state ahead of party politics. And I think this Isaacs, well, they say he's an insider and I guess he is. But that's got to be a good thing for us, don't you think?'

Once again, the camera showed Byron Dennis in front of Earl's Rib Palace.

'And we'll let these ordinary folks have the final word

tonight. From Oklahoma City, Oklahoma, this is Byron Dennis, Fox News.'

Seth Stevens spooned up sugary milk from the bottom of his bowl. He watched the next commercial break, then turned off the TV and finished getting ready for work. It was weird to think of a big news network sending their reporter somewhere as sleepy as Oklahoma. What were they, Afghanistan? Iraq? Then again, if Ira Isaacs's election meant that the Senate would stay Democratic—and if the Democrats really won the presidency—then it did mean something serious. Maybe the troops really would come home from Iraq.

Finally fully dressed and groomed, he knelt down beside the unmade bed and folded his hands to pray. He liked to fix his eyes on the picture of Jesus above his TV set rather than the wooden cross above his bed. He still struggled with what to say when he prayed, but seeing His face somehow made it easier to follow Pastor Grady's advice: talk to Jesus not like he's some fiery being come to judge you but like he's a friend who's there to help you.

Jesus, he prayed, *something bad happened last night and I didn't know what to do. I still don't. I'm listening, Lord, for Your voice.*

He walked down his potholed street, then past a cornfield hemmed in by aging subdivisions, and then along a busy six-lane road lined with fast-food restaurants and strip malls. In cooler weather it took him about twenty minutes, but when it grew warmer he slowed down. If he sweated, the soot from the cars stuck to his skin and he needed another shower before he started his shift. Unfortunately, the employee locker room didn't have a shower.

Finally he crossed the sixteen-acre parking lot and entered the shadow of ShopsMart's massive front wall. Far off to his left, the employees of the garden department were rolling out carts with flats of seedlings and even some good-sized trees. When they were finished, a miniature forest would stand on the asphalt. Bags of peat moss and bark chips and volcanic rock and chemical fertilizer had been left out overnight and ringed the forest like sandbags around a gun emplacement.

He walked through an arcade lined with pop machines, through a set of sliding doors and past the shopping-cart corral, then through another set of sliding doors into the store itself.

ShopsMart's ceiling, corrugated metal held up with massive joists, soared thirty feet overhead. The back wall was 400 feet away. The store ran 550 feet from side to side with forty-five departments, including fifteen grocery aisles and thirty checkouts. The store sold sweaters, frozen waffles, pink plastic castles, basketballs, shotguns, garden hoses, table saws, two-by-fours, dried flowers, cut flowers, prescription medicines, photo portraits, haircuts, lube jobs, made-to-order sub sandwiches, and Mexican food. Seth Stevens was one of 429 employees. He worked in the shoe department.

As he walked through the store, he fished his 'associate's card'—a combination nametag, photo ID, and security key— out of his pocket. He unrolled a lanyard and hung the card around his neck. At the back of the store, at a set of locked double doors, he swiped the magnetic strip on the back of the card and waited for the lock to disengage. He pushed through the doors. At the second door on his left he turned in to the employee locker room. His locker combination was 234— Psalm 23:4. He opened the locker and stuffed his backpack inside.

He swiped his associate's card through the time clock: 9:07. Watching TV had made him late. He went into the warehouse and wended through towering shelves of pallets to the shoe cage. Last night's delivery was sitting on a pallet, swathed in sheets of clear plastic. He took a box knife and started to cut the plastic away from the brown cardboard cartons.

Rob Wingert, his supervisor, came in.

'I thought maybe you were already out on the floor,' he said.

'No, I'm late,' said Seth Stevens. 'I'm sorry.'

'Well, you can say you're sorry, but starting time for your shift is eight forty-five. Someone's got to straighten up before the customers start coming in.'

'I really meant to be on time. It won't happen again if I can help it.'

'Well, did someone else make you late? Is there someone else I should talk to?'

'No.'

'So what do you mean, "if I can help it"?'

'I just meant, you know, I'll do my best.'

'Well, now I'll rest easy. Go police the floor before you unpack this stuff.'

Seth Stevens retracted the blade on the box knife and put it back on the desk in the shoe cage. He walked through the warehouse again and back out to the floor. There were a lot of things he would have liked to say to Rob Wingert but it made him feel better to turn the other cheek. What was so frustrating was that Rob Wingert's concern for the shoe department was an act. He may have looked straight-laced, but when he left the store, Rob Wingert put his nose ring and his earrings back in. He changed into a sleeveless T-shirt that showed tattoos rising from his wrists to his shoulders. And punk rock roared from the speakers of his car.

Rob Wingert had said, smiling, that he was an anarchist. Seth Stevens could only conclude that Rob Wingert's workaday love of rules and order came from a desire to persecute the born-again Christian who worked for him.

The shoe department barely showed any trace of the previous night's shoppers. He picked up a crumpled receipt and a gum wrapper. A child's handprints marked one of the mirrors and some fuzzy blue and pink slippers had fallen off one of the shelves.

He walked slowly through the aisles, neatening skewed boxes and returning an occasional stray shoe to its mate. He tucked the bent corner of a cardboard placard—*We stand on our quality!*—back into its metal frame.

Seth Stevens did hold one trump card: the store's assistant manager, Ryland Wilson, was a deacon at the Free Church of God's Slaves. That was how he had gotten the job: Margo Hofstatter had asked Ryland Wilson to pray on whether Seth Stevens might find a job at ShopsMart. And the answer had been yes. Seth Stevens had only actually spoken with Ryland Wilson at the interview, but they still helloed when they passed each other. And he was certain that a fellow slave of the Lord would take his side against an anarchist.

Satisfied that there was nothing that even Rob Wingert could complain about, he went back into the warehouse to finish unwrapping the pallet.

*   *   *

He ate lunch behind the store. Most employees ate either in the break room or in the food court, but there were also three green picnic tables on a concrete apron next to the loading dock. All the trees within fifty feet of the rear of the store had been cut down, so it was too bright and too hot, but he preferred to eat alone.

He read his Bible while he ate. Being honest with himself, he knew that he ate alone because he didn't like people to watch him. But it was only a white lie, hardly a sin at all, to say that it was because he wanted quiet while he studied the word of the Lord.

He was reading the book straight through from start to finish. In Bible study he had already read the important chapters, but he still felt as though he had a lifetime of catching up to do. How better to steep himself in the Word than to read every word? Unfortunately, it was slow going. Pastor Grady preached from the King James Bible even though there were easier versions to choose from.

Seth Stevens's bookmark was in the Book of Judges, Chapter 3. God, angry with the children of Israel, had caused tyrants to rule over them again and again. Finally he heard their prayers.

> 15 But when the children of Israel cried unto the LORD, the LORD raised them up a deliverer, Ē´-hŭd the son of Gē´-ră, a Benjamite, a man left-handed: and by him the children of Israel sent a present unto Ĕg´-lŏn the king of Moab.
> 16 But Ē´-hŭd made him a dagger which had two edges, of a cubit length; and he did gird it under his raiment upon his right thigh.
> 17 And he brought the present unto Ĕg´-lŏn king of Moab: and Ĕg´-lŏn [*was*] a very fat man.
> 18 And when he had made an end to offer the present, he sent away the people that bare the present.
> 19 But he himself turned again from the quarries that [*were*] by Gĭl´-găl, and said, I have a secret errand unto thee, O king: who said, Keep silence. And all that stood by him went out from him.
> 20 And Ē´-hŭd came unto him; and he was sitting in a summer parlour, which he had for himself alone. And

Ē´-hŭd said, I have a message from God unto thee. And he arose out of [*his*] seat.

21 And Ē´-hŭd put forth his left hand, and took the dagger from his right thigh, and thrust it into his belly:

22 And the haft also went in after the blade; and the fat closed upon the blade, so that he could not draw the dagger out of his belly; and the dirt came out.

23 Then Ē´-hŭd went forth through the porch, and shut the doors of the parlour upon him, and locked them.

24 When he was gone out, his servants came; and when they saw that, behold, the doors of the parlour [*were*] locked, they said, Surely he covereth his feet in his summer chamber.

25 And they tarried till they were ashamed: and, behold, he opened not the doors of the parlour; therefore they took a key, and opened [*them*]: and, behold, their lord [*was*] fallen down dead on the earth.

Surprised as he was by the gory detail, the killing of kings seemed so ancient that it may as well have been a fairytale. He thought about Elder Harbo and wished he knew a chapter to read about preventing bad things from happening. It seemed like something to talk to Pastor Grady about, but he would have to talk to Terry Kinsman first. Terry Kinsman was probably praying on it right now, and he would probably want to talk to Pastor Grady, too. They didn't make confession in the Free Church of God's Slaves, but when they did something wrong they still needed to come clean. Pastor Grady had preached on that more than once.

After lunch Seth Stevens went back to the floor to sell shoes. He wasn't much of a shoe salesman. In fact, his job description specifically prohibited measuring the customer's foot, checking the stockroom for additional sizes, and recommending more attractive styles. ShopsMart, the granddaddy of the big-box stores, had built its empire on the premise of maximum selection with minimum service. Employees in the shoe department were there to stock, straighten, and smile.

This caused some awkward moments. Customers were still not used to the idea that a clerk in the shoe department could not take their size. Settling themselves into the lone chair, they held out their feet and demanded that he measure them. The first time it happened, Seth Stevens had not even known whether to measure the foot with the shoe on or off. By trial and error, however, he had taught himself to be a competent shoe salesman, even if he hadn't been trained for it, wasn't paid for it, and could be punished for doing it. It was easier than explaining. He measured feet. He hustled back into the warehouse—hundreds of yards away— to search for half-sizes. And if he thought of a better-looking shoe, he made sure to let the customer know.

Unfortunately, returns were a constant problem. He could spot a return coming from four aisles away. And he saw one coming now.

The customer was an enormous woman whose hips and thighs were barely contained by a pair of lime-green stretchy shorts. Her panties were clearly outlined. She scowled as she strode toward him, a wrinkled shopping bag whacking the display racks with each swing of her arm.

'You the manager?' she said. 'I need to talk to the manager.'

'I'm not the manager,' he said. 'But I'm sure I can help you.'

She stopped, huffing, and thrust the bag at him.

'These shoes,' she said. 'Junk.'

He took the bag and opened it. Inside was a pair of muddy trainers that had once been white. The soles were held on to the uppers by the tiniest drops of glue.

'I want my money back,' she said.

There was a crumpled receipt in the bag. He took it out and unfolded it. The shoes had been purchased seven weeks earlier. Company policy was clear: unworn merchandise could be refunded or exchanged for a period of six months. Worn but defective merchandise had to be refunded or exchanged within six weeks. He couldn't do anything for her.

'Ma'am,' he said, 'it looks like these shoes have been worn.'

'Of course he worn 'em. That's why we bought 'em. So he could wear 'em.'

'I can only refund your money for unused merchandise.'

'What, you going to tell me I got to take another pair the same shoes? So they can fall apart in another month and a half?'

He steepled his fingers, then realized what he was doing and dropped his hands to his sides.

'Unfortunately, ma'am, I can't do that either,' he said. 'I can only exchange used merchandise—even defective merchandise—for a period of six weeks.'

'So, what? You can't do nothin'?'

'I'm afraid not.'

'Sneakers shouldn't fall apart in no month and a half. He needs 'em to last 'til next year.'

'Of course not. Of course.'

'So then what? You sell me these piece-a-shit shoes and you ain't gonna do nothin'?'

'Ma'am, please, there's no need for language.'

'Oh hell yes there's need for language! You fix this problem or you find me someone who can. I ain't leavin' 'til I get me some money or some new shoes.'

He studied her face. He believed that she meant it.

'Excuse me, please,' he said.

He turned and headed back to the warehouse.

Halfway there, he stopped. What was he doing? Was he actually going to get Rob Wingert? Rob Wingert would repeat the company policy to the lady and he would enjoy doing it. The shoe department supervisor, despite being an anarchist, took perverse pleasure in enforcing ShopsMart's strict rules. Still, Seth Stevens would be off the hook.

But didn't the customer deserve satisfaction? She was unpleasant, but she had paid good money for her son's shoes and the shoes had fallen apart. He wished that fall-apart was an isolated occurrence, but he saw the same thing every few days. Being godly meant following the rules. But what about when the rules weren't right? Was it a sin to break ShopsMart's rules—or was it a sin to help ShopsMart rip the lady off?

He swiped his associate's card, pushed through the door, and went into the warehouse. Rob Wingert was seated at the small desk in the cage, reading a tattoo magazine that he had halfheartedly disguised with an OSHA binder. Seth Stevens lifted a binder containing various store forms off the desk. He found the form he was looking for, removed a copy, and snapped it on to a clipboard.

'Problem?' asked Rob Wingert.

'No problem,' said Seth Stevens. 'Just an exchange.'

Rob Wingert grunted and turned the page. He lifted the binder higher in a failed attempt to prevent Seth Stevens from seeing a picture of a nearly naked woman, her skin wallpapered with brightly-colored occult imagery.

Seth Stevens went back to the floor. The angry customer had apparently tried on half a dozen pairs of shoes, which were now spread out all over the carpet.

He handed her the clipboard and a pen and asked her to please fill out the top half of the form.

'What's this for?' she asked suspiciously.

'For an exchange.'

'I thought you said you couldn't do that.'

He gave her a wry smile.

She seemed to understand. She filled in her name, address, telephone number, and driver's license number. He could almost read what she had written.

She seemed to have had a change of heart.

'I hope this ain't gonna get you in trouble,' she said.

'As long as they don't check the date on your receipt,' he said. 'I can't give you your money back, but at least you can get another pair of shoes. Hopefully these ones won't fall apart.'

He found an identical pair and traded them to her for the ruined ones. He stapled the receipt to the form and handed it to her.

'Just give this to the cashier,' he said.

'Thank you,' she said.

'God bless.'

She glanced at the floor.

'Sorry.'

He wondered whether she was apologizing for making a mess, or for swearing, or for possibly getting him in trouble. He didn't mind. He was glad he'd been able to make her happy. He was pretty sure he'd done the right thing. At least he'd shown this unhappy woman a good Christian example. And if his job was sometimes unpleasant, well, he was lucky to suffer it.

He walked home into the sun. After the refrigerated air of ShopsMart, it felt hotter outside than it was. The traffic was heavy and slow. He walked on the soft shoulder in a futile attempt to avoid the exhaust fumes.

When he got home, his answering machine was blinking. The first call was from Ben Badgeley, wondering if he wanted to watch movies. The second call was from his mother. He deleted her message without listening to it, then called Ben Badgeley back and told him yes.

Then he called Terry Kinsman's cell phone. There was no answer, so he left a message.

'Terry, I just wanted to let you know that I've been thinking about that guy, you know, on Friday, and I'm praying he's all right,' he said. 'I know you probably feel as bad about what happened as I do. If you want to talk about it, well . . . see you tomorrow, anyway.'

He met Ben Badgeley at the 18-Hour Mart and the two of them sat on a concrete wheel stop until Owen Rusk showed up. They bought nachos, slushies, frozen burritos, candy, and bottles of pop, then walked back to Seth Stevens's apartment.

They often got together on Saturday nights. Playing in the Sunday services still made them nervous, and wasting the evening in a mindless way helped them keep their minds off the fact that they would soon be performing three songs in each of two services in front of about 5,500 people.

The DVDs were *Rio Bravo* and *Sands of Iwo Jima*. Pastor Grady had forbidden his congregation from watching PG-13 or R-rated movies. In his former life, Seth Stevens had watched a lot of horror films. Zombie films were his favorite. And though he knew that they had brought nothing wholesome to his life, he sometimes missed the visceral thrill. Most PG movies were made for little kids and their biggest transgressions involved farting. So when they ran out of family-friendly Hollywood hits—they had seen *Groundhog Day* and *Apollo 13* dozens of times—they watched movies their grandparents might have seen in the theater, because the old westerns and war movies were the only grown-up movies they liked that never used foul language or showed nudity.

The really fun part was the junk food. There was no proscription against fried fat. So they gorged themselves, half-watching the movies, talking over the boring parts, until their hearts jackhammered from sugar and caffeine.

That evening it was the same as ever except that Seth Stevens couldn't calm his nerves. This time his fear wasn't coming from stage fright. How could he stand up in a holy place, how could he help lead songs of praise, after what they had done on Friday night?

Three

Before the 9 a.m. worship, the members of Salvation were gathered in the music room when Terry Kinsman walked in. They had tuned their instruments and performed a sound-check nearly an hour ago, then retreated from the stage before the ushers opened the front doors at 8:30 a.m. Sometimes as many as a hundred congregants were waiting outside. The truly devout wanted to sit as close to Pastor Grady as possible.

Owen Rusk clicked an intricate beat with his drumsticks on the back of a plastic chair. Seth Stevens twanged his unplugged guitar while Ben Badgeley plucked and slapped funk riffs on his unplugged bass. Jimmy Gilstrap played melancholy chords on an upright piano. Kirk Swindoll talked to his girlfriend on his cell phone.

Terry Kinsman waited in the center of the room, staring at the floor, until they were all quiet and looking at him.

'I got something I got to say,' he said. 'You all know that I got a temper. I been praying the Lord's help, but Satan is working on me, and I'm weak. I know you all got other things on your mind right now. You need to go out there and play your music and uplift our church and inspire us to walk holy in the name of the Lord. But help me pray first. I want to get right with the Lord before I walk in His holy church again.'

Kirk Swindoll said something into his phone and snapped it shut. He walked over to Terry Kinsman and put one hand on his arm, the other on his shoulder.

'Jesus, I plead Your blood over my friend Terry, over his sins and over my sins,' said Kirk Swindoll. 'Wash away our sins and give us peace, heavenly father, oh Lord, amen.'

'Amen,' said Owen Rusk.

Terry Kinsman closed his eyes and sank to his knees. He raised his right hand and held it palm out. The rest of the band came over and put their hands on him, too. Terry Kinsman swayed slightly as they prayed out loud, their voices overlapping, sometimes synchronizing on a single word: 'Jesus' or 'amen' or 'blood'.

Seth Stevens found room on Terry Kinsman's head, his hand overlapping Ben Badgeley's. He wished he could ignore the touch of skin and instead feel the touch of the divine. He often felt left behind when God's Slaves broke so spontaneously into rapturous prayer. He had never felt so full of goodness that it could burst out of him at a moment's notice. But no one ever called him a slow starter. When he opened his eyes to meet the gaze of the others, he saw only smiles. It felt good to be there. He was sure it would feel even better when he could join in fully.

'Oh Jesus, help our brother, cover him with Your blood,' said Kirk Swindoll. '*Shay may nay fo so popolah. Shay may fay so so popolah. Shay me fa la, no go me fa la, hesh hell shu ma la, shu ma la, shu ma la, Jesus!*'

Jimmy Gilstrap began speaking in tongues, too. Then Ben Badgeley joined in, then Owen Rusk. As their voices rose in a holy babble, Seth Stevens felt a flush first of embarrassment, then of excitement. The first time he had heard the gift of tongues, before he had been born again, he had assumed that it was a hoax. How did a normal person suddenly forget how to speak English and instead use this strange, toddler-like mish-mash of syllables? But that had been before he had seen first-hand the power of Jesus Christ in his life. And before he had heard Pastor Grady preach on the gift of tongues.

'When the seculars look at you and say, "Hey, look at that crazy holy roller redneck talking nonsense," you may fall prey to feeling embarrassed,' Pastor Grady had said. 'When some city folk who come down to see how the Okies live, taking pictures like they're on a safari—when they stare with their mouths wide open when they see you filled with the glory and the power of Jesus Christ, and they hear those funny sounds coming out of your mouth and they say, "That's not normal!"—well, those words may wound you. And you know what? They're right. It's not normal. It's not normal because in these dark times only a lucky few live in friendship with the Lord and walk in a state of grace. No, you are not normal, but we have never tried to be normal. We have tried to walk the perfect path. And look around you, brothers and sisters. That's one lonely road.'

Seth Stevens had never tried speaking in tongues, but he guessed that was the point: it came naturally or not at all. As he laid his hand on Terry Kinsman's close-cropped head and listened to the voices of his band mates, he hoped he would share their gift soon. For most of them it started slowly, with mysterious words slipping in between the English ones. And then all of the words were new. The new words sounded familiar, like regular speech that he just couldn't understand. His band mates' voices rose and fell, grew loud and then quiet. They sounded ancient, or timeless, like angels.

It was only after Terry Kinsman had left the room that he realized no one had said anything about Elder Harbo, the young Mormon missionary who had been chased into the road and hit by a truck.

Seth Stevens liked to watch church services from a hallway that led to the back of the stage. The unlighted tunnel made an S-turn so the congregation couldn't see who was coming on next. Standing only a few steps back, he was practically invisible.

He had never been to church before becoming one of God's Slaves, so he'd had no idea what to expect. The movies usually showed Catholic churches, which he suspected was because the statues of saints and flickering candles looked good on camera. Sometimes, for comic effect, they'd use a Protestant church with a starchy preacher droning on to a pinched crowd of bluebloods. Or maybe a black church where the preacher did backflips in front of an ecstatic choir. He couldn't relate to any of those experiences. But the first time he'd seen Pastor Grady preach he'd been surprised because it felt so familiar. It was kind of like a rock concert.

The Free Church of God's Slaves had come a long way from its origins in a cinder-block strip-mall, sandwiched, as Pastor Grady liked to remind his congregation, between Sodom and Gomorrah: an adult video store and a liquor store. The church had grown so quickly that it changed locations almost yearly, first to a rented high-school gymnasium, then to the store that ShopsMart had outgrown, and finally to a brand new church built from members' tithes.

The new church sat in the middle of a sixteen-acre parking lot, and though it was plain outside—some people said the architect hadn't improved much on the ShopsMart—inside it was state-of-the-art. A cross-shaped thrust stage was surrounded by pews that gradually rose toward all four walls, so that Pastor Grady was surrounded by the faithful and nobody had a bad view. Hidden ramps and mechanical lifts allowed performers and set pieces to be raised and lowered as if by magic. Pastor Grady, his deacons, the choir, and anybody else who went onstage wore headsets with unobtrusive microphones and tiny earpieces. The sound was transmitted to mixing boards in a raised booth over the front door and then broadcasted through a cluster of high-tech speakers suspended over the stage. The ceiling was hung with computer-controlled lights that were fancier than anything Seth Stevens had seen while playing with his old band.

The house lights stayed up until 9:05. Then they began to dim almost imperceptibly while echoey, almost New Age-y music faded up from the speakers. The lights kept going down until the auditorium was lit only by dim aisle lights and by a single spotlight that turned the majestically soaring wooden cross blood red.

The audience hushed. Someone stifled a coughing fit. A cell phone played an arpeggio as someone turned it off. Then, suddenly, in a blaze of lights, the full choir, nearly fifty men and women strong, appeared onstage, singing *The House of the Lord* at the top of their lungs.

Seth Stevens hadn't grown up with church music, either. But he was a music lover, and the first time he'd heard the choir—not dry and brittle like he'd imagined church music would be, but full-throated and joyful—that was when he'd felt he might be in the right place. Pastor Grady's sermons started to sink in after that.

Some members of the congregation clapped their hands. Others stood and swayed, holding their right hands palm out toward the stage. Some danced in place. Some merely smiled.

The choir segued into another song, *We Lift Up Your Name*. As they reached the third chorus, Pastor Grady strode on to the stage, beaming, suddenly the focal point amidst fifty robed, dancing bodies. He sang, his voice inaudible among the trained singers. But the gesture was clear: he was there to worship just like everybody else.

Still singing, repeating the chorus, the choir formed a line and filed down the ramp. The sound man lowered the volume gradually, making it seem as though their voices were growing quieter as they went farther away. The audience applauded and amened until Pastor Grady, still smiling, shushed them.

Finally, the stage was empty. Pastor Grady welcomed them all, told a joke, and then invited Terry Kinsman to the stage with the other four youth pastors. The youth pastors called the children up to the stage. When all of them—from kindergarteners to eighth-graders—had crowded into a seated circle, one of the youth pastors gave a brief sermon about the virtue of honesty. Then they led the children to Sunday school via the doorway at the rear of the stage. While the young people made their way out, Pastor Grady told a funny Sunday school story. They had all heard it before but they laughed anyway.

Seth Stevens watched the children filing by and eavesdropped on their whispers. Terry Kinsman brought up the rear. They gave each other the band handshake, Terry Kinsman's body shielding the exchange from the congregation behind him.

Then it was Salvation's turn to play. The lights went out—all the lights this time.

Seth Stevens followed the glow tape as he walked up the long side of the cross and turned left to where the drum set and amps had risen from the orchestra pit. His hands muting the strings of his guitar, he plugged it in and dialed up the volume.

Pastor Grady's disembodied voice filled the sanctuary.

'And now comes a part of our worship that I know some of you just can't wait for,' he said.

A few teenaged girls yelped in the silence. Their parents shushed them. Pastor Grady chuckled.

'That's all right, parents,' he said. 'No one ever said we couldn't have fun while we praise the Lord. I've read the Bible, well, once or twice'—he held for the laugh—'and if that chapter and verse is there, I couldn't find it.'

The tiny LEDs on the amps and keyboards looked like a technicolor constellation. As his eyes adjusted to the darkness, Seth Stevens could see the rest of the band in place: Jimmy Gilstrap pushing buttons on his keyboard; Ben

Badgeley standing patiently with his bass; Owen Rusk silently twirling his drumsticks; Kirk Swindoll standing at the microphone stand, his head bowed.

'But there is one part I remember pretty well,' said Pastor Grady. '"Make a joyful noise unto the Lord!"'

The lights came up and the band started playing. The audience cheered and applauded. '(To See) His Face' was a mid-tempo number that started with a chiming, swirling riff in which guitar and keyboard played counterpoint. Kirk Swindoll's singing soared above it all, but the music grew louder verse by verse and especially on the triumphant chorus.

> I didn't want a hand to hold
> I didn't want nobody else
> I didn't want to be told
> I didn't want to hear the bells
>
> But I wasn't meant to walk alone
> I couldn't do it by myself
> What I needed was to come home
> And take His words off of the shelf
>
> I'm in Him
> And He's in me
> And I can only be the man He'll let me be
> And I would travel
> Through time and space
> I would obey His command
> Just to see His face
>
> I thought I could do it my own way
> I thought I could throw the past away
> I thought I could travel my own road
> I thought a lot of things but now I know

Kirk Swindoll worked the stage with the canniness of any rock star. The difference, thought Seth Stevens, was that when kids at rock concerts held up their hands, they were reaching toward the singer, creating a false idol. When members of the congregation at church held up their hands, they were reaching out toward their maker. And the singer held his hand up to Him, too.

They repeated the last chorus four times, building a slow but powerful crescendo. Kirk Swindoll played with the phrasing, his delivery deceptively loose. Finally, as the musicians struck the last chord and held it, the singer lowered his head and the lights faded until there were two spotlights: one on the floating cross, one on the kneeling singer.

Applause, amens, and girlish shrieks filled the cavernous church. Then the spotlight on Kirk Swindoll faded and another one came up. Pastor Grady stood in the center of the cross-shaped stage, a Bible in his hand. It was time for the main sermon to begin. There was a quiet tremor as the section of stage under the band began to descend. As they sank into the orchestra pit, the audience disappeared. Pastor Grady's warm and friendly voice followed them.

'When I was twelve years old I had a tough problem to solve. It didn't have anything to do with God, at least not so far as I could see back then. Remember, this was before I was saved. I was a heathen. If God had called me, I hadn't heard Him. And even if I had heard Him, I'm not sure I would have listened to what He said.'

The band waited in the dim light of the pit, keeping quiet so their noise wouldn't carry up into the hushed church. Owen Rusk beat a rhythm on his pants leg while the others sat down in chairs to wait for their next number.

Seth Stevens went through a door, down a short hall, and up a flight of stairs to the back of the stage so he could watch Pastor Grady.

'Now, we were dirt poor, my daddy was a drunk, and my mama was what you call a codependent. We were a regular Oprah family.'

He grinned as the congregation laughed.

'My daddy was between jobs. He was between jobs so often that I sometimes wondered if we should refer to his rare periods of employment as being "between joblessness".'

This line received less of a laugh as the congregants parsed the sentence. Turning stage right, Pastor Grady ambled down one of the short arms of the cross.

'Now, one night, we had a problem: we didn't have any food to eat. The cupboard was bare and we didn't have any money. Now, that may sound like a line from a Mother Goose nursery rhyme, but I mean it. The cupboard was bare, the fridge was bare, the pantry didn't have anything in it but a little mouse staring at the mousetrap, wishing there was some cheese on it.

'And I had five brothers and sisters and we needed to eat. My mama, well, she was afraid of my daddy when he was drinking. And he was drinking. He used to drink canned beer—"High Life" they called it—one after another after another. So because I was the biggest of Mama's boys, she deputized me to ask my daddy to find some food for her family to eat. I really appreciated being asked, let me tell you. I think I would have rather weeded the back forty with a salad fork.'

Pastor Grady was ambling back toward the center of the cross. He adopted the posture of a young boy fearfully approaching his father.

'So I tiptoed up to the couch. Daddy spent a lot of time on the couch. It meant he was closer to the floor if he passed out cold. I tiptoed up. "Daddy, what's for dinner?" I said. And he said, "Ask your mama." And I said, "Mama said we ain't got no food, Daddy." And he must have heard me, because he took the clicker and turned down the volume on his football game. And he looked at me and he said, "Get my fishing pole, go down to the river, and bring back dinner."'

Pastor Grady stopped, his mouth an astonished 'O'.

'Why, I never thought of that! Dinner was waiting for us down there at the river! All I had to do was go down and reel it in.'

Laughter.

'You've all been patient, but I better get on with it. The problem was that I didn't have a fishing license. My mama didn't have a fishing license, my brothers and sisters didn't have a fishing license, and my daddy most certainly didn't have a fishing license. I wanted to go fish dinner out of the river, but I was afraid of that mean ol' fish and game warden, too. So what was I to do? That which was right, or that which was legal? Who was I to obey?'

Pastor Grady came right down the center of the cross, deep into the heart of the congregation.

'You all know Matthew 22:21: "Render therefore unto

Caesar the things which are Caesar's; and unto God the things that are God's." Jesus said it when the Pharisees and the Herodians—let's call them government agents—were trying to "entangle him in his talk". They were sure they had him, too. They asked him, "Is it lawful to give tribute to Caesar, or not?" And if he said, No, don't pay taxes to Caesar, then they were going to cook his goose. And if Jesus said, Sure, pay those taxes, then he would be discredited among his followers, because everyone knew that old Caesar was wicked.

'But Jesus had the perfect reply. And those government agents walked away scratching their heads.'

Pastor Grady sat down on the lip of the stage, dangling his legs.

'I am one long-winded son-of-a-gun. I'm tiring myself out here. So, OK. Ever since then, people have taken Jesus' words to mean that you should follow the law in matters of law, and Jesus in matters of spirit, and grace, and holiness. Pay your parking tickets but pledge your heart to Jesus. But it's not always that simple. Say you're a Christian and you're elected judge. All of a sudden, your belief, the fact that you were saved, the fact that you pray the gospel and walk in the footsteps of Jesus, you're supposed to hang that up with your coat when you report to the office.

'I've got lots of examples: abortion, the Ten Commandments, the Pledge of Allegiance, prayer in school. You all know 'em. So when it's not a parking ticket, when your government forces you into direct conflict with your most deeply held and cherished beliefs, what do you do?'

Mischievously, Pastor Grady extended the microphone toward an old lady in the front row.

'Help me out here, ma'am. What do you do?'

The lady froze, her smile a rictus of fear.

Pastor Grady shook his head and stood up.

'I'm only having fun. You're not the one paid to preach here. Well, I'll tell you what I did way back when I was twelve years old, when I was asked to choose between feeding my family and following a minor governmental regulation.'

Theatrically, Pastor Grady turned his back and began walking toward the rear door.

'I went fishing.'

*　　*　　*

The service was a little over an hour long. After Pastor Grady's spellbinding sermon, one of the deacons read scripture and then there was a laying-on of hands. Salvation played another song, 'There's No Heaven (On Earth)'. Then Terry Kinsman brought a group of eight-, nine-, and ten-year-olds onstage to perform a play about schoolyard evangelism. After that, the choir came back on stage to perform 'I'll Fly Away'. Then everybody—Pastor Grady, the deacons, the youth pastors, the kids, and Salvation—returned to the stage to sing 'Amazing Grace'. Seth Stevens strummed the simple chords on his guitar and sang backup at a microphone with Ben Badgeley. The tech crew brought up the house lights and the audience stood and joined in. Even the tech crew was on their feet, the lights turned on in their glassed-in booth, singing along even if no one heard them.

The old hymn had a simple, almost primal beauty. There were times when playing Christian rock, and even death metal, had felt almost transcendent. But closing the service with 'Amazing Grace', thought Seth Stevens, was truly amazing.

Then the music stopped and people smiled, hugging each other. Tears glistened on some of their faces. Others, overcome with the Spirit, swayed and spoke in tongues, or prayed over one another, laying on hands. Something had happened, something good. Seth Stevens didn't understand it as well as he wished he did, but he was part of something bigger and it gladdened his heart.

Then, at ten thirty, they did it all over again.

Shortly after noon, Seth Stevens stood off to one side of the church entrance, waiting for Margo Hofstatter to come out and take him to Sunday dinner. The sun beat down like the heat from a frying pan. Worshippers came out of the front doors of the church in twos, threes, and fours. They lingered to talk before dispersing into the huge parking lot to look for their cars. It had always seemed odd to him that there were no steps leading up to the front door of the church. Instead, the black asphalt of the parking lot was level with the putting-green grass of the lawn which was flush with the gray concrete of the front walk which led to the short beige carpet of the church without going an inch off level. But then he saw a woman coming out on her electric scooter, her crutches in the back basket, and he thought that maybe function was better than form.

Charisma Brown, blue-eyed and chestnut-haired, broke away from her mother and came over.

'You guys sounded great today,' she said. 'I like the new song. What was it called?'

'"There's No Heaven (On Earth)".'

'It's really powerful. Did you write it?'

He shook his head. Her startling beauty always caused him to forget that he was older and supposedly cooler. He glanced out at the parking lot in order to resist the temptation to look at her large breasts.

She looked away, too. Perhaps she was already plotting her escape.

'I've got to say,' she said, 'I think some of the girls in the audience aren't always thinking holy thoughts when you guys are playing.'

That made him look at her. Her eyes were sunny and her nose was crinkled. Why was she teasing him?

'We're just trying to do the Lord's work,' he said. 'If those girls have something else in their hearts, well, I hope they listen long and hard to our lyrics.'

'Maybe Kirk should sing with a bag over his head or something.'

Seth Stevens felt a pang that Kirk Swindoll had been singled out as the good-looking one. He told himself to stop being vain.

'We asked him to stand behind the drum set when he sings, but he says he can't minister from back there. He has to be right out in front of everybody. What are you gonna do?'

He shrugged, palms out.

She laughed.

'Well, you can't argue with that,' she said. 'I guess that goes for all of you? Kirk's not the only one with groupies.'

Charisma Brown winked and walked away. She had always seemed to like him. He suddenly wondered if he was in love with her. Unfortunately, he was five years older than her. Worse, she was Pastor Grady's niece. He couldn't imagine that anyone, Charisma Brown included, wanted him to ask her out.

Someone tapped him on the shoulder. He turned around and jumped back as Terry Kinsman threw a fake punch.

'Made you flinch,' he said.

'Well, duh.'

The idea of standing still and letting someone punch him in the face didn't strike him as very admirable and he said so.

Terry Kinsman shrugged.

'Listen,' he said, 'Pastor Grady needs some volunteers for a special project. Tonight. I told him he could count on us.'

Seth Stevens was so surprised that he couldn't even think of the right question to ask.

'He can count on us both, can't he?' asked Terry Kinsman.

'Well, yeah, but what the heck are you talking about?'

Terry Kinsman smiled and put his hand on Seth Stevens's shoulder.

'Surprise. Tell you but I'd have to kill you. Pick you up at six?'

Seth Stevens nodded.

'Free pizza,' said Terry Kinsman enigmatically, before strolling away toward his car.

Seth Stevens heard his name being called. Margo Hofstatter stood about fifty feet away, waving him over. He went. He was thinking that doing a favor for Charisma Brown's uncle didn't seem like the worst way to spend a Sunday night.

Margo Hofstatter was his guardian angel. She didn't look or sound like an angel. She stood five feet five inches tall and had a round head stuck on top of a round body like a snowman. Her hair was styled in a spiky look that probably seemed urban to the hairstylists on the outskirts of Tulsa. Her make-up might have looked natural if she had been a stage actress in the footlight era. And her high-pitched voice was incongruously husky from all the years she'd spent drinking and smoking, before she'd been saved by Pastor Grady in his little storefront church.

In turn, she'd saved Seth Stevens. She'd found him living in a storage unit, his addiction to meth out of control.

Back then, Margo Hofstatter wasn't in much of a position to help anyone. She was still getting her own life back together. After her husband took their children and moved in with his parents because of her drinking problem, she had lost her job and then her house. She became a street corner wino only a mile away from the cul-de-sac where she'd lived a comfortable, middle-class existence. One Sunday, Pastor Grady had steered her into his church with the promise of a hot lunch after the service. She had been filled with the Holy Spirit and had begun traveling the road to recovery without the help of any twelve-step programs.

She lived in a rooming house and worked two jobs, slowly piecing together her shattered finances. She attended the Free Church of God's Slaves twice each Sunday and once on Wednesday. When she had a spare moment, she visited her belongings at the storage unit where she'd had them delivered before the bank repossessed her house. She had sold much of the furniture to buy alcohol, but she had kept the things that mattered: photo albums, family records, books, mementos. Sitting in a lawn chair, she would sift tearfully through her boxes, reminding herself of the time when her life had been good and praying that it would be good again.

Seth Stevens was paying thirty dollars per month for the eight-foot by ten-foot unit next to hers. He roamed the streets and alleys of Tulsa at night and returned at dawn to crash or lie twitching on a foam pad on the floor. He had punched extra holes in his belt to keep his pants up. He had weeping sores on his arms from digging at crank bugs. Two teeth had fallen out and, even when he was high, he noticed people wincing at his breath. An emergency-room doctor had told him, bluntly, 'See you in the morgue.'

Margo Hofstatter had heard sounds that made her suspect someone was actually living next door. But Seth Stevens was careful to avoid being seen as he came and went. It was only one evening, as she was taking advantage of a break between shifts to come visit her belongings, that she surprised him as he rolled up the garage-like door part way and walked out, hunchbacked.

Their encounter that night had been brief. Seth Stevens had practically run away when he'd realized she was a Jesus freak. But, she told him later, she knew instantly that she needed to help him. When he came home the next morning, there was a cold meal of a burger and fries waiting for him. He ate it and vomited it up. The next morning, there were cinnamon rolls and a cheap plastic thermos full of lukewarm coffee. The cinnamon rolls stayed down better than the hamburgers. And the third morning, Margo Hofstatter was there, asking if she could take him to breakfast.

It continued like that. She treated him like a feral cat or dog that needed to learn how to trust people. He had slid so far in the previous six months that the analogy wasn't inappropriate. She gave him food, and talked kindly to him, and was careful not to push him too hard. Meanwhile, her own resolve to change grew even stronger. An associate pastor at the church gave her a part-time job as an accountant at his clothing store. She began attending couples counseling with her estranged husband.

Finally, Seth Stevens agreed to accompany her to church. When he didn't have an instant epiphany as she had, she was disappointed. But he did agree to come back the following week. As a grungy, drug-addicted metalhead, he felt like a space alien among the clean-cut worshippers. But no one judged him. Instead, they smiled at him and asked how they could help him. The social cliques of the music scene hadn't prepared him for anything like it. The people he'd known had been quick to share their drugs and alcohol and even quicker to judge those who grew hooked on the high.

Unfortunately, he wasn't able to beat his meth problem through prayer. But Margo Hofstatter called social-service agencies until she found a rehab center with an open bed. He slept twenty hours a day at first, feeling stupid and slow. Gradually, his energy came back. He paced, feeling like he was in jail. He argued with the counselors even though he knew they were right. Agreeing with them too easily would have made him feel like he had no will at all.

The clinic arranged dental work for him. His smile would never look like it used to, but after a half-dozen procedures, it would no longer frighten small children, either.

Four months later he had a tic, a nervous habit of biting the inside of his cheek that sometimes left him tasting blood all day long. But he was clean. He'd even gained twenty pounds, thanks to the regular meals of starchy food.

Margo Hofstatter was waiting when he came out. She had a car by then, and she drove him to a cul-de-sac lined with tiny trees where she was living in a brand new home. Her husband, Bill, was there, and her children, too. Seth Stevens stayed with the family for six months. His tic gradually disappeared. He slept in a corner of the unfinished basement that had been curtained off with old blankets hung from the joists. He worked fast-food for a few months until Margo Hofstatter found him a better job at ShopsMart. Once Seth Stevens had enough money saved up, Bill Hofstatter cosigned his lease on the studio apartment and helped him furnish it from the Salvation Army store. Since then, his presence at Sunday dinner at the Hofstatters' had been what Margot Hofstatter called an 'immaculate assumption'.

Now he followed her to her car. Her husband was behind the wheel and both kids were in the back seat. Tommy Hofstatter was eleven and his sister Tammy was nine. Tammy Hofstatter slid over to the center seat and Seth Stevens climbed in next to her. An only child, he didn't know what it felt like to be somebody's brother. But during his stay in the Hofstatter household he'd begun to feel the way he thought an older brother might feel.

Doors closed, seatbelts clicked, and Bill Hofstatter put the car in gear.

Margo Hofstatter had risen at dawn to cook a Roman-sized meal, then left the hot dishes in the oven while the family went to church. Two hours later, the baked potatoes were withered, the string beans were stringy, and the 'Viva La Chicken' casserole had become a glutinous mass. Compared to microwave burritos and day-old corn dogs from the 18-Hour Mart, however, it was a four-star meal. Seth Stevens ate with gusto, washing the starchy food down with plenty of Bill Hofstatter's mixological specialty, the Arnold Palmer: half iced tea, half lemonade.

Afterward, they sat in white plastic lawn chairs on a concrete pad in the backyard. The sun beat down on their heads. The saplings surrounding them weren't tall or leafy enough to provide meaningful shade. Tommy and Tammy Hofstatter bounced on a trampoline while Margo Hofstatter watched them fearfully and Bill Hofstatter told her not to worry. Kids had been surviving trampolines since olden days.

'It's a shame about that Mormon kid,' said Margo Hofstatter.

Seth Stevens twitched but didn't look at her. He felt his neck flush even in the heat.

'What?' he said.

'I heard it on the radio news this morning, before church. Some Mormon missionary kid, here in Tulsa. Apparently he's missing.'

'Since when?' said Bill Hofstatter.

'Since he didn't come home Friday night. He and this other Mormon boy are staying with this local Mormon family.'

Bill Hofstatter shook his head.

'Probably got some sense in him and run off. Maybe we'll see him next week at Sunday services.'

'Well, I'll bet his family is worried sick,' said Margo Hofstatter. 'I hope they find him.'

Seth Stevens watched a black beetle struggle through the grass.

'Well!' said Margo Hofstatter, clapping her hands. 'Salvation sounded wonderful.'

'Thank you,' said Seth Stevens.

'I know Pastor Grady thinks the world of you boys. He knows there's a lot of young people don't want to get out of bed of a Sunday morning, much less haul their bottoms to church. They sure show up for Salvation, though.'

Seth Stevens was never sure how he should respond to Margo Hofstatter's constant praise. But when he gave the Lord credit, it seemed to make her happy.

'It's the Lord working through us, Margo,' he said.

'Praise Him, amen,' she said.

'Although He works more through Jimmy, since he writes the songs, and through Kirk, since he sings them.'

'It's very modest of you to say so. More Arnold Palmer?'

Without waiting for his answer, she tipped a sweating pitcher of the ocher beverage and refilled his glass. Ice cubes clunked against thick plastic.

'And how's work?' she asked.

'Well, my boss is giving me the usual grief.'

'The Lord has many ways to teach us patience, doesn't He?'

He nodded.

'And how's your apartment? Are you still thinking about moving?'

'Yes.'

'You just let us know if you need anything. Anything at all, Seth. You know I think of you as—'

'I know, thank you, Margo.'

She looked at him, smiling expectantly. He knew what she wanted him to say: that he thought of her as his mother. And sometimes he was tempted. He was grateful to her. In fact, he was pretty sure that he loved her. But he wasn't ready to go farther than that.

'I'll be grateful to you until the end of this life and into the next,' he told her.

He saw disappointment flicker in her eyes.

'Praise be,' she said reflexively.

She turned to watch her children.

'Tommy, stop *bumping* her!'

He watched Bill Hofstatter watching his kids. If he accepted Margo Hofstatter as his mother, would that mean that Bill Hofstatter was his father? He didn't have any experience with fathers. And he didn't know how Bill Hofstatter thought of him. Margo Hofstatter's husband had never expressed any emotion—surprise, pride, disappointment, or disgust—at the fact that his wife had adopted a drug addict during her recovery from alcoholism.

But it was hard to tell what Bill Hofstatter was thinking about anything. If he was taciturn, he was unfailingly helpful, too. He was always the first to lend a hand, always the last to put down his tools. Though he seemed to sit passively, his face almost blank, he existed in a state of perpetual readiness to help others. At the merest suggestion from his wife that the widow across the way needed her lawn mowed, he would back his riding mower out of the garage and attend to the chore.

And yet Margo Hofstatter had said that he had been the one who had put the kids in the car late one night and driven away. So Bill Hofstatter was not always the passive one.

There were times when Seth Stevens wished he was a blood part of their family. Their will to improve themselves and to help others made him certain that their marriage would survive the long haul. And their clean, orderly house gave him a sense of safety that he'd never known, a sense that the grown-ups were in charge. Though he was a grown-up himself now, he still wanted to be taken care of. But he still didn't know if he could simply decide to call another woman his mother.

Seth Stevens watched Margo and Bill Hofstatter watching their children. Her face was closed and frowning. His face was open and smiling. He wondered what parents thought when they thought about their children.

Four

B ill Hofstatter dropped him off at home at five o'clock. Terry Kinsman picked him up an hour later. They drove to the old downtown, to the old church storefront. Seth Stevens had only seen it a couple of times before and not for a long time. The adult video store had closed and the liquor store had been replaced by a tax-preparation service. And there was a new sign on the old church: Citizens for Good Government. The windows were shaded with gray-tinted plastic, but lights were on inside. Terry Kinsman parked in front.

'I thought you said Pastor Grady—' said Seth Stevens.

'This is, but it's for Grady Sheldon, private citizen; not Grady Sheldon, pastor of the Free Church of God's Slaves.'

Terry Kinsman seemed to enjoy Seth Stevens's look of incomprehension.

'See, churches are nonprofit. That means if he's preaching, he can't come out one way or the other on political candidates. But if he wants to contribute his personal time and money to a political action committee, and they get behind someone, well then, he's got the same rights as any citizen. So this doesn't have anything to do with the church.'

They went inside. The former storefront church had been transformed into an office suite with speckled gray carpeting and white walls. In the waiting area were a couch and some chairs, a half-dozen fake-looking houseplants, and a vacant desk with a phone and computer on top of it.

Terry Kinsman led him into the back. As they went down the hallway, Seth Stevens saw a room with a half-dozen cubicles where men and women were talking into phones. They walked past several dark offices and into a conference room where cardboard boxes were piled on a long wood grain-laminate table. Two men were conferring earnestly at

the far end of the room. So far there weren't any faces that
he hadn't seen that morning at church.

The two men interrupted their conversation, smiling.

'Come to do the good Lord's dirty work?' one of them
asked.

'We're here to help clean up Satan's mess,' said Terry
Kinsman.

'Hallelujah,' said one man.

'Hope you brought your shovels,' said the other.

Hundreds of red, white, and blue yard signs leaned against
one wall, their placards upside down and their sharpened
stakes right side up. *Dean Platt: Heartland Values, Common
Sense* they declared.

The two men gave them a map, a list of addresses, two
hammers, and more than a hundred yard signs. Terry Kinsman
and Seth Stevens carried the signs out in armfuls until they'd
filled the back seat.

Terry Kinsman squinted at the map for a few moments.
Then he wedged it into the visor and started the car.

'So Pastor Grady supports Dean Platt?' asked Seth Stevens.

'More or less. He calls politicians an unnecessary evil but
a fact of life. Citizens for Good Government basically supports
the candidate who's most godly. Platt's a Baptist, which we're
not crazy about, but close enough. He's for prayer in schools,
against abortion, and he wants to close the borders before
things get out of hand with the illegals. Ira Isaacs? He's a
Jew, for starters. But he doesn't even go to Jewish church.
He's pro-abortion, pro-ACLU, pro-multiculturalism, pro-
secular everything. Basically he's our worst nightmare. So we
got to get Platt elected. He didn't help himself none when he
told that one lesbian joke, but no way is Oklahoma going to
elect a secular Jew Senator, not if we can help it.'

'So we're doing this for the church, really.'

'Well, don't say that around no one with a tape recorder.
But the law's complete bullcrap anyways. Even judges,
people get upset when they accidentally say the words
"God" or "Jesus". If you've accepted Jesus Christ as your
personal savior, it's in everything you do. How are you
supposed to go to work or anywhere else and not pledge
your actions to the Lord? I swear, people forget that
Christians are citizens, too.'

'Why are we doing this at night? It's like we're sneaking around.'

Terry Kinsman shrugged.

'Because I got to work in the morning.'

When they came to the first address on the list, Terry Kinsman kept the car running while Seth Stevens jumped out and hammered the sign into the front-yard grass. They did this a half-dozen times without seeing any of the homeowners, although flickers on the front windows told them that the houses weren't empty.

Seth Stevens was hammering down a sign, taking care to keep the placard parallel with the sidewalk, when he heard Terry Kinsman's door slam. He looked up. Terry Kinsman ran diagonally across the street and pulled an *Isaacs: Forward Thinking* sign out of the ground. Then he brought the sign back to the car and put it in the trunk. Seth Stevens climbed back in the car, barely getting the door shut before they pulled away from the curb.

'What are you doing, Terry?'

'I'm helping the cause, Seth.'

'But isn't that illegal or something?'

'Whose law do you want? God's law or some secular who wants you to celebrate Earth Day instead of Easter?'

'God's law. Of course.'

'All right then.'

'But shouldn't we fight fair?'

'Do you even hear yourself? Since when have Christians ever been treated fair, from the Romans to the ACLU?'

Seth Stevens didn't know enough history to argue. But when he'd been in bands before Salvation and they'd put up posters for their shows, they'd always taken care to staple them evenly over any posters for other shows scheduled for the same night.

They kept going, putting up yard signs for Platt and taking down yard signs for Isaacs. They listened to KGTO and counted blasphemies. Soon there weren't many Platt signs left in the back seat. The trunk was full of Isaacs signs. Terry Kinsman stole them with zeal, saying things like, 'Another soul saved.'

At twilight, they were about three-quarters of the way through the list. The air was mild and sweet-smelling. Yard lights were coming on and bug zappers were crackling. At the start of the evening Seth Stevens had thought that putting up yard signs sounded painfully boring. But he was enjoying being out, seeing front-window tableaux of quiet Sunday evenings. The trunk was full and Terry Kinsman had started putting Isaacs signs on the floor in the back seat.

Then they reached a block that needed three Platt signs. There were four Isaacs signs already in evidence, two on each side of the street.

'Welcome to Secular City,' said Terry Kinsman.

He put the car in park and turned off the ignition.

'Let's do it to it,' he said.

Noting the addresses, Seth Stevens took three Platt signs and walked to the first lawn. Terry Kinsman ran across the street to the nearest Isaacs sign and pulled it out of the ground. It was a quiet street and the taps of Seth Stevens's hammer sounded louder than usual. By the time he had the first Platt sign in the ground, Terry Kinsman had two Isaacs signs under his arm and was trotting toward the third. Seth Stevens started walking toward the next address on the list.

A sudden whoop made him jump. He turned. Behind them, a police car was crossing the intersection, its lightbar flashing.

Terry Kinsman dropped the signs.

'Run!' he yelled.

Seth Stevens stood frozen in place. He wasn't doing anything wrong. But Terry Kinsman was. Would the police understand the difference? Was there a difference?

Terry Kinsman saw him hesitating. The police car was slowing down, almost between them. Shaking his head, Terry Kinsman raced across the street in front of the police car, forcing its driver to stomp on the brakes to avoid hitting him. The policemen were opening their doors when Terry Kinsman grabbed Seth Stevens's arm and dragged him into the narrow walkway between two houses. Seth Stevens stumbled. Then he dropped his Platt signs and started running, too.

'If they catch us,' hissed Terry Kinsman, 'Pastor Grady's gonna look bad.'

They scrambled over a white board fence and dropped into a backyard. Judging by the ruined grass, a dog lived in that yard, but according to the slack dog trolley, he wasn't home at the moment. The police car's doors slammed and the engine revved as they crossed the yard and opened a gate on to the alley.

Terry Kinsman glanced around, apparently trying to decide whether one policeman would be coming through the yard on foot or whether they would both be flanking them in the car. The police car turned in to the alley and accelerated toward them.

'Split up,' said Terry Kinsman. 'Don't go back to the car. They can't know it's Citizens. We can't make Pastor Grady look bad.'

Terry Kinsman climbed on top of a trash can and vaulted over a chain-link fence into another yard. Seth Stevens could see two policemen in the front seat of the car. He slipped back inside the gate they'd just come out of and latched it. He ran back into the front yard and picked up the dropped signs and the hammer. He ran down the block to Terry Kinsman's car. He considered trying to move the car: if the police came back for another look, they'd see Platt and Isaacs signs lying together on the floor of the back seat.

But the keys weren't in the ignition. He opened the back door and took all the signs out, thinking that maybe there was still some room in the trunk. But Terry Kinsman's car was an older model and there was no button to pop the trunk.

He looked up and down the quiet street, feeling exposed. Someone was drawing back a curtain. From a block away he heard someone say 'Come out of there!' through a bullhorn. Maybe they had Terry Kinsman cornered already.

Seth Stevens dropped the signs on the street and kicked them under the car. He closed the door and ran up the side-walk to the nearest corner, turned away from where he'd heard the police, then zagged across the street again and plunged into another alley.

He stopped running maybe a mile away. His heart was thumping and his breath was ragged. His mouth was dry. He hawked and spat but nothing came out.

He walked into a small park, empty under a bright secur-ity light. He sat down heavily on a merry-go-round. It made a quarter-turn as his weight drew it to its lowest point.

Pastor Grady had followed the rules by creating Citizens for Good Government. And he couldn't be held responsible for the actions of one or two low-level volunteers. But still Seth Stevens knew that Terry Kinsman was right: any news that someone was playing dirty tricks on the Isaacs campaign, no matter how petty, would reflect badly on Citizens for Good Government. Probably on the Platt campaign, too. And maybe even on the Free Church of God's Slaves and its leader.

But if they weren't caught, no charges could be filed. The vandalism might be written off as the work of bored teenagers.

After he caught his breath, he stood up and started walking. He was miles from home. It had been some weekend, he thought. And all thanks to Terry Kinsman.

He was just dozing off in front of the TV, his aching, stinking feet hanging off the side of the bed, when an imperious knock startled him awake.

'Police department. Open the door.'

He went to the door almost without stopping to consider the consequences. What else was he going to do—crawl out the tiny bathroom window and drop down to the ground?

When he released the lock, Terry Kinsman burst through the door, laughing.

'All right, show me what you got in here, God-boy. Bibles? Crosses? You keep your tithes in the cookie jar?'

Seth Stevens wanted to punch him.

'Not funny, Terry.'

He closed the door.

'Take it easy, Seth. I'm a little amped up, is all.'

'So you got away?'

'No, I'm actually in jail now, Einstein.'

Terry Kinsman flopped on the bed, picked up the remote, and started changing channels.

'Albert Einstein: secular Jew who helped us figure out how to blow ourselves to Kingdom Come,' he said, as if reading the back of a trivia game card.

'I mean, I guess we got away with it, huh?'

'I think so. They could of looked in my car and put two and two together and run the plate. But this is Tulsa Police we're talking about, not Scotland Yard.'

'I put the signs from the back seat under the car.'

Terry Kinsman looked up at him, still changing channels.

'I think I broke half of them when I drove off,' he said. 'But good move.'

He stopped on MTV. The program showed nearly naked girls dancing on top of a bar in a crowded nightclub while a fat man in a sombrero hosed them down with a beer tap.

'You think those girls know they're going to Hell?'

They watched in silence for a few minutes. Seth Stevens became aware of a growing erection and walked into the kitchenette. He opened a bottle of pop and took a swig.

'So do you know what happened to that Mormon kid?'

'No, I don't.'

'Margo says it was on the radio that he's missing.'

Terry Kinsman was still staring at the scene of debauchery on TV.

'I was afraid he might have died.'

'He's not dead, Seth.'

'Well, how do you know?'

Terry Kinsman frowned.

'How do I know? I know because I went back there and looked. I know because I called the hospitals. I even called the police. Nobody knew what I was talking about. He must of got back on his bike and rode away. I don't know what else you want me to do.'

'Did you call the Mormon church?'

Irritated, Terry Kinsman turned the television off. He stood up.

'Oh, that's a good one. I wonder how that one would go. "Yes, one of our sweet little Elders got hurt real bad. Who's calling, please?"'

'Well, the police could have traced your number.'

'I'm not stupid, Seth. I called from a pay phone.'

'But don't you want forgiveness, Terry?'

'The Lord has forgiven me. And you were there when you all forgave me. Maybe you didn't, though, way you're acting. Look, I know I need that kid's forgiveness, too. I been having a hard time sleeping. I been praying on it a lot. But that's all I can do. Same reason we ran from the cops tonight. Maybe you want to ruin all Pastor Grady's good work, but I won't. I won't put my stain on him. But anyways they're two totally different things. One, I got my temper up and I sinned and hurt someone. Two, we broke a bullcrap law to help bring this wicked earth closer to God's rule. You see what I'm talking about?'

Seth Stevens nodded.

Terry Kinsman took his keys out of his pocket and jingled them.

'All right then,' he said. 'I gotta go. Praise Jesus.'

'Praise Jesus.'

After Terry Kinsman left, Seth Stevens lay back down on the bed and stared at the cross on the wall. The inside had been jigsawed out so it was more like the outline of a cross; the cinder-block wall was visible through it. The edges and corners had been rounded off and the whole thing had been sanded until it was smooth and supple. It had been stained to bring out the beauty of the cherrywood. It was a pretty cross, nothing like the one Jesus had died on.

He tried praying but he wasn't even sure where to start. After a while he fell asleep.

He made sure to be on time the next morning. But when he arrived at work, Rob Wingert was angry with him anyway.

'What's wrong with this exchange form?'

Rob Wingert held the canary-colored piece of paper up in front of Seth Stevens's face.

Seth Stevens took it and pretended to study it.

'I don't know,' he said.

Rob Wingert snatched it back.

'The date on the receipt doesn't match the date you wrote on the form. Why does that matter? Because it was too late to exchange those shoes. Jesus Christ, I wish you would pay attention.'

Before he had been saved, Seth Stevens had used the savior's name unthinkingly, too. He had used it as mere words, as an epithet, as punctuation. He had used it to humorously raise the stakes in mundane matters: *Jesus Christ, these are some good nachos.* He had no idea how many people he'd hurt by belittling their faith.

'Rob, those shoes had completely fallen apart and that woman is poor. She can't afford to keep buying new shoes every six weeks.'

Rob Wingert's face lit up.

'So you did it on purpose? Listen, Seth, I know you're best

friends with Jesus, but this is a job. Know that word? J-O-B? We're here to make M-O-N-E-Y. If you want to be a Good Samaritan on your own time, on your own dime, be my guest. Buy her a new pair of shoes for Christmas. But when the store buys her a new pair of shoes, I have to make a note of it in your evaluation.'

'Come on, Rob.'

'Store rules. You signed the handbook like everyone else. Or are you too holy to have to play by the rules?'

Seth Stevens sighed.

'Fine, put it down. But I don't regret it. It may have been against the rules but it was still the right thing to do.'

'Does that mean you're going to do it again?'

He shook his head, exasperated. He wasn't going to promise anything.

'You know the policy, Seth. Three infractions in a six-month period and I'll have to fire you.'

'Well, you'll have to keep an eye on me then, won't you?'

'Rest assured that I will.'

Seth Stevens went out on to the floor. He thought that life would be easier if the country was ruled by God's law because then Christians wouldn't have to figure out how to answer all the time. And seculars would be better off even if they didn't know it.

Work went slowly. At lunchtime it was hot and sunny out and the glare from the pages of his Bible made him wish he had brought his sunglasses. He had to quit reading after a little while because he was getting a headache.

Late in the afternoon he heard loud voices coming from a nearby aisle. Bored, he strolled over and peeked around the corner. Two men and a woman were laughing at ShopsMart's teen clothing selection. The woman held a baggy T-shirt up against the chest of one of the guys. A sparkly appliqué read: *Playa*.

'There's nothing more hip-hop than a ShopsMart "Playa" shirt,' she said, laughing.

The other guy was holding up a pair of jeans.

'Look at these,' he said. 'For the gangsta who's afraid his pants will fall down.'

The pants were designed to mimic the fashion of almost-falling-down jeans. But where those kids used belts or hidden

suspenders or sheer nerve to keep their drawers from drop-
ping, the ShopsMart jeans merely mimicked the look: the
waist was high, but the back pockets hung somewhere around
the knees. Add a baggy 'Playa' shirt and who would know the
difference?

Seth Stevens felt a flash of annoyance at their theatrical,
wide-eyed amazement, as if they were anthropologists
descending on a primitive village market.

It wasn't as if the three of them looked normal. They looked
like they were in a death-metal band: tattooed and pierced,
they had shiny blue-black hair and wore black clothes that
had been washed so many times the dye was running out.

Actually, they were in a death-metal band. They were his
former band mates: David Trujillo, Cam McLarin, and Vickie
Lawson.

They saw him looking. They looked back. Vickie Lawson
read his nametag as if she couldn't believe her eyes.

'*Seth?*' she said.

'Hey,' he said.

David Trujillo dropped the jeans on the floor and walked
over. He looked Seth Stevens over curiously.

'Holy shit, Seth. I heard someone say they saw you working
here but I kind of didn't believe it. Bad enough you found
Jesus, but ShopsMart?'

'Hi, David,' said Seth Stevens. 'Nice to see you, too.'

They surrounded him, asking him questions, teasing him
in the manner that had once been so familiar but which now
felt like an attack. When they learned he worked in the shoe
department, they insisted on seeing it. They found the 'Fashion
Athletics' display especially amusing.

He found it hard to keep his eyes off Vickie Lawson. They
had slept together dozens of times before she decided to start
sleeping with David Trujillo again. He wondered whether she
was still sleeping with David Trujillo or if Cam McLarin had
had his turn. Maybe she had even begun to look outside the
band for sexual partners. It was hard to believe he'd been such
a fornicator, and harder to believe that he'd enjoyed it so
much.

'So you're not kidding about this born-again shit, huh?'
said David Trujillo.

'No.'

'At that big church, what's it? Slaves of God?'

'The Free Church of God's Slaves.'

'Sounds like a good album title if you ask me.'

'If you think so.'

'So, no drinking, no drugs?'

'No sex, no dancing, no spitting or swearing?' added Cam McLarin.

'No. I'm trying to live a righteous life now.'

It felt good to say those things when he was with the members of Salvation or with Margo Hofstatter. It felt kind of lame now that he was standing in front of his old friends in the ShopsMart shoe department.

'That's not what you used to mean when you said "righteous",' said Cam McLarin.

David Trujillo stepped closer, guiding Seth Stevens away from the others. He spoke confidentially.

'Was it just to get clean?' he said. 'I know a lot of people need to get born again to get sober. I can see how that would help.'

Seth Stevens wanted to explain how the two were inseparable. How it wasn't as if Jesus' love was a hammer that had helped him break the shackles of addiction. But maybe that was it exactly. And what was wrong with that? What had David Trujillo ever done for him, other than drive him to his dealer?

'I've got to be honest with you, David, I'm a lot happier now,' he said. 'Let me tell you about my relationship with Jesus.'

David Trujillo shook his head. The others shook their heads, too.

'I'm happy you're happy, Seth. But—' he looked around— 'if you're happy working at ShopsMart, I think they put something in your Kool-Aid. I've got to be honest with you, Seth: this God's Slaves stuff sounds like a cult. Anytime you want to come back to Crucifer, just let me know. We've had three different guys since you and none of them can thrash like you did.'

'No, thank you,' he said.

Vickie Lawson put her hand on his arm.

'There's a five-band show at the Elks on Wednesday night. The Black Lodge is coming up from Houston to headline and we're playing right before them. Why don't you just come and listen?'

'Yeah,' said Cam McLarin.

Seth Stevens shook his head.

'I'm going to put you on the list,' said David Trujillo. 'I know you're gonna be there. You're gonna feel that music in your fucking soul and you're not gonna be able to resist. You'll come back to Crucifer.'

Laughing, the three started chanting.

'One of us, one of us, one of us, one of us . . .'

Rob Wingert walked up.

'Is there a problem here?'

'No, no problem,' said Seth Stevens.

'Actually, I have a problem,' said David Trujillo, plucking a fuzzy pink slipper off the shelf. 'I need this in a size eleven.'

'Well, there should be some.'

Rob Wingert scanned the shelf, then shook his head.

'Seth, go look in back. I know we've got a box that just came in.'

'Actually, could you go?' asked Vickie Lawson. 'This gentleman was just about to measure my foot.'

Plopping on to the shoe-fitting stool, she began loosening the laces of her black, knee-high platform boots.

With a tight smile, Rob Wingert started making the long walk to the warehouse.

When he got back, Seth Stevens was straightening the slippers. The members of Crucifer were gone.

'He decided he didn't want them,' he told his supervisor. 'I thought we weren't supposed to check stock for customers.'

Rob Wingert handed him a pair of size 11 slippers.

'We're not supposed to measure their feet, either,' he said. 'So shut up.'

When he opened his door the message light on his answering machine was blinking. He was tempted to hit delete without listening but just to be sure he pressed play. It was his mother.

'Seth, you've got to call me. At least let me know you're getting my messages. If you're not ready to talk yet, well . . . just call me back and let me know it's you. With that weird outgoing message, I don't even know—'

He hit delete. He took a deep breath. He picked up the phone. He put it down.

For years he had answered his mother's calls. She was an alcoholic, in and out of work, on and off the streets. Often he hadn't been able to do anything for her, but he had always listened and offered advice. Usually, he learned during the next call that his advice had already been forgotten. He'd sent money when he could. He knew that she spent it on beer and vodka, but what could he do? She was his mother.

Once he took the bus all the way back to New York to try to help her. She had been weeping, threatening suicide, and begging for rescue. When he got there, she wasn't at the address she'd given. Nor was she at any of her friends' apartments. She wasn't anywhere. He returned to Tulsa to find a message waiting for him. *Please come to New York*, she begged.

He stopped taking her calls after that. There had been nearly two years of silence while he became an addict himself, went to rehab, and joined the church. Then, a month ago, the calls had started again. He wasn't answering. He didn't have anything left to give her. Surviving his own failings was hard enough.

There was a knock at the door. He wasn't expecting anyone.

'Police department! We have a warrant!'

Terry Kinsman was doubled over, laughing, when he opened the door.

'I got you again, didn't I? Didn't I?'

Seth Stevens folded his arms.

'Look, they need more volunteers down at Citizens,' said Terry Kinsman.

'More yard signs?'

'Nope. Something different.'

He didn't say anything. After the previous night, he had thought he was done with volunteering.

'They'll feed us, Seth. Pizza.'

Every man has his price, he thought. His was a slice of pizza. He went with Terry Kinsman.

On the drive over, Terry Kinsman seemed to take Seth Stevens's silence as a challenge and prodded him with questions about his day. After a while Seth Stevens confessed. He told Terry Kinsman about the recent phone calls from his mother.

'You told me she pretty much dropped out of your life,' said Terry Kinsman.

'She stopped raising me a long time ago,' said Seth Stevens. 'But I was the one who cut her off.'

'Your own mother? Holy something.'

'It's hard to live with sometimes. Pastor Grady's always preaching about family and she was all the family I had.'

Terry Kinsman turned off the radio.

'If your mom was a mass murderer, would Jesus still command you to show up at her house for Sunday brunch?'

'He'd command me to still love her.'

'Sure, love. You can give her love if she's on the moon or in Hell or wherever. Think love thoughts, pray for her. But you don't got to hang out with her. What if she spends all her time trying to turn you to Satan?'

'What's love without good works? I just gave up on her. Wouldn't the Christian thing be to keep trying to lift her up, no matter what?'

'Listen, Jesus ran into plenty of jerks along the way. He treated the sinners pretty decent, but He didn't try to save all of 'em. Some people are just wicked.'

Seth Stevens thought of his mother with her bleached hair and her faded T-shirts and her falling-apart scrapbook of photos and flyers. He pictured her sallow skin and her puffy face. He could still hear her voice, which always sounded as if she had spent the previous night shouting to be heard in a bar. She had been a bad girl when she was young, but she wasn't wicked. Alcohol and depression had left her unable to help herself. They had turned her into a black hole that sucked in good intentions until those around her were as empty and exhausted as she was.

'She's not wicked,' he said. 'She's a drunk.'

'How many times have you tried to help her? A lot, right?'

Seth Stevens nodded.

'Not everyone can be saved, Seth. That's why there's gates in front of Heaven. Jesus will accept anyone who accepts Him. Someone says no, well, it wounds His heart but He tries the next person on down the line. The church is a life raft, not a welfare office. Does your mom even want help?'

'Of course.'

'Well, what's she do when you help her? She quit drinking? She get a job? She start going to church?'

'Well, no, but—'

'You did it. Someone gave you a hand up and you took it. You slap someone's hand away, what kind of person are you? Someone who don't have the will to help himself. That's the kind of person Satan wants. He loves the weak. We love the strong.'

They parked in front of Citizens for Good Government. Terry Kinsman turned off the car but didn't open his door.

'And she's not the only family you got left, Seth. What about Margo? What about Pastor Grady? What about all of God's Slaves? What about Salvation? What about me? We're your new family now. You know what's more important than blood? God's blood.'

Seth Stevens stared straight ahead. Out of the corner of his eye he could see Terry Kinsman watching him. It was tempting to let go of his mother for once and for all. But he wasn't certain it was a temptation from the Lord.

'We good?' asked Terry Kinsman.

'Yeah,' he said, nodding. 'We're good.'

They went inside. One of the men they'd seen the night before was sitting at the reception desk. He was cradling the phone against one ear and holding a cell phone against the other. He smiled broadly at them.

'I'm on hold, both lines. You look like you're back for more. Terry, this is Seth, right?'

'This is him.'

The man smiled and, setting the cell phone down, reached out to shake hands.

'Doug Earle,' he said. 'Sure appreciate the help. There's pizza in the conference room. Why don't you guys go ahead and eat before you get started?'

They went back to the conference room. A half-dozen pizza boxes were lined up on the table alongside a dozen warm cans of diet and orange soda. They lifted lids until they found what they wanted, then filled paper plates and ate hungrily.

Doug Earle came in and asked if they were ready. The task that night, he explained, was making telephone calls on behalf of Citizens for Good Government. They had a list of voters who weren't affiliated with either political party. All they had to do was call each person on the list, identify themselves by first name, and read through a poll consisting of ten easy questions.

'Why are we calling, you know—' asked Seth Stevens.

'Unaffiliateds? Because that's who wins elections,' said Doug Earle. 'This country is divided down the middle, Seth. Most Democrats are going to vote Democrat and most Republicans are going to vote Republican. There's five or ten percent in the middle that we don't know how they're going to vote. We don't know why it takes them so long to make up their minds, but we sure want to help them make up their minds to vote Platt as soon as possible.'

Seth Stevens nodded in understanding. The whole thing sounded reasonable.

Doug Earle walked them into what he called the 'call room'. It was similar in size to the conference room but had been divided into a dozen small cubicles, each with a phone, a chair, and a photocopy of the poll.

Across the room, a hand shot up in greeting: Charisma Brown. Seth Stevens smiled at her. He was pretty sure he blushed.

Doug Earle told them that he was going to listen in as they made their first calls. Terry Kinsman volunteered to go first.

Seth Stevens drifted with pretended aimlessness until he was standing by Charisma Brown's cubicle. She was on a call. He half-listened, waiting for her to hang up, but she apparently had a very enthusiastic respondent. She was answering more questions than she asked. Smiling, she drew a wheel in the air with her finger to show how long it was taking.

Doug Earle waved him over. He went over to an empty cubicle, sat down, and fitted the headset over his ears. It had a small microphone so he wouldn't have to use the phone's handset. Doug Earle had headphones that allowed him to listen in.

'OK,' said Doug Earle. 'Read 'em over and then we'll just try one. Easy as falling off a log.'

In the next cubicle, he could hear Terry Kinsman greeting someone with hearty comradeship. He told himself to be natural and not worry about being cheerful. People would see through it if he forced himself, he was sure. It was surprising how nervous it made him to call strangers.

He wanted to delay but Doug Earle was waiting for him. He read the questions and then picked up the phone and dialed.

'Yes, hello?' said an old woman.

'Good evening sir or ma'am,' he said, reading both choices from the script.

Out of the corner of his eye, he saw Doug Earle stifling laughter.

'Ma'am,' said the old woman.

'Sorry. This is'—he almost said *your name here*—'Seth over at Citizens for Good Government. How are you this fine evening?'

'I'm fine. Is this a telemarketing call?'

Apparently it was a common question. A response had been prepared.

'No, ma'am. We're a not-for-profit group of regular citizens like yourself. In the race for Jim Bynum's seat in the Senate, we're trying to make sure that we get the candidate who best serves Oklahomans' needs. Can I enlist your help? We have a ten-question survey that takes no more than five minutes.'

'Well, all right. I'm not sure I'll know all the answers.'

'You can't answer wrong if you just tell us what you think,' he said, extemporizing. 'Question one: Ira Isaacs has spent most of his career in Washington, D.C., while Dean Platt has spent most of his career in Oklahoma. Do you feel that a senatorial candidate should have more Washington experience or should they have spent more time working with ordinary Oklahomans?'

'Well, I'd have to say the second one,' said the woman. 'Ordinary Oklahomans.'

It suddenly occurred to him that he had not been given a pen or paper on which to record the respondents' answers.

'Question two: Ira Isaacs is Jewish, while Dean Platt is a Baptist. Does religion factor into your decision when choosing a candidate?'

'Yes, it certainly does. I'm a Baptist myself. I didn't know that about Isaacs.'

'Thank you. Question three: Ira Isaacs is divorced, while Dean Platt has been married to his high-school sweetheart for twenty-six years. Does a candidate's own track record with marriage affect his ability to speak effectively on such subjects as family values?'

'I would say yes, definitely.'

Seth Stevens glanced up at Doug Earle, who grinned and gave him a thumbs-up.

'Question four: when he was married, Ira Isaacs adopted two black children. Are multicultural values important to you?'

'No, we don't go in for all that around here.'

'Thank you. Question five: Ira Isaacs has been praised for his progressive stances on gay marriage, abortion, and the environment. Does this reflect your own values?'

'I don't even know—by "progressive", you mean what?'

Liberal, mouthed Doug Earle.

'Liberal,' said Seth Stevens.

'Oh, heavens no,' said the woman.

The old woman answered all ten questions, then kept him on the line for another couple of minutes as she shared a few choice thoughts about Ira Isaacs. When Seth Stevens hung up, Doug Earle slapped him on the back and high-fived him.

'Jesus has given you the gift of a trustworthy phone voice,' he said. 'The old ladies will just eat you up.'

Doug Earle left the room.

Seth Stevens sipped from his warm can of orange soda. He listened to the murmur of overlapping voices for a few minutes. Then he dialed the next number on his list.

In two hours he dialed over a hundred numbers. Most of the time he reached only voicemail or answering machines, the targets no doubt suspicious when they saw CITIZENS on their caller ID. Most of those who did answer were elderly. Probably some of them still had rotary phones with actual bells in them. There were some exceptions: an angry young man with crying babies in the background who refused to believe that Seth Stevens was not a sales agent of some kind; a little girl who sang him a song and then walked away from the phone without hanging it up; a teenager who repeated everything he said, sniggering.

He got through the whole survey perhaps a dozen times. Only one of the respondents took issue with its content, demanding again and again to know who Citizens for Good Government actually were. Another respondent seemed confused but tried to answer every question. He wondered if she was mentally ill.

'How can a Jew be a Baptist?' she asked. 'Why did he divorce his high-school sweetheart?'

Or maybe she was just hard of hearing.

The work was interesting for the first hour. After that he started watching the clock even though he didn't know when it would be OK to leave. When Doug Earle came in and thanked him for his time, Seth Stevens practically fell to his knees in gratitude.

It seemed an odd way to serve the Lord. Then again, in olden days the disciples had stood on rocks to spread the Gospel with only the power of their voices. When God's Army had phone banks, it would have been pretty stupid to stand on a rock.

Doug Earle gathered the volunteers in a circle and asked them to hold hands. He offered a short prayer. He asked that they would know the right way, that they would be covered in the blood of Jesus, and that God would prevail and Satan be vanquished.

'And also we pray,' he said with a chuckle, 'that Dean Platt will be elected to the United States Senate this November!'

They laughed with him, and amened, and clapped their hands and praised the Lord.

Terry Kinsman excused himself to use the bathroom. Seth Stevens noted with amusement that there were three empty cans of diet soda on Terry Kinsman's desk. He went out to the reception area to wait.

'How was your night?' asked Charisma Brown.

'All right, I guess. I left a lot of messages.'

'Me, too. I also talked to a gay guy who got really mad at me. He told me he was a personal friend of Ira Isaacs.'

'I'll bet.'

'What about you?'

'What about me what?'

'Any, you know, weird calls?'

He told her about the angry man, the little kid, and the crazy lady.

'That's pretty impressive for your first night. You must have the knack.'

'That's what Doug told me.'

There was an awkward silence. He was afraid that Charisma Brown would walk out the door without his having said one clever thing.

'You come here often?' he said.

He kicked himself as soon as he'd said it.

She laughed.

'Is this a singles bar, Seth Stevens?'

'I mean, you know, do you volunteer a lot?'

She rolled her eyes.

'You might better say I get volunteered. Everybody in Pastor Grady's extended family is expected to do more than just show up at church on Sunday.'

'They take this slavery stuff seriously, huh?'

She laughed again, more warmly this time. She offered him a ride home. Terry Kinsman came out of the bathroom, wiping his hands on his pants and muttering about the paper towel supply.

'I'm going to ride home with Charisma, Terry,' Seth Stevens blurted out.

Terry Kinsman looked disappointed.

'OK, cool. See you in church, then.'

He left. Charisma Brown raised her eyebrows a second time.

'I didn't mean to . . . if you boys had something planned . . .'

'I think he wanted gas money.'

'Good timing for you then.'

Charisma Brown's car was a year or two old but was as clean as brand-new. Without looking in the glove compartment or the trunk, he could see no sign that it was owned by anyone. Charisma Brown seemed to know what he was thinking.

'My mom—Pastor Grady's sister—is a clean freak,' she volunteered. 'I think she thinks that "Cleanliness is next to godliness" is a Bible verse, not just a saying.'

Seth Stevens thought that he would have missed that question in a game of Biblical Pursuit.

The short drive was uneventful. They talked about church and the people they knew there. He asked if she worked or went to school and learned that she was attending University of Tulsa in the fall. Her father had wanted her to go to Oral Roberts University.

'And I said, "Look, you don't have to worry about my faith in Jesus. But a whole school filled with Bible-thumpers? No way. I just want a regular math class, not Algebra of the Bible."'

He tried to think of something to tell her about himself. He couldn't think of anything.

'You've got kind some crazy story, don't you?' she asked. 'Didn't you used to be a Satanist or something?'

This had always been a tricky question for him to answer. It was true that he had played lead guitar in the band Crucifer. It was also true that the lyrics David Trujillo wrote were about monstrous black birds, tides of blood, and zombie armies rising from graveyards to slaughter the living. Some songs were even more explicit, like the one in which Satan plotted his revenge on God. But the band members didn't worship Satan. They were bad—they drank, took drugs, blasphemed, and fornicated—but they didn't think of themselves as evil. They never prayed to Satan, for instance.

But Seth Stevens had discovered that Margo Hofstatter and Pastor Grady and the other God's Slaves were more interested in Satanic lyrics than drug abuse. Which, he conceded, made sense. Lots of people had sinful vices, but not many people sang songs glorifying Satan. And if they hadn't thought of themselves as Satanists, well, maybe that was the devil working through them. Evil people didn't think of themselves as evil, he was pretty sure.

So for his first year in the church, as he learned more about what it meant to be saved, he had let others guide the discussion. They knew more about good and evil than he did, after all. And getting right with God had helped him get off drugs.

It was a lot to summarize and they were nearing his apartment. Charisma Brown was looking at him out of the corner of her eye.

'Yeah,' he said. 'I used to be a Satanist.'

Five

At work the next day, he couldn't stop thinking about Charisma Brown. Their goodnight had been chaste—and would he have expected anything else?—but there had been something about her face, open and smiling, that had hinted at something more. In his wicked days he would have brought her to his room and they would have drunk beer and smoked pot and listened to music and taken their clothes off and fornicated. But in his new life, the same signs meant different things. And if she did like him, what was the next step?

Born-agains did date, even if the way they did it was unfamiliar to him. They told people they were 'going together' and they held hands. But they never kissed and never went anywhere alone. Then they either stopped holding hands or got married.

He liked the idea of holding hands with Charisma Brown. He didn't know if Pastor Grady's sister would be willing to let her beautiful daughter date an ex-drug addict Satanist.

There had been a message from his mother when he came in, of course, which he deleted. She had even called again in the morning, but he had turned down the volume on the answering machine as soon as he heard her voice.

At work, Rob Wingert needled him but he refused to take the bait. He was thinking about Charisma Brown. He was wondering what people would say if they started going together. He knew he was getting ahead of himself. For starters, he didn't even know if she had a boyfriend or not. He hadn't seen her with anyone, so he assumed she didn't. But he didn't see her very often, so that meant nothing.

He spent Tuesday night at home, alone, watching TV. He woke Wednesday morning feeling confused and ashamed. He had been dreaming about making love to Charisma Brown. But Charisma Brown had looked like Vickie Lawson. He took a cold shower. In the shower he prayed for help fighting the lust in his heart.

He wondered if he had dreamed about Vickie Lawson because Crucifer was playing that night. He wondered whether David Trujillo would really put his name on the guest list or whether he had been joking.

Wednesday was his day off. Everyone else in the band would be at work or in school. He opened his door to a thin drizzle of rain. He didn't feel like going out. But he didn't want to stay in his room. He spent the morning sitting on the breezeway outside his door, reading one of the *Left Behind* books that Terry Kinsman had loaned him. He had never been much of a reader, but he guessed the book was OK. It was hard to believe that that was what was going to happen, that people would vanish right out of their clothes and go to Heaven. Of course, no one knew when the Rapture would actually come. Maybe it would be after he had already died.

His neighbors came out around noon, half asleep and smelling of alcohol and cigarette smoke.

The man was chanting: 'Western omelet, Western omelet, Western omelet.'

When the woman saw Seth Stevens she elbowed the man and said, laughing, 'Shut up!'

'What, he doesn't like breakfast food?'

They walked past without acknowledging him. He heard the man call him 'God Boy'. It sounded like a particularly lame superhero.

The rain stopped. Tired of reading, he walked to a bus stop and waited twenty minutes for a bus that took him to the mall. He played some video games, ate a gyro, and returned home in time to get a ride to church from Ben Badgeley.

Wednesday night services were shorter than Sunday services and Salvation only played two songs. The big church was only about half-full, too, and there wasn't as much energy in the room. Pastor Grady still gave a great sermon, but Seth Stevens could tell that he enjoyed it more on Sundays.

Afterward, as the band put their gear away in the music room, Terry Kinsman suggested that they all go to Perkins. Usually they only went on Fridays, after rehearsal. Seth Stevens wondered if the idea was to put the incident with Elder Harbo behind them. But that was precisely why he didn't want to go. It felt like returning to the scene of the crime.

Kirk Swindoll begged off first, saying he had plans already. Jimmy Gilstrap said his wife wouldn't let him. Owen Rusk said he was tired. Ben Badgeley's expression said that he didn't want to go, either, but maybe he felt bad for Terry Kinsman. He looked at Seth Stevens.

'What do you think?' he said.

'I have plans,' said Seth Stevens.

'Oh, man,' said Terry Kinsman.

'What are you going to do?' asked Ben Badgeley.

'I'm going to see a show,' said Seth Stevens.

'A movie?'

'A show-show. Some bands.'

'I didn't know there were any Christian bands playing tonight,' said Terry Kinsman.

'They're not Christian. Just some old friends of mine.'

Terry Kinsman went on high alert.

'You mean old friends from before you got saved? Satanist friends?'

'They don't worship Satan,' said Seth Stevens. 'They're just trying to be cool. They invited me and I was just curious to see how it looked now that I've got my life turned around.'

The rest of the band had already gone. Ben Badgeley sat down on the choir risers as if he were suddenly very tired. Terry Kinsman threw his hands up in the air.

'Seth, what are you talking about? This is Satan putting a trial on your godliness. You can't enter a den of sinners without getting some stain on you. They get you in there, get you surrounded, next thing you know they're sticking a needle in your arm and making you blaspheme the Lord.'

'It's just a show, Terry. It's not some occult ceremony. And if anyone's doing drugs it's going to be backstage or in their cars outside.'

'Just a show? What are they going to be singing about?'

'Heck if I know. It's usually pretty hard to understand the words anyway.'

'Are they going to be praising the Lord?'

'Probably not.'

'Then why go?'

'I go to the mall sometimes, too, and they don't praise the Lord there.'

'That's real funny, Seth, but people don't go to the mall to get a life-changing experience.'

'A lot of people don't go to shows for that, either. Some of them just want to meet girls.'

'And fornicate with them, a sin.'

They glared at each other. Seth Stevens suspected that Terry Kinsman was right, that going to the Crucifer show was a bad idea. But that only made him want to go more.

'Look, Terry,' he said, 'what good is our faith if we can't even survive a single test? I thought that we were supposed to bring the Word and the Truth into the darkest places, to those that know no light?' he added, paraphrasing Pastor Grady.

The youth pastor looked away for a long moment.

'All right,' he said. 'You got to go, go. But you can't go alone. Even the most righteous is vulnerable to the snares of temptation. Take Ben with you.'

Ben Badgeley sat up straight.

'What?'

'You're the most righteous of all of us,' said Terry Kinsman. 'I've never seen you stumble nor fall even once.'

Ben Badgeley's expression said that his most-righteous status was news to him.

'I'd go myself but that kind of music and those kind of people make me sick,' said Terry Kinsman. 'Just physically ill. So you guys go, get it out of Seth's system, and go home early.'

Shaking his head, Ben Badgeley stood up. He took his keys out of his pocket.

'And may you be covered with the blood of Jesus and may He keep you from all sin.'

They amened.

Neither Seth Stevens nor Ben Badgeley said anything as they drove to the Elks Lodge. Seth Stevens wondered why he'd insisted on going to the show. He hadn't been planning on it—at least he didn't think he had been. Had his desire been triggered by his sex dream about Charisma Brown and Vickie Lawson? If so, it was a Satanic trap straight out of the Christian comic books.

Maybe he really was only curious. Or maybe, given the short time he'd known his new friends and family, he was just feeling nostalgic.

As they approached the Elks Lodge, every telephone pole was plastered with red and black posters for the Black Lodge show. He could make out Crucifer's logo, too, but the other bands' names were too small to read. The image on the poster was an elk upside down on an altar with a robed figure thrusting a sword through its breast. The elk's antlers grew like craggy tree roots, spelling out words that he couldn't read from the moving car.

The Elks were going to love that one, he thought, almost smiling. It was an uneasy coexistence. Metal and punk bands, too marginalized to play in Tulsa's bar scene, often resorted to renting out Masonic Halls and Elks, Moose, and Eagles lodges. The graying service clubs needed the revenue, and the bands needed places to play—preferably places where they wouldn't have to be yelled at by bar patrons who preferred REO Speedwagon and Journey tribute bands.

They parked on the street two blocks away. Outside they could hear the echoey thuds and random bursts of music—released by the opening and closing of doors—that told them the show had begun. The entrance was guarded by a burly man with one half of his head shaved to reveal a crooked pentagram tattoo. Seth Stevens and Ben Badgeley tried not to look at it.

Seth Stevens's name was on the guest list. He gave Ben Badgeley four dollars to pay for half of the full cover charge. The doorman drew a sloppy X on each of their hands, a familiar and easy-to-forge symbol that meant, Seth Stevens knew, someone had lost the hand stamp.

They walked past a bar where a handful of half-drunk Elks glared out, then down a hall and up a broad flight of stairs to the ballroom. They opened the doors and were nearly pushed back down the stairs by a wall of noise and hot, humid air. Playing at a conversational volume in an air-conditioned church had made him forget. He was remembering in a hurry.

They went inside. They couldn't even hear the doors slam shut. Knots of people stood in back, the crowd growing thicker toward the stage. A few metal-studded warriors were trying to get a mosh pit going, but it was too early in the evening.

They loped around in a circle like short-track speed skaters, not crashing into anybody.

The band onstage was grinding out machine-gun power chords. Their singer had the death-metal vocal style down, a guttural bark that even the members of Crucifer had jokingly called 'Cookie Monster'. The comparison was valid but not totally accurate. It was possible, for example, to understand what Cookie Monster was saying.

The crowd was full of people wearing band T-shirts and motorcycle boots, with colorful tattoos and diverse hairstyles. A few of them, fans of black metal, had put on corpse paint: white faces with black eyes and lips. When he had been in the scene, Seth Stevens had thought that wearing corpse paint was the height of commitment. Now it struck him as being the metal fan's equivalent of painting his chest for a football game.

It being Tulsa, the crowd was mixed. There weren't enough metalheads to fill the room. They were joined by punks, skaters, stoners, and indie rockers. Given the scarcity of shows, if each group waited for their specific taste in music to arrive, they wouldn't get out much. There were even a few high-school jocks standing in one corner. Every few minutes they made devil horns or pretended to head-bang, just in case anyone made the mistake of thinking that they were there in a non-ironic capacity.

Against the back wall there was a small service bar staffed by two lady Elks. Their frowns showed that they didn't approve of the goings-on but they looked determined to get their beer money anyway. Signs on the walls declared that drinkers would be carded and identified with green bracelets. There were, however, lots of young-looking, bare-wristed beer drinkers.

Seth Stevens nudged Ben Badgeley to get his attention and they went over to the bar and ordered Cokes. The bartender poured them rum-and-Cokes and charged them accordingly. It took shouting and eventually pantomime to get the error corrected.

They leaned against the back wall and watched. Ben Badgeley had never been to a metal show before. He looked frightened. Seth Stevens wondered whether he wasn't drinking a rum-and-Coke after all. The whole scene—loud, thumping music; sweaty, churning bodies; girls dressed in revealing, tempting clothing—was like a flashback to his days of substance abuse.

What troubled him was that he liked it.

When he had been in Crucifer, he had been known as the 'Practice Nazi' because of his insistence that they practice six days a week. He had allowed them to take Sunday off not because it was the Sabbath but because even he had to concede that on Sundays they were too hungover to play well. He told his band mates that they needed the practice, but in truth it was mostly for him. If playing punk rock had helped him forget his problems, playing death metal made him forget himself entirely.

Playing with Salvation helped him, too, but it was different. Even when he felt uplifted he found himself thinking about things, examining the experience. Salvation's music was clean and precise and not very loud. Crucifer's sonic assault had made him feel as though he was stepping outside of his body. But that kind of seductiveness was what made it the devil's music.

According to the artwork on the kick drum, the band they were listening to was called Endless Abyss. They weren't very good, but they were good enough. Seth Stevens let the music pound his body like stormy surf while he resisted the urge to move his head and limbs in time. He tried to wear a skeptical expression like Ben Badgeley.

Endless Abyss stopped playing and began moving their gear off the stage. Ben Badgeley said that he was ready to go. Seth Stevens apologized but said he wanted to wait until his former friends came on.

The second band, Prickthorn, played only one song, but the song lasted for twenty-five minutes. It was like classical music if classical music was played with metal and glass on a blackboard. Still, the composition had unusual nuance for black metal and sometimes became quiet and eerie. At the end of their set, the members of Prickthorn put their still plugged-in instruments down, seemingly oblivious to the howling gales of feedback, and knelt down in a circle on the stage. They bowed their heads. The crowd shuffled forward, curious. Suddenly a huge white flame leapt up from the center of the circle and the lights went black. The feedback stopped.

There was a shriek of genuine fright, answered by mocking shrieks and scattered laughter. The lights came back on. The members of Prickthorn were gone.

'We shouldn't be here, Seth,' hissed Ben. 'This is Satan's work.'

'It's called a flashpot, Ben. It's a pyrotechnic device.'

'I'm not retarded, Seth. I didn't think Satan made the flame. But everyone here is opening their hearts to him.'

'Are you?'

'Of course not.'

'Me neither. Let's praise Jesus in our hearts. And after my old band is done playing, we'll go home.'

Ben Badgeley said amen but he didn't seem convinced.

Seth Stevens decided that Ben Badgeley was right not to trust him. He wasn't sure if he was praising Jesus in his heart or what he was doing. He just wasn't ready to go yet.

The third band, Gnash, was old-school thrash metal. They didn't wear costumes or pretend to worship Satan. They just played fast, precise metal with repetitive choruses. He liked them, too.

Ben Badgeley bought two more Cokes without rum in them. Seth Stevens watched the crowd. Margo Hofstatter had seen some shocking things when she was on the street, but even she would be shocked here, he thought. Any of God's Slaves would be shocked. They weren't blind, and they didn't live in desert compounds, but there was a big difference between seeing a kid dressed like a vampire outside a comic-book store and seeing a whole crowd of them at night. Born-agains who might have pointed and laughed on the street would have cried out in fear at the Black Elks Lodge.

He saw a girl cinched into a shiny black plastic catsuit with silver buckles that climbed from her ankles to her armpits. She was talking to a tall man with a pointy black goatee and black hair waxed into devil horns. He saw a skinhead in a sweaty white T-shirt with vomit on the front of it. He saw a guy, wearing only shorts and combat boots, with tattoos covering nearly every inch of his skin. There were even tattoos on his face. If those people weren't wicked looking, who was? Of course, Satan was said to wear many disguises. Did he sometimes wear a suit and tie? And did good people some-times wear devil horns as a joke?

Finally, it was Crucifer's turn.

'Finally,' said Ben Badgeley.

While Cam McLarin thumped the kick drum as if setting the pace for a funeral march, David Trujillo strolled toward the microphone. Vickie Lawson stood, as always, at the edge of the stage, almost in darkness. The guitar player was an older-looking man with hair down to his waist and a lunatic grin.

The song, *Killing Kindness*, started abruptly, catching the audience off-guard. Even with just one guitar, it sounded massive, thanks mainly to Vickie Lawson's thirty-second notes and rumbling bass chords. People who hadn't seen the band were always amazed that such a diminutive woman could make so much noise.

Seth Stevens knew the song by heart. He'd written it. The fingers of his left hand moved unconsciously, forming the chords and notes against his thigh.

Crucifer sounded excellent. The audience responded enthusiastically, surging forward, moshing, and pumping their fists. The band segued from the first song into the second without pausing. That had always been a point of pride with them: no messing around with set lists and tuning. Just a sonic assault that continued until the audience was exhausted.

After the third song, however, the band stopped. David Trujillo waited until the audience stopped yelling.

'Praise Satan,' he said, smiling. 'Hey, I know some of you are into some pretty weird shit—'

The audience cheered.

'—and we've got freaks of all nations here tonight. We've got gorehounds, sexaholics, and drug addicts. We've got garden-variety drunks and probably some gays. Hopefully some lesbians. Some of you just like to wear black lipstick; that's OK, too. And tonight, we've got genuine cult members in the audience: born-again Christians.'

Seth Stevens's head felt hot as he realized that, not only was David Trujillo talking about him, he was looking at him, too.

'Yeah, our old guitar player Seth is a born-again, but he was cool enough to come here tonight.'

There were a few cheers, a few catcalls.

'What do you say, Seth, you gonna play a few songs with us tonight? Is that OK with Jesus?'

He wanted to.

'Let's go,' said Ben Badgeley.

Seth Stevens nodded at him and started walking toward the stage.

The stage was chest-high. The room was quiet while he jumped and then pulled himself over the edge. In the old days, he had always been nervous before shows. He had sedated his butterflies with alcohol and drugs. Tonight he didn't feel nervous at all. He wondered if it was because he no longer cared if he impressed the crowd.

The new guitar player handed him a Gibson Destroyer, already plugged in.

'I'm Darren,' he said. 'Mind if I play along?'

Seth Stevens shook his head. He dialed the volume down and played a quick scale. His fingers felt fat and slow.

'"Season of Darkness"?' said David Trujillo through the microphone.

Their fastest song. As if Seth Stevens could say no. He nodded.

Cam McLarin clicked his sticks and they started playing. Seth Stevens blew the opening chord and fluffed the first riff. He laughed to show everyone that he knew he had messed up. Things went better from there. It was like riding a bicycle on a curb. Speed was the only thing that kept him from falling off. If he had had time to think about what he was doing, then he would have done it wrong.

And then the song was over. Suddenly he saw the audience pumping their fists. He heard them shouting. He had been looking at his fretboard the whole time.

'Praise the Lord!' bellowed David Trujillo in his best Cookie Monster voice. 'Even Christians can rock! Come back to the dark side, Seth.'

Seth Stevens shook his head, smiling. But before he knew it, they were playing another song, 'Dead Man's Chest'.

> What am I doing here
> Why don't I feel the fear?
> No one is making me
> Oh God, please set me free
>
> And another round
> And another round

And another round
In the dead man's chest

It was a song about a serial killer. He had written it with
David Trujillo between bong hits. Everything they knew about
serial killers came from horror movies and a true-crime novel,
To Kill and Kill Again, that someone had left in their practice
space. They hadn't wanted to become serial killers themselves.
Nor had they been particularly interested in exploring the mind
of a killer. It just seemed like the kind of song that a band
like Crucifer should play.

'Dead Man's Chest' was easier to play than 'Season of
Darkness'. He watched the audience. They were alert, distant,
glazed, transported, euphoric. But for the sweat and the smell,
it was kind of like church.

He played the rest of the set, took a bow, and high-fived the
band. While they packed up their gear, he climbed down from
the stage. The fingers of his right hand were sore. Putting
them to his mouth, he tasted blood. He had skinned the joints
above his knuckles on the strings of the guitar. His pants were
spattered with blood.

A skinhead with a swastika tattooed on his forehead staggered over, slobbering drunk and laughing hysterically.

'Fucking, fucking awesome, dude,' he said. 'You're in the
cult!'

Seth Stevens smiled politely and thanked him. He pushed
through the crowd, looking for Ben Badgeley. He searched
the ballroom, the bathrooms, and the sidewalk outside but
couldn't find him.

Vickie Lawson found Seth Stevens, though.

'We're having a party at Hell House afterwards,' she said.
'Wanna come?'

He shook his head. But when she took his elbow, he allowed
her to guide him back inside.

The members of Crucifer didn't leave the Elks Lodge until
Black Lodge had finished playing. Seth Stevens rode in Vickie
Lawson's car with David Trujillo. It was after midnight and
he was tired. The last set had gone by in a blur. He almost
fell asleep on the way to the party.

Hell House was in a rundown part of Tulsa where the lawns were either overgrown weeds or hard-packed dirt. It was a sagging two-story farmhouse with peeling clapboards and rain-ruined couches out front. Black-clad partygoers filled the porch, drinking keg beer out of red plastic cups. He followed Vickie Lawson and David Trujillo inside. It was strange to be back.

The members of Crucifer lived at Hell House along with an ever-changing rotation of roommates and couch-surfers. Seth Stevens had lived there, too. It wasn't called Hell House because they worshipped Satan there.

'Our house should have a name,' Cam McLarin had said, 'like Animal House or something. Kind of like a death-metal fraternity.'

Then they had watched a horror film called *Hell House* and it had been decided.

In the living room, a teenager in full corpse paint sat on a white plastic chair next to a pasty-faced hair farmer wearing a Metallica T-shirt. They were playing *Resident Evil*. They jerked and lunged in their seats, willing their proxies to ever gorier acts of violence.

When he looked away from the screen his friends were gone. He wandered through the house, feeling like a time traveler. Someone was smoking pot in the kitchen. He stopped and stared at a couple dry-humping in a bedroom with the door open. It had been his room for a while in the old days. A small group of men was huddled around the stereo, arguing about music. One of them held an MP3 player that he had plugged into the stereo. As the argument shifted, so did the playlist, usually mid-song. The volume was deafening.

Vickie Lawson appeared at his elbow. She offered him a foamy cup of beer.

'I know you don't drink,' she shouted over the music.

He grabbed the cup and drank half of it in a half-dozen gulps. The sour taste of cheap beer was like a trigger. More than anything that had happened that night, it reminded him of the way his life had used to be. He had a sick feeling that he'd broken something irreparable. It was too late. He drank again. He felt drunk.

Vickie Lawson laughed while he drank. But when he handed her the empty cup she saw the look on his face and asked if he was all right.

He nodded. Then he followed her back to the keg to get another beer.

Later, he and Cam McLarin sat in the backyard in old lawn chairs with fraying webbing. Cam McLarin lit a cigarette with an oversized flame, scorching the paper.

'So, what?' said the drummer. 'You got all born again and shit just to get clean?'

He'd gotten off meth first and then been born again. Getting clean was difficult but fast. Accepting Jesus was easier but took longer.

Cam McLarin's red-mapped eyes were focused on Seth Stevens's ear. His sweaty face had been unevenly shaved. He seemed unsteady even in his chair, as if he could topple over at any moment. He was shit-faced. He had said so himself, proudly, several times already.

Seth Stevens thought that it was ridiculous to tell someone about his rebirth in Jesus while holding his fourth sixteen-ounce cup of keg beer. But the irony was lost on Cam McLarin. The drummer seemed genuinely if drunkenly interested.

'Not exactly,' said Seth Stevens. 'I met someone who was getting sober from a drinking problem. She got born again, too. The church helped her out. They gave her advice, a place to stay, a job. Then she helped me get clean. I guess helping me helped her, too. She wanted me to come to church. At first, I felt like I had to go for her. But I liked it. I liked the people, I liked going. I even liked the music.'

'You're shitting me,' said Cam McLarin.

'I shit you not.'

'You can swear? You can't swear. Born-agains can't swear.'

Seth Stevens swallowed some more beer.

'We can't drink beer, either.'

'So you're quitting the church?'

'No, I'm not quitting. I'm just fucking up.'

They were silent for a moment. Behind them, in the back yard, a man and a woman started screaming at each other. Neither Seth Stevens nor Cam McLarin had known the couple was there. They turned to look. The man was zipping up his pants. The woman was tugging hers over her hips.

Cam McLarin turned back, uninterested in the argument.

'So you're in a Christian band?' he said. 'Jesus Christ. Have I seen your posters or anything?'

'We usually only play at the church. Sometimes someone will set up a show at a campus center or something. Things work a little different than with you guys.'

'What's your band called?'

'Salvation.'

Cam McLarin shook his head, chuckling.

'Please tell me that you're at least a Christian metal band. Aren't there some Christian metal bands?'

'It's, I don't know, pop.'

'Do you sing, like, "Jesus, I love you sweet Jesus, Jesus you're the one"?'

'The lyrics are better than that.'

'But they're about Jesus, right?'

Seth Stevens wondered if witnessing the gospel while committing a sin would make things come out even. But could he really change anyone else's mind? When he had been using, he hadn't believed in anything. He hadn't needed to. Well, he believed in crystal. When he stopped using, it was like starting over. Everything deserved equal consideration. But how did you change someone's mind if they weren't opening it?

'It's not what you think,' he told Cam McLarin. 'The whole thing. It's not what you think.'

Six

The phone was ringing. He picked it up before he was awake. He heard a man's voice on the other end. It took him a moment to understand what the man was saying.

'Seth, what's going on? Why haven't you been answering?'

He looked at the answering machine and saw the blinking light.

'Terry,' he said finally.

'Me Terry, you Seth. Why didn't you answer?'

'I was sleeping.'

'Sleeping when you're suppose to be at work. What's the matter, did you get messed up?'

He saw the clock: 10:46.

'Shit,' he groaned.

'Don't be cursing at me, Seth. Were you taking dope last night?'

'Come on, Terry.'

'Well, I talked to Ben already and he told me an interesting story, about how Salvation's lead guitarist climbed up on stage with a Satanic heavy metal band at the Elks Lodge last night. When were you planning on telling me?'

'Telling you what?'

'That you're quitting Salvation.'

'I'm not. It just—happened.'

'You're not back with them?'

'No, I just played some songs. And then I stayed too late. I looked for Ben, but he was gone.'

'He wasn't very comfortable, Seth. He was there to help keep you out of trouble and I guess you just didn't want to be helped.'

'I didn't do anything—'

He stopped without finishing the lie.

'Anything what? What did you do? You need to repent for something?'

'Listen, Terry, I'm going to pray on it and we can talk later. Right now I'm late for work.'

'Oh, we will talk later,' said Terry Kinsman, his voice growing small and tinny as Seth Stevens lowered the phone to thumb the off button.

His head felt like it was inside Cam McLarin's kick drum. His sheets reeked of sour sweat. Next door, his neighbors were laughing about something. He stumbled into the shower. The cold water felt like needles on his skin. He deserved it.

It was nearly noon by the time he arrived at work. He had showered clean but was sweaty again from running half the way. He went straight to the floor.

Rob Wingert was talking to Mandy Jenks, an attractive young mother of three who worked in sporting goods. He excused himself when he saw Seth Stevens.

'Glad you could join us,' said Rob Wingert.

'Looks slow,' Seth Stevens said hopefully.

'Not the point. Point is your shift begins at eight forty-five. Got any good excuses for me? And don't tell me you were out drinking. I almost think I'd forgive you for that.'

Seth Stevens didn't say anything.

'Late-night Bible study? Get carried away with your bedtime prayers?'

He stared at the rack of pink and blue fuzzy slippers behind Rob Wingert, wishing that he deserved to feel persecuted. He had fallen on to some kind of middle ground, deserving of no one's respect.

Rob Wingert suddenly tired of berating him. Maybe it was because of his lack of response.

'OK, so, whatever it was that got you in here late this morning, it's strike two, OK? That screwed-up exchange was the first one, being three hours late is the second one. If you screw up again I'm gonna have to let you go. Got me?'

Seth Stevens nodded.

'Got me, Seth?'

'Yes, Rob.'

Rob Wingert walked off.

In frustration, Seth Stevens reached out and swiped a dozen pink and blue fuzzy slippers on to the floor. He stared down at them. It wasn't much of a rebellion. He heard giggling. A little kid was standing nearby, laughing at him.

Seth Stevens knelt down on the floor and began picking up the slippers. He told himself to be a better role model for young people.

The rest of the day was uneventful. He stocked shelves, sold shoes, and picked gum wrappers off the floor. He studied his Bible at lunch. He was almost to the Book of Ruth. He wondered why he had wanted to go to the Crucifer show, why he had gone onstage. Was he a bad Christian? Did he want to be a bad Christian?

It wasn't his band mates' fault that he had become an addict. But it never would have happened if he hadn't been living in Hell House.

When he arrived in Tulsa, he was a skinny, nineteen-year-old punk. He had been traveling to California with a friend prone to mood swings. In retrospect, he thought that his friend probably had bipolar disorder. They had been arguing and when Seth Stevens had come out of the gas station bathroom the car was gone. His money, his clothes, and his guitar were in the car. It was winter and he was wearing a denim jacket covered with patches, pins, and markered band logos.

It took him two hours to panhandle enough money to buy a sandwich. Then he walked to the public library to warm up while he considered his options. He didn't have many. His friends—minus the friend who'd stranded him—all lived in New York. None of them had enough money to help him, anyway. Most of them didn't even have phones. They were gutterpunks like him. And he couldn't call his mother. She was the reason he was going to California in the first place.

He sat in the library, pretending to read magazines, until closing time. He spent the night walking the streets. It was so cold that he was afraid he would freeze to death if he went to sleep. In the morning he stood outside the Salvation Army and panhandled until he had five dollars, enough for a tweed overcoat with shredded lining. He was still cold, but he no longer thought he'd freeze to death.

Over the next few days he acquired a hat, mittens, and enough cardboard to build a shelter under an overpass. He had seen enough homeless people to know how it was done.

He dumpster-dived behind a Pizza Hut to fill his stomach. Through near-constant begging, he managed to get a dollar or two more than he needed every day. If no one stole it from him, he figured he'd have enough for a bus ticket after two months. He planned to keep going to California. Sleeping on the beach in Los Angeles sounded better than sleeping under an overpass in Tulsa.

He was in survival mode. His route ran from the overpass to the library to the Pizza Hut with various panhandling stops in between. The Tulsa cops rousted him almost every day but they never arrested him. When they told him to move, he moved. He discovered that panhandling outside Starbucks was particularly lucrative. Apparently people felt guilty about spending three dollars on a cup of coffee when someone was shivering outside the window.

After about a week he met Cam McLarin. He was standing outside Starbucks, holding a cardboard sign that read '*STRANDED*', when a broad-shouldered blond guy with acne scars, wearing black boots, a black overcoat, and a black stocking cap, walked by on the sidewalk. The blond guy seemed startled to see a panhandling gutterpunk. He stopped.

'You really stranded?'

Seth Stevens said that he was.

'Jesus Christ,' said the blond guy.

He dug in his pocket. He gave Seth Stevens a wrinkled dollar bill and a few coins.

'Good luck, man,' he said. 'I'm Cam.'

'Seth. Thanks.'

And that was it. Two days later, however, as he was walking to Pizza Hut, a wrinkled Geo Metro pulled to the curb. A woman was driving. A man rode in the passenger seat. Cam McLarin was sitting in back. He leaned forward and talked through the front passenger window.

'Dude—what's your name again?—you need a ride?' he asked.

Seth Stevens got in the car just to warm up. When they learned that they were taking him to a dumpster, they insisted that he come home with them.

The three of them—Cam McLarin, David Trujillo, and Vickie Lawson—didn't have much more money than he did. They worked low-paying jobs and shared a house where the wind whistled in through poorly hung windows. But they let him crash on the couch and bought him burritos, ramen noodles, macaroni and cheese. It was Christian charity with a highly ironic result.

When they learned that he played guitar, they exchanged knowing looks and then took him down to the basement where their gear was set up. They were starting their own band, they told him. They thought they might need a second guitar player.

Seth Stevens had fallen into the punk scene because he had grown up around punk rockers. His mother's boyfriends had taught him how to play songs by Black Flag and the Circle Jerks before he was old enough to shave. In high school and afterward, he had joined several different bands and even played at CBGB's before it closed. Punk rock made sense because he was angry at the world. It made sense to him because it was music for poor white people.

He had always associated heavy metal with the suburbs, with fluff-haired losers from New Jersey. He had laughed at the falsetto vocals, at the tight leather pants, at the wannabe biker imagery. But listening to Crucifer rehearse, he realized that he didn't know very much about metal.

They played death metal, they explained. It was dark, angry, and fast. He liked it. A lot of the newer punk bands were too melodic anyway, sounding like pop bands in disguise. He liked old-school punk, like Black Flag, that was ugly and angry. Death metal wasn't melodic. It was ugly. He wanted to play it, too.

David Trujillo was the guitar player. He wasn't very good. He showed Seth Stevens the songs. Without a job to compete for his time, Seth Stevens learned the songs and the style over a period of several months. Death metal was only a little bit more complicated than punk, but it was a lot faster. When he proved to be better than David Trujillo, David Trujillo seemed relieved. He had a hard time singing and playing anyway, he explained.

Though Seth Stevens took some teasing for his musical taste—he was, his band mates joked, the 'token punk'—he was quickly welcomed into the scene. Tulsa was a big small town, and the different musical factions tended to band together for support. Where in New York the punks had spent half their time sitting on sidewalks, discussing who was a poseur and who was authentically punk, the distinctions seemed looser in Tulsa. At most parties there were delegates from the nations of metal, punk, rock, and their various states and counties. The only groups that seemed never to be invited were hippies and preppies who loved jam bands.

If he became a convert by circumstance, he became an evangelist by choice. Over the next year, he immersed himself in death metal. Soon he could speak with authority on not only the genre but its subgenres, on influencers and the influenced. And because he had literally arrived without any baggage, it seemed natural that his new wardrobe looked like that of his new friends. He stopped thinking about California.

Much to his surprise, Midwesterners partied harder than East Coasters. Maybe it was because his New York friends only had drugs and alcohol when they begged or stole them. Or maybe it was simply because there was less to do in a big small town. But beer and liquor were omnipresent, as were pot, pills, and meth.

The members of Crucifer smoked pot, but they rarely did harder drugs. Seth Stevens had tried many things in New York—mushrooms, acid, ecstasy, hash, even heroin—but he'd rarely had the resources to try them twice. He had lived in Tulsa for about two years when a skinny skinhead with rotten teeth took him into the bathroom at a party and smoothed out a small square of foil and heated a line of some granular white stuff with a lighter. Seth Stevens did what the skinhead did and chased the smoke with a straw. As he watched himself in the mirror, exhaling a plume of white smoke, he had the sensation of seeing himself for the first time. It was love.

He loved not having to sleep. He loved the manic conversations that started in somebody's car and ended in strangers' houses, talking mile-a-minute as the sun rose and the day turned a bright, endless sunny blue. He loved the feeling of being a disembodied head navigating a slow-motion movie. Sometimes he even liked crashing—the early stages, before the paranoia kicked in—when he pretended to be a statue while the world accelerated around him in eye-searing technicolor.

And by the time he didn't like the way it made him feel anymore he wasn't able to stop taking it.

* * *

On Friday he was coming back from his lunch break when he turned a corner and had to stop short to avoid crashing into Charisma Brown. Her eyes dropped to his name tag as if she didn't quite believe them.

'Hi,' he said.

'Hi,' she said. 'I didn't know you worked here.'

'I wish I could say I just started.'

She laughed.

'Been a while, huh? Don't worry, I can relate. I've been at Dairy Queen since I was fifteen. I'm assistant manager. I told my friend Ruthie to kill me if I ever agree to be manager.'

Charisma Brown was on her way to college. If she ever did become the Dairy Queen manager, he thought, it would be because she wanted a summer job. She was going to end up in an office or better. If he became a department manager at ShopsMart it would mean that he could get a one-bedroom apartment instead of a studio.

'So,' she said, 'do you like it?'

'Well . . .' he said.

'I was kidding.'

'Sorry. Kind of not used to hearing too many jokes around here.'

'Why don't you get something better?'

'I was lucky just to get this.'

'Go-getter, huh?'

He shrugged, embarrassed. He decided to change the subject.

'What are you looking for?' he asked.

'Unmentionables.'

'Too late,' he said. 'Mentioned.'

'Let us never speak of this again.'

Her laugh was honest, open. He still couldn't shake the feeling that there was a spark between them. It just didn't make sense, though. He was too old, too much of a loser. She was too young, too good. He wanted to ask her to go to a movie. Instead, he pointed in the direction of women's undergarments.

'Aisle thirty-three,' he said.

'Thank you,' she said.

Did her face fall just a little? He couldn't tell.

*   *   *

After practice that night, Terry Kinsman announced that it was 'Perkins time'. No one looked at him. The rest of the band made excuses. Seth Stevens couldn't think of one. He could feel Terry Kinsman's eyes on him and knew that Terry Kinsman was going to ask him a second time. Maybe he would say that they needed to talk. Seth Stevens said he had to go to the bathroom and slipped out the door. He waited by Ben Badgeley's car.

Neither Ben Badgeley nor Seth Stevens mentioned Wednesday night. It was a relief to both of them.

After church on Sunday he was waiting for Margo Hofstatter and her family when Terry Kinsman walked purposefully out of the front doors.

'Pastor Grady wants to see you.'

Seth Stevens suddenly felt nauseous. One-on-one audiences with Pastor Grady were reserved for important people. Most of God's Slaves met him only when they joined the church— or when they were thinking about leaving it.

'But I'm supposed to meet Margo,' he said.

Terry Kinsman shook his head.

'Sorry. Pastor Grady. I'll wait for Margo and tell her.'

'I'm supposed to have dinner at her house.'

'I'll give you a ride. I'll tell her to go ahead without you.'

Seth Stevens walked back into the church against the stream of people leaving. Opening a door labeled 'Church Offices', he passed through into an immaculate and empty reception area. Unsure where Pastor Grady's office was, he kept going, past the reception desk and down the dimly-lit hall.

He passed a half-dozen doors and doorways. Then the hallway dead-ended against a door with a small gold plaque reading *Pastor*. He knocked softly. He heard Pastor Grady's friendly voice.

'Come in.'

He turned the handle and went in. Pastor Grady was at his desk, writing. The pen was fat and looked expensive. The pad of paper he was writing on was clipped into a leather folder. The only other things on his gleaming wooden desk were a leather-bound Bible, a wooden in-box, and a small cloth sack tied with braided gold cord.

Pastor Grady put the pen down and smiled at him.

'Wondering what's in the bag?'

He wasn't, but he nodded anyway.

'Thirty pieces of silver. You know what was bought with that, don't you?'

He nodded again.

'Bet you're wondering why they're on my desk. Those aren't *the* pieces of silver. No one knows what happened to those. And if they did, you can bet that some Papal secret agents would steal them for the Vatican's treasure vault. I keep these facsimiles here as a symbolic reminder. Temptation will always be within reach, especially the temptation for material gain. Sometimes people fool themselves into thinking that they can't be bought because no one's ever tried to buy them. Because they've never seen the silver. But the silver's always there. You get what I'm talking about, Seth?'

'Yes, I think so.'

'Good. You wondering whether those are real silver coins in that bag?'

He shrugged. He felt like a teenager, not knowing what to say. He wasn't wondering whether there were genuine silver coins in the bag. He was wondering why he was in Pastor Grady's office. He half expected to be told to stay away from Charisma Brown.

'Well, if you're a good Christian, you'll never know,' said Pastor Grady. 'But I didn't bring you here for a sermon. Sit down, Seth.'

There were two leather-upholstered chairs in front of the desk. He sat in the nearer one and was surprised at how low he sank down. He looked up at Pastor Grady. The first time he'd come to church, Seth Stevens had expected a bearded prophet. But Pastor Grady was young, clean-shaven, and handsome. He had a slight paunch and a full head of carefully combed hair. Except for his seemingly permanent smile and the laugh lines on his round face, he looked like a businessman. The only unusual thing about him was that his skin was so pale, it looked as if he never went out in the sun.

'Unusual name, Seth. We get a lot more Jacobs. Maybe even more Ezekiels. What church did your mom and dad go to?'

'She, um, didn't go. My dad wasn't around.'

Pastor Grady's brow furrowed.

'Forgive me, Seth. I'd forgotten. But I remember now. Margo told me your story. You can be proud of how far you've come. From atheism and ignorance to being born again in the power and the glory of Jesus Christ.'

Seth Stevens wasn't sure if that warranted an amen or not so he just did it.

Pastor Grady amened back at him.

'But I didn't ask you here to give you a sermon or to discuss popular Biblical names,' he continued. 'I understand you've been volunteering with Citizens for Good Government. How have you found the work?'

He thought about running from the police. He assumed Terry Kinsman hadn't told Pastor Grady about that. He said that he enjoyed the work.

'Political work can be distasteful for spiritual men. But sometimes it's necessary for us to do mundane things to ensure the glory of God in this world as well as the next. Do you know what "mundane" means?'

Seth Stevens said he thought he did.

'Worldly, not spiritual,' said Pastor Grady. 'Yard signs, tele-marketing—God's work is often mundane. Not nearly as exciting as smiting Philistines.'

He laughed.

'I'd say that I miss the smiting, but—before my time.'

Seth Stevens laughed with him.

'You know what you are?' asked Pastor Grady.

'A born-again Christian?' guessed Seth Stevens.

'Certainly that. And there are, praise Him, many, many millions of those. But you're something even more import-ant than that. Many millions of those born-again Christians, well, they accept the Lord Jesus Christ as their personal savior. But they take the saving part too literally. If Jesus has already saved them, why, they don't have any work to do, do they? So they sit on the sidelines. You can sit on the sidelines at a football game, but can you sit on the sidelines in a war?'

Seth Stevens said that he guessed not.

'Well, the French have done it, and the Swiss, but I'm sure glad I'm not French or Swiss. No, you can't. You can't sit on the sidelines during a war. And that's what's happening: our country is at war. It's a war between right and wrong. Between good and evil. Between God and Satan. You're a foot soldier

in the Army of God. God is your commander-in-chief. And
I'm your general. And I thank you for your service.'

Seth Stevens was feeling uncomfortable. Pastor Grady's
speech seemed too big for the occasion. Saying 'you're
welcome' felt wrong, so instead he thanked Pastor Grady.

Pastor Grady smiled.

'Now, in the Christian army, we don't ask much. We ask
that you love Jesus. That you follow orders and do His
will. And that you don't desert. No army can win without
unquestioning loyalty and obedience from its soldiers. Do you
understand?'

He did now. Terry Kinsman had told Pastor Grady something. Not that he had fought the Mormon, and not that they
had run from the police, but that Seth Stevens had gone to
see Crucifer. He felt anger and wondered if his anger was a
sin. After all, Terry Kinsman was just trying to keep him from
doing the wrong thing.

Pastor Grady looked at what he'd written and then closed
his folder. He pushed his chair back and stood up. He walked
over to a wooden panel and tapped its top edge. It sprang
open to reveal a mini-fridge stocked with pop.

'Would you like a Diet Pepsi?' he asked.

Seth Stevens said no, thank you.

Pastor Grady took a can out and closed the refrigerator. He
opened the can and took a deep drink. He sighed and set the can
down on his desk.

'Thank Heaven we're not Mormons, right? Do you like
caffeine?'

'Mountain Dew,' said Seth Stevens.

'As far as I'm concerned, caffeine gives us more energy to
do His bidding.'

Pastor Grady sat down on a corner of his desk. They were
so close they were almost touching.

'Those who follow the Lord will join him in his kingdom
and bask in the light of his glory forever. Those who turn
from the path of righteousness will suffer everlasting agony
in a lake of fire. That's not a story to scare little kids, Seth,
that's the gospel truth. Do you know whose side you're on?'

He nodded.

'Are you on the Lord's side? Are you on my side?'

'Yes, sir,' said Seth Stevens.

Pastor Grady nodded. He took a drink of his pop. He sat down again and opened his folder. He picked up his pen.

'Good,' he said. 'We have more work for you.'

They were halfway to Margo Hofstatter's house when Terry Kinsman asked Seth Stevens why Pastor Grady had wanted to see him. Seth Stevens wondered if he had been wrong to believe that Terry Kinsman had set the meeting up. Maybe Pastor Grady's soldier talk had been a coincidence. Or maybe it was something he said to all the volunteers.

He wanted to believe that, because otherwise Terry Kinsman's question was a lie designed to protect himself. And if it was a lie, Seth Stevens thought angrily, it deserved a lie in return.

'Nothing much,' he said. 'He thanked me for helping out at Citizens and talked about how important it is.'

Terry Kinsman looked over, studying the side of Seth Stevens's head for a moment. Then he turned to watch the road again.

'Huh,' he said. 'That's cool.'

When he was full of ham, sweet potatoes, and Arnold Palmer, Bill Hofstatter gave him a ride home. A few hours later, Ben Badgeley picked him up. Between services, Kirk Swindoll had invited the band to come to his house that night to watch what he called a 'Christian zombie flick'. Earlier, Seth Stevens had been about to ask Terry Kinsman whether he was coming. Then he had decided that Terry Kinsman could do what he liked.

Kirk Swindoll lived with his parents in a large new house on a cloverleaf cul-de-sac in a development where the biggest trees were not much taller than the kids who played under them. He attended Tulsa Community College and said he lived at home to save money. Seth Stevens suspected that he was too comfortable to leave. Bill Swindoll owned an auto dealership and business appeared to be good. New cars filled the three-car garage and the broad driveway as well. Every room in the house was immaculate. The furniture looked as if it had all just come from the showroom.

In the basement rec room, the members of Salvation sprawled on overstuffed leather couches and watched the DVD on a fifty-two-inch high-definition flat-panel TV. Called *The*

Soul Eaters, it was a lot like a regular horror film: after their van broke down, a group of road-tripping teenagers knocked on a farmhouse door and found that the helpful residents were not what they seemed. There were several key differences, however. The teenagers were on their way to Bible camp; the zombies didn't rip and eat flesh but instead tempted the teens with seductive visions of sins; and gross-out gore had been replaced by poorly blocked wrestling and fistfights. Teens who succumbed to temptation found themselves bear-hugged by the zombies while the zombies stole their souls for Satan. It was kind of lame, he thought, but it was still kind of fun. It reminded him just a little bit of the grotesquely thrilling movies he'd watched before he was saved.

And where those gatherings had often ended with everyone either asleep or passed out, there was no danger of that here. In fact, the more Mountain Dew they drank, the more animated they became.

The clock passed midnight and Terry Kinsman hadn't shown up. He wasn't coming.

Seth Stevens enjoyed the gleaming perfection of Kirk Swindoll's house. The refrigerator and pantry seemed to contain a grocery store's worth of food, and they could make as much noise as they wanted without bothering anyone. Even using the toilet was a pleasure. There was no need to hold the handle down until the bowl finally drained and no need to jiggle the handle afterward to keep the tank from over-flowing. As Ben Badgeley drove him home to his dismal apartment, he thought it was good that Satan had never tried to buy his allegiance. Even a nicely furnished one-bedroom was likely to cause a pitched battle between his desires and his better judgment.

When he got home the message light was flashing. His mother, of course. But also Vickie Lawson.

'It was totally awesome playing with you the other night,' she said. 'Any time you want to come back to the band, just let us know. I know I haven't heard your Christian band, but you were, I don't know, made for this, you know?'

Strange that Vickie Lawson had called and not David Trujillo or Cam McLarin. Was it a temptation?

He fell asleep thinking about the words 'born again'. They were good words because they were accurate. In accepting

Jesus, it was necessary to start a whole new life. Living in the past could only remind the saved man of when he was a sinner. It was better to let it go completely.

He decided that he wouldn't call Vickie Lawson back. It went without saying that he wouldn't call his mother.

Seven

On Monday morning he was yawning as he swiped his associate's card at the locked double doors. He had stayed up far too late the night before. Still, he'd made an effort and had arrived at work five minutes early.

Rob Wingert was already in the cage, waiting for him. Ryland Wilson, the ShopsMart assistant manager, was there too, and so was a security guard whose name tag read *Avery Cleveland*.

'Good morning, Seth,' said Rob Wingert cheerfully. 'Got your associate's card with you?'

Seth Stevens held it up dumbly.

'Course you do,' said Rob Wingert. 'Otherwise how'd you get in the store?'

Seth Stevens looked at Ryland Wilson for help.

'Mr Wilson, what's going on?'

'The store was burgled last night, Seth.'

'Someone stole some *shoes*?'

'Not shoes,' said Ryland Wilson unhappily. 'Electronics. Camping gear. They even got into the gun case. Almost ten thousand dollars' worth of merchandise.'

'And you think that I . . . what?'

'We've got your card swipe,' said Rob Wingert. 'What, you didn't think we'd check?'

The scene felt unreal to Seth Stevens. But the unreal was becoming an increasingly common part of his life. He tugged his associate's card and felt the lanyard go taut against his neck. When he wasn't working, he left it on the counter next to his answering machine. It had been there when he'd come home from Kirk Swindoll's the night before. Hadn't it? It had been there this morning.

'What time did I supposedly do this?' he asked.

'There's no *supposedly*,' said Rob Wingert.

Ryland Wilson quieted Rob Wingert with a look.

'The entry swipe was at eleven-oh-seven. The exit swipe was at eleven forty-two.'

He had been at Kirk Swindoll's house until nearly 1 a.m.

'I was with my band the whole time. Just ask them.'

'You're in a *band*?' asked Rob Wingert incredulously.

Ryland Wilson looked at Avery Cleveland.

'Alibis from friends are considered to be somewhat suspect,' said the security guard.

'What about the security cameras?' asked Seth Stevens. 'If you think my friends are liars just because they happen to be my friends, then look at the tape. It wasn't me.'

'The tape's useless,' said Rob Wingert. 'You know that. You wore a ninja mask.'

'Why would I use my own key and wear a mask? It doesn't make any sense.'

Ryland Wilson sighed deeply.

'I'll admit that there's some reasonable doubt, Seth. But even if you didn't do it, the fact is, your key was used to gain access to the store. The employee handbook states that you are responsible for controlling access to your key. That in the event that your key is used to commit a crime you will ultimately be held responsible.'

Though he had only skimmed the seventy-eight-page employee handbook, he had initialed every page as required and signed a statement testifying that he had carefully read the document in full.

'You're going to arrest me based on that?'

'We're not arresting you. The decision whether to notify the police will be made after further review of the evidence. It's in your favor that ShopsMart prefers to avoid negative publicity of any kind.'

'But just try to come into a ShopsMart again,' said Rob Wingert.

Seth Stevens looked at the three men looking at him. If they had been his friends he would have waited for them to start laughing. But they believed, against the evidence, that he was guilty. A few numbers logged by a computer program had tried and convicted him. He groped for an explanation for the mistake. He had a sense that he was overlooking something obvious, that the answer would occur to him as soon as he walked out the door. But he couldn't think of anything.

Would an innocent man make a scene? Or would an innocent man refuse to argue with those who doubted him? He didn't know. He did know that he was sick and tired of working for Rob Wingert.

He lifted the lanyard over his head and held it out in front of him. His associate's card twisted in the cold wind from the air diffuser above them.

Rob Wingert took the card. Ryland Wilson held out his hand. Rob Wingert gave it to him, upstaged.

'Avery will escort you off the property,' said Ryland Wilson.

'Mr Wilson, please don't tell Pastor Grady,' said Seth Stevens.

'Pastor Grady won't judge you. Only the Lord can judge you.'

Rob Wingert rolled his eyes.

Avery Cleveland walked him out of the store at a stately pace, gripping his elbow tightly. The store had just opened and there weren't many shoppers or even coworkers to witness his fall from grace. For that, Seth Stevens said a silent prayer of thanks.

Once the front doors were behind them, the security guard surveyed the vast parking lot and apparently decided against walking him all the way off ShopsMart property.

'Good luck out there,' said Avery Cleveland.

Seth Stevens walked through the slowly filling lot to the six-lane street that brought cars to fast-food restaurants, strip malls, and auto-parts stores. He walked a half-mile and then turned in to an older subdivision whose lots were still only half sold. Where the street dead-ended there was a crash barrier in front of a large pile of weed-covered dirt, maybe fill from long-excavated basements or roadwork. On the other side of the pile was a street that had houses on one side and a corn-field on the other.

He climbed to the top of the dirt pile. He stopped and sat down. Away from the busy arterial streets it was as quiet as the country. A crow cawed in the corn. Songbirds tweeted on a telephone wire.

Now what? he thought.

He felt a sudden craving for meth, so powerful that it was almost as if he was going through withdrawal again. He couldn't do it, of course. Or could he? And why not?

It surprised him that Crucifer wanted him back. Initially, they had responded to the discovery that he was using meth in about the same way they had responded to the discovery that one of Cam McLarin's friends had taken a dump in a cat's litter box: with incredulous mirth. When his moods began jagging with his drug use, at first they ignored the changes. When he became unreliable, they hectored him. When he turned into a thief, eventually stealing some of the band's own gear to pay for a fix, they fired him. When he showed up for rehearsal, rehearsal was already over. David Trujillo confronted him while Cam McLarin and Vickie Lawson studied their shoes.

'Nothing against you personally, Seth,' he'd said. 'Everybody really likes you and all, but we need a guitar player who doesn't fucking steal from us. So until you get your shit figured out, I think you better take a break.'

Seth Stevens had smoked fifteen minutes earlier. He had a manic grin stretched over his bared teeth. It was hard to hear David Trujillo over the noise of his own colliding neurons. By the time he figured out that he was being fired, there was something else to think about.

'And I think you better move out. We need someone who can pay his share of the rent.'

Even death-metal bands practiced charity. Even death-metal bands had limits to the kinds of behavior they would accept.

He stood up and climbed down the dirt pile. He kept walking home. He wondered if his dealer, Indian Charlie, still lived in the same apartment. There was a hard-faced woman with a house full of angry kids, too, that he had bought from. What was her name? Shannon? Sharon? Shauna?

Or he could just go to a liquor store. He could spend the weekend drinking. He could get the pent-up tension of being good out of his system. Then he could sober up, pray, and start over.

Or he could suck it up and keep being good. That was the most frightening prospect of all. Even working at ShopsMart he lived from paycheck to paycheck. By the time he got another job—if he could get another job—he would already be behind in his bills. He would be forced to borrow money to make the rent, money he wouldn't be able to repay.

If getting fired wasn't an excuse to backslide, what was? No one would judge him too harshly. Margo Hofstatter had helped him before and would help him again. But if she helped him again, how could he deny her wish to be his new mother?

He pondered other options. Ben Badgeley was his best friend, maybe his only real friend. But the straight-arrow bass player couldn't begin to know what was going through Seth Stevens's mind.

Who else was there? Terry Kinsman had tattled on him to Pastor Grady. That showed he was paying attention, at least. The two of them had to talk anyway. They had never had much in common, but maybe it would be easier that way.

When he got home he called Terry Kinsman's cell phone. There was no answer. He didn't know Terry Kinsman's address. He called the church, not expecting help. He was thinking about ShopsMart regulations, which prohibited employees from giving out any personal information about other employees. But the church secretary was cheerful and helpful. When he hung up the phone, he had Terry Kinsman's address.

The address, a five-digit number on a county road, didn't mean anything to him. And because he was too poor to own a computer, he couldn't look it up online.

He looked at the clock. He'd been fired before coming on shift and it was still morning. He went out again and rode a bus to the library.

After a short wait for an open computer, he punched the address into a search engine and was rewarded with a map that showed a location on the far outskirts of the city. He requested driving directions and learned that Terry Kinsman lived more than ten miles away. The driving directions were, of course, useless because he didn't own a car. He brought up the website for Tulsa Transit and looked at the routes and schedules. He could get there by bus.

He bought a sandwich, a bag of chips, and a pop and ate lunch at the bus stop. He rode one bus for a little while and then transferred to another one. The second bus had a few tired Latino passengers and Arctic air conditioning.

By the time he got off, forty-five minutes later, he was trembling with cold. He stood at a blacktop-and-gravel intersection and wondered why he hadn't simply left a message for Terry Kinsman. Then he started walking. It was only another mile.

It was mid-afternoon and he was sweating by the time he arrived at the mailbox painted with Terry Kinsman's address. The mailbox was attached to a four-by-four shimmed into a stack of three rusty tire rims. It had one big dent in the side, as if it had been used for target practice by baseball bat-swinging teenagers.

A dirt driveway led past a scrub yard to a double-wide mobile home. Terry Kinsman's car was parked alongside it, under a tree whose red berries stained the hood and windshield. The sun was shining off the windows of the mobile home, making it impossible to see inside.

He climbed the curling plywood steps and knocked on the screen door. There was no answer. He looked for a doorbell. There wasn't one. He opened the screen door and put his hand on the doorknob, wondering whether he should turn it.

There was a loud cracking sound, then another, then another. Gunshots. He turned, lurching back and forth between the wooden porch rails like a hog in a chute. He looked for the shooter. He didn't see anyone. He wondered if he should throw himself off the porch steps on to the ground but didn't do it. He felt stupid for not jumping and embarrassed for wanting to. There were more shots and he flinched. Then he realized that no one was shooting at him. He wondered why he thought somebody might have been.

Cautiously, he made his way around to the back of the double-wide. Terry Kinsman was standing in an unplanted field, shaking spent casings out of a revolver. About thirty yards away from him there was a badly stuffed scarecrow with white paper plates tied over its head and heart. There weren't any bullet holes in the plates.

Not wanting to startle a man with a gun, even a man in the act of reloading, Seth Stevens scuffed his feet as he walked forward. Terry Kinsman turned, startled, then smiled.

'How long you been there?'

'I just got here. I almost had a heart attack on your porch.'

Terry Kinsman started reloading his gun with bullets he pulled out of his pants pocket.

'They say you never hear the shot that kills you,' he said.

Seth Stevens nodded toward the straw target.

'If the shot kills you.'

Terry Kinsman seemed embarrassed. He finished loading the gun and clicked the cylinder back into place.

'I'm better than that. I was practicing turn and fire.'

He lifted the gun with both hands, held it steady, and squeezed the trigger. A new hole appeared where the corner of a mouth would have been.

'What are you doing here?' asked Terry Kinsman. 'I mean, how did you get here?'

'Bus. And walking.'

'You must of really wanted to see me.'

Seth Stevens scratched his neck. He toed the dirt.

'I got fired today.'

'It was that Antichrist boss of yours, wasn't it?' said Terry Kinsman.

'They said I stole a bunch of stuff, guns even. That I used my key to get into the store last night.'

'Couldn't of been you. You were with the band.'

'That's what I told them. They said friends aren't good alibis. But that it doesn't matter anyway because it was my key.'

Terry Kinsman glowered at the scarecrow. It looked as if he was thinking about shooting it again.

'The day they won't listen to a Christian man,' he said angrily.

He turned and started walking toward his house. He stopped and looked back at Seth Stevens. He smiled suddenly.

'I bet you need to blow off some steam,' he said.

Seth Stevens followed him back to his house. They climbed steps made out of milk crates and went in through a sliding-glass back door. He wasn't sure what he'd expected of Terry Kinsman's house. This wasn't it. Decorated in shades of brown and beige, it was compulsively clean. The threadbare furniture looked unchanged since the 1980s and the walls were hung with framed oil paintings of ducks, deer, and elk. A gun case stood under a picture of a praying Jesus and next to a large, rough-hewn wooden cross. A framed Christian flag was centered on the wall nearby.

Terry Kinsman unlocked the gun case and put his revolver in a drawer inside. He closed the door and relocked the case. He left the room for a minute and returned with two strange-looking assault rifles. They were cross-hatched with green-and-black camouflage paint and had bulbous magazines attached to their tops. Grinning, he handed Seth Stevens one of the rifles and a pair of workshop goggles. Seth Stevens wondered why it was goggles and not ear protectors.

'Paintball,' said Terry Kinsman. 'You're gonna love this.'

They went back outside and started walking toward a big stand of trees about 200 yards away. The gun was surprisingly heavy. As they walked, Terry Kinsman showed him how it worked.

'You got two hundred balls in the hopper. Safety on and off. You're gonna want to keep it off once we start. You don't got to cock it or nothing. Pull the trigger and it shoots.'

They entered the shade of the trees, pushing through a tangle of undergrowth. In less than a minute his clothes were covered with twigs, stickers, and bugs. He had never shot a paint gun, let alone a real gun, but blasting away at some targets did sound like fun.

'I been playing around in here since I was a kid,' said Terry Kinsman. 'Some of my old forts is still in here. I even used to look at my daddy's *Playboys* out here. When he found me and whipped me, my mom whipped him and made him throw them out. You can bet he prayed real hard on it.'

'You grew up here?' asked Seth Stevens.

'Ever since I was six.'

'Do your parents still live here, too?'

Terry Kinsman's tone grew flat.

'Some trucker was charging his cell phone and didn't see them. They was stopped at the tollbooth.'

Seth Stevens didn't know what to say. Putting his hand on Terry Kinsman's shoulder didn't seem like the right move when they were carrying paint guns.

'I'm sorry, Terry. That's horrible.'

Terry Kinsman looked at him.

'I don't know why Christian people always say dying's so bad,' he said. 'They were right with Jesus when they went. They're with Him now.'

Seth Stevens wondered how many Christians believed in a Heaven that was as real as the real world. He believed in Heaven but thought that it must be more like a dream, like some kind of flickering half-sleep.

'No, you're right,' he said. 'It's just . . . well, you must miss them.'

'Here's the last fort I made,' said Terry Kinsman, stopping to point.

At first Seth Stevens thought it was just a pile of rocks and branches. Then his eyes adjusted to the dappled light and he saw three distinct rooms that would accommodate even a teenage-sized boy.

'Camouflage,' said Terry Kinsman, grinning.

A thin trail appeared and they followed it. About fifty yards along they came to a fire ring where scorched pop cans lay half-buried in powdered ash.

'Come out here sometimes to think,' said Terry Kinsman. 'Not too buggy out, I might even sleep out. Peaceful out here.'

They were completely walled in by green. Seth Stevens had lost his sense of direction. Even with the trail, he wasn't sure he would find his way out.

'OK,' said Terry Kinsman. 'There's lots of natural cover, of course, but I've dug some foxholes, too, and made some walls and stuff. You can't get lost 'cause there's fields all around. Way I play is: three body shots and you're dead. You get shot in the leg, you can't use that leg. Both legs, you got to stay where you are or crawl with your arms. And so forth. You go off that way and I'll go off that way. Then we circle back and try to find each other.'

Terry Kinsman pointed directions.

Seth Stevens was still processing the fact that they were going to shoot at each other.

'Does it hurt?' he asked.

'Yeah, kind of,' said Terry Kinsman. 'Like if someone gives you a dead arm. That's what makes you not want to get shot.'

He slipped his goggles on.

'You ready?'

Seth Stevens couldn't think of an objection that didn't make him sound like a wimp, so he nodded. Cradling the paint gun in the crook of his arm, he put on his goggles.

Terry Kinsman marched off into the bushes.

'Count two hundred before you turn back,' he said.

Seth Stevens left the trail. Even though the goggles were clear plastic, he felt half-blind. The ventilated shields at the top, bottom, and sides distorted his peripheral vision. His head seemed as if it was floating just above his body, making him feel likely to trip and fall.

Nevertheless, he picked up his pace. He only remembered to start counting after he'd already taken a few dozen steps. He turned to look before he remembered that it was cheating. But Terry Kinsman had already disappeared.

He ran, his scalp prickling with adrenaline. He didn't think he was going to enjoy himself. But he did want to win the game, if only because he didn't want to get hit with a paint-ball. If Terry Kinsman enjoyed it, well, he'd try to give him something to enjoy.

He came to a huge fallen tree, its exposed roots dry as driftwood and clotted with dirt and leaves. He crouched behind it, starting his count at fifty and giving up at a hundred. He waited until his breathing slowed and then decided he had waited long enough. He crept along the tree trunk, careful not to brush against the large red ants who followed an invis-ible road spiraling around its girth. When he popped his head up for a look he half expected a paintball to thunk his goggles. But nothing happened.

Trying to fix the location of the fire ring in his mind, he slipped off to his left. Terry Kinsman would probably come right after him, he thought. If he circled around, he might be able to come up on Terry Kinsman from behind.

He went left and forward, left and forward. Five minutes later he was completely turned around. When he expected to be approaching the fire ring he found himself instead at the bank of an overgrown creek with a muddy trickle in the bottom. He backtracked and tried to correct his route but found himself in the middle of a dense thicket. There were criss-crossing trails, whether made by deer or Terry Kinsman he didn't know. With nothing to lose, he chose the one on the right and crept forward. The woods may have been small, but it seemed to him as if they could play for hours without finding each other.

The trail led to another fort, small but sturdily built. A shoulder-height wall had been constructed out of carefully fitted rocks, then turned into a lean-to with a lattice of woven saplings. The leaves on the branches were now brown and dry, but when it had been built, the structure would have been nearly invisible.

There was a rustle in the bushes and he stooped and went into the fort. He crouched down and listened, trying to slow his breathing. He heard birds, insects, an airplane far over-head. Was that a twig snapping? He wasn't sure. He regretted going into the fort. He couldn't see out, and if Terry Kinsman was indeed outside, all he would have to do was wait until Seth Stevens showed himself and then start shooting. Maybe the thing to do was to sit still long enough that Terry Kinsman couldn't be sure he was inside. If Terry Kinsman was even out there.

Several damp boards had been laid on the ground to make a floor. There was a folded-up lawn chair, its tubing rusted and its webbing tattered. There was a small stone altar, too, about two feet high and made with flat stones that had been mortared with mud. Withered flowers lay on top of it.

One of the boards was much smaller than the others, about one-and-a-half by two feet. The initials T.K. had been carved into it, along with various dates that may have corre-sponded to Terry Kinsman's visits. Seth Stevens did the math. The earliest date put Terry Kinsman there in the seventh grade.

He pulled at a corner of the board and it came up, almost turning to damp sawdust in his hands. Millipedes and earwigs writhed under the edges, and clusters of larvae lay there, slick and white. But a hole had been dug under the center part of the board. There were badly mildewed books and magazines: a fantasy novel, illustrated Bible comics, a swollen copy of *Left Behind*, and, underneath all of it, a copy of *Club International*. The picture on the cover showed a man having anal intercourse with a woman. Terry Kinsman's father hadn't read *Playboy*, and the magazines hadn't gone out in the trash, either.

Seth Stevens lay the board down over the hole again, wishing the signs of his snooping weren't so easy to read. He hoped that Terry Kinsman had simply forgotten to get rid of this sin of his youth.

He inched his way to one end of the fort and peered out. He didn't see anything. He decided to go.

As he straightened up he heard a popping sound. Red paint splashed on the lean-to, hard enough to rattle the branches.

Seth Stevens put his head down and ran, blundering into the underbrush, weaving, stopping short and then finally diving on to his stomach.

'And He shall smite them with the edge of the sword; He shall not spare them, neither have pity, nor have mercy,' shouted Terry Kinsman behind him.

Seth Stevens lifted his head and peered over a plant. He couldn't see anything. It was hard to tell where Terry Kinsman's shouts were coming from.

There was a stand of trees ahead of him. He wriggled toward them on his belly, knowing that he was making the bushes move. Terry Kinsman's paint gun popped a few more times but Seth Stevens suspected he was just shooting to shoot.

He reached the trees and stood up. Sticking the barrel of his gun around a tree trunk, he squeezed off a few blind shots, just to give Terry Kinsman something to think about. But there was no return fire. Nothing happened for a few minutes. He sneaked repeated looks but couldn't see anything. Sighing, he decided just to charge and get it over with.

But before he could step into view, there was a popping sound and it felt as if someone had punched his leg. A bright red blotch blossomed on his thigh. Terry Kinsman had circled around behind him.

He started to run.

'Can't run on one leg!' shouted Terry Kinsman.

Mid-stride, he started hopping. He hopped about three times before he tripped and fell on the ground. He landed on the gun, hurting his ribs. But his thigh hurt worse.

There was another pop and another punch. His other leg. He was a paraplegic soldier. He sat up, shouldered the rifle, and squeezed off a dozen shots toward where he thought Terry Kinsman was.

Another shot hit him in his right bicep. His gun arm.

'Let's see you shoot left-handed!' shouted Terry Kinsman.

He dropped the gun. His eyes watered from the pain. Awkwardly, he picked up the gun with his left hand. Terry Kinsman finally broke from his cover, running toward him, zigzagging, daring him to shoot. He could barely hold the gun. There was no way he could hit a target. He shot anyway. Terry Kinsman ran toward him, flushed, smiling, his eyes bright.

'Onward, Christian so-*hol*-diers!' he sang. 'Marching off to war! With the cross of Je-*he*-sus! Going on before!'

When Terry Kinsman was almost at point-blank range he lifted his gun and shot a half-dozen times, all of his shots hitting Seth Stevens in the chest. It knocked the wind out of him, but he stood, throwing the paint gun down in disgust. He stalked away, turning his back so Terry Kinsman couldn't see his face.

Terry Kinsman stopped singing.

'Seth, you mad? Hey, don't be mad.'

He kept walking. He was thinking about the bus ride home, wearing his ruined red clothes, the bruises turning purple underneath.

Terry Kinsman picked up the gun and trotted after him.

'You did pretty good for your first time. You'll get the hang of it. Sorry I got carried away. It's just, when I'm playing, I pretend like I'm, you know, fighting evil. Listen, the dye washes right out. I'm telling you, right out.'

Seth Stevens quickened his pace.

Terry Kinsman finally stopped.

'Well, look, you can keep walking, but I gotta tell you, you're headed toward Missouri. My house is the other way.'

Seth Stevens stopped, his chest heaving, all the anger and tension of the day and the last week escaping. His laughter sounded like sobs.

He stayed for dinner. Terry Kinsman lit a fire in a rickety grill and they cooked hot dogs and ate them with macaroni and cheese and potato chips. They drank flat Mountain Dew from washed-out plastic cups that advertised the 18-Hour Mart. The sun went down, leaving behind a glow that looked like a grass fire on the horizon. Radio towers blinked lazily under the blinking red lights of a landing plane under the blinking white light of a satellite. There were few stars in the heavens.

Terry Kinsman stirred the disintegrating coals.

'Ever since I was a kid, I felt called to the Lord,' he said. 'But I never felt like it was enough to just, you know, pray. People are always talking about you got to fight for what you believe in. But our country, what do we fight for? I mean, we go into Afghanistan and take care of the mullahs, then we go into Iraq and take care of Saddam. And we win, right? What's the very next thing we do after we bomb their country flat? We rebuild it. We rebuild everything, even their mosques. Do we build any churches? Course not. We got a president who says he's born again who talks about respect for the Islam faith. People say, well, he's got to say that, it's politics, you know he thinks different. But you know what? I don't care. Those Muslims, they'd put a bomb on a baby and blow up a hospital, they hate us so bad. It's like some modern-day Crusades, except they know it and we don't. People talk about some religious Disneyland, everybody holding hands and singing, but that's never gonna happen in a million years. Old days, you conquered a people, you made them worship your god. And that's exactly what we should be doing. I'd join the army if I thought it'd do any good. Growing up, when I'd play paintball and shoot guns and stuff back here, in my mind I was thinking I was a soldier in the Army of God. And I still feel that way.'

Seth Stevens swallowed more pop. Now it was warm as well as flat. He told himself to stop drinking it. Then he drank some more.

'Do you think Dean Platt is, I don't know, better?' he asked.

Terry Kinsman snorted.

'Platt, he's more religious than most, I believe that. But he's a politician and that's only gonna get you so far. The whole thing with Citizens is just a smokescreen. There's more stuff planned than you know. Heck, than I know. I'm just a foot soldier. But there's generals nobody even knows about. They've talked to me specifically. They got a master plan to bring the country back to God. And believe me, it's more powerful than getting a one-vote majority in the Senate.'

Seth Stevens looked at Terry Kinsman. The reflection of the dying fire made sparks in his eyes. He wondered if Terry Kinsman was telling the truth. If he was, the bigger question was when the master plan was going into effect and whether it was going to work.

'Don't worry about yourself, Seth. You stay loyal to the church and the church will stay loyal to you. There's paid work at Citizens. I can probably get you some of that. And on the unpaid side, well we got plenty more to do. You're still in, right?'

It would have been an excellent time to say no. But he learned that later. At the time he said yes.

Eight

When Seth Stevens entered the music room before the Wednesday night service, Terry Kinsman was there. He had told the other members of Salvation what had happened to Seth Stevens at ShopsMart on Monday. They shared Terry Kinsman's outrage. Led by Kirk Swindoll, they laid their hands on Seth Stevens and prayed over him. Being the center of that kind of attention had never been easy for him, and his pleasure was mixed with embarrassment. He told himself to relax and, as the babble of tongues swallowed him up, he began to feel better. He thought maybe he understood why it was impossible to speak plain English when talking to Jesus: plain English didn't have the right words. And even though the words sounded like nonsense, their meaning was clear. Seth Stevens breathed in deeply, and when he breathed out, he found himself speaking with the gift.

'*Hallelujah so ko ra sha, so ko ra sha la la la la, oh praise Him, praise Him . . .*'

He wasn't sure how long it lasted. But when it was over he was wrung out and euphoric.

Salvation's part of the service went smoothly. The feeling of well-being had stayed with him. And when he heard his own name in Pastor Grady's list of those who needed special prayers, he looked out on the enormous church and saw that he had been given a wonderful new family. They stood with their hands held high in supplication or sat with their fingers steepled. Their eyes were open and closed, their lips moving and still. They didn't ask what Seth Stevens's troubles were. They knew that he needed help, and they prayed.

After the service, Terry Kinsman told him that Pastor Grady wanted to see him again. Seth Stevens nodded. It seemed almost natural. Terry Kinsman said he would find Ben

Badgeley and tell him to go ahead, that he would give Seth
Stevens a ride home.

Pastor Grady was waiting for him.

'I only have a minute tonight, Seth, but I've learned that
you might be in a time of trial. Are you?'

'I'm not sure. I think so.'

'Are you tempted by sin? Are you questioning your faith
in Jesus?'

'I was yesterday. But today—here at church—I feel a lot
better.'

Pastor Grady chuckled.

'Church has a way of doing that. But when you walk out
of these doors, are you going to be OK?'

'I think so.'

'Remember that we're always in church. The very world is
a cathedral to God. We build these nice buildings in His honor
and because we like to get together with like-minded people.
But you should behave as if you're in church no matter where
you are. And you should take that feeling of safety and power
with you, too.'

He thought about it. It made sense.

'Seth, did you steal from your employer?'

'No, sir.'

Pastor Grady looked him in the eye for a long moment. He
nodded.

'All right then. Between two Christian men, our word is
our bond. I think you're being tested. I don't know why, but
God does. Sometimes He wants to know if our belief is more
than mere convenience, if we're pledged to Him as fiercely
as He is pledged to us. Sometimes He's working on something else. He doesn't reveal the blueprints of His grand plan
until we meet Him in paradise. You OK with that?'

'Yes, sir.'

Pastor Grady patted him on the back.

'Good man.'

Pastor Grady looked at his watch. Then he knelt down on
the carpet.

'Pray with me, Seth.'

Seth Stevens knelt down, too. Pastor Grady offered a short
prayer asking for patience and forgiveness. They amened and
stood up.

At the door, as Seth Stevens was about to leave, Pastor Grady put a hand on his arm.

'I understand that it's not like ancient times, Seth. I don't say "biblical times", because the Bible is for always. But even if God is testing you, we don't expect you to sit outside the city wall in sackcloth and ashes. Until you get back on your feet, why don't you work mornings at Citizens for Good Government? I'll ask them to put you on the payroll, starting Monday. It's not much but it'll keep you off the streets.'

He thanked Pastor Grady.

'We take care of our own, Seth.'

He left the office and closed the door. As he walked down the hall he sensed someone beside him. He turned. It was Charisma Brown.

'What are you doing after church on Sunday?' she asked.

'Do you have a secret door you come out of?' he asked.

She smiled.

'Maybe. What about Sunday?'

'I have to eat dinner at Margo Hofstatter's like usual,' he said.

'How about Sunday night?'

'Doing what?'

She shrugged.

'Drive around, watch TV, whatever.'

He thought he should find an excuse not to see her. But maybe having a beautiful nineteen-year-old ask him out wasn't a temptation. Were all good things temptations and all bad things tests?

'Sure,' he said, starting to give her his address.

'I remember,' she said. 'I'll pick you up at eight.'

Then she turned and went back down the dimly lit hallway.

Sunday was blistering hot. At Margo Hofstatter's they had closed up the house and turned on the air conditioning. Instead of watching her kids bounce on the trampoline they watched them watch a cartoon Bible story.

'I don't like the way they do the battles in this one,' she said, twisting her hair. 'Too violent.'

Bill Hofstatter swirled the ice in his glass. He shook his head.

'What do you want? They left out the blood. Even in biblical times people bled when they got whacked with a sword.'

'Well, we're not whacking people with swords anymore, are we? I think they should just skip over the battles and get to the teachings. Love thy brother and whatnot.'

Bill Hofstatter shrugged. He held up his empty glass. Margo Hofstatter got up to get him a refill.

'I keep thinking about that Mormon kid,' she said from the kitchen. 'His poor family. I mean, they probably know people whose kids are doing their missionary stuff in some place in darkest Africa. So when their boy got Oklahoma, they must've thought, "Well now. Lord be praised!"'

'The Mormon faith is a cult,' said Bill Hofstatter.

'He's still their child,' retorted his wife. 'Even cult members have families.'

'If they can't find him, he probably ran away,' said Seth Stevens, wanting to believe it. 'Maybe he wanted out of the cult.'

Margo Hofstatter considered this.

'Well, when he gets where he's going, I hope he sends someone a note so we can all stop worrying about him.'

At six o'clock, Seth Stevens was strumming his acoustic guitar when there was a series of sharp knocks on his door.

'Police! Open up!'

He slid off the bed, unlocked his door, and tugged it open. He walked back to his bed and picked up his guitar without looking to see who was there.

'Come in, Terry.'

'One of these days it's really going to be the police, Seth. That how you're going to answer it?'

'You think they're going to throw us in jail over some yard signs?'

'Secular law don't always see eye to eye with Christian law. And anyways, you can get arrested even when you didn't do nothing wrong. You got fired for nothing, didn't you?'

Seth Stevens didn't answer. He didn't want to go over it all again.

'Anywho, you ready to go?' asked Terry Kinsman.

Seth Stevens hit a sour chord and grimaced.

'Can we be back by eight?'

'Why, you got to get up early tomorrow?'

'I have a date. Sort of.'

'You mean Chastity Brown?'

'What do you mean by that?'

'Nothing. I guess you guys hit it off.'

'I haven't been, you know. I mean, she's—'

'Practically royalty, I know,' interrupted Terry Kinsman. 'But I guess if Pastor Grady didn't cut your hands off by now, then you got sanctioned.'

'It's not, I mean, we're not—'

'You don't got to tell me, Seth. I know you're a Christian man.'

He nodded stupidly.

'OK, back by eight it is, then,' said Terry Kinsman. 'Job's kind of quick tonight anyways.'

'What, no yard signs?'

'No yard signs.'

'No telephone calls?'

'Just the one.'

'About what?'

'Put your guitar away. I'll tell you in the car.'

Terry Kinsman was looking around the apartment as if searching for hidden microphones. He peered under a lampshade, then turned the phone over and examined its base.

'Oh come on,' said Seth Stevens. 'You don't think . . .?'

'I don't think nothing. Let's talk in the car.'

Fifteen minutes later they were in Terry Kinsman's car, headed north. The sun was getting closer to the horizon but the day wasn't getting cooler. Without air conditioning, the car felt like an egg on a griddle. Seth Stevens held his hand out the passenger window, surfing it up and down on the oven-hot currents of air.

Terry Kinsman talked while he drove. All Seth Stevens had to do, he explained, was to call one phone number and repeat two sentences.

'Who's going to pick up the phone?'

'A newspaper reporter.'

'What do I tell them? Vote Platt?'

'You tell them this: "Ira Isaacs sexually harassed his secretary three years ago. Look into it."'

'Did he?'

'She says he did.'

'Well, if it happened three years ago, why haven't any of

the newspapers found out about it already? That'd be a pretty hard secret to keep.'

'Well, the complaint was made on Friday. The papers will find out about it eventually. This just kind of speeds things up a little bit.'

'Why did she wait so long?'

'Guilt, shame, stuff like that. I dunno, maybe she repressed the memory. Her therapist told her she had to get it off her chest, so she's filing charges.'

'Well, how do we know about it?'

Terry Kinsman signaled a turn. His lips curled into a smirk.

'Let me guess,' said Seth Stevens. 'She goes to our church, doesn't she?'

Terry Kinsman pulled into a no-name gas station on the old state highway and stopped in front of a filthy pay phone. The triangle-shaped plastic flags that ringed the lot had been ripped to tatters by the wind.

'She does.'

'Did she ever even work for Isaacs?'

'Course she did. He was her hero, too. Then he fondled her breasts and buttocks on three separate occasions, which she wrote about in her diary, and she began to question her lack of any kind of a belief system. She's with us now.'

'So if all this really happened,' said Seth Stevens, 'why are we driving out to the middle of nowhere to make the call?'

'Look, Ira Isaacs may be a Jew in Oklahoma, but he's a powerful man. There's always a chance he could suppress this, maybe say she's crazy or something. I don't know. We just want to make sure they take a look. We're giving the free press an opportunity to do their duty. They don't, isn't nothing we can do about it. We're making an anonymous call because if they know we know her it's gonna look suspicious. Like you found out yesterday, just because you know someone, people assume you're going to lie for them.'

Terry Kinsman took a handful of quarters from his pocket. Seth Stevens stared at the silver coins.

'Don't know if I'll be on the phone that long, but thanks,' he said. 'What's the number?'

Terry Kinsman gave him a torn corner of newspaper with a phone number written on it. The area code was 202.

'This isn't local, Terry.'

'Let's just say that the *Tulsa World* isn't exactly Woodstein and Goldberg.'

'Woodward and Bernstein?'

'Whatever.'

He got out of the car, walked to the poorly sheltered pay phone, and dialed the number. A computerized voice told him to deposit $1.75. He pushed the quarters into the slot one at a time, listening to the faint electronic hiccups that told him the coins had registered.

The phone rang. A man answered.

'National desk.'

'Ira Isaacs sexually assaulted his secretary three years ago,' said Seth Stevens. 'Look into it.'

How had *assaulted* slipped into the sentence?

'Who's calling, please?' said the man on the phone.

Terry Kinsman had told him to just hang up.

'Who's calling, please?'

The man sounded tired but interested.

'A friend,' he said, and hung up.

A friend? Where had that come from? It sounded like something from a spy movie. He went back to the car.

'Go OK?' said Terry Kinsman.

He nodded.

'Good. Now let's get you back to your hot date with Chastity Brown.'

'Charisma.'

'Right. Charisma. Wonder if she was a boy they'd of named her Charlie?'

He waited for her in front of his building. It was too late to pretend that he didn't live in a dump, but he could preserve some of his dignity by not letting her see how small and run-down his apartment was. Also, it seemed like a good idea to avoid being alone with her in a room with a bed. The road to righteousness detoured around the pitfalls of temptation. Or so he had read on the church's reader board a few months earlier.

Charisma Brown arrived just a few minutes late, honking hello even though they had already made eye contact. As he lifted the door handle he found himself wondering if he would ever stop being the passenger in other people's cars.

'So where to?' she asked.

'I was hoping we could do something real Midwest,' he said. 'Like tipping cows or climbing a water tower.'

'This is pork country,' she said. 'Out here we tip pigs. Besides, what does a New Yorker know about cow-tipping?'

'That's why I wanted to try it. To lose my virginity.'

It sounded stupid leaving his mouth, but he was still caught off guard when her smile faded.

'Is that some kind of a joke?'

'What? No. What are you talking about?'

She studied his face, then put the car in gear.

'I'm in that group, Sworn to Wait? I took a pledge to keep my virginity until I get married. Some people think that's funny, even Christians.'

'I'm sorry, Charisma. I didn't know.'

'Sorry that I'm a virgin?'

'Of course not.'

'You're probably not a virgin.'

There didn't seem to be a safe way to answer the question, so he didn't answer. He wished they hadn't gotten started on the subject.

'You've probably had sex lots of times, back when you were a Satanist,' she continued. 'Do you still have premarital sex now?'

'No.'

'It's OK, Seth. It doesn't matter what you did, only what you are now. Sometimes I think half of God's Slaves are former drug addicts or whatever.'

'I wasn't trying to tease you. It was just a stupid joke. Honestly.'

'I thought maybe Terry said something to you. He used to tease me a lot when I was in high school. Until I told Uncle Grady to make Terry leave me alone. Being the pastor's niece kind of stinks sometimes, but sometimes it has its perks.'

He watched the cars coming toward them, headlights starting to come on even though there was plenty of daylight left.

'Have you ever played miniature golf?' she asked abruptly.

He confessed that he hadn't.

'That's a good, wholesome Midwestern thing for us to do. Mini golf and Dairy Queen. And with plenty of people around so we're not tempted to do anything bad. We'll pop your cherry.'

Until she laughed, he had considered asking her to turn the car around. Then, relieved, he laughed with her.

He was surprisingly bad at miniature golf. Though it looked easy, he finished every hole several strokes over par. Twice he hit the ball so hard that it left the miniature fairway entirely. The first time, it landed in a decorative bed of volcanic rock. The second time, his ball took a funny hop off a picnic table, jumped the fence, and rolled into the parking lot. He searched for it until the large owner of a large pickup truck asked what it was, exactly, that he thought he was doing under someone else's vehicle. When he came back empty-handed, Charisma Brown offered to share her ball with him. He told her that he would rather watch her play, which was true.

The awkwardness at the start of the evening hadn't lasted long. But he continued to stumble over his thoughts and words. Charisma Brown may have been fresh-faced and pretty, but she was hard to read. When she talked about her virginity pledge or the church, she sounded like the poster child for doing the right thing. At other times she seemed to be teasing him, and her repeated references to his sinful past life betrayed an interest that struck him as flirtatious. But she never winked once. He would have thought that she was playing a game with him but she didn't seem like the type who played games. He suspected that she was more intelligent than he was, too, which made him doubt his readings of her behavior even more.

After the game, they went to Dairy Queen. Seth Stevens asked for a plain vanilla cone. Charisma Brown ordered a banana split with extra nuts, extra cherries, and extra whipped cream. When the order-taker saw who was ordering, she tried to give them the treats for free. But Charisma Brown insisted on paying the full price, minus her employee discount.

They sat on a sticky picnic table and watched the traffic.

'You probably think I'm some kind of groupie stalker,' she said.

'I thought you made fun of Salvation groupies.'

'Not a Salvation groupie. A Satanist groupie. Ever notice how born-agains are the ones who want to talk about Satan all the time?'

He hadn't. But it seemed at least partly true.

'Being good just isn't as exciting as being bad. That's why there's so many bad people.'

'A lot of them get born again, though,' said Seth Stevens.

'But I kind of think that, for some of them, it's like they get tired of being bad, so they might as well be good.'

'Isn't that kind of jaded?'

'Hang around the church long enough, you'll see some people come and go more than once. Thing is, I envy them. I know it's a sin, but being good all the time, you feel like you're missing out. Even when being good means you get to go to Heaven and being bad means you have to go to Hell.'

'But you get to sin right now,' said Seth Stevens, 'and you have to wait until you die to go to Heaven.'

'That's it, isn't it?'

Charisma Brown ate her banana split methodically, getting ice cream, banana, and toppings in every spoonful. She had a smudge of chocolate syrup on her upper lip that had so far evaded her napkin. He considered telling her about it but decided not to. It made her even more attractive. What he really wanted to do was lick it off.

'Funny thing is that the Free Church of God's Slaves is full of people who've done all sorts of stuff. There's reformed alcoholics, drug addicts, and sex addicts, wife-beaters and child-beaters, car thieves and everything. There's even one guy who went to prison for manslaughter. In my family we don't have any of that. My dad was class president, honor roll, valedictorian, you name it. My mom? She's never even said a single curse word in her *mind*.'

'That's pretty lucky,' he said.

'Of course it is. And I pray to Jesus every night to forgive me for wishing somebody in my family would screw up once in a while so I don't feel like I have to hold my breath my whole entire life.'

Seth Stevens's ice cream was melting. He licked up the runny parts and then took a bite of the cone, shivering when his front teeth sank into the ice cream. He finished it in a few more bites so he wouldn't have to bother with it anymore. He wondered why he hadn't ordered something that he really wanted. He also wondered why it hadn't occurred to him that God's Slaves didn't all walk around thinking holy thoughts all day long. Maybe if he had been raised in the church he would have known better.

'I know I'm going to feel terrible telling you all this after you tell me that you were an orphan or something,' said Charisma Brown.

'My mom used to draw my blood every Saturday night and share it with her vampire friends.'

Charisma Brown froze with her spoon in front of her open mouth.

'Kidding.'

She shook her head, smiling ruefully. She put her spoon down.

In fact, he'd had a childhood that many high-schoolers would have killed for: no supervision, no responsibility. Jan Stevens had been a fifteen-year-old living in suburban New Jersey when an older boyfriend took her into New York City to see the Ramones play at CBGB's. A social outcast in her hometown, she identified with the band and its fans and returned home five hours past her curfew and with a new plan for her life. She spent the rest of her high-school years commuting to the city to go to shows and hang out on the streets, sometimes running away from home for days at a time, desperate to establish her credentials as an authentic punk rocker.

When she finally graduated from high school—she wasn't punk enough to drop out, she later joked—she moved to the city for good. She crashed on couches or shared tiny apartments with large groups of friends, moving whenever the money or goodwill ran out. For a year she was the steady girlfriend of the guitarist of a band that had once opened for Richard Hell & The Voidoids. After that she dated a series of increasingly dimmer luminaries. They were always musicians. She had shown her son photographs of herself onstage, too. When band members were in short supply she was sometimes recruited to stand behind the band, holding a microphone or a guitar.

She dabbled in drugs, mostly speed and heroin. She had once told him in a moment of candor that she made a lousy heroin addict because she was a shitty thief: she could never steal enough to support her habit. Alcohol, however, was so cheap as to be almost free. By 1984, a year that provided a modest boost in profits to the designers of punk-rock T-shirts, she had made several trips to rehab, dragged there each time by her furious father, who seemed to find her wherever she went. By then she was living mostly on the street.

It was in rehab that a doctor had informed her that she was pregnant. A friendly nurse explained the timeline and tried to help her retrace her steps, but Jan Stevens was never even able to come up with a theory as to who the father might be.

She spent the rest of her pregnancy at home, watched carefully by her parents. Five months after giving birth, however, she ran away one last time, taking baby Seth with her. And this time, her father didn't come looking for her.

Seth Stevens had learned all of this from the source. His mother loved to talk and didn't believe in keeping secrets. She did her best to settle down, but her version of family life wasn't one that his friends—even New York gutterpunks—could relate to. Living in a one-room cold-water flat in the Bowery, he walked to school by himself and, when there was food, made his own meals. He sometimes came home from school to find three leather-jacketed punks passed out on his floor and sometimes he found no one at all. He sometimes woke to the distinctive sound of his mother having sex—carrying on a one-sided conversation while a man grunted on top of her. More often he woke to the sound of her puking in the shared bathroom down the hall.

When she was drunk she was funny and exuberant and when she was sober she was cold and angry. And when she was hungover, she was prone to maudlin monologues. She knew she was a horrible mother. She knew she had to stop drinking so much. She was so sorry. She kissed his hair and squeezed him and cried while he held his breath against her halitosis.

That's OK, Mom, he said. *I know you love me.*

I do love you, Seth, she said. *I do, I do, I do.*

He drank while he was in high school, but no more than the other kids. He did some drugs. But it hadn't been until he got to the Heartland that he got hooked.

While deciding how to answer Charisma Brown, Seth Stevens realized that he had two conflicting impulses. His first impulse was, as usual, to withhold information. He had always been embarrassed by his upbringing, by his mother's abundant character flaws, by his failure to learn from her mistakes. The second impulse was new: he wanted to tell Charisma

Brown all the gory details. But he wasn't sure why he wanted to do that. Was it because he felt it would be meaningful? Or was it because he wanted her to think he was cool?

'Why did your parents name you Charisma?' he asked.

She laughed.

'I don't know. I guess they hoped people would like me. Why did your mom name you Seth?'

'She didn't name me. My grandma did. My mom told me she was "weirded out by the whole giving-birth thing" and couldn't make up her mind. I guess the front-runners were Iggy, Bowie, and Lydon. So I could be a cool baby or something.'

'She wanted people to like you, too.'

They sat, both of them thinking about his silence.

'Rough childhood, huh?' she said.

He nodded. Then, surprising himself, he told her some things. Not the worst stories, but not a made-for-TV version, either. Just enough to give her an accurate picture.

When he stopped, she stared at the traffic for a while. Then the Dairy Queen's lights clicked off and they sat in the bruised glow of a streetlight.

'I guess it's not that cool to be cool, huh?' she said.

'Not my kind of cool,' he agreed.

'How does it feel,' she asked, 'being in Salvation? Eating ice cream and playing mini golf?'

'Pretty good,' he said. 'I mean, sometimes it doesn't feel as intense. But sometimes just eating ice cream seems intense, too. I think I've forgotten half of the stuff that happened to me before.'

She leaned toward him. Her eyes were glistening with tears. She kissed him tenderly on the lips. They regarded each other seriously and then kissed again. She pressed her face against his shoulder.

'I thought you were, you know, celibate,' he said.

'It's just kissing,' she said, pressing closer. 'It's just kissing.'

Nine

When he showed up at Citizens for Good Government, no one was sure exactly what he should do. There were only three people there—Doug Earle and two others—and while they clearly knew he was coming, it was equally clear that they didn't have any work for him. They gave him a list of light cleaning tasks that it took only an hour to complete. Then they suggested that he sit at the front desk and act as the receptionist. But when calls came in, every phone rang, and Doug Earle usually answered before Seth Stevens could. There was no walk-in traffic. The job was clearly pure charity.

There was a computer there, a grinding relic that, judging from the stickers, had once belonged to someone's kid. But it was connected to the Internet. He opened a browser and did some news searches on Ira Isaacs. There were plenty of articles about his fundraising efforts and Oklahoma credentials, but nothing about sexual harassment. As if a newspaper could put a story like that together over a single Sunday night.

Even though he had no computer of his own, he did have an e-mail account. A well-intentioned librarian at the Tulsa public library had signed him up for it during his homeless days, thinking it would help him keep in better touch with his friends. He had been too polite to tell her that he didn't think his friends used e-mail, and even if they did, he didn't know their addresses. He checked his in-box once in a while, but all he saw were a few hundred pieces of spam. He used the address mostly when he needed to create an account in order to visit the various sites that interested him.

Logging into his e-mail account, he clicked rapidly through several screens of solicitations before deleting them all. What was *cl@ll$*? he wondered. Who wanted to see pictures of a *wrinkled granny fingered by young stud!!!*? Sometimes church people used these e-mails as examples of the moral degeneracy sweeping the land. But it was hard for him to imagine a human being opening such an e-mail, much less writing one. It was harder still to see it as the work of Satan: to seduce the righteous, wouldn't Satan's work have to be more beautiful?

He visited the site of the *Tulsa World* and searched for 'Jason Harbo'. The only result was an article several days old. It said simply that the search for the missing Mormon missionary was ongoing. On impulse, he searched 'Terry Kinsman' and, to his surprise, saw eleven results. The first nine were notices about Terry Kinsman's activities as youth minister, mostly as a director of plays and social activities for the kids at church. The tenth article was a short news item.

LOCAL MAN CHARGED IN ASSAULT AT BASEBALL GAME
Police charged a local man, Terry Kinsman, 21, with assault after an incident at Midwest Harvest Supply Field, home of the minor-league Okla-Homers baseball team.

According to the police report and to witnesses, Kinsman was heckling Lloyd Cornish, a fan of the visiting Branson Missouris who was watching the game with his niece. The heckling was said to have started during the fifth inning.

During the seventh inning, with the verbal abuse continuing unabated, Cornish walked over to confront Kinsman. Witnesses agreed that while Cornish was still speaking Kinsman punched him in the face.

Cornish received several more punches and then fell to the ground, where Kinsman kicked him until observers intervened.

Cornish, a veteran of Operation Desert Storm, has a prosthetic left leg and also a metal plate covering a portion of his skull, both a result of injuries received during his military service.

Witnesses told the *Star* that Cornish's injuries were not immediately apparent given that Cornish was wearing long pants and a baseball cap. Kinsman remains in the county jail following a failure to post bond.

The article didn't mention the Free Church of God's Slaves, although Terry Kinsman might not have been a member at the time the article was written. Maybe his troubles had, like Seth Stevens's, led directly to his joining the church.

The eleventh article was about the accident that had killed Terry Kinsman's parents. All of the details matched with the story Seth Stevens had already heard except one: Terry Kinsman had been there. The reason he hadn't died, too, was that he had climbed out of the car to pick up a quarter that his father had thrown and missed. He had been kneeling behind a concrete bollard when the crash happened. He had seen it and been spared. He had been nineteen.

It seemed a terrible way to receive the Lord's mercy.

Seth Stevens suddenly felt guilty for surfing the Internet when he was getting paid to work. He closed the browser, then went back to Doug Earle's office and asked again if there was anything more for him to do. Doug Earle found a box of envelopes that needed to be stuffed with informational flyers. Seth Stevens lugged the box to the conference room and set up on the long table, grateful to have something with which to occupy himself.

Even though he was only being paid to work until noon, he stayed until one o'clock in order to get the envelope-stuffing done. No one was around to see his self-sacrifice, however, as the others had gone to lunch at 12:30. He briefly considered staying until they returned so they would know that he had put in extra time, then dismissed the thought as vanity. Pastor Grady had preached that the truest charity was performed with the recipient in complete ignorance of the benefactor's identify. If the Free Church of God's Slaves put its name on its charitable works, he said, it was not for the glory but to serve as a calling card for lost or like-minded souls.

But Seth Stevens couldn't leave: he didn't have a key to lock up with. After a twinge of annoyance at being forced to stay, he sat down at the reception desk to surf the Web some more.

The door opened and a man walked in. The man was average height, with skin like crinkled gray tissue paper. He was wearing a charcoal suit with a white shirt and a red and blue striped tie. He nodded at Seth Stevens and kept walking toward the back.

Seth Stevens had never seen the man before. Probably the man worked for Citizens, but what was the point of sitting at a reception desk if he allowed everyone to simply walk past?

'Excuse me, can I help you?' he said.

The man stopped and turned.

'New here?'

Seth Stevens nodded.

'I'm Seth,' he said. 'I'm only here part-time.'

'Nice to meet you, Seth,' the man said.

The man turned again and walked down the hall. He went into an office and closed the door.

It was only after the door closed that Seth Stevens realized the man had not given his own name. But there was no point in chasing him. Walking in as if he owned the place, the man had to at least work there. And, at any rate, Doug Earle would return soon. At least he hoped it would be soon.

Doug Earle and the others were laughing when they walked back in, the men holding Styrofoam cups of pop, the woman holding a Styrofoam clamshell with her leftovers.

'You're still here,' said Doug Earle.

'I couldn't leave,' said Seth Stevens. 'I don't have a key.'

Doug Earle slapped himself on the forehead.

'For crying out loud,' he said. 'Seth, I'm sorry.'

'Some guy came in and went into an office. I felt kind of funny letting him, but he acted like he owned the place. He has gray hair and he's wearing a gray suit.'

Doug Earle's smile tightened.

'I think I know who you mean. He's a consultant. He can rub people a little wrong sometimes.'

The other two workers had already gone into the back. Doug Earle craned his neck to see what Seth Stevens was looking at. It was just the start page for a search engine. Doug Earle thanked him and told him he'd be paid on Fridays. He encouraged him to take an extra can of pop with him 'for the road'. He seemed anxious to go and meet with the consultant, so Seth Stevens grabbed a can of pop and hit the road.

The week passed uneventfully. After everything that had happened, he was grateful for a boring routine. He worked at Citizens in the mornings, helping out when needed and surfing the Web the rest of the time. He looked for new stories about

Ira Isaacs and Jason Harbo but didn't see anything. He played with Salvation at Wednesday and Sunday services and at rehearsal on Friday night.

The one thing that wasn't routine was the time he spent with Charisma Brown. She told him she wasn't ready to introduce him to her parents yet. He wasn't ready to introduce her to his neighbors yet, either. So they met in a park, at an ice cream shop, and, once, at a movie theater where they watched a PG-13 romantic comedy. They held hands the entire time, and the clinch of sweaty palms reminded him of 'going with' a girl in eighth grade. Only that time they'd been watching an R-rated movie in Times Square. And that girl had been a freshman in high school, a smoker, who encouraged him to put his hand up her shirt to feel her breasts.

It was funny. Now that he was born again, he spent his time doing things that he would have derided as kid stuff even when he was a kid. His old, secular life had been built around the desire to gain experience. The more experience he had, the more grown-up he felt, and the more grown-up he was in his friends' eyes. But the experiences they had wanted had mostly to do with sex, drugs, and punk rock. In one way, trading sex for ice cream felt almost embarrassingly saccharine. But in another way it felt like the truest possible definition of 'grown-up': he wasn't counting on chemicals to tell him how to feel.

The age difference between him and Charisma Brown seemed far less important than he had thought it would. And not expecting sex took a lot of pressure off their time together, too. It was true that there was a lot he still didn't know about being a Christian. But Pastor Grady used the word 'peace' a lot. And for a week Seth Stevens felt peaceful.

The guys in the band—except Kirk Swindoll, who kept a busy social calendar—teased him about spending less time with them. To appease them, he invited them to watch movies at his apartment the following Friday, after rehearsal. Kirk Swindoll had plans, of course, but Ben Badgeley and Owen Rusk accepted. Even Jimmy Gilstrap said that his wife would allow him to come for a little while. Terry Kinsman had something to do first. He would come if he could and would call first to make sure he wasn't too late.

They hit the 18-Hour Mart first and bought pop, nachos, and candy. Owen Rusk detoured home to pick up some DVDs he had recently bought. Then they converged on Seth Stevens's apartment. Thankfully, the neighbors were out.

Halfway through the first movie, the phone rang.

'That's probably Terry,' said Owen Rusk.

'I got it,' said Ben Badgeley, who was closest to the phone.

Seth Stevens paused the DVD. On the TV screen, a man who had been running across a busy street froze in mid-stride with a city bus bearing down on him.

Ben Badgeley lifted the receiver and said hello. He listened. His eyes widened. He said that Seth Stevens was there and then held out the phone.

'It's for you,' he said. 'It's your mom.'

'I didn't know Seth had a mom,' said Owen Rusk.

Jimmy Gilstrap punched Owen Rusk on the arm.

Seth Stevens thought about telling Ben Badgeley to hang up. Instead, he traded the remote control for the phone. He stretched the cord as far as it would go as he retreated to the kitchenette. The cord didn't reach very far.

'Hello?' he said.

It sounded as if his mother was choking back tears.

'The only way I get you to answer the phone is when a friend of yours answers by accident,' she said.

He didn't say anything. Simply hearing her voice live, not on a recording, seemed to alter the chemistry of his brain. It was as if the past two years had only been two days. It made him feel like his former self. Had he really turned his life around?

'Seth, say something.'

'What do you want?'

'I want to talk to my son. Are you going to hang up on me?'

'Do you want money?'

He could feel his friends' eyes fixed on him. He stared at a stain on the back wall where a two-liter bottle of pop had exploded months ago. He had never been able to scrub it entirely clean.

'Do you want to tell me you hate me?' said Jan Stevens. 'Because if you do, let's just get it over with now.'

'No.'

'Well, good. And I don't need money, either. Maybe we've said those things to each other enough times.'

'What do you want?'

'I just want to talk to you, Seth. Maybe you don't believe it, but I miss you. Don't you miss me, too?'

'No,' he said. 'I don't think about my old life. Things are finally going good for me now.'

He heard her breathe in sharply. Or maybe she was smoking.

'Things are going good for me, now, too,' she said. 'Well, that's a lie, things are pretty shitty, but at least they're shitty in a new way. OK, in case you hang up on me, I'll make it quick: I'm sober and I've been sober for seven months. There's this program, they helped me get a job and an apartment. The apartment is a shithole and the job is retarded, but hey, one day at a time, right?'

He wished his friends would go outside but he didn't want to ask them to do it.

'I'm not supposed to hang out with my old friends, you know, the usual advice I always ignored,' she continued. 'I mean, half of 'em are dead, but I get the point. The people I got to know in the program, well, let's just say the only thing I have in common with them is that we all have difficult personalities.'

He was squeezing the phone so tightly that his hand was cramping.

'I have to go,' he said.

'Wait wait wait,' she said. 'Just give me one more fucking minute, OK? So, yeah, to this point most of my life has been shit, I know, I know. And most of the people I know aren't worth knowing. And my dad was probably right when he said I should never have been born. But, Seth—what am I trying to say? I guess I'm just trying to say you deserve a better mom, but I'm your mom and you're my kid and so can we just not hate each other, please?'

It was so tempting to give in. But he knew what would happen. The same thing always happened.

'Do I have to come out there?' she said. 'Because I will, you know. I can't afford it right this minute, but I'll come out there and stand outside your door until you at least admit I'm your mom.'

'Mom,' he said, 'have you accepted the Lord Jesus Christ as your personal savior?

'Not this shit again,' she groaned.

'Mom, please don't use profanity.'

'OK, I'll try not to swear, but I'd like to have a conversation about our messed-up little family without bringing Jesus Christ into it.'

'Mom, I have a new family now. And Jesus Christ is part of my family. You're welcome to be a part of it to, but you're going to have to repent your sins and be born again into the glory of the Lord.'

'Are you going to keep going like this?'

'Our time on this earth will last only a moment, but when we are reborn in the next world we will live forever in His glory.'

'Amen,' said Ben Badgeley and Jimmy Gilstrap quietly.

'Seth, if you're going to talk like some robot, then I'm going to hang up.'

'Mom, the church will help you,' he said. 'You're going to keep sinning until you renounce Satan. But Jesus loves you. I love you.'

She had hung up before he said the last three words. He hung up, too. He put the phone down and then sat on his bed, tears welling at the corners of his eyes.

'That is so messed up,' said Owen Rusk.

'Start the movie,' said Seth Stevens.

'I think we should pray,' said Ben Badgeley.

'Just start the movie.'

Terry Kinsman never did call that night. When Seth Stevens called Charisma Brown the next day, he told her about his mother's phone call. He knew that, given her storybook family life, she wouldn't really understand what he was feeling, but he told her anyway. He told himself that he did it because he wanted to see if she would say something different from Terry Kinsman. But maybe he just he wanted her to feel sorry for him.

'I know you're thinking I can't understand what you're going through,' she said, 'because I have such a picture-book family and everything.'

He said he hadn't thought that at all. She ignored him.

'And you're basically right. I know she's your mother, Seth, but she just sounds so horrible. I don't know how she could treat you like that.'

'Sometimes I think that, you know, she did the best job she could.'

'She could have done a better job. You don't have to make excuses for her.'

'I know.'

'And you did the right thing. I mean, honestly, you don't owe her anything, but you did the right thing, the Christian thing. Because you're right. She won't find peace until she accepts Jesus Christ.'

'She won't do it. You should hear her, Charisma.'

'Even the worst sinner can be redeemed.'

'I know. But a lot of the worst sinners don't want to be.'

'It must be scary for you, thinking she's going to Hell.'

The thought hadn't occurred to him. He felt guilty, realizing that he hadn't been worrying about his mother so much as he had been worrying about himself. He pictured her bound in rusty chains, anchored in a lake of fire, screaming in agony. She didn't deserve that, of course. But if she wasn't afraid of it for herself, why should he fear it for her?

'Am I going to see you tonight, Seth?'

It was the one question he could answer with confidence.

That night they drove to a small town outside Tulsa and climbed the water tower, joking as they did that it was the most stereotypical Midwestern date that ever was. At the top, they peered over a rusted metal railing at the ground below, giddy from adrenaline. They inspected the scrawlings of the lovers and delinquents who had preceded them. *Shauna hearts James. Tulsa Krew 2007. Egan is a fagot.*

The heavens were full of man-made lights. The moon and stars seemed pale in comparison. Tulsa glowed on the horizon like the fire in a crater left by a bomb. They held tightly to each other, kissing fervently, their hands daring them to release their grasp and see where their fingers might go.

He thought later that it was as if he had never been kissed. Knowing that they would not have sex focused everything on the touch of their lips, the feel of their bodies through their T-shirts. It was as if they were drunk on kissing. They kissed for at least an hour and when they finally stopped it was as if by the shared knowledge that if they didn't stop they would commit a carnal sin the very next moment. He felt so dizzy that he wasn't sure he would be able to climb down the water tower.

'Seth, I know you're going to think I'm crazy,' she said, panting a little, 'because this is way too soon for anyone to ever say something like this, but have you ever thought about the kind of girl you want to marry? I mean, would you want to marry someone like me?'

He started kissing her again. She was crying. He started crying, too. Hot tears slicked their faces and salted their lips. Finally his mouth hurt from kissing so much.

'I'm not crying because I'm sad,' she said.

'I know,' he said. 'Me neither.'

She was right. It did seem crazy. But from then on he was unable to think of his future without imagining being married to Charisma Brown. At the same time, he was pretty sure he couldn't marry her. At least, not until he figured out what normal married life was supposed to be like.

Ten

He was sitting at the reception desk, playing a computer game called *Satan's Invaders*—a slightly altered version of the old *Space Invaders* arcade game—when he heard someone shout 'Hallelujah!' Then he heard an 'Amen' and an 'About time!'

Doug Earle appeared in the doorway.

'You'll want to see this,' he said.

Seth Stevens went back to a small office where Doug Earle and two others were crowded around a TV. On the TV, Byron Dennis, identified as the Fox News Midwest correspondent, was standing in front of a storefront. Sun glinted off the plate-glass window.

'I'm standing outside the Oklahoma City Senate campaign office of Congressman Ira Isaacs. It was here that Isaacs, then Holly Lee's employer, fondled her breasts and buttocks on three separate occasions, ignoring her distressed pleas for him to stop, according to Lee. Lee says she was a "yellow-dog Democrat" in whose eyes the party could do no wrong. But that's changed since her groping at the hands of the party's star candidate, as she told me in an interview at her home in nearby Tulsa.'

The scene shifted to a tidy suburban living room. Holly Lee was a pretty cheerleader type with frosted blonde hair. Byron Dennis sat opposite her, the camera looking over his shoulder.

'My Lord!' said one of the Citizens. 'Isn't that . . .?'

'Yep,' said Doug Earle.

'Your claims are truly shocking,' said Byron Dennis. 'And I imagine that this secret was as hard for you to live with as it is for us to hear about. Why come forward now?'

'Well, to be honest, Mr Byron, I didn't think I was ever going to say anything. Where I come from, the values I was raised with, it's just sort of shameful even when it's not your fault. And next to the truly awful things that are happening all over the world, like children starving in Africa, what happened to me just didn't seem so important. I thought it was a matter between Ira Isaacs and his conscience.'

'And yet you came forward.'

'Well, as you know, a reporter did contact me—'

'Connie McGarrigle from the *Washington Post*,' interjected Byron Dennis.

'—yes, that's right. And she asked me point blank whether anything had happened. And, well, I was raised not to make a fuss but I was also raised not to tell a lie. And since then it's just been unbelievable how many people have called me to offer their support and prayers.'

Seth Stevens reached out for the wall, his head swimming. Had his anonymous phone call really set the whole thing in motion? If, as Terry Kinsman had said, 'she's with us now', then why hadn't Holly Lee just come forward on her own? Why did he have to tip off the media? So she could act surprised? Or had Citizens for Good Government planted the story without her knowing?

Doug Earle watched the interview with a smile, urging the revelations on with mouthed words and playful jabs and upper-cuts. It looked as if the story was news to him. But of course it wasn't news to him. If Terry Kinsman had known, then Doug Earle would have known, too. Unless Terry Kinsman's talk of taking orders from upper levels was more than idle boasting.

'This is a very serious charge to make against a man in a position of great authority,' Byron Dennis was saying. 'What proof do you have?'

'Well, there's my diary for one,' said Holly Lee. 'And I told one of my girlfriends about it at the time. She can vouch for me. There's also the timeline. Why would I have quit a job I loved all of a sudden like that?'

'Yet you claim that there were three incidents, over a period of as many months.'

'Yes, but each one got worse. And the last time just put me right over the edge. I quit the next day.'

'Did you contact the authorities?'

'Ira Isaacs was in a position of authority and I found that

he was not to be trusted. Let's just say that I was distrustful of all authority for a while.'

'This really marked a turning point for you.'

'You can say that again.'

'I understand that you're no longer a Democrat—that you're now a registered Republican. You've even become a born-again Christian.'

'The Lord gave me comfort when no one else could or would, Mr Byron. But I believe that a person's faith is a private matter.'

Byron Dennis told her that he respected her feelings. He thanked her for her time and wished her the best.

Seth Stevens let Doug Earle and the others high-five him and then walked dazedly back to the reception desk. It was hard to make sense of the story. He was grateful that there were people above him who could.

He spent the rest of the morning on the computer, reading about Ira Isaacs and Holly Lee. Every article contained essentially the same information. The rapid growth of the story amazed him. Even news sites from Europe, Africa, Asia, and Australia were covering the story. His stomach was upset, the way it sometimes was before he went on stage. He tried to tell himself that it all had nothing to do with him, that others had had the information and that anyone could have made the phone call. But the power of that phone call was frightening.

When Doug Earle and the others got ready to go to lunch, he took that as his cue to leave. This time, however, they invited him to come with them. He hesitated, worried about spending money.

'This one's on Citizens,' said Doug Earle. 'It's a strategy session.'

Though they did talk the whole time about the day's news and how it would affect the Platt campaign, the meal felt more celebratory than collaborative. Doug Earle ordered a steak and encouraged the others to do the same. They drank giant cups of pop, lemonade, and iced tea that the waitress kept refilling whether they asked her to or not. For dessert they ordered cheesecake, chocolate mousse, and pecan pie. Seth Stevens couldn't remember the last time he'd eaten so much food.

They had coffee with dessert. Doug Earle offered a toast.

'To Ira Isaacs, who should be a better man, but as long as he's not, I'm glad he's running against our candidate.'

They amened, drank their coffee, and finally stood to go.

Doug Earle even gave him a ride home. When he walked in the door, his apartment was dark and stiflingly hot. He had pulled the shades before he left in the morning but he couldn't afford to run the air conditioner when he was away. And having a bed in his only room was a curse, he thought: the idea of sleep was always right in front of him.

Keeping the blinds closed, he turned the air conditioner on low and lay down. He felt suddenly exhausted.

He woke in the late afternoon, his head thick and his thoughts slow. He took a shower and tried not to think of Charisma Brown. It was difficult. The water was ice-cold by the time he was finished.

He got dressed and turned on the TV. The liberal-versus-conservative team on Fox News was arguing about Ira Isaacs.

'First you guys have a president who can't keep it in his pants, and now you want to elect a senator—and we all know he would be the most important senator of the next two years, because he gives you the majority—who can't keep it in his pants, either,' said the conservative. 'Yes, it's early. Yes, we don't have all the facts. But as we've seen time and time again, where there's smoke, there's fire.'

'As you said yourself, we don't have all the facts,' said the liberal. 'I think it's a good time for all of us to withhold judgment.'

He watched for several hours, changing channels each time a station moved on to another story. In the early evening there was breaking news. Several stations interrupted their coverage to carry Ira Isaacs's press conference live.

The congressman stood at a wooden podium in front of a blue curtain. Camera flashes went off continuously, like fireworks. There was a moment of dead air while Ira Isaacs studied something—his notes? his fingernails?—on the podium. Off-camera, someone asked an unintelligible question. Someone shushed the speaker.

Ira Isaacs looked up. He appeared confident and at ease. Maybe he had a clean conscience, thought Seth Stevens. Or maybe he had no conscience. Maybe his expression was the mark of a good liar. Seth Stevens thought that if someone had accused him of sexual harassment, he would have been worried even if he had nothing to worry about.

'Ladies and gentlemen of the press, thank you for assembling on such short notice,' said Ira Isaacs. 'I'll be brief. Yesterday, the *Washington Post* printed a story quoting a woman, Holly Lee, as saying that I behaved inappropriately toward her. It is true that Holly Lee was employed in my Muskogee office for a period of eighteen months. In our interactions, which were limited, our conduct was professional. As for the reason for her abrupt departure, all I can say is that it was as much a mystery to me then as it is now. I must apologize but I will not be available to answer further questions at this time. Thank you.'

Back in the studio, the anchor and his panel of experts were whipped into a frenzy by Ira Isaacs's seeming reluctance to deny the charge categorically.

'He blundered there, Bill,' said one expert, a professor who studied apologies. 'Here he has the chance to offer an airtight, unambiguous rebuttal, and now the only thing people are going to talk about is, "Well, why did she really leave?" "If not because he harassed her, then why?" "And if he didn't harass her, why not say so directly?" Politics is no place for the high road.'

Seth Stevens wanted to talk to someone. Charisma Brown was at an aunt's birthday party and he wasn't sure if he should confide in her, anyway. Which left Terry Kinsman.

After a dinner of two frozen burritos, he made the call.

'Terry, have you been watching this?'

'Watching what?'

'TV. The Ira Isaacs thing.'

'Oh, yeah, of course.'

'Doesn't it make you feel kind of funny?'

'Funny how, Seth?'

'Well, knowing that—'

'Knowing that Bob Platt's going to probably win? That makes me feel great.'

'It's just that—'

'Hey, Seth? Hate to say it, but I can't talk on the phone right now.'

Seth Stevens finally realized why Terry Kinsman was acting strangely.

'Oh, OK,' he said.

'But we can get together. Why don't I drop by and see you at work tomorrow?'

Seth Stevens said that sounded OK. Terry Kinsman hung up.

Terry Kinsman was afraid his phone was tapped. It seemed crazy. Then again, a couple of weeks ago, Seth Stevens would have thought that making a phone call that changed the national news was crazy, too.

There were several more people at Citizens for Good Government the next morning. New volunteers, explained Doug Earle. There was a higher level of activity, too, as if the news of Ira Isaacs's misdeeds had energized the organization. For once, there was plenty of work for everyone. Seth Stevens kept busy stapling, folding, and stuffing. He ran letters through a franking machine. He loaded paper into the copier and emptied the trash. And the phone rang so often that he was even needed to answer it. His effectiveness as a switchboard operator was limited by his not knowing people's names and extensions. But no one seemed to mind as he put call after call on hold and then walked into the back to locate the desired recipients and tell them which line to pick up.

Late in the morning, Doug Earle gave him a handwritten list of office supplies and a $100 bill. Would he mind driving to the store? Doug Earle seemed surprised when Seth Stevens reminded him that he didn't own a car, and aghast that he didn't know how to drive.

'Where did you grow up, Seth? New York City?' he asked.

The answer mollified him.

Seth Stevens said he didn't mind walking. The store was only a mile away.

Doug Earle thanked him profusely and returned to the back.

Outside, it was hot and dry with a steady wind. Small puffs of cloud flew overhead, their shadows strafing the city like airplanes. Traffic was light and the sidewalks were empty. After twenty minutes of getting peppered with airborne grit, he reached the store. It was cold inside, its long aisles deserted, its piped-in music too loud. But there was something reassuring about the sterility of the wares. Even the Army of God needed these weapons, he thought: three-ring binders, manila folders, whiteboards. Even the seculars, too. A dry-erase marker is no better or no worse than the man who uses it, he thought, almost making himself laugh.

Doug Earle's $100 bill didn't cover the charges, and Seth Stevens only had a few singles in his wallet. He had to put back some things. It took several tries to reach the correct amount, and the cashier shook his head tiredly each time Seth Stevens told him to take something off.

It was the middle of the lunch hour when he returned. He could see as he approached that Doug Earle's car was gone from its usual parking space. He hoped they hadn't locked him out when they left for lunch.

The street across from Citizens was lined with six or eight storefronts, most of them showing 'For Lease' signs in their dirty windows. Halfway down the block, however, in front of the former *Junior Executive Men's Fashions*, a dark sedan was idling. He noticed it because no one ever parked on that side of the street. The strip mall that housed Citizens had plenty of spaces for its customers.

Terry Kinsman got out of the sedan and started across the street toward Citizens. The car pulled away, coming toward Seth Stevens. The gray man, the consultant, was at the wheel, dialing his cell phone with his thumb.

Seth Stevens met Terry Kinsman at the door.

'Hey, Seth, I was just coming to see you,' said Terry Kinsman.

'Who was that that dropped you off?' asked Seth Stevens.

'Just a guy I know. He was a friend of my dad's. I got a flat so I called him for a ride.'

'I thought he worked for Citizens. A consultant or something.'

Terry Kinsman's looked him in the eyes.

'Who said that?'

'Doug Earle.'

'Doug Earle said that? I don't know, maybe he's right. We didn't talk about it. Lots of people help out in this town. Lots of people go to church, too. Nothing special about that.'

'What's his name?'

Terry Kinsman laughed.

'Man, you're curious. Hey, you want a hand with those bags?'

He gave Terry Kinsman a bag to carry. The door was unlocked. Several volunteers were working through lunch. They took the office supplies through to the supply closet and unloaded the bags. Seth Stevens left the receipt on what he thought was probably Doug Earle's desk. He wondered who the gray man really was and why his identity might be a secret.

'Did you know this Isaacs thing was going to get so big?' he asked Terry Kinsman.

'Who knows anything, Seth?'

'You mean we can't talk about it here, either?'

Terry Kinsman hung his head in mock exasperation. Then he led Seth Stevens out the back door and into the alley. They sat down on a stack of weathered wooden pallets. Robust weeds sprouted from cracks in the pavement.

'Seth,' said Terry Kinsman, 'we shouldn't talk about any of this at all unless we're away from our homes and away from Citizens.'

'It's not illegal, is it?'

'It's the truth is what it is. Illegal, well, a government lawyer can make just about anything illegal. We just got to be smart, is all. To be careful.'

'But it worked, right? Isaacs will lose the election? Platt will win.'

'Lord didn't give us the ability to see the future, Seth. He gave us the will to try to work it in His favor. Until we know the future, we got to work to try and make it so.'

'You mean there's more planned?'

Terry Kinsman grinned.

'Let's just say, you didn't see nothing yet.'

'Who's that guy who gave you a ride?'

'I'm going to call him "Uncle Frank" for now. When he wants to meet you, you'll meet him.'

'I met him already.'

'He tell you his name?'

'No.'

'OK then. Uncle Frank.'

Embarrassed by his lack of heartland survival skills, Seth Stevens asked Charisma Brown to teach him how to drive. That evening they went to the parking lot of the abandoned ShopsMart—the one that had for a while been home to the

Free Church of God's Slaves—so he could practice. He was surprised at how easy it was.

'At least, it's easy with an automatic transmission,' said Charisma Brown. 'With a stick-shift it's a lot harder.'

He spent an hour driving in the parking lot, looping around lampposts, pulling into and backing out of the striped parking spaces. When she judged him ready, he drove to a nearby street to learn parallel parking. That was much harder. With his teacher leaning out the passenger window, he tried again and again to get the angle right as he cut in toward the curb.

'My dad says think of it like one big motion,' she told him. 'He says just pull up next to the other car and then just, like, recline back into your spot.'

'He says "recline"?'

'He does.'

Seth Stevens couldn't do it that easily. He corrected, over-corrected, and soon found himself stuck, the passenger door of Charisma Brown's car resting gently against the bumper of the parked car.

'Just go nudge the wheel left, roll forward, and then straighten out,' she told him.

'If I mess up your car, I can't pay to get it fixed,' he moaned.

Charisma Brown punched him on the arm, making him yelp.

'All right, city boy, get out.'

Probably some guys would have been humiliated by having to let their nineteen-year-old girlfriends get them out of a parallel-parking jam, he thought. But those guys weren't falling in love with Charisma Brown.

He put the car in park, opened the door, and got out. She slid over the armrest and took the wheel. She pulled forward, then backed up until her car was neatly alongside the parked car once again. Then she put her car in park and climbed back into the passenger seat.

'Can't we be done?' he asked.

'You have to park it right one time. Then we can be done.'

Taking a deep breath, he got back behind the wheel.

She was lying. After he finally parked the car, she made him do it three more times so he wouldn't forget how. After that, they drove around on residential streets so he could get used to being behind the wheel. While he drove, she rested her hand lightly on his seat back, then casually moved it to his shoulder. When she told him not to be afraid of getting close to the cars on the side of the road, she touched his arm. And when her arm got tired, she rested her hand on his knee.

They ended up back in the parking lot of the abandoned ShopsMart. The wind had died down and it was just another hot, humid night. Swarming bugs haloed the security lights, occasionally coming in through the car window to buzz around their ears. They waved off the bugs without breaking their kiss.

Seth Stevens felt exposed in the bright, empty parking lot, but he knew that that was why Charisma Brown had chosen it.

'This feels so right,' she murmured, 'that I'm tempted to do something so wrong.'

The week went by quickly. The activity at Citizens continued. Doug Earle even asked him to stay late two times despite not knowing whether he was authorized to pay for the extra hours. Seth Stevens agreed, still feeling grateful for the work. He spent his afternoons watching TV, playing guitar, and wishing that Charisma Brown's summer job didn't demand forty hours per week. It felt strange to have so much time on his hands. He knew he'd need to look for a full-time job himself—the money from Citizens was barely enough to cover rent and groceries—but he worried about having even less time for driving lessons and kissing.

He spent evenings with Charisma Brown, at church, or at band practice. Margo Hofstatter had heard about his 'going with someone' and invited him to bring 'the pastor's super niece' to Sunday dinner. His own mother had stopped calling. Each time he came home to an unblinking answering machine, he felt both relief and longing. He didn't want to talk to his mother, it was true. But the dark LED symbolized the growing distance between them. Was this really the end of their relationship? He had visions of Jan Stevens moving to Tulsa, Oklahoma, wearing long sleeves to hide her tattoos, getting a short permanent like Margo Hofstatter. He saw her reading the Bible, baking casseroles, tending a garden.

The vision of his mother baking a casserole made him laugh, actually.

At the Sunday service he could see Charisma Brown clearly—her family sat in the first and second pews at stage left—and he played poorly. First his fingers fluffed the opening riff to 'Grace of (His Eyes)'. Then, when the band was singing harmony at the end of 'Judgment Gate (Triumph)', he forgot to count choruses. The rest of the band stopped on the same beat but he kept singing. His voice rang out in the silence until he realized his mistake and shut up. It was only half a dozen words, but still, laughter rippled through the church. He could see Charisma Brown's sister whispering to her.

Pastor Grady absolved him.

'I don't blame Seth for not wanting to stop. Praising the Lord is a tough habit to break.'

But still he felt humiliated. He felt better when he saw Charisma Brown mouth the words *I love you*.

Her sister saw it, too, and threw an elbow that made Charisma Brown gasp.

Fortunately, it was the last song of the second service. He didn't think he would have been able to play another note.

Before Pastor Grady offered the closing prayer, the kids from the Sunday school returned to perform a play. Terry Kinsman had mentioned his role as the director, but Seth Stevens hadn't even known what the play was called: *Judgment Day*.

The sanctuary lights dimmed as several deacons put scrims and props into their proper places. Then small figures began making their way onstage, not without a few stumbles and giggles. Once they found their marks, though, they stood still and fell silent.

In the hall at the back of the stage, Terry Kinsman appeared behind Seth Stevens, holding a clipboard and nervously twiddling a pencil between his fingers.

When at last all was ready, the room went black. Battle sounds burst forth from the PA system, the rattle of automatic rifles, the pops of pistols, and the boom and crump of artillery. Men shouted and women screamed.

A child's voice rose above the din.

'It is the near future. America has descended into anarchism. The seculars that rule the government have outlawed religion. Good Christians rise against them, fighting for the right to be left in peaceful worship. But Satan has poisoned the minds against them. All they can do is fight—fight, and pray for the return of the Lord Jesus Christ. The end times have begun.'

The battle sounds grew even louder. The lights came up, red and yellow and bright white. A half-dozen pint-sized soldiers sprang from their hiding places, aiming toy rifles and jerking the muzzles to pantomime firing.

The play was short, about fifteen minutes, and it was soon evident that it had been written by the students, probably with some structural work by Terry Kinsman. The rebel fighters were surrounded by soldiers from the secular army who, when they weren't fighting, drank whiskey, listened to gangsta rap, and spoke suggestively about women. In the Oval Office, the President schemed to turn the nation's churches into 'cathouses'. And a young boy and girl, both of them filled with righteous spirit, warded off near-constant entreaties from their classmates to 'get with it' by smoking pot, having sex, and blaspheming Jesus.

The play ended with a drunken man, played by an eleven-year-old, verbally abusing his long-suffering, pious wife—who, perhaps twelve, stood a half-foot taller than him. Then there was a clap of thunder and the lights flickered before going off for about five seconds. When the lights came up again, the husband was holding his wife's empty dress. He looked up, as if watching his wife ascending into the clouds. Then he looked out at the audience as he delivered the final line: 'The rapture has begun.'

The play was poorly written and amateurishly acted, as anyone would expect from a bunch of kids. But the sight of the husband holding his wife's empty clothes had a powerful effect on Seth Stevens. What would it be like, he wondered, to know that the person you loved the most would be taken from you in an instant, and that you would be apart not only for the rest of your life but for all eternity?

Actually, he decided, he had a pretty good idea what that would feel like.

The congregation applauded thunderously, rising to their feet the same way they did when Pastor Grady drew them up with his palms open to the heavens. The kids bowed, then bowed again, then trooped offstage. Then they trooped back on for an encore.

'Nice job, Terry,' he said.

'Thanks, Seth. We been working on that for so long that it's like I can only see the mistakes. But they did pretty good.'

'They did great. See you later.'

'See you tonight, actually. We got an important job to do. I'll pick you up at nine.'

Terry Kinsman left and Seth Stevens watched the kids climbing down off the stage to hug their parents. Some of them posed for pictures, their faces still young despite the blood-and-mud make-up, their bodies small in the adult costumes. He didn't ponder Terry Kinsman's 'important job' for very long. He was already wondering what Charisma Brown and Margo Hofstatter would have to talk about during Sunday dinner.

Football, as it turned out. The Hofstatters had long been disappointed by Seth Stevens's inability to grasp the nuances of Golden Hurricane lore and strategy, but Charisma Brown knew chapter and verse. He sat amazed but grateful as she discussed the Hurricane's long history of disappointment and mediocrity—despite recent improvements, even die-hard fans knew that the team would never equal the success of the Sooners— with all the ease of a sunburned jock.

'I thought they'd never stop talking football,' she said as they drove away.

'You faked it pretty well,' he said.

'That's one of those moral gray areas, I guess. I know all about it because of my dad and my brother and everyone else in the family, but I never really got into it. So if it seemed like I like it, I guess that was kind of dishonest.'

'Little white lies to make people feel good seem pretty Christian to me,' he said. 'But I would have never in a million years guessed that you didn't spend your Saturdays waving gold, blue, and crimson.'

He was afraid he would have to tell a little white lie himself, about what he was doing later that evening. He hoped to avoid it. Charisma Brown had impulsively decided that, now that she had met his de facto family, it was time for him to meet her family, too. They drove to her house, arriving just in time to see Bill Brown firing up his barrel-sized gas grill.

'Ribs,' he said, shaking Seth Steven's hand. 'Hope you brought your appetite.'

Seth Stevens wasn't sure which was harder: spending more time making small talk or eating another Roman-sized meal. Bill and Sandy Brown were friendly but lacked Margo Hofstatter's gift of gab. Despite the well-attended table—the four of them were joined by Charisma Brown's brother and sister, aunt and uncle, and three cousins—most of the meal took place in silence. Between polite requests for margarine, or salt, or more pop, the Browns made brief inquiries about Seth Stevens's lineage, line of work, and favorite linebacker. But Seth Stevens didn't have Charisma Brown's knowledge or ability to fake it.

After dinner the men played two-on-two basketball in the driveway, a semicircle of concrete with a regulation-sized key painted on it. He was recruited to play with Charisma Brown's dad against her brother and a cousin. After he missed ten shots in as many minutes, Charisma Brown suggested that the two of them go inside to look at family photo albums.

'Good hustle, Chief,' said Bill Brown, slapping him on the butt. 'Jump shot needs a little work.'

Seth Stevens didn't jump at all but stood flat-footed when he shot the ball. Growing up, the basketball teams at his schools had been populated by impossibly athletic black and Puerto Rican guys. Trying out had seemed as ludicrous as applying to NASA.

He was drenched with sweat. The other players had taken off their shirts but he hadn't felt the time was right to show them his tattoo. Covering fully one-quarter of his back, it depicted a white-faced ghoul riding a surfboard on a wave of flames. He had gotten it while he was tweaking and couldn't remember why he had chosen it. Sometimes he forgot it was even there until he glimpsed it in the mirror. Seeing it always made him feel a pang of embarrassment.

They went inside. The air conditioning turned his sweat cold. The immaculate house made him feel dirty.

'I'm not going to make you look at old pictures,' said Charisma Brown.

'I don't mind,' he insisted.

'Please,' she said. 'I just hate it when they give guys the boyfriend treatment.'

Of course she'd brought other guys home. But he didn't want to know any more than that.

'Basically,' she continued, 'if I leave you out there with them, they'll keep trying to chase you off. They don't think anybody's good enough for me.'

'They're right.'

'That's sweet.'

They kissed quickly, breaking it off before they could be discovered, then went into the family room and turned on the TV.

He watched the clock nervously. He didn't want to lie about why he had to leave. But he didn't want to tell her what he was doing with Terry Kinsman just yet. And, truthfully, he had no idea what they were going to do that night.

Fortunately, Charisma Brown saved him. At twenty minutes before nine o'clock, she stretched and yawned.

'I hate to say it, but I'm sleepy. Do you mind if I take you home?'

'That's OK,' he said, thinking, *Praise the Lord!*

She dropped him off on the street in front of his building. He walked through the parking lot to his stairwell, surprised to see that it was dark.

'Hands up!' said a voice.

His heart jackhammered.

Terry Kinsman stood up from the steps where he'd been sitting.

Seth Stevens wanted to punch him.

'You want to surprise someone, wait in the dark so he's coming at you from the light,' said Terry Kinsman. 'Good as being invisible.'

He screwed the light bulb back in.

Seth Stevens winced in the sudden glare.

'Can you please stop trying to scare me? Why don't you save that for people you don't like?'

'Problem with most people is they're not ready for things,' said Terry Kinsman. 'Robbers, cops, sudden death. You should be ready for anything at any time. But be right with God just in case you're not ready.'

Seth Stevens followed Terry Kinsman into the alley, where his car was parked next to the dumpsters. Terry Kinsman didn't turn his headlights on until they had reached the end of the alley and turned on to a side street.

'Where are we going?' asked Seth Stevens.

Terry Kinsman's teeth gleamed in the light of the dashboard controls.

'Guess.'

'Pastor Grady's house.'

'Nope.'

'Bob Platt's house.'

'Nope. But closer.'

'Ira Isaacs's house.'

'Now that's really close.'

They drove to Interstate 44 and got on, going west.

'We're going to OK City?' asked Seth Stevens.

'Bingo.'

'Why? What're we going to do there?'

'How's your love life?' asked Terry Kinsman suddenly.

'Good.'

'Yeah?'

'Look, Terry, I know why you call her Chastity now. And I don't think it's very godly of you.'

'Did I call her Chastity? Just a slip of the tongue. You know there's a Chastity goes to God's Slaves? And a Charity, too? They're sisters. I always get them mixed up with Charisma.'

Terry Kinsman could be maddeningly hard to read.

'Well, I hope so,' said Seth Stevens.

'I hope you don't think I'd lie to you, Seth. But speaking of truth, you told her what it is we do for Citizens?'

Seth Stevens shook his head.

'Probably best if you don't. Girl like Chas—Charisma, I mean—might not understand.'

'I barely understand, Terry.'

'Well, me either, sometimes. But that's why we got men like Pastor Grady to guide us in the way of righteousness.'

'And Uncle Frank.'

'Right. And Uncle Frank.'

Eleven

Driving seventy-five miles per hour on the nearly empty freeway, they reached Oklahoma City just before 10:30. They had stopped en route for jumbo Mountain Dews and now Seth Stevens needed to use the toilet. He asked Terry Kinsman to stop at a gas station. Terry Kinsman said no. He drove instead to a deserted city park and told Seth Stevens to pee in the shadows behind a graffiti-striped baseball dugout.

Terry Kinsman kept looking at his watch. He seemed agitated. He insisted that they kill some time at the park before they went wherever it was they were going. No, they couldn't go to a restaurant for French fries and coffee. No, they couldn't go find an arcade.

They sat in the dugout, watching bats gorge themselves on the clouds of insects that darkened the security lights beyond the outfield fence. The bats were so quick that it was impossible to count them. There could have been a dozen or only a few.

Terry Kinsman still wouldn't say where they were going. Seth Stevens stopped trying to guess.

Finally, a cloud passed over the moon and Terry Kinsman announced that it was time to go. They drove to a quiet downtown block that looked somehow familiar. Then, as Terry Kinsman turned the corner into an alley, Seth Stevens realized why: they had just passed Ira Isaacs's office.

'Terry, what are we going to do?' he asked.

'We're going to let people know that they shouldn't elect a sexual harasser to the U.S. Senate.'

'But don't they know that already? From the TV news?'

Terry Kinsman stopped the car behind a building with barred windows facing the alley. The building's security light was out, making Seth Stevens wonder if Terry Kinsman had been there already.

'It's all "alleged" this and "supposably" that. It could take years before the truth comes out and everybody believes it. And this morning Isaacs went on the politics shows and said he was the victim of a quote-unquote right-wing conspiracy. He practically said it was Christians out to get him.'

Terry Kinsman turned the car off but left the key in the ignition. He switched off the dome light. Seth Stevens followed his lead as he climbed out of the car, eased his door shut, and walked around to the back. Terry Kinsman opened the trunk. Inside were a long prybar, several cans of spray paint, and a duffel bag. In the duffel bag were black boiler suits, black gloves, and black balaclavas.

'Put these on,' said Terry Kinsman.

'But, if he said, aren't we . . . ?'

'Yeah, it'd be a conspiracy theory if it wasn't conspiracy fact. Look, we're just going to make a mess, make it look like people are mad. People *are* mad.'

Seth Stevens put on the boiler suit. His hands were shaking. When he pulled the balaclava over his head he felt even more nervous because he couldn't see or hear very well.

Terry Kinsman was ready before he was. They walked down the alley and across a quiet side street to an unmarked fire door. Slotting the broad edge of the prybar between the door and the frame, Terry Kinsman took a deep breath and pushed forward.

There was a loud groan as the latch guard bent outward. Working the prybar in deeper, Terry Kinsman pushed again. The door crumpled around the lock but still the deadbolt held.

Terry Kinsman rocked back and forth, causing irreparable damage to the door. The door groaned, shrieked, and finally burst open.

Seth Stevens expected a clanging alarm, but the night grew quiet again.

Terry Kinsman pulled a flashlight from his pocket and they went in.

It was just an office suite, much like the one at Citizens but obviously more crowded and more lived in. The back hall was lined with bankers' boxes, the ones on bottom slowly being crushed by the weight of the ones on top. A bulletin board was so papered with drooping memos as to be useless. There was a mountain bike in the break room and dirty sneakers under a desk. The office walls were white and empty as if no one had had time to decorate.

Terry Kinsman handed Seth Stevens a can of spray paint.

'OK,' he said. 'Just mess things up, you know, and write some stuff like, "No sickos in Senate", and "I believe Holly Lee". I'll get the front.'

Terry Kinsman gave him another flashlight and then disappeared down the hall.

He switched on the flashlight and played its beam over the walls. He'd done bad things before, of course, like selling stolen CDs so he could buy meth. It had never occurred to him to become a vandal.

He went into the nearest office. The desk was covered in foot-high stacks of paper. Take-out wrappers and empty go-cups littered the floor. If he trashed the place, he wasn't sure the office's resident would even notice.

A wavering flashlight beam came down the hall. Terry Kinsman was behind it.

'What are you waiting for, Seth? Come on. We got five minutes.'

And then he was gone again.

Seth Stevens raised his spray can to the white wall. He tried to remember what Terry Kinsman had told him to write. The longer the phrase, the smaller the letters would have to be. It was a small office.

Shame on Isaacs, he thought.

He shook the can. The bead inside moved sluggishly at first, then more easily as the paint thinned. When the rattle was high-pitched, he pressed the button on top of the can and started writing.

He was making the *I* when he heard something. He stopped painting and listened. There was a hollow boom as someone bumped a file cabinet. A high-pitched clatter as plastic in-boxes hit the floor. Grunting.

He made his way cautiously into the front. In a large, open room with a reception area and a half-dozen cubicles, Terry Kinsman's flashlight beam swung wildly. He was wrestling with someone. They were both still on their feet, silhouetted against the light from the street.

Who was the other person—a security guard? An office worker? He wondered why whoever it was didn't call for help.

He wondered if, like him, the person was in such disbelief that the fight was happening that they were too embarrassed to call for help lest the whole thing be revealed as imaginary.

Terry Kinsman and the other man were evenly matched. They were both grappling, perhaps, in order to keep the other one from having room to throw a punch. They were stumbling, clumsy in the lack of light.

They smashed into a task chair that skidded and spun. They knocked over a trash can and a brochure spinner.

Seth Stevens didn't move. He didn't know what he would do if he did move.

'John!' said Terry Kinsman. 'Help me, John!'

Who was John? He was John. Terry Kinsman was reminding him not to use his real name. He probably would have.

'OK,' he said, stupidly.

He moved forward. He wasn't a fighter. He guessed he would try to pull the other man off Terry Kinsman so they could both hold the other man down.

The other man looked up and saw him coming. He was older than them but not by much. He had frizzy hair that touched the tops of his shoulders.

Seth Stevens felt sleepy and weak. He didn't think his arms would obey him. But there they were, grabbing the curly-haired man, wrapping around his arms at the elbows, pulling him away from Terry Kinsman.

'Hold him,' said Terry Kinsman. 'Hold him!'

The curly-haired man swung his body around, trying to shrug off Seth Stevens's arms. Seth Stevens could barely hold on.

Terry Kinsman opened desk drawers, shining his flashlight inside them, tossing their contents with his free hand.

'What are you looking for?' panted Seth Stevens.

'Tape. Duct tape or something.'

The curly-haired man lurched hard and Seth Stevens lost his grip and then his footing. The curly-haired man pulled away. By the time Terry Kinsman's flashlight came up, the curly-haired man was striding toward the front door.

'Stop!' shouted Terry Kinsman. 'I have a gun!'

But the curly-haired man didn't stop. He hammered the panic bar with both hands, throwing the door open.

Terry Kinsman followed as far as the doorway. He looked out and shook his head.

'Fuck!'

'What do we do now, Terry?'

The youth minister looked down the street again. Then he closed the door and started yanking open the long venetian blinds that covered the front windows.

'We finish the job.'

Seth Stevens swallowed bile.

'But the police. He's going to get . . .'

'Three minutes. Let's go. Trash the place.'

Terry Kinsman began spray-painting huge letters on the glass.

Numbly, Seth Stevens started emptying drawers and knocking over chairs.

Finally, Terry Kinsman was done. They ran down the back hall. Near the break room, Terry Kinsman took a fire extinguisher off the wall and pulled the pin. He pulled the trigger and the hallway filled instantly with fine white powder. Coughing, they stumbled out the back door and then ran breakneck toward Terry Kinsman's car.

In the passenger seat, Seth Stevens felt suddenly sleepy. He wondered if he was going to pass out. As Terry Kinsman started the car, they heard sirens, already uncomfortably close.

'Don't worry, I memorized the escape route,' said Terry Kinsman.

They drove away on side streets, then through a residential district. They took off their gloves and masks and wriggled out of their boiler suits, then drove into an alley and pushed everything down to the bottom of someone's trash can.

Just when Seth Stevens was completely lost, a freeway on-ramp appeared in front of them.

'Where did that guy come from, Terry?'

'Who knows. He was probably working late and heard us come in. He probably turned off the light hoping we wouldn't see him. I don't know who was more scared, him or us.'

'Me. I was the most scared. I don't want to do this again.'

Terry Kinsman looked at him, surprised.

'You don't?'

'I just, I don't know, Terry, I don't feel comfortable.'

'Well, if we don't do it, who will? You want to let the seculars take everything over? You want this country to go to Hell? To be filled with drunks and druggies and abortionists and illegals and everything?'

He thought of his mother. He thought of himself.

'You don't ask to be chosen, Seth. You may not even want to be chosen. But when God does choose you, you answer the call.'

The car rolled past the outskirts of Oklahoma City. Had he been chosen? And if so, who had chosen him? God? Or Terry Kinsman?

'Besides, I don't believe this scared stuff. I know you like doing the right thing. I just think you're scared to let yourself enjoy it.'

He thought about that, too. He wondered if Terry Kinsman was right.

When he turned on his TV the next morning, the story was already several hours old. He felt afraid. On a sleepy street in the middle of the night in the middle of the country, two men unknown to the world vandalized an office. And then the world knew all about it. It was like throwing a stone over a wall and waking up to learn that he'd hit the President.

Byron Dennis was standing in front of Ira Isaacs's office once again. Behind him, a length of yellow police tape drooped across the front door. People lifted the tape and ducked under it as they went in or out. Behind the plate-glass window stood a small group of policemen, men in suits, and one curly-haired man wearing a T-shirt. It took Seth Stevens a moment to read what Terry Kinsman had spray-painted across the front window. From outside, it looked backward.

'HANDS OFF OUR WOMEN', it read.

'Only a short time has elapsed since allegations of Ira Isaacs's sexual misconduct were made public,' said Byron Dennis. 'And yet, last night, the Senate hopeful's Oklahoma City campaign office was vandalized.'

The show's producer cut to a camera moving slowly through the mess, panning and zooming as if in response to off-camera commands: show this, show that.

'Earlier this morning, we were allowed inside for a brief look. Although nothing was stolen and the official damage estimate is low, you can see that normal operations will be disrupted for some time as the cleanup takes place. Spray-painted on the inside of the front window was the message "Hands off our women". And further inside, in the office manager's office,

were the words "Shame on I"—a message that we assume
was left unfinished.'

The producer cut back to Byron Dennis, live.

'Tim Phillips, a paid intern, was working late when he was
surprised by the vandals. He told me earlier that when he
heard the back door being pried open, he turned off the lights
and crouched under a desk.'

Footage again, this time of the curly-haired man standing
in front of the office. The light looked like dawn. Tim Phillips
had a red bruise under one eye that looked as if it would turn
black.

'I was working late,' he said. 'And I heard this sound like
metal ripping. And I realized someone was probably breaking
in. So I turned off the lights and hid under my desk. But when
I heard the guy come into the room I panicked and stood up.
I just wanted out of there.'

'And then you grappled with the assailant?' asked Byron
Dennis from off-camera.

'Yeah, we kind of wrestled a little bit. And this other guy
came in and pulled me off. We fell over and I got up and ran
out. I think the first guy wanted to tie me up or something.'

'That's quite a bruise you've got there.'

Tim Phillips touched his cheek.

'Yeah, not sure when that happened. It all happened pretty
fast.'

'Do you have any idea who the intruders might have been?'

Tim Phillips grinned.

'People from the Platt campaign? I don't know.'

'OK, that's enough!' said a stern voice off-camera.

Byron Dennis faced the camera, live again.

'Isaacs campaign staff, in a formal statement, said that they
will leave identification of the culprits to the police, and that
they in no way suspect operatives of rival candidate Dean
Platt of this or any other unlawful activity. Reached by cell
phone, Dean Platt's campaign manager expressed his sympathy
for Ira Isaacs. From a troubled Oklahoma City, this is Byron
Dennis reporting.'

Seth Stevens changed channels, keeping one eye on the
clock. He would have to leave for Citizens soon. A local station
was covering a different story that was equally arresting: Jason
Harbo's mother had come to Tulsa to find her missing son.

'Disregarding advice from authorities, family, and even her own church, the mother of a Mormon missionary missing for over a month has come to Tulsa to organize a volunteer effort to find her son. Jeri Lynne spoke with Sandi Harbo yesterday.'

The mother was short and heavy with sand-colored hair and skin that grew flushed as she spoke.

'My son may be dead,' she said. 'I know that, it's a fact. But until I hold him in my arms again, alive or dead, I won't have closure. And I wouldn't be worth the name mother if I didn't do all that was in my power to help bring my son home.'

Seth Stevens sat frozen, the remote poised in mid-air, as he watched the rest of the story. Sandi Harbo called for anyone with knowledge of her son's whereabouts to come forward. She gave a telephone number, an e-mail address, and a URL where citizens could go to share their information. She held up a full-color flyer and said that volunteers planned to hang 5,000 of them in Tulsa and Tulsa County, and along the Interstate throughout the lower Midwest.

'He was doing the Lord's work,' said Sandi Harbo. 'And if the Lord took him from me then I must be at peace with that. But if Satan is to blame, then there will be hell to pay.'

Seth Stevens was late for work.

Over the next two days, the efforts of the Find Jason Task Force were very much in evidence. Telephone poles had one, two, or even three flyers staple-gunned to their trunks. Grocery-store bulletin boards had stacks of flyers hung from loops of wire with hand-printed notes reading *TAKE ONE!* Radio hosts took calls from Sandi Harbo and her volunteers. The *Tulsa World* ran a front-page article. The mayor, the police chief, and, for some reason, the manager of ShopsMart all pledged that Tulsans would help find Jason Harbo.

Seth Stevens couldn't imagine what had happened to the missing Mormon missionary. If Jason Harbo had died after being hit by the truck, an ambulance would have been called. And Sandi Harbo would have waited in Utah while her son's body came home.

Many of the news stories mentioned an interesting detail: missionaries always traveled in pairs. But the night he disappeared, Jason Harbo had told his partner, Dan Lewis, that he didn't feel well. Dan Lewis had kept their next appointment, taking a Book of Mormon to a young couple who had requested a copy, while Jason Harbo supposedly returned to the home of their host family. But Jason Harbo had never come home.

If Terry Kinsman was right, if the shame of belonging to a cult had caused Jason Harbo to run away, then maybe he had gone to Perkins alone to mull things over. But why hadn't he at least called his mother to tell her he was all right? As angry as he had been at his own mother, even Seth Stevens had called her to tell her he had wound up in Tulsa, Oklahoma.

It seemed strange, but now that he was working at Citizens for Good Government, he wasn't studying his Bible anymore. At ShopsMart, working for an antagonistic supervisor, the scriptures had seemed like a rock to cling to. Now that he was surrounded by godly people, he felt as if their goodness would simply rub off on him. But Pastor Grady had always preached that the more a man knew, the more he needed to learn. A little bit of knowledge, he sometimes said, was more dangerous than none at all.

Seth Stevens vowed to have his Bible with him at all times. It was a tattered, second-hand copy he'd gotten from Margo Hofstatter. She'd dog-eared dozens of pages, highlighting the verses that moved her in neon pink and occasionally scrawling notes in the margins that he struggled to decipher. But his name was in it, too. She'd written it under her own inside the front cover.

Now he put it in his backpack every morning. He read during the slow times at Citizens and for half an hour in the afternoon. And sometimes he and Charisma Brown read chapters to each other, too, when they weren't kissing and trying desperately not to do more.

He was reading the second Book of Samuel and trying to keep straight the details of King David's reign. But if he felt lost, the simple act of opening the Bible gave him some peace. He needed that. More and more, he began to feel that it was only a matter of time before his door came off the hinges with a police battering ram behind it.

By Wednesday night, everyone in the band knew about the Find Jason Task Force. They talked things over in the rehearsal room before the service while their fingers went mechanically through the motions of tuning guitars and tightening drum heads.

'So what happened, exactly?' demanded Kirk Swindoll.

'We told you before,' said Seth Stevens.

'Tell me again.'

He resisted the urge to say, *Who are you, the cops?* Instead he said: 'Terry got into it with this missionary kid—the one on TV. He was ragging on him, calling Mormons a cult. Then, when we were getting into our cars, the kid came out to unlock his bike. They got into it again and Terry punched him. The kid got up and got on his bike. Then when he was turning out of the parking lot, he got clipped by this truck.'

'Not run over?'

'Well, it hit his tire but it didn't run over him. He landed on the side of the road.'

'And he was wearing a helmet?'

'Yeah. I think.'

Suddenly it was hard to remember whether Jason Harbo had gotten his helmet on or not. If he had gotten it on, had he taken the time to snap the chin straps?

'So it's not our fault. I mean, Terry's fault.'

'Not really, no. Of course not.'

'So we should have told them what we know a long time ago.'

'They might say it was Terry's fault because the guy was trying to get away from him,' said Ben Badgeley.

'But fault for what?' said Kirk Swindoll. 'Nobody even knows what happened. The guy disappeared. Maybe he got brain damaged and wandered off into the wilderness. Maybe someone's taking care of him somewhere.'

'We should turn Terry in to the police,' said Jimmy Gilstrap. 'It's our Christian duty to tell the truth and to cooperate with the government except where it conflicts with our beliefs.'

'What are you, a brochure?' said Kirk Swindoll. 'Maybe we shouldn't do anything. If Terry didn't do anything, it could still wreck the band because you guys were there. And it could wreck the church.'

'What wrecks the church is not following your conscience and doing what you know is right,' said Jimmy Gilstrap.

'You guys weren't even there,' said Ben Badgeley. 'I don't think you should decide. Seth, what do you think?'

He was still trying to decide what he thought when the door opened and Terry Kinsman walked in.

'What?' he asked. 'What?'

'The Mormon,' said Owen Rusk.

Terry Kinsman closed the door behind him. He sat down wearily in a plastic chair.

'This is a test,' he said. 'Repeat: only a test.'

'What do we tell his mother?' asked Jimmy Gilstrap.

'We don't tell her nothing. She wants to know where her son is, and we don't know where he is. Circumstantial, this looks pretty messed up. I got in a fight with a guy and now he's missing. But that's all it is: a coincidence, and a pretty messed-up one. Day after it happened, I called the hospitals, I even called the police. They didn't know nothing. Now, we could go to the police and tell them what happened at Perkins. And me, and Seth and Owen, and Salvation, and the Free Church of God's Slaves are going to get tarred with it.'

'That's what I said,' said Kirk Swindoll.

'Or we can keep quiet and keep good Christians from getting unfairly smeared yet again. Whatever happened to that Mormon, we can't change it. So we need to stand our ground and let whatever happens work itself out.'

Terry Kinsman stood up.

'Anyone got a problem with that?'

He looked around the group, meeting the gaze of each of them in turn.

'I don't have a problem with it,' said Kirk Swindoll. 'I think you're right.'

Jimmy Gilstrap, outnumbered, looked away.

They played poorly that night. The congregation didn't seem to notice, applauding with almost as much fervor as they usually did. But the band didn't look at each other. Owen Rusk played behind the beat, Seth Stevens flubbed a bridge, and Kirk Swindoll forgot the second verse of a song and sang the first one twice. All that, thought Seth Stevens, and Terry Kinsman wasn't even on the stage.

After they were done, while Pastor Grady was still offering the closing prayer, Seth Stevens hurried to the rehearsal room. He put his guitar away and collected his backpack, wanting to be gone before the band returned.

He went outside, circled around to the front of the building, and went in through the main entrance. The service ended and the crowd began slowly filing out. He scanned faces, looking for Charisma Brown. More than anything, he wanted to be with her.

'Seth!'

He turned. Cam McLarin stood at arm's length, grinning, smelling of beer.

'Cam,' he said. 'What are you—did you . . .?'

'Did I need the word of the Lord? Nah. We just came to catch the show.'

Suddenly, David Trujillo and Vickie Lawson were there, too. David Trujillo grinned and punched him on the shoulder.

'Christian *rawk!*' he screeched. 'I had no idea, Seth, no idea at all.'

'Hi, Seth,' said Vickie Lawson.

'You muffed that bridge, though,' said David Trujillo.

'I liked the one about Jesus,' said Cam McLarin. 'Oh, wait, they were all about Jesus.'

Parishioners were parting around them like a stream around a rock. He was sure they could hear every word. He felt like a rock. He stood there, struck dumb.

'David and Cam,' said Vickie Lawson, 'maybe you should lighten up a little.'

'Is this why you won't come back to the band?' said David Trujillo. 'The kids and the old ladies? Dude, you were getting *pussy.*'

Several men slowed, taking in the scene.

'I think you should go,' said Seth Stevens.

'What, do churches have bouncers these days?'

'We're called deacons,' said one of the men.

David Trujillo and Cam McLarin looked up. They were surrounded by a half-dozen angry-looking men. The members of Crucifer weren't wearing their stage clothes, but even in black jeans, black T-shirts, and black leather boots, they looked like a motorcycle gang that had crashed a christening. A very small motorcycle gang.

He thought that the members of Crucifer had thought it would be funny to go to church. Just like punks, metalheads often made their own entertainment simply by showing up in places where their presence was incongruous. The annoyed looks they provoked were payback for the many times they had felt outnumbered and persecuted themselves. But their expressions suggested that they had miscalculated.

'I think you guys should go,' said Seth Stevens again.

'Great idea,' said Vickie Lawson.

Cam McLarin looked ready to go along with whoever made the decision. But David Trujillo stood his ground.

'Are you guys threatening us?' he said. 'That doesn't sound very Christian to me.'

'You're in our church,' said the deacon. 'You better respect us in our church. We don't come to your wherever and mess with you.'

'Oh yeah?' said David Trujillo. 'This guy—' he pointed at Seth Stevens— 'came to our show. And then he partied with us afterward. We sing the praises of Satan, and he was bringing us down, man.'

Several people gasped at the use of the word 'Satan'. Mothers hurried their children out the door. But everyone else was slowing or had stopped. And still more people came through the doors behind them. The vestibule was packed.

Seth Stevens flushed. He saw Charisma Brown peering through the crowd, looking confused.

'Don't speak that word in here,' said the deacon.

'Satan! Satan! Satan!' shouted David Trujillo, a wild look in his eyes. 'You all gonna melt now?'

Vickie Lawson was pushing toward the door. The crowd parted easily. With her platform boots and with her teased blue-black hair, she towered above them.

'Damn you to Hell!' said someone.

The deacon and the other men rushed forward, reaching for David Trujillo and Cam McLarin. A woman screamed. As the crowd surged backward, pushing through the nearest available doors, Seth Stevens found himself standing in open space, between the scrum and the onlookers.

It was a short fight. David Trujillo and Cam McLarin threw a few punches, but, getting worse than they gave, seemed almost content to be dragged out the door and down the church steps.

Picking themselves up, they retreated to the parking lot, glaring and straightening their clothes. Behind them, Vickie Lawson's car came slowly toward them through the dispersing crowd.

'I told you we shouldn't have tried to rescue him from the cult,' said Cam McLarin to David Trujillo. 'We should have got a professional.'

Several of God's Slaves were praying, their eyes closed and their hands out as if to ward off the members of Crucifer. Seth Stevens felt Charisma Brown's hand on his shoulder and grasped it gratefully.

'Who are those people?' she asked as David Trujillo and Cam McLarin got into Vickie Lawson's car.

'My old friends,' he said. 'You know, the Satanists.'

Twelve

The sky had been flat gray all day. The air had smelled of rain but not a drop had fallen. Now that it was night, the lowering clouds blotted out the moon and stars. As he rode away from church in Charisma Brown's car, water speckled the windshield. Within a few minutes the rain was coming down in buckets and the frantically working windshield wipers were unable to keep up.

They pulled over to the side of the road and waited. The rain was cool and the windows fogged over. Charisma Brown turned the air conditioner on full blast. Only when they were shivering could they finally see enough to drive again.

'I want to go to your apartment,' she said.

'Do you think that's a good idea?' he asked.

'Probably not. But I just want to be alone with you and I don't want to sit in this car in the rain.'

She drove to his building and parked below his apartment. As they walked up the stairwell they heard laughter and smelled smoke. His neighbors were sitting on the breezeway, watching the water swirl and pool in the parking lot.

'Hey, Reverend,' said the man. 'Coming in for a little Bible study?'

'Hey,' he said stupidly.

When they were inside and he had locked the door, Charisma Brown pointed through the wall at his neighbors.

'Those are your neighbors?'

'Uh-huh.'

'Are they always so disrespectful?'

'That's them being polite,' he told her.

She shook her head, amazed at how people could be.

He wished he had known she was coming over. He would have washed his dirty plastic cups or at least picked his clothes up off the floor. But after the scene at the church, it didn't bother him as much as it would normally have. He doubted she was still titillated by his dark past after seeing his friends get thrown out of church.

He offered her a chair and got her a soda. She sat down, her eyes roving the room as he quickly tidied up. He noticed almost after the fact that his answering-machine light was blinking. He was sure it was his mother even though she hadn't called since their fight.

'Things sure have been weird lately,' she said.

He agreed, thinking that she meant their relationship and the incident at church. But then she surprised him.

'First all this stuff with Ira Isaacs. And now this missing Mormon guy.'

He turned his back and ran some water in the sink to hide his shaking hands.

'What's weird about those things? Stuff like that happens all the time.'

'Well, maybe politicians grab their secretaries' butts all the time, Seth, but people in Tulsa don't go missing *all the time*. Don't be jaded. But what I was going to say is, what's weird is my dad. When the Isaacs thing happened, he laughed. That's not godly, to laugh at sinners or the sinned-against. And then when they did one of those stories about the Mormon guy's mom, he said that maybe they should have both stayed at home in Utah.'

'Your dad isn't always like that?'

'I don't think so. Or maybe I just don't know. It's just— can you stop washing the dishes for a second?'

He shut off the tap and turned around.

'Sorry.'

'And sit over here. This is important.'

He went over and sat across from her on a corner of the bed. She was looking directly into his eyes. It was hard to meet her gaze.

'I hope you don't take this wrong, like I think you're some kind of freak or something, but—'

'No offense taken,' he said.

She laughed.

'I'm not good at saying important stuff. It's just that, since I met you, since I got to know you, it's got me thinking about things. I mean, you're the kind of person—or the kind of person you were, anyway—that I was always afraid of. My friends, we'd always laugh about guys like you in high school because it was easier to call you losers than to admit we were afraid of you. But now that I know you, it's just got me thinking about how many people there must be that seem so different but that are really good inside.'

'I wasn't saved then.'

'Right, but now you are. What chance did you have then? I just think we should all remember that people aren't neces- sarily what we're looking at. Maybe we should look at them and think about what they can be.'

'So we shouldn't laugh at Democrats or Mormons, no matter what they do?'

'Well, they decide to do what they do, of course. But maybe some day they'll do better.'

When he lived in New York, Seth Stevens had gotten to know a few college girls. Like his mother, they were from comfortable homes but wanted to spend time in the rougher parts of the city. Some of them made friends with the gutter- punks, sharing food, money, and even space in their dorm rooms. They always found cause to regret it—usually after their CD collections were stolen—but he had heard many of them talk in a similar way.

'It sounds like you're getting ready to go away to college,' he said.

'I think I'm ready,' she said. 'I have more questions now than I ever did.'

He put on some music. Complaining that her chair was uncomfortable, she joined him on the bed. Soon they were lying close together. Recent events slipped away and they joked and laughed, talking happily about inconsequential things. In a little while they were kissing.

When they had been alone in other places, like the water tower or her car, it had been easier to stop at kissing. Lying in his bed, he could think of nothing except taking her clothes off and fucking until they were sweaty. His erection was so hard it hurt. He angled his hips away from her so she wouldn't feel it against her thighs. He wanted to sin. He wanted to be good. After being rescued by Margo Hofstatter, Charisma Brown was the best thing that had ever happened to him. He wanted her desperately. But he was filled with the fear that, if they sinned together, their love would be ruined. Wasn't she thinking the same thing? Why didn't she save them both and stop?

She was kissing him more passionately than she ever had. She was holding his face in her hands and moaning softly.

He started to think that everything was up to him. That if he only kissed her, they would only kiss. That if he took her clothes off, she would willingly do more. It was a responsibility he didn't want. He needed her to set the boundaries. But, as when he was in high school, he wanted the freedom to try. He would honor her denials.

Then she took his hand and placed it on her breast.

'Are you sure?' he said.

'Yes,' she said, closing her eyes.

He touched her gently. She tensed, then relaxed. She seemed to be going farther away from him, surrendering her body while her mind retreated.

They kissed harder. Her hands stroked his chest, his back, his hips. He grew bolder, brushing her nipples with his thumbs. Even through the fabric of her shirt and bra, he could feel them respond.

Almost without thinking he put his hand between her legs. She squeezed her thighs together, bringing his hand closer to her. She sighed deeply, almost groaning.

She took his hand and began to guide it under the waistband of her pants.

'Wait,' he said.

She froze. Her eyes opened wide.

'Oh, Jesus,' she said. 'What am I doing?'

He wasn't sure why he'd stopped her when he wanted to keep going. Maybe he was afraid that she was doing something she didn't really want to do. He hoped that he was good enough for that to be his reason.

Burying her face in his shoulder, she started to cry.

'Oh, Seth,' she said. 'I just don't know what I want. I mean, I know what I want. And I think it's wrong. But what if it isn't?'

He held her tightly. He felt like crying, too.

After she left, he took the longest cold shower of his life. It took him an hour to fall asleep. Even then, he did so only with the simultaneous distractions of TV and music.

In the morning he took the second-longest cold shower of his life and then walked to work.

He wondered if he was having what Pastor Grady called a 'crisis of faith'. Then he remembered a sermon in which Pastor Grady had preached that sometimes people questioned their belief in God because they were in fact questioning their belief that they were able to do what God wanted.

God, he thought ruefully, must want Seth Stevens and Charisma Brown to get married soon.

Though they hadn't talked of marriage since the first time, it seemed to be only a sentence away from most things they said. He couldn't imagine anything better than marrying her. He also couldn't imagine anything more unlikely. Bill Brown would serve Seth Stevens up as the main dish at his next barbecue—his grill was certainly big enough to handle the job. Seth Stevens had to get a car and a full-time job before anyone would take him seriously. A husband couldn't ride in his wife's passenger seat or wait in her dorm room while she went to class.

He spent the morning in a daze. When Doug Earle said he could go home, he left immediately.

Stopping at a fast-food restaurant for lunch, he ordered a double cheeseburger with bacon, fries, and a jumbo Mountain Dew. He read his Bible while he ate, 2 Samuel 14, nearly cursing when he got some ketchup on one of the pages.

> 14 For we must needs die, and [*are*] as water spilt on
> the ground, which cannot be gathered up again; neither
> doth God respect [*any*] person

He went home and tried to write a song about Charisma Brown. The lyrics were so bad that he recognized their badness even despite his love for her. He pulled the page out of his spiral notebook and tore it up. Then he tried again. By dinnertime he had aborted seventeen songs.

He walked to the 18-Hour Mart and bought a frozen mini-pizza and a bag of cheese curls for dinner. When he came back, there was a police cruiser parked across the street from his building. There were two policemen sitting in the front seat. His first instinct was to run.

Running makes you look guilty, he thought.

I am guilty, he thought.

Tightening his jaw, he walked into the parking lot. He didn't turn to see if the policemen were watching him.

They're probably just taking a break, he told himself. And even if they were waiting for someone in the building, probably half the tenants could have been arrested for something. Seth Stevens knew what drug-dealing looked like and there was drug-dealing going on in at least two units.

Even though he made it inside without hearing an order to freeze, he was still too nervous to eat. When the timer went off, he turned off the toaster oven without taking the pizza out. He tried peering through a crack in the curtains to see if there cruiser was still there, but the angle was wrong.

He watched TV.

When the phone rang, he jumped.

'Don't you check your messages?' said Terry Kinsman.

The light on his answering machine was still blinking. He hadn't noticed it since coming home the night before.

'What is it, Terry?'

'I need to talk to you. Do you remember what I said about being invisible?'

He didn't.

Terry Kinsman sounded annoyed.

'Do you remember where I parked that one time, when we went to do the thing?'

The sentence made him want to laugh, but he did remember. Terry Kinsman was talking about the night they went to Oklahoma City. He had unscrewed the light bulb in the stairwell and sat in the dark. His car had been parked in the alley behind the building.

'I do now.'

'Good. See you.'

The line went dead.

Why was Terry Kinsman being so vague? He was afraid the phone was tapped, but this set a new standard for paranoia.

Seth Stevens used the toilet. He washed his face. Suddenly hungry, he folded the cold mini-pizza in half and wrapped it in a paper towel. After turning his light off, he cracked the door and looked out.

The police cruiser was still there.

If Terry Kinsman was concerned about the police, he wouldn't have mentioned it in case they were listening. And the police were clearly watching the building. Maybe they were watching Seth Stevens, maybe they were watching someone else. But they certainly had reason to watch him. So he had to assume that that was what they were doing.

Crouching down, he opened the door wider and squeezed through. The width of the breezeway would keep him from being seen from below as long as he stayed low and hugged the wall. He pulled the door closed, not bothering to lock it, and crawled, using his elbows to pull himself forward. If his neighbors came out there was going to be an awkward conversation. He thought that he should let go of the pizza but, now that he had gone through the trouble of bringing it, he really wanted to eat it.

He reached the stairwell. Even with the light bulb burning, he couldn't be seen from the street because the stairwell was enclosed. At the bottom, he went through a short passageway that led on to the alley.

Terry Kinsman's car was not by the dumpsters. But as he stood peering into the gloom he saw parking lights blink on and off far down the alley.

He walked to the end of the block, crossed the street, and went into the next alley. Terry Kinsman's car was parked in front of someone's garage.

Seth Stevens opened the passenger door and got in.

'Took you long enough,' said Terry Kinsman. 'What is that, pizza?'

'You can't have any. This is my dinner.'

'Didn't want any. Some soldier you are.'

Terry Kinsman started the car.

Seth Stevens took a bite of the cold pizza. The crust was like cardboard. The pepperoni slices were like rubber. He kept eating anyway, not wanting to hear what Terry Kinsman would say if he threw it out the window.

'Is this about the cop car?' he asked.

'We're gonna have to meet like this from now on. Just to be sure. I got no idea why that cop car's sitting there, but we're gonna have to assume it's you.'

'What do we do?'

'Act normal. Sneak out the back. If they ask us anything, we don't tell them nothing.'

'You had me sneak out to see you just to tell me I have to sneak out to see you?'

Terry Kinsman smacked the steering wheel with the flat of his hand.

'Seth! Quit kidding around!'

Keeping his lights off, Terry Kinsman drove to the end of the next block. He turned left, away from Seth Stevens's building and the waiting police car. He drove a half-block and then finally turned on the headlights, swerving to avoid a startled possum. He laughed.

'That little guy must of thought the headlights was a chariot of angels, coming to take him away. Now he's got to eat garbage another night.'

'OK, so what's going on?' asked Seth Stevens.

'We got our marching orders.'

'What, they want us to go to Oklahoma City again?'

'I can't tell you where we're going. Not until we're on the road. We leave Monday night at midnight.'

The spy fantasy seemed exaggerated even for Terry Kinsman.

'Can you just talk normally, please?' said Seth Stevens. 'I mean, OK: we're doing some secret, illegal stuff. I feel weird about it, but it's not like I have any better ideas so I'm taking everyone's word that it's what we should be doing. But can we please not pretend that we're some kind of James Bond guys? We steal yard signs and spray-paint stuff, for crying out loud.'

He expected Terry Kinsman to be angry with him. But the youth minister only smiled. He kept driving, making a seemingly random series of lefts and rights on quiet, residential streets. A bicyclist appeared ahead, invisible except for the loops made by the orange reflectors on his pedals.

'I know you don't want to realize this is big as it is,' said Terry Kinsman. 'I don't blame you. It's kind of hard to take it all in, sometimes. But this is big as it gets. We're bringing the country back to the Lord and we're making the national news.'

'So what, this time we're going to burn down Ira Isaacs's house?'

'Uncle Frank says there's been a change of strategy. He says the Isaacs stuff is important, but it won't make a big enough difference.'

Seth Stevens tried to imagine what else they could be asked to do. He couldn't think of anything.

'This is gonna be a remote operation,' said Terry Kinsman. 'We're supposed to pack camping gear: backpacks, sleeping bags, canteens, flashlights, stuff like that.'

'What are we going to do? Have a sleep-over paintball party?'

'No, it won't be paintball. You should try not to be so sarcastic, Seth.'

'But I don't have any of that stuff, Terry.'

'You don't have a sleeping bag, even?'

'No.'

'Well, I got a lot of that stuff from when me and my dad used to go hunting. Might smell a little funny but there's nothing wrong with it. Whatever you do, don't go and buy new stuff. They track your receipts, it's circumstantial evidence.'

'I wasn't planning on it.'

He realized with some surprise that they were only a few blocks away from his building. They had come in a wide, irregular circle and were nearly back where they had started. Terry Kinsman dropped him off a couple of blocks away and made him promise to walk in through the back alley. They would meet in the same place at midnight on Monday night.

As Seth Stevens started to get out of the car, Terry Kinsman slapped his own chest and said, in the manner of a Marine saying '*Semper Fi*': 'Army of God!' He held out his fist.

Seth Stevens bumped fists.

'Army of God,' he said quietly.

His thoughts the next day were a hopeless muddle. He wanted to tell Charisma Brown about his secret life but had no idea how to start. More than that, he feared her judgment. If he lost her, he wasn't sure if even Jesus' love could keep him going.

He didn't have a chance to talk to her anyway. She was busy, first with work and then with family obligations. Seth Stevens wondered what it was like to have parents who regularly counted on her presence.

After work, he went to Taco Bell. He read his Bible over a deep-fried taco combo. He wondered why believing in God sometimes felt so much like work. When he was getting clean, he had thought that being born again would mean being bathed in a holy light for the rest of his days, that the world would look, feel, sound, and taste different. And it had seemed that way for a while. But that might also have been the euphoria of getting clean.

He desperately wanted God to talk to him. If he couldn't hear His voice, he at least wanted his path to be made clear. Wasn't that what God was for? To be a rock in troubled seas? Or was a life of faith a series of tests for which he would never know the correct answers?

Everyone talked about how it was possible to worship God anywhere. At home, at work, even in a fast-food restaurant. But maybe it was harder to hear God in some places.

He took a bus to church.

The door was open. He knew it would be. Pastor Grady spoke often of his 'literal open-door policy'.

'Other churches,' he would say, 'have visiting hours. You know who else has visiting hours? Hospitals and prisons. I like to think that the Free Church of God's Slaves is a more welcoming place than a hospital or a prison.'

Pastor Grady would preach about the concept of sanctuary, how churches had once been places where the faithful could pray whether in the darkest night of the soul or simply late at night. That was before churches became afraid of thieves and vandals, crackheads and tweakers.

Anyway, the door was open. Seth Stevens went through the vestibule into the sanctuary. It was empty and silent. From rehearsals, he was used to being in the church when there weren't many other people there. But then he was only in the annex, a two-story building with offices and function rooms. He had never come into the sanctuary.

Daylight warmed the tall, cross-shaped stained-glass window that rose up behind the stage. He walked up the center aisle and sat in the front row. He thought that maybe he should kneel as they did in Catholic churches in the movies. But there was no kneeler. The theater-style seats did recline, however, so he lay back and stared at the lofty, vaulted ceiling. The air conditioning was turned off and dust motes moved so slowly they seemed suspended.

It was utterly silent. No joyful noise was being made. No

honking cars, no roaring jets intruded. Even if God's voice was a whisper he would still hear it.

But maybe God was waiting for a question.

Seth Stevens had too many.

He thought he might have dozed off but he wasn't sure. Rousing himself, he went to a water fountain in the backstage area and drank deeply, wetting his hands and rubbing them over his face and neck.

He was tempted to talk to Pastor Grady. He wasn't sure how much Pastor Grady knew, so he wasn't sure how much he could ask. But he wanted to be told that everything would be all right. And he was pretty sure that Pastor Grady would tell him that, no matter how vaguely he expressed his troubles.

He walked back to the vestibule and then tried the door to the church office. It was an open door, of course.

Inside, he saw Jackie Mory, the church secretary, walking toward the far end of the hall. She was holding an empty coffee carafe. She turned off the hallway and disappeared.

He wasn't sure whether he should wait for Jackie Mory to come back or whether to simply knock on Pastor Grady's door. Would he be turned away because he didn't have an appointment? Tentatively, he started down the hall. If he didn't see Jackie Mory by the time he reached the door then he would go ahead and knock.

He could hear water running. Jackie Mory was rinsing out the carafe. There was a light in a doorway on the right-hand side of the hall.

Pastor Grady's door started to open. Seth Stevens got ready to announce himself.

The words died on his lips.

The man backing out of the door was not Pastor Grady.

It was Uncle Frank.

Seth Stevens stepped quickly through the lighted doorway and found himself in a small kitchenette.

Jackie Mory was filling the carafe with water. She looked surprised to see him.

'Is it . . . Steven?'

'Seth Stevens,' he said.

He craned his ears. He could hear Pastor Grady and Uncle Frank talking, but he couldn't tell what they were saying.

'Can I help you with something, Seth?' said Jackie Mory.

The silence while he struggled to answer might have lasted only five seconds. It seemed to last five minutes.

'Is there a lost and found?' he asked.

She smiled.

'Yes, of course. It's in the reception area.'

She walked past him and back up the hall. He followed her.

'What did you lose?' she asked.

He glanced over his shoulder. Uncle Frank was gone. Pastor Grady's door was swinging shut.

Jackie Mory walked quickly, even in high heels.

'Um,' he said.

'What was that?' she asked without looking back.

'A guitar tuner.'

They had arrived in the reception area. She set the carafe on her desk. Shaking her head, she opened a cabinet door and tugged out a large cardboard box. It seemed to be full of winter hats and puffy, insulated gloves.

'Don't think we've seen one of those,' she said. 'But you should look. I suppose it could have come in when I was out.'

He pretended to look through the box while she finished making the coffee. Then he thanked her and left.

Now he had another unanswered question.

Terry Kinsman didn't come to rehearsal that night. His absence defused some of the lingering tension. But as they got ready to play, Jimmy Gilstrap kept his eyes on his keyboard and spoke only when spoken to.

The mood was workmanlike. They warmed up by playing their three most popular songs, songs Seth Stevens was so familiar with that he could have formed the chord changes in his sleep. Then they worked on a new song, 'Moving the Mountain'. Jimmy Gilstrap had written the music and as he played it they listened, occasionally adding a riff, a beat, or a run of notes as they tried out ideas for their parts.

Then they broke the song down into its components: verse, chorus, bridge, solo, intro, outro. As the instrumentalists roughed out an arrangement of the verse, Kirk Swindoll half-sang, half-mumbled over the top.

Before long, Jimmy Gilstrap complained that the mumbling

was distracting him. Kirk Swindoll defended himself, saying that he couldn't be expected to make up the lyrics on the spot.

Besides, he said, wasn't 'Moving the Mountain' some kind of Muslim reference? Didn't the false prophet Muhammad say, 'Bring the mountain to me?'

After they had argued for a while, Ben Badgeley suggested that everyone take a break. Jimmy Gilstrap said he didn't need a break. He stayed at his keyboard, grumbling, while the rest of them went down the hall to use the vending machines.

When they came back, Ben Badgeley suggested that they wait until next week to work on the new song. In the meantime, Kirk Swindoll could develop his ideas for the lyrics.

'Fine,' snapped Jimmy Gilstrap.

They drew up a short set list—just seven songs—and played them in order. To an outsider, the band would have sounded fine. But Seth Stevens missed the uplifted feeling that the music had given him so recently. Before the last song, 'I Want to Know You', he cleared his throat.

'Guys, can we play this one like we're filled with the Spirit? Maybe if we pretend, it will really happen.'

Embarrassed, the rest of the band nodded. Owen Rusk clicked off the tempo and they started playing. Slowly, the music began to gel. Seth Stevens closed his eyes, trusting his fingers to find the way. Kirk Swindoll's voice changed subtly and instead of just hitting the notes, he sang at concert pitch. The rest of the band responded, locking into the beat, adding the little touches and flourishes that they so often did on Sundays.

When he opened his eyes he saw that he wasn't the only one smiling. Relief coursed through his body. Just this, a song of praise, has so much power, he thought.

When they were done they high-fived and amened. Then they played it again.

That weekend he found it hard to concentrate. He kept thinking about Terry Kinsman and their secret mission, about Pastor Grady and Uncle Frank. He knew he didn't have enough information to understand what was happening but that didn't stop him from trying. More than once, Charisma Brown asked him where he was. He was sitting beside her but that was no answer.

On Monday afternoon he was alone. He played guitar, read his Bible, and packed a change of clothes in his backpack. He felt he should prepare himself for something but he didn't know how. He ate dinner. He looked at the clock. Midnight seemed an eternity away. He didn't want to wait in his room.

He had a strange idea. He laced his shoes and went outside. The falling sun glinted orange on the knob as he pulled his door shut. He went downstairs and started walking.

He walked for forty-five minutes. Some of the drivers turned on their headlights. Finally, the Perkins sign appeared ahead.

He cut across the parking lot to the front door and went inside. The air conditioner was set to Arctic. Violins played Simon and Garfunkel's 'Bridge over Troubled Water'. An arcade game waited for children, its mechanical claw splayed over a colorful necropolis of small furry animals.

On the bulletin board, a stack of Find Jason Task Force flyers hung from a loop of wire.

A waitress seated him in a booth. Like the night that Jason Harbo had gone missing, the restaurant was practically empty. It would get busy later, after the bars let out. He remembered that from the old part of his life.

He ordered coffee and an ice cream sundae. He wasn't sure why he'd come. It wasn't as if the Mormon would be sitting in the booth where Seth Stevens had first seen him, drinking decaf and eating a piece of pie. He couldn't imagine what had really happened. But maybe the answer was in front of him. Maybe he had resisted searching for the truth.

His order came. He took a sip of coffee, then a bite of ice cream, and kept going that way. Hot and cold, sour and sweet.

The police had surely talked to the restaurant staff. Unless no one remembered the Mormon missionary who had eaten there alone. Unless no one saw the fight in the parking lot. Or maybe they had and that was why the police were waiting outside Seth Stevens's building. But then what were the police waiting for?

He finished eating. He took the check up front and paid the cashier. He went outside.

It was dusk. The western sky was blood red and streaked with clouds. The hot, humid air reminded him of the locker room at the public swimming pool. Sweat dampened his skin.

After staring at the empty bike rack, he walked slowly

through the parking lot, retracing his steps. At the lighted arrow that steered drivers into the parking lot, he paused, looking off in the direction that Jason Harbo had ridden.

As on that night, traffic was sparse. During the day the road groaned with traffic. There were trucking yards one way, the airport the other, and the Interstate between them.

He walked along the road at the very edge of the shoulder. He wished he would have waited to see what happened after Jason Harbo got hit by the truck. If he had picked up his bike, had he ridden away confused? Or had he intentionally pointed his bike at a new horizon?

The truck's driver either hadn't seen him or hadn't stopped. But if he had been killed, someone would have found his body beside the road. And Sandi Harbo would never have come to town.

Seth Stevens stopped.

On a power line, a crow bounced and cawed. Then it dropped down into the tall weeds and disappeared. A moment later, it flapped out of the weeds and alighted on the power line again. Between the Perkins and the next developed lot, a yard full of semis, was a huge lot, maybe 300 yards wide, with a big sign facing the road: *12 ACRES, ZONED COMMERCIAL, WILL SUBDIVIDE*. The lot itself was grassy and weedy, pocked with pools of stagnant water.

The crow dropped off the power line again. It reappeared another moment later, a worm in its mouth. Bobbing its head, it worked the worm down its gullet and cawed loudly.

He walked off the shoulder, pushing through the thigh-high weeds toward where the crow was feeding. He was barely a few yards in when he smelled it, a stench like fresh feces and rotting meat.

He gagged but kept going.

The crow dived again. He got a visual fix on the point where it landed and pressed forward. The smell grew worse. First he cupped his hand over his mouth. Then he lifted his T-shirt and slipped the elastic neckband on to the bridge of his nose. The T-shirt hung like a mask. It didn't diminish the smell much but the idea of it helped.

There was trash in the weeds: beer cans, pop cans, fast-food wrappers. His feet were lost in shadows.

He came to a small, weed-choked ditch. The water in the

bottom looked like burnt engine oil. He was practically on top of where the crow was feeding but he couldn't see anything.

Then he saw it.

A hand.

Black, bloated, missing some of its flesh. Sticking out from under a weathered-gray sheet of plywood.

He started to pray. Aloud. He didn't recognize the tongue he was speaking in.

As if in a trance, he lifted the plywood.

A cloud of insects boiled out. He dropped the plywood. The light was failing. But in one glimpse he'd seen what he needed to see.

A blackened, swollen corpse. Wearing a white, short-sleeved shirt. With a nametag still pinned to the pocket.

Thirteen

At midnight he was waiting in the alley. The police car was still parked on the street out front. Terry Kinsman's car turned in to the alley and crept toward him with only its parking lights on. The yellow-orange lights flickered past trash cans, cinder-blocks, dumpsters, and a dirty white picket fence. Terry Kinsman slowed just long enough for Seth Stevens to get in and then rolled forward again. The tires popped gravel.

The dome light hadn't come on when he opened the door. But the illuminated dials of the dashboard lit Terry Kinsman's face like a ghost. He was wearing a tight camouflage T-shirt, its sleeves tight on his pale biceps.

Seth Stevens looked into the back seat.

'Where's the camping stuff?'

'The trunk, duh. We get stopped for speeding, I don't want some cop to ask if we're going camping.'

Instead of heading toward the Interstate, Terry Kinsman drove to church and parked right in front. Seth Stevens followed him up the steps, through the front doors, and into the sanctuary. It was almost pitch black. Red exit signs burned over the doors.

Terry Kinsman walked to the front. He climbed on to the stage and knelt down below the enormous, soaring cross. The stained glass window glowed dimly from the security lights in the parking lot.

'Kneel, Seth,' said Terry Kinsman.

He knelt, then again followed suit as Terry Kinsman steepled his hands and closed his eyes.

'Jesus,' said Terry Kinsman, 'show us, your warriors, the path of righteousness. Help make us strong against our enemies. And give us Your heavenly light to guide us. Let the godless fear the godly. And let us make America a holy land once more. One nation, under God, amen. We pray in your name.'

The hairs on Seth Stevens's arms prickled. He half expected to hear an answering voice.

Terry Kinsman stood up, his eyes still closed, and reached out toward the cross.

'JESUS!' his voice boomed out. 'Show us, your warriors, the path of righteousness!'

He repeated the rest of the prayer.

Seth Stevens was starting to feel uncomfortable. He wondered if he should leave so Terry Kinsman could have a private moment with God. Then Terry Kinsman grabbed his hand, raising it toward the cross.

He repeated the prayer a third time, his voice growing hoarse. Then he spoke in tongues. Seth Stevens could only listen dumbly.

Terry Kinsman was overcome with Spirit. He babbled, half-singing and half-crying, until his voice rasped and his lips were flecked with spittle. He let go of Seth Stevens's hand and fell to his knees. Then he threw himself to the floor and lay prostrate before the cross. After a while he stopped moving. Then he fell silent.

Seth Stevens thought that he shouldn't touch Terry Kinsman. Maybe he was afraid of interrupting the strange communion. Or maybe he was afraid that Terry Kinsman would leap to his feet, speaking in tongues, and then fly around the sanctuary like some holy spirit.

He climbed down off the stage. He sat in a chair and waited until Terry Kinsman sat up. The youth minister seemed dazed, uncertain of his surroundings. Then he, too, climbed down off the stage. Together they left the church and got into the car.

They drove toward the Interstate. At the on-ramp, they stopped at a Hardee's drive-through for cheeseburgers and crispy curls. Then they got on the Interstate, going east. Terry Kinsman drove with one hand and ate with the other.

If Jason Harbo's body had been lying hidden in the weeds, it would have been reasonable to think that it was all an accident. He had been killed when he hit the ground. The force of the blow had been enough to throw him into the weeds along a road where only oddballs like Seth Stevens walked.

But Jason Harbo hadn't fallen under the piece of plywood. And where was his bike?

And what if the crash hadn't been enough to kill him?

The most likely scenario, he thought, was that Terry Kinsman had gone back to the road that night and found Jason Harbo's body lying in the weeds close to the road. He had dragged the body into the ditch and covered it with the piece of plywood. The bike was probably nearby, also hidden.

Had he done it to protect Salvation? The Free Church of God's Slaves? Citizens for Good Government?

Had he simply been scared?

Seth Stevens wondered if the fact that he had called the police would jeopardize their mission. Did it matter? And what was their mission?

After he had stopped vomiting, he had walked back to the road and then away from the Perkins until he found a large truck stop. Using a pay phone next to a bank of blooping video games, he called 911, whispered the location of the body, and hung up. He knew that his vomit was DNA evidence—kicking dirt over it was probably a futile gesture— but he also thought that it might be only circumstantial evidence. He had simply thought that Sandi Harbo had deserved to learn her son's fate. He had decided not to tell Terry Kinsman.

Terry Kinsman finished eating. He balled up the rectangle of foil from his cheeseburger, swerving a little, and threw it into the back seat.

'I got something to confess,' he said.

'I know,' said Seth Stevens.

'I got you fired from ShopsMart.'

'What?'

'What'd you mean, you know?'

'What? Nothing. I just—why?'

'You obviously weren't happy working for that atheist.'

'Rob Wingert is an anarchist.'

'Same difference.'

'Does Pastor Grady know?'

'That I broke into ShopsMart? Course not. He can't know stuff like that. But I knew he'd offer you a job. Fact, he was the one who told me, "Seth needs to get closer to the church." He was worried about you.'

Seth Stevens watched the broken white center stripe shoot toward them. He thought of tracers, the fiery bullets he'd seen in films about Vietnam.

'How did you do it?' he asked. 'Did you steal my associate's card?'

'Copied it.'

'You what?'

'This stuff's all out there on the Internet, Seth. People set up fake ATMs, you put your card in and punch in your number, ATM tells you, "Sorry, out of cash." You get your card back. But when you put the card in, they copied the magnetic stripe and your PIN number. I spent some time IM-ing with this one guy, he sent me the instructions how to copy magnetic stripes. You were on stage one time, I told the kids I had to go to the bathroom. I went to your backpack and got her done.'

Terry Kinsman looked at him, trying to read his expression.

'Are you mad or what?'

'It's just, they called me a thief. With my record, I could have gone to jail.'

'They wouldn't of pressed charges. ShopsMart hates bad publicity.'

Seth Stevens pictured Terry Kinsman in the music room, digging through his backpack, looking for the associate's card.

Terry Kinsman looked at him, taking his eyes off the road for a frighteningly long time.

'Well, do you wish you were back there? At ShopsMart? Working for that God-hater?'

'I don't know if he hates God. He hated me, I think.'

'Do you wish you were still working for him? And not for Citizens?'

'No,' said Seth Stevens. 'Of course not.'

'That's right,' said Terry Kinsman. 'Of course not.'

After an hour or so they left the Interstate and drove to a campground. Terry Kinsman drove past the gatehouse, where a large sign with block letters pointed out the drop box for nighttime check-ins.

'Shouldn't we check in?' asked Seth Stevens.

'That's why we're at a campground,' said Terry Kinsman. 'So we don't have to check in. Sometimes, Seth . . .'

'But won't they check the campsites in the morning?'

'Time they come around, we'll be gone.'

Their headlights flashed on RVs, pop-tops, and tents as they looked for an empty site. The campground was crowded. Most of the campers seemed to have electricity. Finally, they found a site. It was far from the toilets and close to the highway.

Terry Kinsman approved.

'Off the beaten path. We have to make a quick getaway, we can just drive through the weeds to the highway.'

He left the motor running and the headlights shining while they set up the tent, drawing angry shouts from a man nearby. Terry Kinsman shouted back and the man backed down.

Seth Stevens had no idea how to set up a tent. He stumbled around, getting in Terry Kinsman's way, until he was finally ordered to stand back. He stood, stupidly, holding a bag of tent stakes until they were called for.

Fortunately, Terry Kinsman knew what he was doing. Soon the car was turned off and they were zipped into their sleeping bags. Seth Stevens had thought that he might have trouble sleeping, but he was out as soon as he closed his eyes.

It was only a few minutes later, it seemed, that Terry Kinsman woke him up. The olive green tent smelled like socks. It was just light enough to see.

'What time is it?' asked Seth Stevens.

'Around five.'

'You've got to be kidding me.'

'You want to stick around and make friends with the witnesses, be my guest.'

Seth Stevens groaned. He did the math and calculated that he had gotten three and a half hours of sleep. Instinctively he wished for the hyperspace thrust of meth. Or even the warm adrenaline of a cross-top.

Terry Kinsman was already dressed. He unzipped the tent and slipped out. There was a scrape of gravel and then a soft nylon sound as one of the guy lines slipped off a stake. One corner of the tent drooped.

'But I gotta take the tent with me,' said Terry Kinsman.

Seth Stevens was sweaty. When he brushed the tent wall his hand came back wet with condensation. Sighing, he wriggled out of his sleeping bag, getting out of the tent just before Terry Kinsman let go of the last guy line.

Five minutes later they were creeping around the loop that led to the campground exit. An early riser, drinking coffee in a lawn chair outside the door of his RV, waved a cheery greeting. Terry Kinsman stared straight ahead and kept driving.

'Don't give them anything to remember you by,' he said.

'But what if they remember you not waving?' said Seth Stevens.

'That all this is to you, a big joke?'

'Of course not. I'm just trying to have some fun.'

They stopped at a gas station food mart for breakfast. Terry Kinsman parked 200 yards away and they paid in cash. He had filled up the tank at his usual gas station, he said, at his usual time.

'Sure, our faces are on the video here,' he said. 'But someone would have to come look at the video. We don't use a credit card, they won't know we were here.'

'You really think that someone's looking for us?'

'Not yet, they aren't. But they're gonna for sure.'

'Why?'

'Tell you when we get across state lines,' said Terry Kinsman.

'Why's that?'

'No reason.'

'You just like keeping secrets?'

'I just like keeping secrets.'

They ate their rubbery egg-and-bacon sandwiches, the grease soaking through the paper wrappers. Terry Kinsman chugged orange juice while Seth Stevens unscrewed a bottle of Mountain Dew.

As far as he could tell, they were driving toward the northeast corner of the state. Where the western part was flat and dry, the eastern part was hilly and green. They followed winding two-lane highways through small towns where half of the storefronts were empty. They crossed rivers that were little more than rock-dotted trickles. Every now and then, huge flocks of little black birds would explode out of the trees, their flight a wheeling, kaleidoscoping movement that left him dizzy. He wished he knew the names of birds. Or trees. He was pretty good with bands and books of the Bible, he thought ruefully, but that was about it.

They passed antique malls, nut stands, and a gas station that still had old-fashioned pumps. They saw a junk dealer who sold scrap metal, lawn statuary, and big chunks of raw glass. The sun was bright and the clouds were thick and cottony. When a cloud passed overhead it was like stepping into the shade of a tree.

One minute, Seth Stevens felt content to be driven. The next, he felt angry at not knowing where they were going.

They seemed to be nowhere in particular when he saw a sign that read: *Welcome to Missouri!*

After a while they came to a small town. The needle on the fuel gauge was riding just above the orange zone. Terry Kinsman stopped the car next to a public park and told Seth Stevens to get out.

'Gas station's just up ahead. It'll be more confusing if sometimes there's one of us, sometimes there's two of us.'

Seth Stevens got out. He was still wondering whether Terry Kinsman's fear of being followed was justified. He decided that it depended on what they were going to do when they got to wherever it was they were going.

Watching the car drive off, he wondered if he should leave before Terry Kinsman came back.

The town was quiet. An angry mother herded her three kids out of a video store and into a car. An old man, Mexican or Indian, pedaled past on a mountain bike. A police patrol car rolled lazily down the street, its driver's-side wheels riding the center line.

The police car passed him and then slowed to a stop. Its reverse lights came on. The driver backed up until he could speak through his open window. All Seth Stevens could see were mirrored aviator glasses and a brushy mustache.

'New in town or just visiting?' said the policeman.

'Just visiting.'

'Where you staying?'

He was caught off guard by the questions. Why would a policeman question someone sitting on a park bench?

'I'm not. Staying. I'm just waiting for my friend. He's getting gas.'

'And you wanted some fresh air, huh?'

'Yeah. Wanted to stretch my legs.'

'Well, welcome to our town.'

The policeman drove off. Was this the kind of small town that threw vagrants in jail?

He stood up, feeling self-conscious. He thought that he should stretch his legs for real so he wouldn't be made a liar. He strolled through the park. It didn't take long. It was the size of a small-town city block. There was a gazebo, a playground, and a large concrete circle with turtles that sprayed water out of nozzles on their backs. A skinny man with a potbelly and a ponytail stood on the grass, urging his daughter to play in the water. He wore black jeans and cowboy boots. She wore a pink swimsuit and water wings. On the playground, two boys were throwing handfuls of pea gravel at each other and laughing.

Seth Stevens circled the park two more times. He sat on the steps of the gazebo, picking off pieces of blistered white paint. He wasn't wearing a watch. But Terry Kinsman was taking far too long to fill up the tank.

The man with the ponytail carried the still-dry little girl to an enormous pickup truck and lifted her in through the driver's-side door. She crawled across the bench seat and he climbed in after her. The door closed. They drove away.

The two boys' gravel toss turned into a fight. After yelling at each other for a little while, they left, too, walking about twenty yards apart.

The sun grew hotter. He got hungry.

Finally, Terry Kinsman drove up.

'Where were you?' asked Seth Stevens as he climbed into the car. 'A cop asked me what I was doing here.'

'You didn't tell him anything, did you?' asked Terry Kinsman.

'I told him everything I know. Which doesn't amount to much.'

'Ha ha.'

'What took you so long?'

Terry Kinsman gave him a sidelong look.

'I saw you talking to that cop and I figured I better drive around a little, make sure he was gone.'

'You were gone more than an hour.'

'Well, he's gone, isn't he?'

Terry Kinsman handed him a limp, grease-spotted paper bag. He opened it and found two corn dogs, French fries, a stick of beef jerky, and a Mountain Dew. The food was room temperature.

'Sorry the pop got warm,' said Terry Kinsman. 'Didn't know I'd have to drive around so long.'

Seth Stevens was hungry. He ate the food even though it tasted like damp cardboard. He had originally imagined that the mission would be just an overnight trip. Now he wondered how many nights it would last. Two? Three? Seven? He wondered, too, how long it would be before Terry Kinsman revealed their destination to him. One moment he wanted to throttle Terry Kinsman until he told. The next moment he was perversely content to wait.

Maybe there was no mission. Maybe Terry Kinsman just wanted his company. Maybe they were just going to drive the back roads of the United States, stealing an occasional yard sign.

Somehow he knew that wasn't true.

He realized that he'd forgotten to bring his Bible. He asked if Terry Kinsman had brought his. The answer was no. He asked if they should look for a church.

'There aren't no other churches like ours,' said Terry Kinsman.

'Maybe we should stop to pray sometime, then.'

'You want to stop to pray, fine by me. But you think warriors turn around and go back to church? You think they stop in the middle of battle, kneel down, and pray? God is with us, Seth. Jesus, He's riding in the back seat. We can talk to Him right here, we don't even need to pull over. I'm gonna pray right now. You do it, too.'

He prayed, keeping one eye on Terry Kinsman. He was irrationally afraid that, if Terry Kinsman prayed while he was driving, he would close his eyes.

They passed under the Interstate. They saw a black cinder-block building with a sign painted on the side: *ExotiXXX Gentleman's Club*. It was mid-afternoon, but there were a half-dozen cars in the parking lot. An SUV was signaling to turn in. Terry Kinsman followed it.

'What are you doing?' asked Seth Stevens.

'Hold on, just wait.'

Terry Kinsman pulled up next to the SUV. A large black man, wearing a backward driving cap and a gold chain, opened the door.

'Excuse me,' said Terry Kinsman.

'What is it?' said the man.

'How does it feel to know you're going to Hell?'

Seth Stevens shrank back. He expected the man to pull a gun.

'Excuse me?'

'I said: how does it feel to know you're going to Hell?'

The man stared, his eyes invisible behind wraparound sunglasses.

'Shit,' he said. 'You don't know anything about me.'

'I know you're going to Hell,' said Terry Kinsman. 'Unless you repent and accept Jesus Christ as your personal savior.'

'I believe in Jesus Christ.'

'Do you believe he wants you stuffing dollar bills into the underwear of naked women?'

The man stared at Terry Kinsman.

Seth Stevens was ready to open his door and run.

The man looked at the door of the strip club. Then he looked back at Terry Kinsman. He shook his head.

'Shit,' he said. 'Can't believe this.'

He climbed back into his SUV.

'Pray on the Bible,' called Terry Kinsman after him. 'And don't curse. He don't like cursing, either.'

The SUV backed up in a quarter-circle, then accelerated out of the lot. Terry Kinsman followed at a moderate pace.

'That,' he said, 'is some old-time evangelizing.'

Seth Stevens's mind relaxed, but his body was slow to get the message.

'I thought you said we shouldn't do anything that would make anyone remember us.'

'I know. I just couldn't help myself. I think I got to him. He realized that it would be an offense to God if he went in and looked at those women.'

'He's probably just going to come back later. He just felt guilty because we were there.'

'Pastor Grady says that the way you imagine someone else sinning tells you how you sin yourself.'

'What's that supposed to mean?'

'Never mind. Look, Seth, I been a Christian a lot longer than you. I seen a lot of people come to Jesus. And I can tell you for a fact, that man's going to go home and think about the fact that he's not right with God. You'd be surprised. Black people can be very religious.'

*   *   *

They drove all day and into the evening, keeping to two-lane highways. Their progress was slow. In small town after small town they were forced to crawl along and wait at stoplights that directed nearly nonexistent traffic. The road curved and sometimes seemed to double back on itself.

Terry Kinsman's mood alternated between righteous anger at the sinning he saw on the roadside and beatific detachment that suggested he was above it all.

Seth Stevens grew quieter and quieter. He wasn't sure how much longer he wanted to stay in the car. He pictured Charisma Brown lying alone on her bed, dialing his number.

They ate pulled-pork sandwiches in the car, then walked up to a Dairy Queen and bought dessert. On the sticky green picnic tables, engraved with generations of initials, a cross-section of small-town society had gathered: teenaged lovers, taciturn moms and dads, thick-bodied bikers. The bug zappers hanging from the eaves worked overtime.

Shortly after nightfall, on a long stretch of wooded, hilly road, Terry Kinsman adjusted his rear-view mirror.

'Cop's been following us for twenty miles,' he said.

'Probably going the same way,' said Seth Stevens.

'Nuh-uh. I tried slowing down, speeding up, he keeps hanging with me.'

'What would he possibly be following us for?'

'He knows.'

'Great. The cop knows and I don't.'

He realized that Terry Kinsman was accelerating toward the crest of a hill.

'Well, don't *speed*, Terry,' he said.

But the needle moved steadily clockwise. At the crest of the hill, Terry Kinsman stomped on the accelerator. The engine responded with a high whine and they hurtled downward. The car shimmied on the rutted asphalt.

Seth Stevens turned in his seat, looking behind them.

'He ain't even noticed yet,' said Terry Kinsman. 'He's smart, lying about three hundred yards back or so.'

The speedometer passed ninety. In a moment they would begin climbing another hill.

Behind them, a halo of headlights showed that the police car was nearing the top.

'What do you think, Seth?' asked Terry Kinsman. 'We going to make the top of this second hill before he comes over?'

No, he thought. No, of course not.

Suddenly they were climbing. Terry Kinsman downshifted. The car lurched and the engine's whine became a scream. Something smelled hot. They were flying up the hill.

Behind them, there was light at the top of the hill.

They topped the second hill. Just before they sank out of sight, Seth Stevens saw the police car's two headlights shining. And then they were gone.

The car hurtled through the night. Then Terry Kinsman stepped on the brakes. Seth Stevens reached out to the dashboard.

'Can't skid,' said Terry Kinsman.

But they were stopping too fast. Seth Stevens's whole body came off the seat, held in place only by the seatbelt. He glimpsed an unmarked turnoff to a gravel road.

Terry Kinsman turned the wheel. The car slewed on to the gravel road, hammering up and down. The car's heavy undercarriage yo-yoed on its suspension, straining away from the cab. Only their seatbelts kept them from hitting the roof. Seth Stevens couldn't see. The road was a blur of rocks and tree trunks.

Then it wasn't a road. It was just a gravel circle ringed by trees.

'Man!' yelled Terry Kinsman.

He stomped on the brakes again and turned the wheel. There was no way to stop in time. The car dropped off an embankment. Seth Stevens heard snapping wood as they crashed through a stand of saplings. Then there was a sickening thump and they stopped.

Terry Kinsman turned off the engine and killed the lights. He rolled down his window.

They listened.

They heard a car rolling down the highway, the fat asphalt sound of an under-inflated tire, the automatic transmission downshifting as the car accelerated up the hill.

'You OK, Seth?'

Stunned, he looked down at his legs. They were both attached. His arms worked, too. He touched his face. He didn't feel blood.

'Yeah.'

'Blessed be.'

'Terry, what if that car wasn't following us?'

'Trust me, he was.'

'Well, what happens when he realizes we're not in front of him anymore and comes back?'

'He's gonna think we're in front of him for a while anyway. If he does come back, he's gonna have other side roads to check out. Meanwhile, we're gonna be headed back the other way.'

Terry Kinsman turned the ignition key. The car started, but the engine idled too fast and made a grinding sound. He put the car in reverse, looking over his shoulder at the short gravel embankment, the snapped saplings frozen in the reverse lights. The car lurched backward and stopped. The steering wheel seemed loose in his hands. The engine was making sounds that Seth Stevens had never heard before.

'Get out and push,' said Terry Kinsman.

Seth Stevens opened the door and climbed out, stumbling in the ruined underbrush. He got behind the car and put his hands on the trunk, pushing as Terry Kinsman gunned the engine. He turned backward, putting his butt against the rear bumper and pushing with his legs. The car lifted and settled on its damaged suspension. The wheels kicked rocks and wood chips against his legs. The car didn't move.

Terry Kinsman got out and slammed his door.

'Jesus saves us, Satan screws us,' he said. 'Let's go.'

They walked along the shoulder of the highway, ready to bolt into the trees at the sight of headlights. But no headlights appeared.

After a mile or two they came to a dirt driveway. Three metal mailboxes clung to a post that leaned precipitously toward the asphalt. Terry Kinsman turned in to the driveway. Seth Stevens followed.

The first house they passed was a well-kept Colonial with white clapboard siding and dark shutters and trim. Lights blazed in the windows. On a concrete pad, a car and a truck gleamed under a brilliant security light.

'Nuh-uh,' whispered Terry Kinsman.

The second house was a double-wide prefab whose windows

were dark. But the only vehicle near it was a jet-ski that was padlocked to a large tree with a loop of thick chrome chain.

They kept walking.

The driveway ended in a loop in front of a low, squat house that looked hand-built. If its plywood walls had ever been painted, there was no color left to tell the tale. An old black Chevy truck with oversized tires and a dented canopy was parked in the shadows on the left side of the house. On the right side of the house, TV light flickered in a darkened room.

In the front yard, a large dog collar was tethered to an iron stake by a length of slender steel cable.

'Dog's inside, that's good,' whispered Terry Kinsman.

'For what?' asked Seth Stevens.

'We need a car, less you want to walk a few hundred miles.'

'Steal it?'

'The Lord will make it up to them when they get to Heaven, if they show up.'

They had walked a few steps closer when he had a more practical concern.

'Do you know how to hotwire a car, Terry?'

'You think I'm some kind of car thief? We need the keys.'

They crept to the truck. Seth Stevens waited for the dog to start barking and the lights to come on.

Terry Kinsman lifted the truck's door handle and eased the door open. It gave a dry groan. They froze, listening. But nothing happened. Terry Kinsman opened the door the rest of the way and searched under the floor mat and the seat.

'Well, lookee here,' he said.

He pulled an old-fashioned looking revolver from underneath the seat and stuck it in his belt. Then he climbed up into the cab of the truck. He flipped down the visor, pulled out the ashtray, and opened the glove compartment.

'No key,' he hissed.

Seth Stevens started to back away from the truck. He felt relieved to have an excuse to abort the theft.

Terry Kinsman grabbed his arm.

'The house.'

The side door was blank steel. There could have been anything on the other side. Anything including a large German shepherd whose collar and leash were lying useless in the yard.

'What if it's locked?' he said hopefully.

'Just try the handle,' whispered Terry Kinsman. 'People usually leave their keys by the door or on the counter.'

Seth Stevens walked to the door. Blood thundered in his ears. He turned the handle. The door was unlocked. He pushed and it opened quietly. He opened it all the way.

Moonlight through a window showed a sink with a few dirty dishes in it. Newspapers were stacked on a chrome-legged table. Through a doorway and down a hall he saw the light from the TV. The volume was turned up loud. A cop show. A drug bust in a housing project in a big city.

He stepped inside. He looked at the kitchen counter, praying to see a ring of keys just lying there. Instead he saw unopened junk mail. He took another step and looked at the back of the door. He had been in homes where jigsawed wooden keys had small metal hooks for all the household's keys. On the back of the door was a scrawled note. He squinted, straining to read it in the darkness.

REMEMBER TO FEED DOG, it read.

The dog that would smell him any second.

His fear was like white noise. He stepped farther into the room. Then he saw the keys lying on the table, partly covered by a corner of newspaper. He took two more steps and grabbed them.

In the living room, the show went to commercial.

'Want something?' said a deep voice.

The other party must have shaken his or her head. There was no reply. An easy chair ratcheted shut.

Seth Stevens took long strides toward the door, tottering on the balls of his feet. He heard footsteps in the hall. He slipped through the door and pulled it shut, careful not to release the bolt until the door was snug in the frame.

Terry Kinsman saw the keys in his hand.

'Nice work,' he said.

Seth Stevens wrapped an arm around him and half-dragged him to the far side of the truck.

The kitchen light came on, flooding out through a window beside the door.

They crouched behind one of the big tires, their eyes wide. If the homeowner noticed his keys missing, if he happened to glance out his window and see his truck door hanging open . . .

Even through the wall they could hear the sounds of the man getting a snack. The floorboards groaned under his weight.

Terry Kinsman reached for the keys.

'We got to go now,' he whispered.

'Wait until he goes back into the other room.'

'He's gonna hear the truck start no matter what room he's in.'

Seth Stevens shook his head. He wrapped his fist around the keys.

Terry Kinsman shook his head. They waited.

After a minute they stopped hearing sounds from the house. But the kitchen light stayed on.

Terry Kinsman crept around the truck and peered through a corner of the window. He shook his head. Seth Stevens didn't know whether the head shake meant that the man was gone or the man was still there.

Terry Kinsman came back.

'He's gone. Now give me the keys.'

While Terry Kinsman went around to the driver's side, Seth Stevens opened the passenger-side door. He put one foot on a friction-taped step and climbed up and in. The cab of the truck looked clean but smelled peculiar, a pungent combination of air freshener and body odor.

They left their doors open. Terry Kinsman slotted the key. Seth Stevens braced himself for the engine's rumble, for the owner's shouts, for a harrowing drive back to the main road.

Terry Kinsman turned the key.

Nothing happened.

'What's wrong with it?'

'Kill switch,' said Terry Kinsman. 'Got to be. This guy don't have another car. He wouldn't sit out here with his only truck broke.'

When Seth Stevens had been using, he had sometimes hung around other addicts who stole cars. He had heard them talk about kill switches, little toggles that interrupted the current to the starter. Kill switches were especially popular among gearheads who owned easy-to-hotwire classic cars.

Even with the light from the house, the inside of the cab was dark. They ran their hands over the underside of the dashboard, over the sides of the seats, over the headliner.

Seth Stevens opened the glove compartment.

'Seth, look,' said Terry Kinsman.

A shadow fell over them. On the other side of the kitchen
window, a big, shirtless, bearded man was staring at them as
if he wasn't quite sure what he was seeing.

Seth Stevens's fingers found a little plastic toggle switch
in the glove compartment. He pushed it so hard that it snapped
off.

'Go,' he said.

Terry Kinsman turned the key. The engine chugged and
then roared to life. The house door opened and the man stood
framed in light, a big belly hanging over the waistband of his
jeans.

'Go!' said Seth Stevens.

Terry Kinsman gunned the engine but left the transmission
in neutral. He pressed the revolver into Seth Stevens's hand.

'Show him the gun.'

'What?'

'*Show him the gun*. Tell him to get back in the house.'

His hands shaking, Seth Stevens rolled down his window
and reached the heavy gun out. It felt like trying to hold a
sandbag on the end of a broomstick. He thought he said something but his voice was inaudible over the engine.

'Back in the house!' shouted Terry Kinsman. 'We need to
borrow your truck.'

Blankly, the bearded man closed his door. Terry Kinsman
shifted into reverse and popped the clutch. The truck lurched
backward, nearly stalling, and then bounced down the road,
spraying dust and rocks. Terry Kinsman swung the wheel and
skidded to a stop, then ground gears until he found first and
gunned it again. They sped back toward the highway.

Seth Stevens practically threw the gun into the glove
compartment. He slammed it shut.

'I bet he don't even have a dog,' muttered Terry Kinsman.

Fourteen

They drove back to the ruined car. Terry Kinsman stood with his hands on his hips and surveyed the wreck.

'Leaving a car is bad as leaving DNA,' he said. 'I'd burn it but the fire would help them find it sooner. Only thing in our favor is nobody might find it awhile. You get the plates while I get the stuff.'

Terry Kinsman had a multi-tool in his own glove compartment. Seth Stevens used the screwdriver to remove the front and back license plates while Terry Kinsman opened the trunk and started moving their gear to the back of the truck.

When he stood up he saw Terry Kinsman lifting gallon-sized jugs of water out of his trunk.

'When did we get this water, Terry?'

'I got it at that last town, while you were in the park.'

He hoisted the jugs. The smudged and peeling labels advertised a store brand of distilled water.

'The labels are dirty.'

'Probably why they were twenty percent off.'

Puzzled, Seth Stevens helped move the rest of the jugs. There were nearly two dozen in all.

When the truck was fully loaded, Terry Kinsman started his car and put it in gear. He was only able to drive it ten feet further into the woods before the engine died for good.

'Guess it'll have to do,' he said.

He slammed the door. They got into the truck and drove away.

Terry Kinsman insisted on driving what he called an 'evasive stratagem'. They backtracked for about half an hour, then took a small county road that led them to another county road and then eventually the freeway. After an hour on the freeway they rejoined the state highway and continued on in their earlier direction.

The truck's fat tires and jacked-up transmission seemed to make it harder to drive. Terry Kinsman handled the steering wheel as if he were in a TV movie, correcting and overcorrecting as the tires rode the edges of the valleyed asphalt.

The engine was noisy, making it hard for them to hear each other. But they were too tired to talk much. Seth Stevens's eyelids kept falling, although they rose rapidly when he realized that Terry Kinsman was falling asleep, too. They decided to pull over and sleep. In the next small town they found a used-car dealership with a line of jeeps and trucks at the back of the lot. Terry Kinsman parked in the line and Seth Stevens tied a balloon to the truck's antenna. He wished he had a grease pencil so he could write *LOW MILES—RUNS GREAT!* on the windshield.

Terry Kinsman claimed the bench seat, so Seth Stevens climbed into the back, pushing duffle bags and water jugs out of the way until he had a long narrow space in which to lie down.

The air was stuffy and the ribbed metal floor was hard under his back. He fell asleep as soon as he closed his eyes.

They slept past dawn. By the time they woke up, the sun had heated the truck like an oven. He sat up and reached for a jug of water.

'Wait on that,' said Terry Kinsman from the front seat. 'I got a canteen still.'

He took the canteen, swallowed some bath-warm water, and handed it back through the connecting window. His bladder was aching. He pushed open the rear hatch, which he had left unlatched, and climbed on to the back bumper.

A woman with teased hair was standing at the back door of the dealership with keys in her hand.

'You boys had better be gone by the time Jerry gets here,' she said. 'He'll call the cops.'

'Yes, ma'am,' said Terry Kinsman. 'Gone in sixty seconds.'

They drove the speed limit until they had passed the town line, then stopped at a gas station to use the toilet and buy breakfast. After a little while they passed a church.

'The Church of Jesus Christ of Latter-Day Saints: The Mormons,' said Terry Kinsman in the voice of a TV announcer.

Seth Stevens's next words were out of his mouth before he knew what he was saying.

'Why didn't you tell us what happened to Jason Harbo?'

'What happened to the who?'

'Elder Harbo. The Mormon. At Perkins.'

'Tell you what happened? I don't know what happened.'

'I do.'

Terry Kinsman looked over. He shook his head. He looked at the road again.

'I didn't want you all to have to carry the weight of my sin.'

'Is that it, Terry?'

'I didn't tell you for the same reason I told you not to tell anyone in the first place. To protect Salvation, and God's Slaves, and Citizens.'

'So you hid his body.'

'It's not like your soul walks the earth unless you're buried in consecrated ground.'

'There was a bird eating him, Terry.'

Terry Kinsman gripped the wheel. He leaned on the horn with both hands. Then he pushed the accelerator to the floor.

'Man, Seth!' he said. 'Do you have any idea what's going on?'

'What's going on with what?'

'"What's going on with what?"' Terry Kinsman mimicked in a high falsetto. 'What's going on is a war between right and wrong and good and evil. A holy war. You think it's yard signs and Senate candidates. But the stuff Pastor Grady talks about isn't fairy tales. Satan walks among us and he wears many disguises. If we win, we can ensure the reign of God on earth. If we lose, well, Ancient Rome is going to look like a toddler party at Chuck E. Cheese. The whores, fornicators, and idolaters will run the most powerful nation on earth. Elder Harbo, well, I feel bad for his mom, but you know what? He's a casualty of war. And there's going to be a bunch more casualties of war before this thing is through.'

The truck was going faster and faster. It lurched back and forth on the highway. Terry Kinsman passed a car heading into a blind curve.

'So if Dean Platt wins then it's OK because there will be a God-fearing Senate majority?' asked Seth Stevens.

'Forget all that. Look, we're trying to elect Platt, course we are. Isaacs gets into office, I'm going to puke. But even if we win in Oklahoma, we might lose in Minnesota. Or

Oregon. And anyway, what's a one-vote Senate majority if we lose the Presidency?'

Instinctively, Seth Stevens reached for an armrest. There wasn't one. He grabbed the door handle instead. As if he would jump.

'But aren't we going to lose?

'Maybe. Probably.'

'So why does any of it matter?'

'We might lose, but the President isn't going to leave the White House.'

'What are you talking about?'

'Because Muslim terrorists are going to strike the heartland. The president will declare martial law. Check out Executive Order 12919. And do you think they're going to still hold elections when they're waiting for the next attack?'

The white stripe came at them like machine-gun fire. Terry Kinsman passed two cars at once. He kept driving in the left-hand lane.

'Terry, slow down.'

An approaching car blipped into sight.

'Terry, slow down.'

He could hear the other car honking. They were going to crash.

'Terry, you're drawing attention! Slow the damn car down!'

Terry Kinsman grinned. He stomped on the brake.

The tires squealed as they skidded, fishtailing. Terry Kinsman fought the truck over to the shoulder. He pulled off the asphalt and stopped. He grinned.

'Now you're thinking like a soldier.'

Seth Stevens pictured Terry Kinsman at night, dragging Jason Harbo's body deeper into the weeds.

'Was he dead when you found him?' he asked.

'I hid the body, Seth. I didn't kill him. Exactly what do you think I'm capable of?'

'I don't know.'

Seth Stevens's mouth was dry. He reached for the canteen on the floor. It was empty. He reached into the back and grabbed a jug of water. He started unscrewing the cap.

'I wouldn't drink that, I were you,' said Terry Kinsman.

'Why?'

'Because we're the Muslim terrorists.'

*   *   *

Terry Kinsman pulled on to the highway again, once again obeying the speed limit. He began to explain their mission. Seth Stevens sat, stupefied, and listened.

They were driving to Canterbury, Ohio, a small town chosen for the fact that its water supply was unguarded, easily accessible, and close to the faucets of its citizens. The water jugs, said Terry Kinsman, contained Giardia. The parasite had been incubated by a biologist who had attended the Free Church of God's Slaves until family issues had caused him to leave Tulsa and move to the small town where Terry Kinsman had gone alone to buy gas. They would pour the infected solution into the town's water reservoir. At the scene, they would leave a note in which a group called 'al-Qaeda in America' claimed responsibility.

But weren't there real terrorists out there? asked Seth Stevens. Why should they become terrorists themselves?

Terry Kinsman explained that of course there were real terrorists out there. Islamic fundamentalism was just as real a threat from without as secular humanism was from within. But despite the President's declaration of war on terror, the country had not yet realized they were truly at war. Homeland Security was a joke. A single act of terror now could save them from a dozen, worse terrorist attacks later. It was a wake-up call, nothing more.

But wouldn't people get hurt?

Of course people would get hurt. If no one got hurt, no one would listen. But suffering diarrhea, cramps, and vomiting was better than being vaporized by a suicide bomber.

But what if making some people sick in Ohio wasn't enough to change everyone's mind?

They weren't alone. Others would be carrying out similar missions, creating the image of a coordinated attack by foreign terrorists on U.S. soil.

What would the other attacks be like?

Terry Kinsman said he didn't know and didn't want to know. It was important that members of each cell not know the members of any other cell. That way, no one could incriminate anyone else. If one plot was foiled, the others could still proceed. Coordination, he said, came from above.

Above?

Terry Kinsman wanted to know if Seth Stevens had ever heard of the Embassy of Christianity.

Seth Stevens had not.

The Embassy of Christianity, Terry Kinsman explained, was on Embassy Row in Washington, D.C., right there with the embassies of actual countries. Its ambassadors worked for the U.S. government, in the State Department, the Department of Justice, the Pentagon, even the White House. They believed that Christians had a moral obligation to witness their faith at church, at home, and on the job. Some of the Christian ambassadors were very highly placed. They would be on hand to urge the President to follow the proper course of action. If the President failed, there was a backup plan.

'Is Uncle Frank a Christian ambassador?'

'You might call him a senior ambassador,' said Terry Kinsman.

'You really think this is going to scare everybody enough that all this is going to happen?'

'Yup.'

'How can you be so sure?'

'Seth, what's the date?'

He rarely knew the date. He didn't read the newspaper, and beyond the day of the week, such information held little value for him. He was aware that summer was almost over.

Just then they passed a gas station with a blinking reader board. It flashed the temperature: 78 degrees. It flashed the time: 9:32. It flashed the date: September 10.

Terry Kinsman asked if he was going to help. Seth Stevens said that he would. Terry Kinsman prayed aloud while he was driving. Seth Stevens praised and amened, but when Terry Kinsman's prayer turned to tongues, he heard it differently than when he had heard it before. The gibberish didn't sound heavenly. It sounded false and presumptuous of God's love. And so instead of worrying that Terry Kinsman's rapture would cause them to crash, he began worrying about how to stop Terry Kinsman before he poisoned the water in Canterbury, Ohio.

Before Terry Kinsman had told him where they were going and what they were doing, the trip had seemed to be taking forever. Now it seemed to be speeding by. The truck's owner had attached a small digital clock to the face of the truck's original clock, which was broken. Every time Seth Stevens looked at it, expecting a minute to have blinked by, ten more had passed.

Without seeing a map, he had no idea how many more miles there were to drive. Terry Kinsman seemed to have memorized their route. And when were they to poison the well? He assumed it would be under cover of darkness, but that was all he could guess.

Should he try to stop Terry Kinsman by himself? Or should he escape and get help? Hours passed and he couldn't decide.

Finally he decided that he would empty the jugs and refill them with plain water. Then he could go along with the plot. When nobody got sick, he could claim ignorance as well as Terry Kinsman.

But, even though he gave no indication that he didn't believe Seth Stevens's pledge of allegiance, Terry Kinsman wouldn't leave him alone. He never left the truck unless Seth Stevens did, too. They urinated together, picked out food together, and stretched their legs together.

The day raced on in a blur of half-eaten fast food and stolen glances at the clock. Around dinnertime he saw a sign: *WELCOME TO OHIO: WITH GOD, ALL THINGS ARE POSSIBLE.*

'Terry? What if we're wrong?' said Seth.

'Wrong about what? Serving God?'

'No. What if we're doing it wrong?'

'Know what makes a soldier a soldier?'

'A helmet and a gun?'

'A soldier follows orders. If every soldier thought he was a general, you know what we'd have?'

He thought maybe it would be better to keep his response light.

'A problem with chain of command?'

'Man! Stop joking, Seth. Chaos, that's what. Not everybody has to make the big decisions. It's something to be grateful for. We got Pastor Grady, Uncle Frank, a whole bunch of other people we haven't even met yet. They got this stuff worked out. They might be wrong, but they're closer to right than I would be. And who else are you gonna trust? A Jew? A Mormon? An atheist?'

'I just don't think God wants us to hurt people.'

'What, you don't think Christians never hurt people?'

'No, I know, but—'

'Read on your Bible, Seth. Old-time Christians, they never wanted to hurt nobody. They just wanted to worship the one true God. But when people wouldn't let them, look out. We been persecuted a lot, but we fight back, too. And that's what's happening today. Instead of Pharaoh, we got seculars who say we can't honor our Lord in schools and in government. Like Pastor Grady says, those are even more important than church, you want to reach people. Because if you're in church, you're already on the right side.'

He knew, of course, that he would never be able to argue Terry Kinsman out of it. He had never been good at arguing. And what moral virtue did he have anyway? He was a drug addict. He was a musician. He had never been sure of his way. Terry Kinsman had always been sure of his.

When they passed a park with a picnic area, Seth Stevens said that he had to use the toilet.

'Again?' asked Terry Kinsman. 'You just went like half an hour ago.'

'I've got to take a dump,' said Seth Stevens. 'My stomach feels funny. Maybe I'm getting nervous.'

Terry Kinsman grumbled, but he pulled over. He opened his door, too.

'You probably don't want to come with me,' said Seth Stevens. 'This might get ugly.'

Terry Kinsman chuckled and pulled his door shut.

Seth Stevens walked into the park to a green wooden pavilion with restrooms at the back. He went to the men's room and pretended to tug on the door handle.

'Locked,' he shouted.

Behind the park was a stand of trees. Once he was in the trees he would keep going. It was Ohio, not Alaska. There would be fields and houses on the other side. He would ask for a phone. He would call the police and tell them what was going to happen in Canterbury. They would be waiting when Terry Kinsman arrived.

He nodded his head toward the trees, grimaced, and started jogging. He slowed when he reached the tree line, picking his way carefully through the undergrowth.

Twenty feet in, he stopped. The trees went on as far as he could see. He had twenty-seven dollars in his wallet and the clothes on his back. But he had to go. Every second counted. He took a deep breath and started forward.

He heard crashing in the brush behind him. He turned. Terry Kinsman waved a roll of toilet paper.

'Should of pulled harder on the door handle,' he said. 'It sticks, but it's not locked. You probably want to wipe, anyways.'

He threw the toilet paper. It unrolled partly in the air, a comet with a flapping tail. Seth Stevens missed the catch. He bent down to pick it up, then brushed leaves and dirt off it.

'I'll leave you to it,' said Terry Kinsman.

His footsteps crunched away, but not all the way out of the brush.

Seth Stevens crouched, cursing and praying, and pretended to defecate.

He decided that the only thing to do was to go along, all the way, and then try to stop it at the last minute. Terry Kinsman was bigger and stronger than he was, but he wouldn't be expecting a fight. Maybe Seth Stevens could spill some jugs on the ground, or pour them in the wrong place. If not, a lot of people were going to get sick.

They drove through central Ohio, following the winding two-lane trail of black asphalt. They drove past high schools, banks, and churches. They drove past V.F.W. Posts and Elks Lodges and Masonic Temples. They saw evening crowds at Dairy Queens and miniature golf courses and batting cages. Everyone seemed determined to wring summer dry. They saw a Pop Warner football team practicing under lights. They saw multiplexes and fast-food restaurants and shopping malls. They saw a family of five going into a McDonald's, all of them wearing the American flag on their clothes.

Behind them the sun fell to the horizon like a burning tower. Its reflection in the rear-view made a rectangular burn on Terry Kinsman's face. When Seth Stevens looked into the passenger-side mirror he was blinded.

At around eleven o'clock Terry Kinsman pulled into a wooded picnic area. He drove on to the grass and then parked behind some trees.

'Almost there,' he said. 'May as well get a little sleep.'

Seth Stevens crawled into the back as before. This time, however, he was hesitant to even touch the plastic jugs. He knew he would have to actually drink from them to get sick, but he didn't want to take any chances.

The weather was changing. It was still warm, but the air was drier, and with the side vents open it was almost comfortable under the canopy.

He didn't sleep. He wasn't sure when he would sleep again. He imagined Charisma Brown in bed, asleep. Or, better, awake and thinking of him. His answering machine would be blinking with messages from her. Until now, they hadn't lasted a single day without talking on the phone at least once. Would each message be more worried than the last? Or would each message be more angry?

After a while he heard Terry Kinsman's breathing grow deep and even. Outside the truck, the metallic whine of a cicada almost drowned out the chirping of crickets and the burping of frogs.

He counted the plastic jugs. There were twenty-one in all. He wondered if there was a reason for the odd number. He found himself getting drowsy against his will. Just a few more minutes, he thought.

He startled awake. He had no idea how long he'd nodded off. Now was the time. He could throw open the back door and have half the jugs emptied before Terry Kinsman was even awake.

He sat up and began inching his way to the back of the truck bed. The truck tremored with his movements. His short breaths sounded like gasps.

Finally, he was close enough to push on the hatch. It didn't open. Had the latch slipped shut? Or had Terry Kinsman locked him in?

The back door was composed of two pieces: a flimsy glass-and-aluminum hatch that lifted up and a sturdy steel tailgate that opened downward. There was a keyed, T-shaped handle on the outside that opened the hatch, allowing the tailgate to open. No accommodation for passengers had been made on the inside of the canopy. But it would be possible to turn the handle by pulling on two long rods that slotted into either side of the canopy.

Carefully, grasping one rod in each hand, he pulled them toward the center. It was harder than it looked, but eventually the handle turned. At the last moment there was a loud creak as a rusty spring compressed.

In the cab, Terry Kinsman snorted and stirred.

Seth Stevens held the rods, his forearms trembling with the tension. It would have been easy to get out if only he didn't have to do it quietly.

Terry Kinsman quieted again. Seth Stevens pushed the glass hatch out, moving it as slowly as he could, careful not to let go. He had to shift his position as the hatch rose higher, making the truck shake again. He ended with his torso half out of the back. When he let go and the hatch held still, he let his breath out in a long, relieved sigh, then sucked in more air. He hadn't realized that he had stopped breathing.

The tailgate release was a chrome handle that had to be pulled up before the tailgate could go down. He pulled up. He felt the lock mechanism turn and let go. He heard only a dull, low-pitched click. He pushed the tailgate down. The jointed metal arms that supported it complained but he pushed so slowly that their groans seemed almost subsonic.

Finally the back of the truck was open. The night seemed immense. He picked up a jug of water and slithered out of the back. The truck lifted a little as he slipped to the ground.

He unscrewed the soft plastic cap.

'Seth?' said Terry Kinsman.

'I have to pee,' said Seth Stevens.

He tipped the jug, measuring out a stream that sounded about right for a nighttime wake-up. But it lasted too long. Terry Kinsman's door opened violently. Seth Stevens upended the bottle, shying away as the infected liquid splashed on his shoes.

Terry Kinsman grabbed the jug.

Seth Stevens pulled back, splashing himself again. He kept his mouth closed and prayed that would be enough. Then he let go—the jug was almost empty, anyway—and Terry Kinsman stumbled back.

They stood, trying to see each other in the darkness, and then Seth Stevens reached for another jug, laying his torso across the tailgate and extending his arms.

Terry Kinsman grabbed him by both shoulders, pulled him out, and threw him to the ground. Seth Stevens climbed to his feet and felt something bony strike him under the eye. He fell on his butt. He felt a sharp pain in his ribs, and then another. Terry Kinsman was kicking him. He curled up, trying to protect himself, then changed his mind and started crawling away. A kick caught his tailbone and almost lifted him off the ground.

'Who got to you?' shouted Terry Kinsman. 'When did you start working for them?'

Seth Stevens scrambled on all fours, unable to get away fast enough to stand up. Terry Kinsman followed him, kicking with every other step.

'What did you tell them? What do they know?'

'I didn't tell anybody anything,' said Seth Stevens, panting.

Something cut his hand. Broken glass, maybe. They were in the trees. It was dark. If he could only get a few steps ahead, he thought, Terry Kinsman might lose him.

'Who got to you, Seth?'

He went head first into a tree trunk. He sat down. Campfire sparks floated inside his eyes. He smelled sap. He tasted blood.

'You did, Terry,' he said. 'You got to me.'

Terry Kinsman stopped kicking.

'What?'

Seth Stevens's tongue felt thick.

'You did. Everything. I thought you were right. But I don't think this is right. Hurting people.'

Terry Kinsman was quiet for a moment.

'People get hurt, Seth. They always will. In this life, and, a lot of them, in the next, too. We're trying to help. Don't you see? I can't believe you can't see that.'

The sparks slowly embered out. His eyes adjusted to the starlight. He saw Terry Kinsman in silhouette, his shoulders slumped.

'I pray Jesus' blood on your immortal soul, Seth,' said Terry Kinsman. 'I hope I see you again by His side, in His house, clothed in purity and all your sins forgotten.'

Seth Stevens wondered if Terry Kinsman had had time to grab the gun. His hands were lost in pools of shadow.

Terry Kinsman moved suddenly. A branch cracked under his foot. Seth Stevens's bowels almost let go.

Then Terry Kinsman walked away through the bushes. He slammed the tailgate, hatch, and driver's-side door of the truck. The engine rumbled and the parking lights glowed to life. Terry Kinsman drove away.

A minute later the cicadas started up again. Then the crickets, then the frogs.

Fifteen

He limped out of the trees. His head ached and his body throbbed in a dozen places. His stomach churned, too; one of Terry Kinsman's kicks had caught him in the scrotum. He sat on a picnic table until the nausea passed. Several cars passed on the highway. None of them saw him. The truck didn't come back.

OK, he thought. Back to Plan A.

But what would he say? The local police might send a car to the water reservoir. They would never believe that the whole country was about to be attacked. He wasn't sure he believed it himself.

He doubted that he could put the nation on high alert with one phone call. But then he had done so much with one phone call already.

Of course, the best way to prove the truth of his claims was to give his name and admit his own role. But would they give him immunity? He had been to jail before, for stealing to support his habit. He hadn't been there long but he had seen enough to know that he never wanted to go back.

Was it enough to simply stop Terry Kinsman? Or was that a sin of omission?

In the end, he chose to let circumstances decide. He washed his face and hands at a spigot near the picnic shelter. He finger-combed his hair. Then he started walking down the highway.

Cars slowed but didn't stop for his thumb. He saw the drivers peering at him as if sighting an unfamiliar species. Probably no one hitch-hiked anymore except serial killers, he thought. Or was it the other way around? Maybe no one picked up hitch-hikers except serial killers.

Half-afraid, he half-prayed to see a police cruiser. But there weren't any. There were only passenger cars and delivery trucks. Once, a carload of high-schoolers stopped on the road ahead of him, only to start driving as soon as he caught up with it. Laughter, shrieks, and taunts trailed the car like exhaust. It stopped again, but he stopped, too, waiting until it pulled away for good.

Finally, he saw a sign: *Canterbury, 7.*

He had no idea what time it was, perhaps between 1 and 2 a.m. Terry Kinsman would be done by the time he got there. Maybe he was already done. Seth Stevens half-expected to see the black Chevy truck roar past him, going back to Oklahoma.

He wondered if Terry Kinsman would offer him a ride.

He wondered if he would accept.

He kept walking.

The black sky was streaked with violet when a car stopped. It was an old Jeep Wagoneer, driven by a gray-haired man in a flannel-lined denim jacket. The back seat of the Jeep was piled high with newspapers.

'Need a lift?' the man said.

Seth Stevens, footsore, wondered where he needed to go. Terry Kinsman would have told him he was creating a witness. He wondered if it mattered anymore.

'Can you take me to the water reservoir?' he asked.

The man probed his ear with his little finger.

'Water reservoir? What do you need to go there for?'

'I'm camping out with my friends. I got lost.'

'Can't camp at the water reservoir,' said the man. 'That's city land.'

'I know,' said Seth Stevens. 'We were just, you know, drinking and messing around. We don't even have tents. But, I went for a walk and got lost.'

The Jeep's engine idled throatily. Its timing was irregular. The man shook his head and grimaced.

'Get in,' he said.

It wasn't far. They didn't even have to drive through the town. But the turnoff wasn't marked in any way that Seth Stevens would have understood. After a mile on the highway and two miles on black asphalt, the man let him out at a locked gate. A sign beside the gate read: *Bow Lake.* No fishing, swimming, sailing, or camping were allowed due to the fact that Bow Lake was a municipal water supply.

He thanked the paper carrier for the ride. The man grunted, made a slow three-point turn, and drove off.

Seth Stevens slipped under the gate and started walking up a gravel road. The air was chilly. He was hungry and tired. He knew he was too late. And he had had a memorable encounter with a witness who would be able to place him at the scene of an act of terrorism. At least the nation would know that al-Qaeda in America looked just like them.

The gravel crunched under his feet. He passed a picnic area with a rusting iron grill and three warped tables. A sudden *thunk* made him jump. A raccoon peered out of a trash can, hissed loudly, and resumed digging.

He walked to the edge of the water. The dawn sky was violet and, away to the east, pale blue. The reservoir was small. Maybe a half-dozen acres, he thought. As if he knew how big an acre was. He couldn't see its source and wondered if it was spring-fed. Small as it was, how could twenty-one gallons of anything poison it? And how would Terry Kinsman have done it? Would he have just dumped it into the middle?

He scanned the placid surface for a boat. He didn't see one.

Away to his left, the gently curving shoreline narrowed to a 'V'. It was overgrown there. Was that the direction of Canterbury? He returned to the road and kept walking.

A few hundred yards further, he saw an overgrown track leading into the bushes. Even in the dim dawn light he could see tire tracks and snapped twigs. He followed the track.

He had only gone a little way when he saw the truck, black and hulking against the silvery water. Had Terry Kinsman had a hard time finding the reservoir? Or had he been waiting for the morning light? And where was he?

Trying to walk quietly, Seth Stevens stepped into the brush and worked his way to the shoreline. Then he went toward the truck. After a few minutes he had circled around and had the water at his back and the truck in front of him. Was Terry Kinsman sleeping in the cab?

Then he saw the sluice channel, low in the bushes and covered with a bowed basket of chain-link fence. Terry Kinsman knelt beside it, his fingers steepled, praying. The plastic jugs lay on the grass beside him. Seth Stevens was about to start forward when he realized the jugs were uncapped and empty.

Then he heard a motor. A white van with tinted windows was creeping up the track, its lights out. He looked at Terry Kinsman. The youth pastor was reading something written on a white piece of paper. Seth Stevens crouched down.

The van stopped behind the truck. Two men got out. They were wearing puffy white HazMat suits that covered everything but their faces. Their feet, hands, and hair were contained. Seth Stevens wondered if he was hallucinating. Or maybe he was having a vision.

Terry Kinsman heard the van's doors close. He stood up and turned around. Surprised, he stumbled backward. He crumpled the piece of paper in his hand.

'You Homeland Security?' he asked, his voice carrying in the quiet. 'I didn't do nothing.'

The first man stopped in front of Terry Kinsman. The second man went behind him, peering at the sluice channel.

'Relax, Terry,' said the first man. 'We're with the Embassy.'

'I didn't know nobody was going to be here.'

'We're just watching over you. Making sure everything goes OK.'

'It went OK, all right. Done as done.'

Terry Kinsman gestured to the sluice channel. The second man wasn't looking at the water anymore. He was standing behind Terry Kinsman. Elastic pulled the HazMat suits' hoods close to the men's faces. It would have been extremely hard to tell anyone what they looked like.

'What about your friend?' asked the first man. 'Seth?'

'We had a fight. He chickened out. I left him because I couldn't trust him.'

'You left him? Where?'

'Park about ten miles up the road,' said Terry Kinsman.

'When?'

'Last night. Midnight, around there.'

The two men exchanged a look and nodded.

'What's with the HazMat suits, anyways?' asked Terry Kinsman.

The first man smiled.

'DNA. We were never here, right?'

Terry Kinsman nodded.

'Right. But what about—'

His words were strangled. The second man had a piece of nylon cord around his neck and was pulling it tight. Terry Kinsman's fingers dug at the cord, unable to get under it. His legs kicked out front and back. The first man stepped away. The second man leaned forward to keep his own legs out of reach. He kept the cord tight.

Some sound must have escaped Seth Stevens's lips. Suddenly both men were looking at him. He stood, knowing he made a fine target, silhouetted against the silver water of Bow Lake.

'No gun,' said the second man quietly.

Terry Kinsman stopped fighting. He went to his knees, then pitched face-first into the ground and lay still.

Seth Stevens ran. He didn't look back. He raced along the shoreline, away from the track, the road, the gate. Thick bushes forced him off the shore and into the water. The cold water made him gasp. He stumbled on slippery, round stones. He splashed and fell, then got up and ran again. His jeans were wet and heavy. His sneakers felt like sponges.

He stopped, panting, and turned.

He didn't see anything. The shoreline was tranquil. A bird tweeted. No one pursued him. No bullet ripped through his chest. As if he had been dreaming.

But Terry Kinsman was lying dead back there. And something terrible was working its way into the town's water supply. Something worse than Giardia. They wouldn't have killed Terry Kinsman for giving a town diarrhea.

He found a break in the underbrush and climbed out of the water. The trees stopped at a rail fence. On the other side of the fence was a pitted cow pasture. He climbed the fence and started running across the pasture. On the other side of the pasture was a street with a half-dozen widely spaced houses.

Panting, he ran faster, still expecting a shot to ring out. Maybe the second man had not meant that Seth Stevens was not carrying a gun. Maybe he had meant that they were not supposed to shoot him.

But even if they weren't going to shoot him, they still wanted him dead.

He climbed a fence into a backyard strewn with bright plastic children's toys. He walked under dark house windows to a street where pickup trucks were parked on a dirt shoulder.

At the end of the street, the white van glided past the turnoff, then backed into view again.

He ran across the street, through a vacant lot, and plunged into a cornfield. A dog barked nearby and was answered by another.

The cornstalks rose above his head. Their broad leaves whipped his face and arms. He broke taut spider webs as he ran. It was dusty. He felt claustrophobic. He felt lost.

But it was a small cornfield. In a moment he was out the other side, digging in his heels to avoid falling into an irrigation ditch. A little further down, the water passed through a culvert under a dirt road.

He stepped down the bank and into the water. It was only shin-deep and warmer than the reservoir. He splashed to the culvert, bent down, and peered inside. It was about three feet high. Hoping there weren't any snakes living in it, he bent down and crawled inside.

The fit was tight, but he was able to sit with his knees drawn up to his chest. With the day growing lighter, he doubted the men in HazMat suits would search for him on foot. It seemed better to stay put than to provide a moving target.

The dogs barked for a while and then stopped. The sky grew bright. His eyes grew accustomed to the dark. He watched twigs and water bugs drift downstream and get caught on the dam made by his legs. He heard birds and, for a while, planes.

After a while the planes stopped.

Several times he heard distant sirens. He had no idea how much time was passing. He was hungry. He began to imagine that he would not be able to uncoil his body to stand up. After a while, he fell asleep.

When he woke, the light outside the culvert looked like afternoon. He crawled out, waiting on all fours until his cramped muscles relaxed. His hunger made him nauseous. But the hunger helped him. It gave him an idea of what to do next.

He thought of breaking into one of the quiet houses nearby. But he knew from experience that even quiet suburban houses often held life. Behind those blank windows, people were home, watching TV. They had security systems, dogs, and guns. Instead he decided to do what he had most often done when he was homeless. Even small towns like Canterbury, Ohio had Pizza Huts.

He walked into town. The streets were nearly empty. And then he came to the town center. National Guardsmen patrolled with their M16s held at port arms. Jeeps and heavy trucks were parked with two wheels on the sidewalk. A police station, a medical clinic, a high school, and a church stood on adjacent blocks. While he watched, an ambulance screamed up to the clinic. The EMTs unloaded a woman on a gurney and wheeled her toward the clinic. A man in a blue work shirt met them at the door of the clinic. He shook his head. The EMTs wheeled the gurney across the street to a large Red Cross tent on the lawn of the high school.

By the police station, three TV news trucks were parked in a line, their telescoping masts raised high in the air.

Seth Stevens walked through it all without receiving a second glance. There were worried and curious townspeople here and there and, except for having damp jeans and soggy feet, they looked a lot like him.

He walked over to the Red Cross tent. Teams of doctors were performing triage. It looked as if they were treating urgent cases right there on the lawn and sending anyone who could walk into the high-school gymnasium. One patient was convulsing, fighting wildly as the doctors tried to intubate her.

Behind the tent, five body bags lay on the grass like rotten fruit. He wondered if Terry Kinsman had believed what he said about Giardia.

He recrossed the street, feeling weak but no longer hungry. In front of the Fox News van, Byron Dennis was preparing to do a standup. Seth Stevens wondered how he could have arrived so quickly.

The cameraman counted down to live.

'More scenes of terror from small-town America,' said Byron Dennis. 'In what we are learning is merely one horrifying episode on what many people are already calling nine-one-one-two—referring to this as a second September Eleven—unsuspecting residents of Canterbury, Ohio—a town whose previous worst tragedy was a freight train derailment that killed the engineer and a brakeman—have been poisoned simply by drinking the water coming out of their own taps.'

Byron Dennis' heavily powdered face glowed almost orange. A tired-looking man knelt in front of him, using a large silver panel to reflect sunlight on to the reporter's face. A man in a blue button-down shirt stood a little way off, speaking animatedly but inaudibly into his phone.

Seth Stevens suddenly wondered if he was in the background of the shot. He moved to the side of the camera. Then he wondered if he should have bothered. When the search for al-Qaeda in Canterbury began in earnest, they were bound to find him, even if they weren't looking for born-again Christians from Tulsa, Oklahoma.

'Despite the growing body count, we're still short on specifics at this hour,' continued Byron Dennis. 'I've spoken with a number of federal, state, and local officials—from the regional director of Homeland Security to the chairman of the local water board—and they all agree that the most pressing need is to tend to the sick and wounded while trying to find out whether we can expect more terrorist attacks today.

'But what I have been told is that the water was infected with a chemical agent of some kind. The agent attacks the nervous system of infected people much as nerve gas does when it's inhaled. Those living closest to the Bow Lake water reservoir, where the agent was introduced, have suffered the gravest symptoms, up to and including death. Those farther down the pipes, so to speak, display milder symptoms. It is these people for whom medical workers hold out the most hope. And, of course, the water system has now been shut down.'

Byron Dennis touched his ear.

'Yes, Harris?'

He listened, nodding several times at the unwinking camera eye.

Seth Stevens imagined Byron Dennis' image bouncing off a satellite into peoples' homes, appearing next to Harris Trent's, framed by crawling stock prices and sports scores. Like terror, television magnified the acts of individuals a million-fold.

'Well, you certainly would think so,' said Byron Dennis, replying to the tiny voice in his ear. 'But experts tell me that America's public water utilities are in fact vulnerable targets.

The infrastructure is aging, security is minimal, and political will to safeguard facilities is nonexistent. On top of that, the terrorists appear to have done their research carefully. They selected a town whose water system dates back to the 1930s. There's very little done to the Canterbury water other than chlorination and fluoridation, which obviously weren't enough to take out the poison.'

The reporter's face froze as he anticipated the next question.

'Yes. A note was recovered at the scene. Although the media has not yet been granted access to that note, a sheriff's deputy told me, under condition of anonymity, that it was signed "al-Qaeda in America", as have been the other notes around the country on this horrible day. In what may or may not be a significant detail, the deputy told me that the note appeared to have been first crumpled into a ball and then smoothed out before ultimately being weighed down with a rock and left at the scene. A sign of hesitation? Only the terrorist or terrorists know for sure.'

Again, the expectant look.

'Yes, that's true.'

Again.

'Thank you, Harris. Reporting live from Canterbury, Ohio, the latest scene of America's heartland heartbreak, I'm Byron Dennis.'

He held his grave look until the man with the camera nodded. Then his face relaxed and simply looked tired. Seeing Seth Stevens in his peripheral vision, he glanced over. Their eyes met. Byron Dennis nodded. Seth Stevens walked away.

Despite everything, he was hungry again. He didn't want to spend his last few dollars, but he had changed his mind and didn't want to dumpster-dive, either.

A large awning on the lawn of the church shaded several tables and a handful of folding chairs. The chairs were all empty. He walked over. On the tables were half-empty boxes of melting chocolate donuts, warm turkey sandwiches, and crushed bags of cookies and potato chips. There were stacks of Styrofoam cups and large dispensers of coffee, iced tea, and lemonade. He guessed the food was for relief workers and volunteers. He didn't care. He sat down and ate two sandwiches and some chips and cookies. He drank four cups of lemonade. Afterward he felt dozy but resisted the temptation to lie down in the grass and sleep.

Instead he walked to the library.

Amazingly, it was open, although the woman at the desk looked at him with a sad half-smile and red eyes rimmed with tears. He half-smiled back and then followed a sign to the toilets. The drinking fountain outside the men's room had duct tape wound around the faucet and handle. It occurred to him that bottled water might suddenly quadruple in value.

None of the public computer terminals were in use. Indeed, the whole library seemed empty. The screen savers showed slide shows of downtown Canterbury. The photos appeared to have been taken at dawn on Sunday. There weren't any people in them.

He sat down at the computer and opened a browser. He went to the Yahoo home page. He couldn't bear to click on any of the headlines.

Sniper Kills 8, Wounds 32 at Flea Market
Tanker 'Went off Like a Bomb'
IED in Parking Garage
National Guard Mobilized in 17 States
President Blasts 'Second 9/11'
No Suicide Bombers This Time
American al-Qaeda? Ohio Suspect Sought
Amazingly, there were already editorials:
Terror on the Cheap
Were We Sleeping?
9/11 Redux
Will the World Care This Time?

There were pictures, audio, video. His stomach turned. He thought he might vomit. He swallowed it down.

He logged in to his e-mail account. There was a message from Charisma Brown. The subject line read: *Where are you?*

He opened the message. Without reading it, he clicked reply.

I love you, he typed. *I need your help.*

Then he told her where to come get him.

Sixteen

The library closed at six o'clock. He killed time until then, wandering the stacks, returning to the computers every ten minutes to check for a return e-mail from Charisma Brown. Finally the teary-eyed librarian asked him to leave, having already flicked the lights off and on for his benefit.

He stood on the front steps of the library. The sky had clouded over and thunder grumbled in the distance but no rain fell. As the sky darkened, the flashing lights of emergency vehicles made the entire town feel like the crime scene that it was.

No one gave him a second look. Apparently they were still looking for brown-skinned terrorists, the immigrants or children of immigrants who had formed al-Qaeda in America. But it was too risky to stay in town. If any of the hundreds of security personnel moving about—police, deputies, National Guardsmen—found him sleeping in the park, they would be bound to ask him questions. And even innocent questions might lead them in the right direction.

He thought maybe he should turn himself in but thought that he should pray on it first. Terry Kinsman had said that the diplomats of the Embassy of Christianity also worked for the government. He didn't want to die in a jail cell before even coming to trial.

He found a grocery store and spent half of his money on bananas, Pop-Tarts, and bottled water. The bottled water was rationed: one gallon per customer every twelve hours. He heard a clerk explaining to an angry mother that no, she couldn't count all of her children as customers. But more water would be delivered soon.

Carrying his purchases in a plastic bag, he headed back to the picnic ground where he and Terry Kinsman had slept in the truck. The men in the white van would not expect him to go back there, he reasoned. And it was the only place he knew to direct Charisma Brown.

He trudged along the side of the road, walking backward when he heard an approaching car, sticking his thumb out for everything but emergency vehicles.

After he had gone a mile a minivan pulled over. The driver was a worried-looking man with thinning hair who opened the passenger door without asking where he was going.

Seth Stevens climbed in. In the back, three shouting children were strapped into booster seats. When the man asked if he had lost anyone in the attack, the man's concern was almost too painful to bear. Seth Stevens started sobbing. The man reached across and gripped his shoulder as the children suddenly quieted down.

To explain his crying, Seth Stevens lied and said that he had lost someone. To excuse his lie, he told himself that Terry Kinsman was that someone. He knew it didn't count.

The man said that he had lost someone, too: his elderly aunt. He said that they should be strong and keep their faith in God. He said that those who worshipped Allah were lost souls who needed Christian love now more than ever.

Seth Stevens sucked air, his chest heaving, and blinked away hot tears.

The man dropped him off at the picnic ground without asking why he was going there. Seth Stevens held the van door open, thinking he should explain.

'I just need to be alone,' he said.

'I understand,' said the man. 'Pray to Jesus. I call it the miracle cure.'

But Seth Stevens couldn't pray. He watched the van drive off and thought that God knew everything; there was no need to remind him.

In the morning he walked stiffly into the sunshine and sat down, staying there until the chill was gone. He hadn't slept much. There were strange sounds in the trees. And then there was his conscience.

He ate two Pop-Tarts and a banana. He drank some water and started back to town. No drivers stopped to offer him a ride this time and he arrived three hours later, footsore and tired.

He went to the library. It wasn't open yet. He waited until

10:30 a.m., when the librarian he'd seen the day before parked her car on the street out front.

'You again,' she said, seeming to will her voice to breezy familiarity.

'Me again,' he agreed.

He followed her inside and went straight to the computers. They had been shut down the night before. He waited anxiously as the librarian turned on the lights and booted up her own terminal, then finally came over to the public computers and turned them on, too. She entered the password six times and then stepped back.

He felt her staring at him as he brought up the Yahoo home page, so he pretended to read some articles until she went away. Then he read his e-mail.

I'm leaving now, she had written. *I love you, too.*

Relief washed through his body. He wanted to shout, Hallelujah. He settled for a smile.

He mapped directions from Tulsa to Canterbury, which gave him mileage and driving time. He checked the date stamp on Charisma Brown's e-mail and did the math. He had no way of knowing how often or for how long she would stop. But if she drove on the Interstate, he estimated that it could take her as little as half of the time it had taken him and Terry Kinsman to get there.

Glancing up, he saw that the librarian was talking on the phone. She glanced up, too, and saw him looking at her. She looked away quickly. Too quickly, he thought. And why would she need to talk with her whole body angled away from him? He was too far away to hear her.

His relief left as quickly as it had come. With his hands shaking, he closed the browser. Then he reopened it and cleared the page history and the cache memory. Then he closed it again and powered down the computer.

When he passed the circulation desk he mustered a cheery smile and waved goodbye. The librarian lowered the phone to her lap.

'Did you need me to help you find something?' she called after him.

'No,' he said. 'I'm all set.'

He walked swiftly to the doors. Whoever she was talking to had told her to delay him. He left without delay.

A siren whooped as he walked down the library steps. An ambulance sped past. He cut around the side of the library to the alley. He followed the alley, crossed a street, then went down another alley. He turned on to a side street and zigzagged until he was in an unfamiliar part of town.

He saw a laundromat, a locksmith, and a bowling alley. The laundromat's window had a hand-written sign reading *FREE WASH FOR RELIEF WORKERS*. The letters on the bowling alley's sign spelled out *RELIEF WORKERS PLAY FREE*.

It was dark and cool in the bowling alley. No one was standing at the counter and no one was bowling on any of the eight lanes. Wooden cues were crossed on the green cloth of a pool table, and three arcade games blooped and chittered. One of them alternated a short melody with the words, 'The gauntlet is down! Cage match!'

He wanted to stay off the street for a little while. Probably they would look for him on the streets nearest the library. They wouldn't expect him to stop to play games.

The ball return on the pool table had been locked open so no coins were needed to play. He rolled the cues to one side and lifted balls on to the table, setting them inside a flimsy plastic triangle. He chose the straighter of the two cues and leaned the other one against the wall. He sawed the cue back and forth and then broke the rack. The balls separated a little. None of them went into a pocket.

A door opened at the back of the alley, beside the pinsetting machines. A man wiped his greasy hands on a red rag.

'Hi!' he said. 'I'm just in the back. Lane three's broke again.'

The man disappeared, leaving the door open.

Seth Stevens played for awhile. It took him twenty minutes to sink all the balls. He racked and broke again.

He felt his chest constricting. Here he was, in a cheerful little bowling alley, playing a harmless game. It was almost as if the world wasn't falling apart outside.

After forty-five minutes he stopped playing. He wasn't sure whether he was hiding out or trapped. He looked around, wondering if there was anything he needed to take with him. A pool cue? He wasn't planning on fighting anyone.

His eyes settled on the cash register. He willed himself to walk out the door before the thought could sink in.

He had to get back to the picnic ground. But walking along-side the road would give the police seven miles' worth of free chances.

There was a rundown house across the street. Three whole junked cars and pieces of others were spread out over the boulevard, the driveway, and the front yard. A couple of old bicycles leaned against a graying white picket fence.

As quickly as he had walked away from the cash register, he walked across the street and tugged the top bike free. It was a ten-speed, a heavy brand once sold by a major mail-order catalog. The tires were squishy but, as if by a miracle, they were rideable.

He walked the bike to the street. He swung his leg over, pushed away from the curb, and started pedaling. The derailleur clicked and thunked as he worked the shifters. Finally he found the right gear. The wheels started turning. He steered toward the edge of town.

He interrogated himself. Had he ignored the cash register because he couldn't imagine how money could help him? Had he decided to steal the bike because he could?

He told himself he would leave the bike behind. That someone would find it and it would be returned to its rightful owner.

He couldn't remember the last time he'd ridden a bike. It was harder than he remembered. Of course, he was an out-of-shape twenty-four and the tires were soft. He weaved along the shoulder. Cars whizzed by. When trucks passed, he felt the pressure drop pulling him toward the traffic lanes. If he died on this bike, he thought, would that be a message from God?

He was lathered in sweat by the time he reached the picnic ground. It was a warm afternoon, so he stripped to his under-wear and slapped water on his body from the spigot. In the toilet, he took off his jeans and underwear and then pulled his jeans back on. He washed his underwear, socks, and shirt and spread them on bushes to dry.

The remaining food and water were in the trees where he had left them. The sugar from the Pop-Tarts made his teeth hurt and his stomach ache but he ate them anyway.

He settled in to wait.

He moved his wet clothes from sun to sun throughout the day. When there was no more sun finding its way to the ground he put them back on even though they were still a little damp.

His water bottle was empty. He was starting to have visions of bacon double cheeseburgers but resisted the urge to follow them.

Dusk was turning to night when he heard the crunch of tires on gravel. He crouched in the bushes, leaves obscuring his vision.

A car door opened. A seatbelt alarm chimed.

'Seth?' she called. 'Seth? It's me.'

He ran to meet her, not noticing the branches that scratched his face.

They drove an hour north before they stopped to eat. Charisma Brown chose a Perkins. He didn't contest her choice. Inside it looked like they all looked.

They found a quiet booth in the back and held hands across the tabletop. She looked tired, even without the light from above making shadows below her eyes. When the waitress came, they ordered cheeseburgers.

In the car, she had asked him which part of his past had caught up with him. Was it the drugs? Was it the Satanists? She prayed, she told him, that it was nothing to do with the Mormon, whose body had been found the night he had disappeared.

'All Tulsa was talking about it,' she said. 'Until the terrorists attacked.'

When he told her he was with one of the terrorists, she almost drove off the road.

Now he told her everything. He stopped frequently to apologize and tell her that he loved her. He had gone along without thinking hard enough, he said. He had assumed that what came from the church was right. He had had no idea where it was all going.

She looked him in the eye.

'I believe everything you say,' she said. 'Except I'm not sure I believe everything Terry told you. Maybe he was lied to. Or maybe he lied. Uncle Grady isn't perfect, but Christians just don't do stuff like that.'

'Terry said he was a Christian. And I saw what he did with my own eyes.'

The food came. He ate his cheeseburger without stopping to talk. He asked for a refill on his Mountain Dew. He ate his fries and most of hers. She said she wasn't feeling hungry.

The waitress cleared their plates.

'What do we do now?' asked Charisma Brown.

'What should we do?'

'I don't know.'

'I think I want to tell the truth. Go to the newspapers. But I need time to think about how to do it. Terry said that the Embassy of Christianity had high-ranking members from every branch of government. Which means that—'

'Which means that the government could be behind everything. I just don't know if I can believe it.'

'Not the whole government. Some of the people who work for government. Look, I don't know if I believe it, either. But why would he make something like that up?'

'To sound more important? A lot of people will make things up to give them more power over other people.'

'That's what the atheists say.'

'I know. But that's—different.'

He got up and went around to her side of the table. He sat down next to her on the bench seat. She leaned her head on his shoulder.

'There's only one thing I'm sure of,' he said. 'That we should be together.'

She nodded, sniffling a little, and kissed him.

'Me, too,' she said.

As they left the seating area he noticed a man reading the *Canterbury Ledger.* The front-page headline read: *IN OUR PRAYERS TONIGHT.*

Charisma Brown paid the bill while he used the bathroom. He looked bad. He was afraid he smelled worse. He washed the dirt off his face and then wiped under his arms with a wet paper towel.

In the parking lot he saw the man with the newspaper again. Now he was sitting in a parked car and talking on a cell phone. Seth Stevens looked at the racks of newspapers outside the restaurant: *USA Today*, the *Toledo Blade*, a real-estate classified, and an auto trader.

He looked at the man's car: a white Ford Taurus.

He got into Charisma Brown's car. They drove away. Ducking down, he turned in his seat and watched out the back window. When they were almost out of sight of the Perkins, he saw the Taurus come out of the lot and turn their way.

He almost told her that they were being followed but decided not to say anything. He could be wrong, and there was no point frightening her until he knew for sure.

He had hoped to make it to Canada before he called the newspapers. But security would be tight at the border, he knew, because of 9/11 2. And if they were being followed already, then there was nowhere they could run. How had they known to follow Charisma Brown? He had made things easy for them, he supposed, by sending the e-mail from the Canterbury library. Or maybe Citizens for Good Government had keyloggers and they had been checking his e-mail ever since he'd started. Maybe he had been stupid and saved his password there.

They drove north for another hour and then stopped at a budget motel on the outskirts of Toledo. He thought he had seen the Taurus several times en route, but it was hard to tell with headlights shining in his eyes.

Charisma Brown paid for the room while he waited in the car. He told her to use cash and to give a fake license plate number. She hesitated but agreed.

'They looked at me like I was crazy when I said I'd pay cash,' she said when she was done. 'But they took it.'

They drove to the parking spot in front of their room. As he carried her suitcase inside he paused on the threshold, scanning the parking lot. He didn't see a white Taurus. Maybe he was imagining the pursuit. Or maybe the driver had dropped back once he saw them check into the motel.

He locked the door, fastened the chain, and wedged a chair under the door handle. The whole setup looked as if it would last for about three kicks.

Then he turned and Charisma Brown was kissing him hungrily. He kissed her back. They lay on the bed and kissed and groped each other for nearly an hour. Each time it seemed as if they were going to go further one of them would say something and they would stop. They would have a short conversation about something else, a way of talking each other down. Then they would start again. His erection felt like an iron rod.

Then she pushed him away, her eyes closed.

'Do you want to?' she whispered.

'Of course.'

'I want to.'

'Now?'

'Yes.'

He hesitated. He wanted desperately to do it. But he was afraid she would regret it in the morning. He really loved her.

'Are you sure?'

She opened her eyes and kissed him. She nodded seriously.

'I know it's a sin,' she said. 'But what if we never get another chance?'

She unbuttoned her blouse, then sat up and shrugged out of it. She lay back down again and unbuttoned her jeans. He tugged them down slowly. The jeans pulled her panties with them, exposing a curly thatch of dark pubic hair. She pulled her panties back up.

'Now you,' she said.

He stood by the bed and stripped down to his underwear. He wished he had taken a shower. He felt like a virgin. But when he had lost his virginity he had been so drunk that he had vomited afterward.

She stared at the erection tenting his briefs.

'Turn out the light,' she said.

He crossed the room and flipped the switch, stealing a glance through the curtains at the parking lot. He wondered if they were out there, if they were listening or somehow looking through the walls. He went back to the bed.

Their skin was goose-pimpled from the air conditioning, so they lifted the coverlet and slipped into the cool sheets, snuggling their warm bodies together. They kissed some more. Then he reached behind her and fumbled open the snaps of her bra.

She stifled a sob.

'Do you want me to stop?' he said.

She shook her head violently.

'No,' she said. 'No, no, no.'

He pulled down her underwear and then she pulled down his. She touched his penis nervously, trying to guide him to her, then let go.

'You do it,' she whispered.

It was thrilling to be naked with her, finally touching her most intimate place. He had expected her to be wet. But maybe she was nervous. She winced when he started to penetrate her. He spit in his hand and tried to make them both wetter. Then he tried again. She seemed to retreat inside of herself. He asked again if he should stop. She told him no, two times. He pushed harder. She gasped. Then she wrapped her arms around his torso so tightly he could hardly breathe. Then she pushed back.

He woke and reached out for her. The bed was empty. He opened his eyes. The room was lit by a gray shaft of light coming through a crack in the curtains.

She was kneeling beside the bed, her back to him, her head bowed.

He listened for her prayer but she wasn't whispering. Whatever she had to say was between her and God alone.

Despite everything, he was surprised to find that he still believed in God. It was his faith in man that had been shaken. He mistrusted the rapture he had sometimes felt at church. And he suspected that it was he himself, not God, who had caused him to babble in a foreign tongue. But when God's Slaves stood together, wanting to be good and to do good works, that was something real. And when Margo Hofstatter had tried to do God's will by helping him, that was real, too. He didn't know what God looked like or wanted any more than Pastor Grady did, but he thought that maybe God wanted them to be kind to each other. And maybe that was enough.

He hoped Terry Kinsman had been given a second chance at the seat of judgment.

He waited until Charisma Brown was done with her prayer before he spoke. She was already half-dressed, wearing a T-shirt and panties.

'Are you sorry?' he asked.

She startled and turned around. Her eyes were red. She smiled.

'No. Are you?'

'No. I just—'

'You just don't want to hurt me. Seth, you've hurt a lot of people, even if it wasn't on purpose. But you haven't hurt me.'

He stared at her, aching with longing. She was so beautiful and so kind. If he could be with her, he knew he could be happy forever.

And then he knew what he had to do.

They showered and dressed separately. He used her razor to scrape the scruff from his cheeks and chin. She had brought some of her brother's clothes for him. They were too big but at least they were clean.

When they pulled out of the motel parking lot, a Ford Taurus fell in behind them. This one was black, not white.

He wondered how the hero in a spy movie would handle the situation. Probably by telling Charisma Brown to make a sudden right, then an immediate U-turn so they could watch the other driver's reaction. More probably the hero in the movie would take one glance in the rear-view and know. Seth Stevens knew, too.

What he didn't know was why they were following him. They had found him. If they wanted to take him, they could have done it during the night. So maybe they wanted to see where he was going.

He also didn't know who they were. But, ironically, if they hadn't broken down the motel-room door, they were probably not law-abiding members of government. They were probably with the Embassy of Christianity or one of the other groups that had organized 9/11 2.

But no matter who or why, they wanted him. They couldn't have had any interest in Charisma Brown—unless they thought he had told her something. So the more he told her, and the longer they stayed together, the more she was at risk.

They drove in silence, holding hands over the emergency brake. Sometimes he saw the Taurus behind them and sometimes he didn't. They were headed toward Detroit. With luck, they could pass into Canada with the outbound commuters at rush hour. At least, that was the plan they had agreed on.

They stopped for gas an hour later. Charisma Brown was about to pull into a small service station when he pointed her to a busy truck stop across the road. There would be less chance of being remembered, he said. When they pulled up at the pump, the Taurus stopped to refuel, too.

Charisma Brown got out and unscrewed the gas-tank cap.

Seth Stevens stood outside his door and stared at the Taurus. Its driver was a middle-aged man wearing a striped golf shirt and tan chinos. He was paunchy and balding but held himself like a cop.

Seth Stevens stared. The man didn't look.

Charisma Brown swiped her credit card and lifted the nozzle out of the pump. The man did the same thing.

Seth Stevens kept staring. The man glanced up. He saw Seth Stevens looking. He looked away.

Charisma Brown pulled the trigger. There was a hollow sound as gas rushed into her empty tank. Seth Stevens walked around to her side of the car. He told her that he needed to use the toilet. He kissed her, squeezed her hand, and turned away, hot tears already rolling down his cheeks.

He went into the truck stop. To the left was a combination grocery, hardware, and auto-parts store. To the right, past a small arcade, were hallways leading to showers and a diner. He walked toward the showers, then went past them and out a back door. Squinting in the sunlight, he saw a vast lot lined with idling semis.

He walked forward. The air shimmered and rippled over the black asphalt. The enormous trucks were white, black, and sparkly red. They rumbled and hummed. An approaching truck slowed with an exhalation of its brakes.

Some of the trucks had chrome silhouettes of naked women on their mudflaps. One of them had a decal on its trailer door. Under the word 'Risen', the decal showed Jesus' tomb with the rock rolled away.

He remembered hearing about the 'Risen Truckers' from Margo Hofstatter. They were born-agains who had become disgusted by the immoral lifestyles they witnessed on the road. Many truckers took speed, bought prostitutes, and broke the law if it helped them make more money. The Risen Truckers identified themselves to each other by decals and tattoos. When they found each other, they held impromptu prayers and Bible studies.

Seth Stevens walked alongside the trailer until he reached the cab. He stopped, looking up at the door. It was impossible to see inside. Should he knock on the door? What if the driver were sleeping inside?

'Help you, son?'

He whirled. Behind him stood a man with a torso like a bull and legs like a calf. The man stood warily, as if his fears of trouble were often realized.

Seth Stevens wasn't sure how to proceed.

'I saw the Risen decal,' he said.

'Uh huh?'

'I was glad to find a Christian.'

'And why's that?'

'I need help, sir. Just a ride. Can you give me a ride out of here?'

'Why's that?'

'Someone's chasing me.'

'Why's that?'

'I can't tell you. Believe me, you don't want to get messed up in it.'

'Drugs?'

Seth Stevens shook his head.

'I swear, no.'

The trucker looked him up and down, then took a few steps closer.

'You've accepted Jesus Christ as your lord and savior?'

'Yes.'

'And you renounce Satan and his evil works?'

'Yes.'

The trucker shook his head, as if at his own folly, then walked past Seth Stevens. He unlocked the door of his cab and climbed up.

'Other side,' he said over his shoulder.

Seth Stevens ran around to the other side and climbed up into the cab.

The trucker's name was Van Ford.

'Name like that,' he said, 'how could I been anythin' else but a trucker?'

He was going south and east. Seth Stevens said that that was fine by him, perfect, actually. Van Ford peppered him with questions about the Bible, glancing over from time to time. Seth Stevens got a few wrong, but he must have gotten enough right to pass. Van Ford started to relax. He offered Seth Stevens a Slim Jim and some Mountain Dew.

'Sorry I seemed so unfriendly,' he said. 'You wouldn't

believe the people I run into out here: punks, drunks, druggies, trannies, thieves, skeeves, sickos, and dick-o's. Seen
people'd slit your throat for the gas in your tank, people'd
whore their own sisters, mothers, daughters, brothers. People
who take the name of the Lord in vain like they was sayin'
and. Lord tells us to keep our heart open to our fellow man,
and I try, but let me tell you, you got to keep it locked at
nighttime.'

The words rolled off his tongue as if rehearsed. Seth Stevens
imagined that Van Ford had told his story thousands of times
over the years.

Like most born-agains, he had a tale of woe. He had been
a beer drunk, prone to fits of temper and fighting. When he
raised his hand against his wife, though, he had heard a voice
commanding him to stop. The voice, he said, of God.

Seth Stevens stared through the windshield, glancing over
and nodding as if he was listening. His chest felt empty. He
had done the wrong thing in leaving Charisma Brown. How
could he have not even told her he was going? Every few
minutes he cleared his throat to tell Van Ford to stop the truck
and let him off. But he didn't say anything. The truck kept
rolling down the freeway.

'Somethin' in your throat, Seth? Need another Dew?'

He nodded even though he didn't. Van Ford reached into a
cooler he kept by his seat and fished out a can of Mountain
Dew that was bobbing in melted ice. The water dripped on
Seth Stevens's jeans.

'So what's your story?' said Van Ford.

Seth Stevens knew this cue. At God's Slaves, newly met
acquaintances told their worst sins first, then told how they
had triumphed with the love of God. It had taken him aback
at first. Even among the gutterpunks, the Hessians, and the
tweakers, the worst secrets—abuse, incest, rape—took a long
time to come out. Sometimes they never did, and the person
with the secret would disappear or die without telling their
story. But born-agains didn't seem to fear that darkness.
Beating the Devil was their badge of honor. The story of spiritual death and rebirth was their handshake.

Seth Stevens had told his story many times. He could do
it in three to five minutes. He knew which details to include,
when to hurry the chronology, where to end it. His story had

always been popular at church because, while sins of theft, violence, drunkenness, and drug abuse were common, very few stories included homelessness and heavy metal. And the fact that he was from New York City was in itself enough to drop the jaws of many Oklahomans.

He didn't feel like telling his story but he told it anyway. It took longer than usual, as Van Ford prodded him with questions whenever he tried to go too quickly.

'So that's it?' asked Van Ford.

'That's it.'

'Seems like there's a big gap there. Way we left it, you was in church. Now you're in a truck.'

'I told you, Van, I can't tell you what's going on. You're a nice guy. I can't let you get hurt.'

If Van Ford didn't believe this, he didn't let on. He nodded and scratched his clean-shaven chin.

'No, fair enough. I appreciate that, Seth. I want to help you, but I'm not sure my wife would want me goin' to jail for you. But there's one part of the story we can fill in: where you're goin'. You're goin' back to New York City to see your mama, huh?'

The thought had never even occurred to him. But he said yes anyway.

Seventeen

They drove straight through to Cleveland. Van Ford bought Seth Stevens a late lunch while his trailer was being unloaded at a large distribution center. Then they drove down to Akron to pick up another load. The load wasn't ready, so Van Ford bought him an early dinner while they waited. Then they drove into Pennsylvania. Around midnight, they pulled over at a truck stop so Van Ford could get four hours' sleep in the back of his cab. Seth Stevens stayed in the passenger seat, dozing and watching the other trucks come and go.

They reached Harrisburg at dawn. Van Ford said that it was as close to New York as he was going. He was headed south to Baltimore. They stood on the damp asphalt outside the bus station and exchanged goodbyes. Van Ford pressed five twenties into Seth Stevens's hand, 'for a bus ticket and some food'. Then they prayed together. Seth Stevens liked Van Ford's prayer. It was quiet, with no speaking in tongues and no hand-waving.

Holy Father who art in Heaven
Watch over Seth and guide him in the right path
That he may walk righteous and treat his fellow man
As good as he deserves to be treated
We are all sinners, Lord
Not worthy of your sight
But forgive us our sins that we may
Sit by your feet in Heaven.

They amened. Van Ford surprised him by giving him a hug. Then Van Ford climbed into his truck. He gave a blast of the air horn and waved as the long trailer swung out on to the street. It occurred to Seth Stevens that he had never asked Van Ford what he was hauling.

He went into the bus station. The ticket windows were shuttered. He sat down on a bench and waited until one of the windows opened at 8 a.m. Then he went over and asked for a ticket to New York City.

As he had come further east, he had noticed more signs that the country was on alert. Highway patrol cars idled in truck stops. Flags flew at half-mast. And traffic signs informed drivers that Homeland Security had declared a red alert.

The clerk at the window was Seth Stevens's age, clean-cut and skinny. He quoted a price and, while Seth Stevens counted out the money, asked to see some ID.

Seth Stevens had never applied for a driver's license, of course. All he had was a generic ID issued by the state of Oklahoma. The clerk eyed it intently.

'Long ways from home, huh?' he said.

'I'm traveling. That's why I'm in a bus station,' said Seth Stevens, immediately regretting it.

The clerk looked wounded.

'No need to get snippy with me,' he said. 'Everybody's on edge. You should be, too. You should thank me for asking to see your ID. I'm the one's keeping you safe.'

'No, you're right,' said Seth Stevens. 'Sorry.'

The clerk made sure to enter his address and phone number before handing back the ID. He printed the ticket and counted back the change in silence.

The bus came at 9:20 a.m. Seth Stevens killed time outside the station until 9:10, then went to the gate and walked directly on to the bus.

As they pulled out, he saw the clerk standing in the station doorway, scanning the tinted windows of the bus.

Seth Stevens leaned away from the glass.

He arrived in Port Authority at 2:45. He felt lost for a moment, like a tourist. Then his memory returned and he found his way to the subway and got on a train to the Bronx.

His mother had moved more times than he could remember, but she had given him the most recent address during her current bout with sobriety, so he thought she might still live there. He changed trains once and in late afternoon arrived at a four-story walk-up on a quiet, littered street.

The buzzer appeared to be broken. He sat by the door and

waited. After a while, a heavyset woman sighed up the steps with shopping bags bumping her thighs. She set the bags down and fumbled for her key. When he offered to hold the door for her she turned and began berating him furiously in a Jamaican accent.

'Now why would I let some little white boy steal his way into my building just because he has a smile and ask politely? Why? Go on with you!'

Chastened, he backed all the way down to the sidewalk. When she went inside he climbed the steps again. A little while later a teenage boy with unlaced shoes slapped out of the door, noticing but not caring that Seth Stevens slipped in behind him.

He went upstairs slowly. Like most of the places his mother had lived, he had never been there. It had been just an address on a piece of paper. Now he saw a stairwell with too many doors on each landing. Most of the light bulbs were missing but he could still see how dirty the carpet and walls were. Gang members had markered their elaborate runes on to the paint and even the wood. From behind a door with four locks on it came the sounds of a popular trial show. Something to do with a purebred puppy that had been sold without papers.

Finally he stood in front of 4C. He knocked.

'Who is it?' came the answer.

'It's me,' he said. 'Seth.'

'Who?'

'Your son, Seth.'

The door opened a crack, tethered by a security chain. He saw a warm brown face with a gimlet eye. The woman with the groceries.

'You that lady son? Janet?'

He nodded.

She sighed. She looked down and shook her head. Then she unfastened the chain.

His mother was drinking again. She had been evicted from the apartment. The program had given the apartment to the Jamaican woman, who refused to tell Seth Stevens her name. When she arrived, she said, his mother was still there, drunk and angry. Two male social workers carried Jan Stevens downstairs and sat with her on the stoop. They asked if she needed to go to the hospital. She said no. They asked if she needed food. She said no. They reminded her that she had violated the program's rules three times. There were other women trying to get their lives on track, too, and now it was their turn to try. Jan Stevens asked the men for money. One of them gave her ten dollars and told her to buy food. He told her she was welcome to reapply for the program's waiting list.

Seth Stevens listened, feeling a familiar numbness flooding his body. When the woman was done talking, he nodded and started for the door. He couldn't think of anything to say.

'Don't you wanna ask where she is?' said the woman.

He stopped.

'Do you know?'

She shook her head.

'Not for certain. But the program has a kitchen, you know, for homeless. Maybe you ask there. Maybe she goes there again.'

Now he sat on a bus that was hiccupping its way through rush-hour traffic. The program, he had learned, was run by a church. A Catholic church. Not that his mother would have given it much thought. She might have noticed the statues of the saints.

The church and its buildings took up half a block. The large, rough-hewn stones of the church itself were blackened with the soot of more than a century. The other buildings were made of slim blonde bricks and looked as if they had been built in the 1950s. When he arrived, a blade of sun was cutting through the surrounding mid-rises to light up the stained-glass window in the front of the church. But it was hard to see the intricately cut and colored panes behind the scarred and weathered Plexiglas that protected them.

He found the door to the soup kitchen and joined the line for dinner. He stood behind an exhausted-looking black woman with three tired children and in front of a white-bearded man who looked like a Depression-era hobo. The smell of alcohol seeped from the man's pores. It reminded Seth Stevens of the way his mother used to smell in the morning.

At the door, a middle-aged woman in a tracksuit was vetting the new arrivals. She greeted many of them by name. Others she moved out of the line with a pointed finger, where they were frisked by a white-haired man whose build suggested he might have been a wrestling coach. Still others she turned back with a shake of her head. Her manner was friendly but professional. With her left hand she clicked off new arrivals on a plastic counting device.

She pointed Seth Stevens over to the coach. The frisking was swift but thorough. He might have gotten a pocket knife through but he doubted it.

Then he was in the dining room. It was the size of a high-school cafeteria. There were maybe 150 people and room for twice as many. They queued at steam tables with sneeze guards, where three hair-netted women ladled food on to their plates. Then they sat down at long, low tables that looked as if they had come from a high-school cafeteria.

He had thought about asking the workers if they knew his mother. Even surrounded by so many hard-luck cases, he found the prospect embarrassing.

But he was not too proud to eat. He joined the line and was given meatloaf, mashed potatoes with gravy, and carrots that had had the orange cooked out of them.

He walked up and down each row of tables. He didn't see his mother. He sat down and started to eat.

There was a television behind a cage on the wall. Its picture was fuzzy and jittery. The sound was too low to hear. But he could see pictures of soldiers, tanks, and fighter planes. The soldiers were marching in front of the White House. The tanks were crossing the Golden Gate Bridge. And the fighters were streaking past the Empire State Building. It occurred to him that, even though he had been traveling through the country, without watching TV he had had no idea what was happening.

He heard raised voices at the front door. A woman's voice, insisting that she was not drunk. She promised she wasn't, she swore it, she swore to God she wasn't.

He turned. The woman at the door clicked her counter, shaking her head. A bony brunette lurched past her and into the room.

The woman was his mother.

He had thought he might run to her. Instead he sat and watched. Carefully, as if the floor were the deck of a ship at sea, she circumnavigated the room until she found the end of the food line. Once in line she stopped paying attention. Only the nudges of the man behind her kept her moving forward. She took a tray, a plate, and a glass of lemonade and carried them carefully to a table. His table. She set the tray down too hard, spilling a little.

She was across from him, only seven seats over.

He cleared his throat.

He watched her eat.

She seemed so much older than when he had seen her two years earlier. Up close, he saw that her dark hair was threaded with gray. Her skin was sallow and lined. She had a fat lip and a yellowing bruise on her cheek, and the skin on the backs of her hands was red and scaly.

The bruise, he thought, could have come from a fight. It could just as easily have come from a fall. She had always been prone to both kinds of bruises.

She ate slowly, sleepily. She didn't look up from her plate, making it hard at times to tell whether her eyes were even open. But she kept eating, first the meatloaf, then the mashed potatoes, until she had finished them both. She left the carrots untouched.

None of the diners had prayed before eating, he noticed. He had forgotten to pray, too. There was a five-foot-tall crucifix on one wall, with a thick, gilt-edged Bible lying open on a reading stand below it, but other than that, there were few reminders that they were being fed by a church. He had heard of soup kitchens where meals were only given after sermons. Maybe the sermon was still to come.

His mother set her fork down next to her plate. She bowed her head as if in deep thought or silent prayer. After a moment he realized that she was sleeping.

He rose, ready to wake her up. But first he had to decide what he would say to her. Why had he come here? Was it because, after all that had happened, he had realized that he was just a boy who needed his mother? Was he so desperate for a safe haven that he was willing to put his hope in someone so hopeless?

The shell of a woman before him would keep him safe from nothing.

Or had he come here because of what Charisma Brown had said, because he had hurt a lot of people? He knew it was true. Had he come here to blame his mother for it? To blame her weakness for his weakness, her failures for his failures?

Or had he come here to help her? That was what it meant to be a Christian, he thought. To help those who could not help you. To forgive those who could not forgive you.

On the TV on the wall, the President was talking. Behind him stood a wall of uniforms, olive, khaki, camouflage, black, and white. He rested his hands on a podium with a picture of the White House on it. Superimposed on the screen were the words: *PRESIDENT'S MESSAGE TO NATION*. In the dining hall, no one was watching.

He imagined the words he could say: *Mom, I'm sorry.* Or: *Mom, I forgive you.* Or: *Mom, we're going home.*

He imagined standing her up and walking her out. But where would they go? They were both homeless now. And was he strong enough to carry her? Hopelessness drained his strength. His arms felt leaden.

She was wearing a hooded sweatshirt, men's work pants, and filthy white sneakers. She probably had a punk band's T-shirt on underneath the sweatshirt. Somehow she had always managed to hang on to those. Her clothes were dirty. She was sleeping rough somewhere. She had almost certainly run out of couches to crash on.

He wanted to wake her up and talk to her. But he couldn't imagine the right ending for the conversation. He couldn't think of anything to say that they hadn't said before. He felt different now, but he didn't know what to do that was different.

People were finishing their dinners. They stood and carried their trays to a row of large trash cans. They shook their plastic dinnerware into the cans and banged the trays to loosen uneaten food. They stacked the trays on battered metal carts, then filed out through a door he hadn't noticed. Over the door was the word *Sanctuary*.

So there was a sermon.

His mother's back rose and fell, her breathing deep and regular.

On the TV, the president was still speaking. New words were superimposed on the screen: *MARTIAL LAW; ELEC-TIONS SUSPENDED*.

In the dining hall, no one was watching.

On the TV, the President bowed his head in prayer. Behind him, the generals did, too.

'I forgive you,' Seth Stevens told his mother.

Then he walked out through the door marked *Sanctuary*. He walked through the church and outside into the cool evening. Helicopters chopped the air overhead. Sirens rose and fell and rose again.

Eighteen

His new plan was simple: call the *Washington Post* and tell them everything. Executing the plan would be more complicated. The reporters might have a hard time finding evidence to support his claims. He would have to help them. After all, he was evidence himself. He would show up in person.

It was ten o'clock when he reached Penn Station. He bought a ticket to Washington, D.C. The train would leave at 3 a.m. and arrive at 7 a.m. He waited in the station, visiting the men's room frequently to slap cold water on his face. Not wanting to draw attention, he resisted the urge to lie down on a bench. He wished he had inherited his mother's ability to sleep sitting up. That would have been one worthwhile inheritance, anyway.

When he did doze off, he was prodded awake and asked for his ticket by some National Guardsmen who were patrolling the station. He had been asked for his ID when he bought his ticket, but the ticket alone seemed to satisfy the Guardsmen. They looked like high-school teachers, like union laborers, like college students. Some of them looked bored. More of them looked excited.

At one point he decided to go outside to clear his head, but a Guardsman stopped him at the revolving door.

'Curfew,' he said. 'You're gonna have to stay in here.'

Seth Stevens returned to his bench and tried to sleep with his eyes open.

At 2:45 a.m. he found the track and boarded his train. Soldiers were patrolling the platform with barking dogs and using angled mirrors on long poles to peer under the cars. Conductors were checking tickets and IDs against a list.

The train pulled away half an hour late.

He found a seat in an almost empty car and leaned back,

grateful to have four hours to sleep. The train glided out of the station. He was unconscious before the train went aboveground.

He woke up not knowing where he was. Then he remembered: the train. He looked out the window. The sun was up. He had no idea where the train was. He saw trees, freeways, overpasses, strip malls.

There was a new man sitting in his car. The man was reading the *New York Post*. When he lowered the paper to turn the page he glanced at Seth Stevens. The man looked familiar. He smiled and raised the newspaper again.

In a way, Seth Stevens had never really believed that they were following him. It seemed almost egotistical to believe that he was that important to anyone. But, of course, in a backward way, he was.

He remembered where he had seen the face before: in a Ford Taurus. The man had a habit of buying newspapers in the towns where he started following Seth Stevens. They had gotten his information when he bought the train ticket. Or maybe even when he bought the bus ticket in Pennsylvania. For people who were running the country, a small piece of information like that would be easy to obtain.

The train began to slow down. He stood up. The newspaper didn't move. He yawned gratuitously, then sauntered off in search of the toilets. If he had had a backpack, he would have left it on his seat.

He used the toilet and then took a seat in another car. The man hadn't followed him. Of course, there could be other men.

He looked out the window. He had had a notion that the train would glide past the Washington Monument, the Capitol Building, the White House. But the nation's capitol looked like just another city, one that lay low and flat in the bright late-summer sunshine.

When the train stopped in the station, he was waiting by the door with a small knot of the other overnight travelers. He got off with them, matching his stride to theirs, trying to stay in their midst. But within fifty yards the knot had unraveled and he was alone.

He quickened his pace, then suddenly stopped and pretended to tie his shoe. He looked behind himself. The man with the paper was tying his own shoe, the *New York Post* tucked under his arm. Their eyes met. The man with the newspaper grinned.

Seth Stevens took off at a fast walk. Without even thinking where he was going, he weaved between other passengers, slipped through sliding doors, ran, stopped, doubled back, and then pressed himself against the wall beside a shuttered newsstand. He waited five minutes. Ten.

He had a vision of himself on a monitor screen, pressed against the wall. The technicians watching the monitor were laughing. Another screen showed a red dot for each of the agents following him. The red dots were converging.

He told himself he was being paranoid. He dug the fingernails of his right hand into the flesh of his left forearm. It helped a little. He started walking again, looking for a phone.

He asked a man pushing a gray plastic tilt truck. The man pointed. Seth Stevens ran. Miraculously, a bank of old-fashioned phone booths appeared. He entered the first one and closed the door. A discolored rectangle showed where a phone had once been bolted to the brass.

He tried the next booth. There was a phone. There wasn't a phone book. Amazingly, he remembered the phone number for the *Washington Post* newsroom. He lifted the receiver and dialed. A computer voice told him to please deposit fifty cents. He dug in his pocket and found one quarter and two dimes. He pushed the coins through the slot. The computer voice asked him to please deposit five more cents. He checked his pockets again. He didn't have a nickel. He banged the receiver into the cradle, then lifted it and did it several more times. His breath was coming quickly. Blood thundered in his head. He could hardly think.

He lifted the receiver again and dialed the operator. A computer voice asked, in infuriatingly casual tones, how it could assist him.

'Collect call,' he said.

'I think you said that you would like to make a collect call,' said the computer voice. 'Please answer "yes" if this is correct, "no" if this is incorrect.'

'Yes!' he shouted.

With maddening slowness, the computer guided him through the process. He dialed the number he wanted. He spoke his name. Then he waited while the phone rang.

'National desk,' said a sleepy voice.

He heard the recording of himself saying, 'Seth Stevens.'

'—is trying to make a collect call,' continued the computer voice. 'Please press one to accept the charges. Press two to decline the charges.'

There was a snort at the other end of the line.

'Listen to this,' said the sleepy voice to someone. 'First ring of the day and it's a collect call. Un-freaking-believable.'

Seth Stevens suddenly wondered if the man could hear him, too.

'Hi!' he shouted. 'Don't hang up! Don't hang up!'

'Who is this?'

'I did not register your response,' said the computer voice. 'Please press one to accept the charges. Press two to decline the charges.'

'Listen, I'm in a phone booth and I don't have change. I have a story about 9/11 2. I know who's behind it.'

'Me, too, pal. Because guess what? They confessed already.'

'They what?'

'Al-Qaeda in America. Maybe you don't read newspapers or watch TV.'

'I did not register your response. Please press one to accept the charges. Press two to decline the charges. If you do not select either option, the line will be disconnected.'

'It's not. It's us. It's Christians. The Embassy of Christianity.'

The man paused.

'I called before, about Ira Isaacs. From Oklahoma. That was me—I was the one who called.'

'What's your number there?' asked the man.

Seth Stevens found it and read it off.

'Thank you,' said the computer voice. 'Goodbye.'

The line went dead.

He expected the phone to ring right away. It didn't. He slumped down to the floor, where at least he was hidden from passersby. He tried to guess how much time was passing. Five minutes? Ten? Fifteen?

The phone rang. He reached up, snatched it off the hook, and pulled it down to the floor with him.

'Hello?'

He heard a different voice than before. A woman.

'Seth Stevens?'

'Yes.'

'What's your tip again? The guy who answered the phone didn't believe you.'

Seth Stevens told her.

'I don't believe you, either.'

'I have evidence. I mean, I don't have evidence, but I can tell you things that you can verify. That's what you do, right?'

'Listen, we've gotten hundreds of calls from people telling us they have hot information about 9/11 2. Even after we take out the flying saucers, there are still too many for us to investigate. So don't waste my time.'

'I'm not. But you have to meet me. They're following me. I'm hiding in the train station but I think I lost them.'

'They're *following* you? You've gotta be kidding me.'

He wished he had something to say that would cut through her cynicism and doubt and make her realize that what was happening was real. He wondered if there had been other callers whose truth was ignored because it was simply too frightening to be believed.

'I'm not,' he said.

She sighed. Then she gave him a time and an address.

'I'll meet you for lunch,' she said. 'If I like what I hear, it's my treat. If my jaded reporter's sixth sense doesn't start to tingle, we're going Dutch.'

'What's your name?' he asked.

'Connie McGarrigle,' she said.

He remembered.

'You wrote the story about Holly Lee and Ira Isaacs.'

'You know how to read, that's a start.'

'I'm in the Free Church of God's Slaves.'

She was silent for a moment.

'OK, that's interesting,' she said. She repeated the details of their meeting, this time more slowly.

'What do you look like?' he asked her.

'Katharine Hepburn as a power forward. What do you look like?'

'I'll be the one who looks scared and needs a shower.'

'Looking forward to it,' she said.

The line went dead.

He opened the phone booth door and looked out. He didn't see anyone. Wishing he had asked for directions, he started running.

He saw a clock: 7:52 a.m.

He turned a corner in to a crowded concourse. Travelers were streaming through the doors. In the center of the floor, four National Guardsmen stood in a circle, facing out, scanning the crowd.

Seth Stevens pushed through the people and out the doors. At the curb, a beat-up Mazda with a taxi light on top was letting a passenger out. He jumped in. The taxi driver turned and smiled. A skinny man with a bald head the color of a coffee bean, he barely seemed to fit inside the small car.

'Where to, Mister?' he said.

Seth Stevens didn't know. It was too early to go to the restaurant, but he wanted to find out where it was. Hopefully without creating another witness.

The address that Connie McGarrigle had given him was on the 2300 block of Massachusetts Avenue Northwest. He told the driver a number 1000 higher, thinking he would walk down.

The driver eyed him dubiously.

'You sure, Mister? What do you need there?'

'Just go, please?'

The taxi started to move.

Seth Stevens emptied his pocket. He had eight dollars. On the seatback in front of him, a map divided the city into zones and explained the charges from zone to zone. It didn't help him any. He didn't know which zone he was in and he didn't know which zone he was going to.

'I have eight dollars,' he blurted out.

The driver looked at him in the rear-view mirror.

'That is not enough.'

'Can you take me part of the way? Take me eight dollars closer.'

The driver shook his head.

'I will take you there. Maybe someday you can do a favor for me.'

Washington had a different feel than New York. He had read somewhere that no building was allowed to be taller than the Washington Monument. He didn't know if that was true, but he didn't see any skyscrapers, either, just endless walls of medium-height buildings. It made him think for some reason of the Pentagon, a building that he had only seen in pictures, but whose hallways must have been long enough to form a city.

The taxi stopped in a leafy area, in front of a nameplate for the Embassy of the Apostolic Nunciature of the Holy See. He surrendered the last of his money, thanked the driver, and climbed out.

He walked past the walls and fences of secluded buildings until he crossed Rock Creek. Then it was as if he was in a city again. He saw a few early tourists and some students but most of the people on the street were dressed for work. They carried briefcases, newspapers, and coffee. They looked crisp, clean, and confident. He imagined that many of them worked for government, both American and foreign. Martial law was in effect but work must go on.

The blocks seemed long. He was tired. He saw the embassies of Turkey, Japan, and South Korea, of Lesotho, the Marshall Islands, and Latvia. There were many others. He counted down the addresses, watching for the restaurant where he would meet the reporter. He saw a discreet neon rainbow in a window and was surprised at a gay bar's proximity to the outposts of diplomacy.

Then suddenly he saw two huge Christian flags lifted like sails in the morning breeze. He saw a brass plate bolted into the wall: *EMBASSY OF CHRISTIANITY*.

He looked across the street and saw the restaurant, Café Gepetto, where Connie McGarrigle had said she would meet him. What was going on? Was the location just a coincidence? Or was the reporter having a joke at his expense? Or did she hope he could identify people coming and going from the Embassy of Christianity?

What if Connie McGarrigle was a Christian ambassador?

If they had set a trap for him, he had one thing in his favor: he had arrived before they expected him. He backtracked to a nearby corner where there was a cluster of newspaper boxes. He had to wait twenty minutes before someone bought a *Washington Post*. Then he lunged forward and caught the spring-loaded door before it snapped shut.

The man who had bought the newspaper stopped and stared. He wore an expensive suit with a pink shirt and a pink-striped tie.

'That's theft, you know,' he said.

'I don't have the money,' said Seth Stevens.

Shaking his head, the man held out two quarters.

Seth Stevens took the quarters. He closed the newspaper box. He pushed the quarters through the slot. He opened the box and took a newspaper.

'That's better,' said the man as he walked away.

Seth Stevens scanned the front page of the paper. Then he laid it on the box and opened it. He started turning pages, his eyes jumping from byline to byline. Sid Klein. Janet Pederson. Royce Willeford. Stephan Lees. Shirin Manfour.

Finally, on page twenty-three of the front section, over a six-inch column about Homeland Security's decision to keep the nation's alert level at red, he saw her name: Connie McGarrigle.

It didn't prove anything. Someone named Connie McGarrigle worked for the newspaper. Whether she also worked for the Embassy of Christianity—or whether she was really the woman who would be meeting him—was impossible to say. He had hoped that there would be a picture of her.

He told himself he was being paranoid. But why had she chosen a restaurant right across the street from the place he needed to avoid the most?

Because even if she believed him that Christians were responsible for 9/11 2, she would have no way of knowing that these particular Christians were responsible. And, for all he knew, the *Washington Post* was right around the corner. For all he knew, she ate lunch at this restaurant every day.

He walked back up the block and stood on the sidewalk in front of the Embassy of Christianity. Blinds were drawn behind the windows. Inside the front door he could see a plush-carpeted reception area with comfortable-looking chairs. The business hours had been painted on the glass in gold: 9 to 5, Monday through Friday.

He looked across the street. Café Gepetto didn't serve break-fast. On the sidewalk, stacked chairs and folded tables were threaded by long, locked loops of silver cable.

He wished he could go into the restaurant right away, to take a table and sip water until Connie McGarrigle showed up. He was afraid that if he walked away he would never get back, that he would disappear and his story would never be told.

A long black limousine pulled up to the curb. The driver got out and circled to the curbside passenger door. He opened it.

Seth Stevens gaped as Uncle Frank got out, then turned and offered a hand to Pastor Grady. The two men started for the embassy entrance. A pert, professional woman had appeared inside and was unlocking the doors for them.

Pastor Grady, smiling, looked up and down the block. He saw Seth Stevens. His smile softened and his eyebrows furrowed.

'Seth?' he said.

Uncle Frank turned. Uncle Frank recognized him.

Seth Stevens ran. As he ran, he kept turning to look and staggering off course. Uncle Frank followed him to the first corner, a cell phone already at his ear. But then Uncle Frank stopped. Seth Stevens kept running. He kept turning to look. He couldn't see if he was being followed. He smashed into a lamppost and was spun around. He hobbled along, gritting his teeth at the pain in his shoulder.

He lost them. He got lost.

He went into an alley. Halfway in, he found a stack of broken-down cardboard boxes. He sat down.

He waited.

While he waited he thought about Pastor Grady. He believed that Pastor Grady was a good man, or at least wanted to do good. He wondered how much Pastor Grady knew. He thought about the Free Church of God's Slaves and the thousands of people who came twice each week to listen to Pastor Grady. Though nothing Pastor Grady had said had ever led him to believe that it was acceptable to hurt people in God's name.

He felt strangely comfortable in the alley. The spray-paint, the dented security doors, the trash, the bugs—it all reminded him of when he had been an addict. Things had been simpler then. He had one overriding need and he existed to fulfill it.

If only life were so simple again, he thought ruefully.

He decided not to miss his meeting with Connie McGarrigle. He didn't know where else to run. And even if he knew where to go, he didn't know how to get there.

He waited. It was quiet in the alley. He waited until he thought an hour had passed and then he waited another hour. Then he crept to the edge of the alley and asked a woman walking by what time it was. Ten fifteen, she told him.

He waited another two hours and then asked again. Now it was eleven thirty. He thought that probably he should wait until noon before he left, just to make sure the reporter was already there.

He couldn't wait. He stood up and started walking. He asked directions to the restaurant. He was there in ten minutes. There was nobody on the street in front of the Embassy of Christianity. He doubted that they would be at the windows watching for him.

He went to the front door of Café Gepetto. The hostess frowned at him when he asked for a table. He told her he was meeting Connie McGarrigle. The hostess frowned at her reservation list. But Connie McGarrigle had called ahead. The hostess seated him inside.

The restaurant was empty. He drank water and ate every piece of bread in the basket: dinner roll, sourdough with dill, black rye, pretzel bread, and something he didn't know the name for.

A busboy refilled his water and brought another bread basket.

The clock ticked. Several tables filled up. Seth Stevens started going over his story, trying to think of the most efficient way to tell it. The facts got jumbled up. He wasn't sure which parts were the most important. He couldn't remember the order in which things had happened. But Connie McGarrigle would be able to help him make sense of it all. Unless her real motive was to keep him from telling his story.

He tried to anticipate her questions. One in particular came to mind. At the end of it, after he had told her everything, perhaps after she had sheltered him in her apartment while the newspaper published a week-long series of articles, she would ask: do you still consider yourself a Christian?

I believe in God, he would say, but I'm not sure if I still believe in church.

A man came in and sat alone at the bar. He was carrying a newspaper, the *Washington Post*. He smiled at Seth Stevens. Seth Stevens knew him. He felt his forehead getting hot.

He looked at the clock on the wall: 12:05.

He looked out the window: Uncle Frank was helping Pastor Grady back into the limousine.

At the bar, the man with the newspaper snapped his cell phone shut.

Seth Stevens pushed his chair back and bolted. He scattered

furniture and pulled down a heavy chrome hat rack behind him.

Outside, on the sidewalk, his eyes pulsed in the bright sunlight. The limousine was pulling away. The man with the newspaper was coming after him.

Just down the sidewalk, two bike messengers were sitting cross-legged in the shade of a planter, unwrapping large, foil-covered burritos. Their bikes leaned against the edge of the planter, pointed toward the street.

Seth Stevens grabbed one, still running full tilt. He squeezed between parked cars and got one foot on the pedal, then swung his other leg over. The bike was a ten-speed that had been stripped of everything but seat, frame, and tires. There weren't even brakes.

He heard footsteps slapping the pavement. The bike messenger was behind him, not saying a word, just running, reaching out for Seth Stevens and his bike.

Seth Stevens strained against the pedal, fighting a low gear and an incline. The messenger's hand was close. For several long seconds he thought he would lose the race. Then he turned a corner and started going downhill. He pulled away.

The bike felt like a child's toy but it was fast. Relieved to be getting away, he almost didn't see the red light. How did he stop with no brakes? He slid off the seat and dragged first one foot, then both feet. The bike came to a stop in a cross-walk. An angry pedestrian scolded him. He looked away.

The light changed. He started pedaling again. He needed to get to another phone and call Connie McGarrigle to reschedule their meeting. It was one of many things he wished he'd done differently.

Then he thought of Charisma Brown. The only thing he would have done differently with her was that he wouldn't have left her at the truck stop. He would have gone to Canada with her. He pictured them older, in a home of their own, with three kids that they loved and worried about. She was probably back in Tulsa now, worried about him or angry with him. He wished he wouldn't have to wait to explain.

He didn't know what street he was on, but traffic was moving swiftly, the lights well-timed. He was careful of the parked cars on his right, scanning the side-view mirrors for faces, watching the doors for signs that they would swing open. With the traffic on his left it was like being caught in a logjammed river during spring runoff. He let the current carry him. At the next red light, he thought, he would pull over.

He was thinking about Charisma Brown again when the white van sped up behind him.